WALDGEIST

A Gothic Tragedy

RICHELLE MANTEUFEL

Waldgeist: A Gothic Tragedy

Copyright @ 2020 by Richelle Manteufel

Second Edition @ 2024 by Richelle Manteufel

All rights reserved.

This book or any portion thereof may not be reproduced or transmitted in any form, including electronic or audiobook, without the express permission of the author except as permitted by U.S. copyright law. For permission requests, contact richellemanteufelbooks@outlook.com.

All portrayed incidents, agencies, and characters are fictitious. Any resemblance to actual identities is coincidental.

None of this publication's content was in any way generated or supplemented with AI.

Published by Man Devil Press in the United States of America.

Paperback ISBN: 979-8-9910190-1-9

Editor: Kaitlyn Keller

2024 Edition Cover Design by Miblart

Art "The Ringmaster" by Elizabeth Bradley

Content Advisory

This novel contains depictions of character death, physical abuse, trauma bonding, psychological disturbance, demonic possession, witchcraft, depression, tobacco and alcohol use, and swearing. Reader discretion is advised.

CONTENTS

and selfish. The contortionist, the soldiers, and the weight-lifter could all claim more active attendance than I was able to claim.

At the time, I had been concluding my training with visits to the equestrians' post, where Mathilda and her troupe circled in preparation. As Mathilda's slight stature was of concern, Erbanhue and the master had speculated until the conclusion of a double-bareback act was reached. Mathilda was caught *pre-accidenta* by the co-rider. All persons of medical knowledge stood at the ready. Thus they prospered.

I am ashamed to admit that no feelings of warmth for my fellow workers provoked these visits. Sentiment and sympathy were foreign invaders in Erbanhue's Traveling Theatre. No one wanted them, so no one proposed them.

But there is no one to blame, Reader. It was a problem of emotional economics that fed on an all-pervasive cycle. It was safer to have a heart of stone than to go about making friends.

On the night in question, this doleful apathy drove me away from my feeble attempt toward society. I walked alone. The sumptuous darkness that enshrouded me was most welcome. In the dark, the wagon was not a wagon, the trees were not trees, and the cries of the slim menagerie were a thousand miles away.

As I twisted my hair about me like a scarf, I doted on Memory. I stamped within her sober brows the image of my beloved Sophie. Sophie the dominant, the lumbering, the shrewd, the one gorgeously clad in bold gray hide! Not two weeks ago she had been sold – my poor darling, the only creature I had been fond of – so that the troupe could eat.

That evening's stale loaves and toughened steaks were seasoned with private tears. I could not eat when my precious elephantine daughter was torn from me. I would have been content nibbling crumbs and starving rather than seeing her go... but *she* could not have been nourished by crumbs.

Go she must; go she did. I pined for a fortnight before the wine of apathy restored itself at my lips. A grown woman like me, sulking about an elephant!

Instead, the trees were my companions. I passed my arms about them with sisterly fondness. No doubt if anyone witnessed this charade they would have labeled me a half-wit.

No matter. Doused in temperate affection and bitter worry, I wrapped both arms around the trim trunk of a young maple and rested my cheek against it. Outwardly stern and uncommunicative, inwardly whimsical and wondering, I quietly asked it what we ought to do.

Winter came quickly. It was always a question of survival each time the cold season commenced, but that year it was worse. Audiences, already thin enough, thinned even more both in number and generosity. Some of us, not above the pastime of beggary, abandoned our posts to plea for scraps. Others from our troupe were suspected of thieving. Others bought up sellable goods all spring and summer long, just so they could be resold in the cold time.

I attempted to buy and sell fairly as stealing was a sin of my past, not my present. But do not think too highly of me, Reader. Selfishness, a sullen temper, and vanity (though I had, indeed, precious little to be vain about) were not exempt from my trials. Indeed, they attend me to this day.

A glance into any mirror would reveal a bedraggled, gaunt young maiden. She was too old for her years, with wilting threads of hair and dull eyes too large in her stony face. Despite a bizarre immunity to illness and a stubborn tenacity, she did not expect a long life. It was settled by statistics that my ill-fortuned troupe and I should die of either madness, injury, or starvation, and most likely a combination of all three. That is, if we did not slay ourselves first... like poor Tola, who threw herself into the lake (so it was believed) ... or the stable-boy August, who poisoned himself with the contortionist's supply of weaponry, of which the tactless lad had refused to be rid.

This same Indian contortionist preserved the lad's corpse as long as possible to study the toxin's bloodless penetration. I quivered, reclaiming my mind from this memory.

I let my arms fall away from the tree. Poor, faithless August had been nobody's friend, and in that I could claim some measure of resemblance. In his youth he had clung to me, but I had not been tamable. I am not amiable. Of all my sins, I regret my detachment the most. An attachment disorder, some have termed it.

The ghost of August exists in my mind. Sometimes I talk to it, but more often I feign disinterest. To feel too much guilt would assuredly shorten my life. To die by rivers or poison arrows is not my inclination. I thought it more likely that I would die by injury, vaulting too high or with too much vigor, and snapping my misanthropic neck in two as I justly deserved.

God must only ripen my soul with a little more wearing - a little more misfortune - and to Hell I shall go, with all due ceremony imbued. Any tears shed would be unmerited.

Be it so.

Who am I to dictate unfairness to a god? Or preach to him my sense of his reckless unamiability? When I myself am so little amiable! *Nein*, hypocrisy would not save me (nor has it ever saved anyone).

I trod objectless around the next tree, studying my bare feet as they flattened dead leaves. I yawned. My chapped lips split. To relieve the pain, I grabbed a branch and crushed it with fingers slim, like minute rods of iron, effectively distracting myself.

I gazed upward to the sun. I determined from the waxing light that our stale gruel would soon be prepared for its unenthusiastic consumers. I wondered if anyone would be able to eat it.

While cold enhances the appetites of the healthy, it seems to flatten the pangs of the poor in spirit. Snapping off a pittance of bark, I placed it between my lips and chewed, silencing the portion of my brain that registered flavor.

It was horrendously cold. Dressed in a ragged cotton gown, I deliberately forced each numb foot forward to walk. A second freezing shudder bent my limbs. The intensity of it forced a gasp from my bleeding mouth, and I started up, suddenly aware of the splinters in my gums and the dry, choking effect of snacking on wood.

I fell to my knees and coughed, spitting out the remnants and wondering why I had attempted to eat bark. I stared at the grass. My throat constricted with chilly puffs. My eyes inspected the mindless attempt at a snack, all bedewed in saliva and falling sleet.

The bark was black as night, and the flavor was leathery and bitter. A few drops of blood fell on it as I watched. Coughing still, I slipped my fingers into my mouth to extract embedded wood, exploring by touch the wilderness of worn little teeth. My fingers came away victorious though bloodied and shaking. I hadn't felt the tugs.

I stood. For the third time, a powerful tremor of pure cold disturbed me. Something about the waves of arid chill did not seem *natural*. I turned and fled. No longer did I care how crowded our fire would be, or how loudly Trinna would jabber, or how dourly Erbanhue would curse and spit. I wouldn't even mind how terribly the tasteless gruel, strangely doctored by the contortionist's herbage, would scent the air. I *had* to get warm.

The harsh gruel stung the new wounds in my mouth. I could not drink it.

"You will not eat?" Chaske probed, stabbing my side with his crude spoon.

I shook my head. Night had fallen, knitting my jaws shut. It pained me to speak.

"Ungrateful wench," muttered Erbanhue, downing his bowl. His flashing eyes damned me over its brittle edge. "She's better fit for the gutters, and we'd have one less mouth to feed. Devil curse the women!"

Pardon the speech, Reader; this was mere classic talk from him.

As usual, no one replied. "They're all sitting in wait to lead mankind to hell," he obligingly continued, uncorking a frosted bottle and draining its contents.

I calmly arose and shuffled away from the circle, eyeing the bottle with cool distaste. Among other jealously-hoarded souvenirs, Chaske also kept *medicine* - i.e. a meager supply of drink - which he only deposited into Erbanhue's palms at threat of eviction or manslaughter. It was therefore quite rare to see the Dragon otherwise than either sober and angry, or intoxicated and angrier. It was part and parcel of him until the end of his days... which the Indian predicted would be very soon.

Here, we camped about two minutes' walk from a brown creek. Its flow was steady enough at the time to keep it from freezing shut, although icy shards collected at its sides, clinging like moss. I pierced my visuals right and left before bowing at the stream and dunking my utensils until their contents dispersed. While washing, I mumbled a tune under my breath, a miniature prayer to the elements to supplement our survival. It was strange, I know. But how many of us are *not* strange when alone?

"Lange?"

Sighing, I turned on my heels and assessed the Indian. With typical inherited skill he had followed me without noise. "Yes?"

"The gods of our land have not abandoned you," – continuing in his chopped, bland strain. "Bless you they can, and they will."

"I do not understand," I answered, my stunted English not so pronounced as it would later be. "I do not know your gods."

"But they and the lands are one, they are same. You *do* know them."

"Indeed, you're deeply mistaken."

"They know *you*. I wish to teach you; will you learn?"

Again, I pronounced a negative.

"I see. You are not ready. But ask me when you are, *Fräulein*. There is a god here," making a vague gesture deep into the woods, "And I sense him. He wishes to bless you."

Fräulein. He dared to call me this? I cringed, my heart crying out in rebellion to the absent Fatherland accents, so basely missing from my former prefix. "Leave me be," I said, stepping away from him.

"Do not be childish, Yasmin. Do not reject him. Would you incur his wrath?"

"*Lassen Sie mich allein!*[1] I do not know this god. I know one, and He knows me, and I will die young. *Ist das nicht genug?*[2]"

The Indian shrugged. In flagrant imitation of Erbanhue, he turned neatly upon his heel and strode away.

---

1. "Leave me alone!"

2. "Is this not enough?"

I coughed with dissolving rage. An ache spread through my body; I reveled in the petty warmth that attended it. Anger stirs up my blood pleasantly… to give in is natural and welcome. I crouched over my utensils to inspect my grievance.

Why should his beliefs disturb me so? If one believes in Nothing, then nothing should make one angry. Perhaps I was more lonely than angry, and Anger was a diversion.

Whatever the reason, whatever the cost, it was the only balm I had… that and hot tears. Speak of it not, I believe my eyes were wet.

A sneeze rattled my sore throat. I covered my mouth. Surprised and a little alarmed, I saw the stain of blood come away with my hand, splattered from nose to mouth. I stooped again to clean my face, ignoring the pulsing sensation that grew from my fingertips through my body. *Perhaps I am ill.*

My weakness, indeed, Mr. Indian? Childish, am I?

Schwäche ist eine Beobachtung.[3] I may cut a stunted figure, and yet I am neither dead nor dying. He will see me practice with undiminished ardor. Come, Dragon! Inspire me with thy pain!

---

3. *Weakness is merely an observation.*

Chapter Two

Lillias

The sun rose crisp and dauntless. I arose feeling restored despite a long night, for the Ringmaster and Sallix had amused themselves with another provoking battle over costs and profits. They seldom agreed about anything, yet they managed to keep us alive by their strenuous efforts.

For once, Master Hue was pitched as hay from a fork, and Sallix emerged victorious with the rum; the Indian always relished an impromptu performance.

With a sulking ringmaster (the lifeblood of our group), no engagements, and empty pockets, it promised to be a profitless day. I determined to make the best of it.

I began at the far end of the creek, washing myself and my dress. I then attempted to sew together a torn, faded shawl, but it was rapidly approaching a state of utter helplessness. This shawl was once an article of mine, but I was reengaging its use for the shoulders of young Lillias Vosquez, the twelve-year-old equestrian and our most popular performer. Most vital to the troupe was her continued health and strength.

That day, the chill in the air was desert-dry. It made little difference to pause every few minutes and drink from my cracked wooden bowl. My mouth tasted of cotton, and my frail skin was assaulted by arctic gusts from all angles. I ignored Winter's declamations as well as I could, sewing and mending with caution.

Bored with the endless straight stitches, I sewed on her initials as well. *L. E. V.* Lillias Evangelina Vosquez. Fancy enough for an orphan child. Someone must have loved the poor, beautiful, fawn-like creature.

I had some trouble with the letters. A brief sneer of distaste wrinkled my demeanor. I never did learn to like sewing. To distract myself I stared at the stones, the showering leaves, or the whispering, chattering sleet, imagining all of nature to be fully invested with sentient and solemnent faculties. *That* is conversation. Entirely lost in thought, the intricacies of sewing escaped me. My fingers were numb; I did *not* feel the perverse, wayward tracks of the sewing-pin, leaving a trail of bloody dots in its wake.

Good! I had completed the distasteful task. Next came thoughts of presentation. Should I present the shawl as a trifle, with a manner of easy nonchalance? Should I slip into her tent and leave it nestled in the straw where she slept? I had slight experience in giving presents.

I gnashed my worn teeth together in consternation. A renewed pang was my reward as my gums resisted the pressure... The pain and the thin article in my hands called up a remembrance.

Before me rose the image of August, the stable-boy. I had once watched in perfect indifference as he gathered leaves together, attempting to keep warm. Something inside of me whispered that I had enough to do to look out for myself. I had nestled close into my threadbare shawl, averting my eyes.

This very shawl I now held with chapped hands, insipid and reluctant. I forced myself to imagine Lillias even colder than I, and I bade my unwilling feet to go to her tent.

I nearly tripped over tiny Mathilda as she came rushing out. "She's very poorly, miss," Mathilda sighed. "Could you spare her a little supper? Is there any milk to be coaxed out of that goat?"

"Not so, and I have not a crumb to bless myself with," I answered. "Let the child have this." And I passed over the shawl.

Mathilda put me to shame as her tired faced beamed over. "Thank you, Miss Yasmin! This will be hailed as a blessing from our dear Lillias. Oh, miss, you've done a good deed, that you have!" Here she added a profuse demonstration I could have lived without. Mathilda dashed back in, the shawl trailing behind with a half-hearted flutter, like a weary flag of truce.

Having nothing left to do, I wandered away. Snow began to fall. I squinted at the dark trees beyond the whiteness of laced flakes, picturing tall spirits and dancing elves hiding among them. Garland County is beautiful in its own reclusive, strange, blood-thinning way. One tree in particular reminded me of a supple, dark native, winding its arms into the sky...

This tree's bark bore streaked ebony tones. It seemed familiar. Approaching it, I recognized it as the tree I passed only the day before; yes, there was the chip off its bark, about as high as I stood. This was the tree I had absently made a meal of.

Pondering, I lifted my hand and pressed it against my aching jaw. In fact, now that my attention was drawn to that region, I noticed that my mouth was sorer than before. It was a toothache, perhaps. But then, had it affected every region? Running my tongue along its perimeter, I could not find one section that was unswollen. I frowned.

My hand dropped away and rested on the tree.

A shudder - stark and sudden and cold - convulsed me to my bones. I fell backward, stifling a cry of shock and pain. Was the tree itself a harbor for the winter chill? I believed I had absorbed all the wrath of winter by merely touching that tree.

Upon closer inspection, I was mystified. It was a strange tree. It could not have been more dismal if it had been made to order. It was not a maple, nor a pine, nor an oak, nor indeed any tree that I had ever recognized. It was slender as a birch, yet taller than any of the same, and dark as fate. It tapered down to paler, gray branches, sharp as needles.

As I gazed upon it, I thought of ghost stories and terrors in the woods at night. All trees like this one, I reasoned – rising proudly at first, then crippled and struck with odd woodsome diseases – trees like this one must conjure up those fearful tales of ghosts and ghouls, and even wood gods, as the Indian worshipped. Nature itself is a source of countless superstitions.

My brittle finger gently traced the open wound in the bark. Musing still, I returned to the creek to stare at the water. I have always enjoyed how water moves, how it makes its burbling presence known. I knelt beside it, tucking the skirt of my dress around my knees, and I felt content. If I listened hard enough, I could hear the snow.

"Miss Yasmin?"

Disturbed twice over at the creek. However, my mood quickly stabilized, for *this* voice was welcome to my solitary ears. "Hello, Lillias."

The child brightened. "You know my name?"

At this darling astonishment, I smiled. "I am not deaf, *mein Kind*. I often hear Erbanhue call your name. He tells you to practice with Shatze."

Shatze was the darling of our regiment *Equus Caballus*. She was the only show horse with an equal temper.

"Yes, she is my favorite." Lillias came near, shyness coloring her fresh countenance. I admired her dark, crinkled hair and wistful cinnamon eyes. I wished I had been a pretty child.

She motioned; I looked and saw the poor, dilapidated shawl between her hands. "Please, Miss Lange, I didn't know this was your shawl. I wouldn't have taken it if I knew."

"Call me Yasmin. Miss Lange is too formal."

Lillias beamed abright once more. "Since you say so, Yasmin. But please, I must return your shawl to you. It is too pretty to give away, and surely you need it!"

The child's innocent gaze betrayed her discomfort. She silently marveled at my thin summer dress, wet with melting snow-blood. My mind discarded her latter assertion to dwell sorrowfully on the former. I quietly placed a hand on the scrap of raiment.

For a beautiful young girl - the pride of our troupe - to term a gray cloth, thin as parchment with sideways blue stitching, as "too pretty to give away!" This was a statement of our affairs beyond any other.

Its succinctness pricked even Yasmin Lange to her center.

On an impulse, I leaned over Lillias and cradled her shivering body. "*Du bist ein Schatz!*[1]" was all I could manage.

Not understanding my words, Lillias was content to stand quietly and enjoy the embrace.

From that moment on, we were friends. Her way of following me about was troublesome at times, especially since she was yet ill and coughed a great deal. Despite her indisposition she performed well, with a smile all hearty and unwavering.

---

1. You are a darling!

Perhaps this was the source of my admiration for her. I *could not* smile while I worked.

I succumbed to the preference of calling her *Liebste* when occasion suited, or else *Das Insekt* when it did not. She answered to both by instinct, never quite discerning that *Insekt* was my term for her when I had tired of her company. I rarely petted her, often scolded her, and never at any moment flattered her, but she did not need flattery. She knew she was pretty. She often expounded the fact to my face.

"You do not love me, Yassy!" she pouted, after trying and failing to insert her hand into mine. "Am I so pretty that you cannot love me for jealousy?"

"Indeed, artless one! I love nobody," I replied.

"Why?" – her frank inquiry.

"Because it is impractical in our line of life."

"Ah, I do not believe that! Outside you are thorny, but inside you are tender." Here she slipped her hand into mine. And I could not withdraw my hand, nor did I stir when she laid her head on my shoulder.

Chapter Three

I Have Seen It Move!

All winters seem eternal. At length, with a great heave of relief and new life, spring arrived. Erbanhue's Circus prepared for better days as snow melted to mud, mud bred vegetation, and vegetation invited floral additions to grace our bitter path.

I perched on a stump and combed my hair, affecting satisfaction with its dull, ashen strands. I heard first a stifled cough, then the call: "Yasmin! Yassy, dear!"

Such was Lillias' term for me.

"You do not come quietly even in the early times." I sighed, setting down the comb and confronting her. "What ails Her Highness now?"

I spoke with sarcasm, for Lillias' bright cinnamon eyes were alight with joy. "Sallix told me that Shatze is..." (she leaned in to whisper,) "She's *expecting*." Tittering, she leaned back again, rocking to and fro on her heels.

I smiled at her lowered words. "There is no need to writhe into a fever. It is perfectly natural. Perhaps it will bring us good fortune."

"Oh, I am sure it will! What shall we name the foal?" Ducking her head, she coughed into her cupped hands and murmured an apology.

I shook my head. "I do not know. Must we name it? Why do you ask me?"

"Because you always think of interesting names. Did you not name the little apple grove we discovered last month, down to the smallest tree? And they were such clever names! You named Shatze too, didn't you?"

"Thou flatterest me, Lillias. But I do not care for your placations at six in the morning; get thee gone!"

Lillias was capable of a most marvelous pout. But she knew me too well to tease me further. She sped off, likely bent on ministering her satisfaction upon Chaske, who often humored her when I would not.

While watching her, I regretted the fact that young August was no longer present, for he would have been better company for Lillias than either the Indian or myself. My spirit, frequently bent on criticism, was not the best companion for a child. At times, I was obliged to send her away.

Not for the world would I have shown my convictions to the darling child. I kept them locked safely away, to be dragged from me only when communication was requisite. I hoped I was wrong in my foreboding... Indeed, all humankind courts silence in the plea of *perhaps* being wrong. We all answer to Lady Philautia[1]; never in haste do we abandon her.

But in this case, I did not believe that Shatze's promised foal would be with us for long. I supposed that Erbanhue meant to sell it. This would

1. Love of the self, or regard only for one's advantage.

break the tender heart of Lillias more thoroughly than any illness or loss... And she is yet ill. No, I could not prepare her. I would be certain first.

If only I wielded the power of persuasion over Erbanhue! It would be well used in the child's behalf. Sighing, I sectioned off sections of my hair to braid it. It must be out of my way, for today we were to travel.

While traveling to a new station, my task was to fetch water for the horses in two buckets and carry them on a rod between my shoulders. Sometimes I abandoned the buckets and selected a large, disused pitcher. Perched on my head, I balanced it after the fashion of the gypsies.

Wrapping my feet in knotted cloth, I walked to the steady brown stream to fill my pitcher. I was sorry to leave this stream. It had been my friend and confidant through that lonely, strange, uneventful season. It understood what it meant to be ever-stretched, ever-reaching, never resting, and forever craving a purer existence.

Multiple trees gazed at me from its reflective surface. They were all as still as ice; there was no wind. And yet I started and stared, for the dim branches of the tall ebony tree had moved.

Had they not? Did my eyes deceive me? Did my weary, fanciful, morbid brain conjure up a living thing from the depressed recesses of my thoughts?

I looked at it. All was cloaked in silence. *Nein*, I had seen something move. Perhaps there was a squirrel in the branches.

But it was not so... it *was* the tree itself. *It was moving.* It flexed its needle-like branches like a hand, coming toward me!

I froze, choking on terror. All poise and pride were abandoned as I launched myself up, water spilt, and I ran away. Fear caused me to commit the sin of the decade by invading the tent of Master Erbanhue himself (goodness knows why), and latching onto his rock-like arm. "Do go, go and see it! *Mein Gott!* I have seen it move!"

My sin was instantly repaid by a slap across the face. "Woman! Why do you throw yourself at me?"

Panting for breath, I held my pulsing face between my hands and stared at the ground. I could not speak.

"Well?" The Dragon raged. "Can't you see I'm busy?"

"It was nothing, sir. Something startled me-"

"No, it *is* something; it is shameless stupidity. Get on, thoughtless woman. Get the water for the horses. *Now!*"

There was no help for it. I abandoned the tent as quickly as I had intruded upon it, blindly grabbing the damaged pitcher. I returned to the stream, stooping and sloshing, preferring to risk dashing my brains out among branches rather than turning my eyes within range of the Black Tree.

Whether the following events I shall write have *everything* to do with that Dark Tree, I cannot say for certain.

But I *suspect*. Yes, I suspect it entirely.

You will see why.

Do not imagine, Reader, that I am the type to be afraid of noise and nature. It is true, however, that I often lament my parents' removal from the Fatherland to come to America, for this land seemed dismal enough to me. But perhaps it is not their fault. It may be mine.

My parents, Alarik and Beryl Lange, escaped the crop famines of Europe in 1847. My father was a decent farmer. He ought to have reaped, sown, and been happy. But having a sort of nameless proclivity for machinery, and hearing many tales of the plans of industrial America, he soon abandoned his failing crops for the drudgeries of American cities. My mother and I suffered the consequence.

However, allow me to attempt fairness. It might have been worse. After a year or two of abject poverty... years during which I was conceived and born... Alarik Lange came to the light, confessed that fascination is *not* the same as genius, and bought "Lauber's Restaurant" at a fair price. Although he was not good with people, he was good with foodstuff and beer. Between his work, and the spirited service of my mother, we improved.

Imagine me at seven years of age. I had not developed well. I was often sickly and this made me fretful and morose.

Beneath a general cloud of petulance and cynicism, I bred strange ideas. Somehow I conceived the notion that my father did not love me because he wished I was a boy. Due to this amiable psuedofact, our relationship was not heavenlike. We never hit or quarreled, but still less did we kiss or embrace. We lived and let live.

By contrast, my mother held my heart in her capable hands. I worshipped her with all my might and main. Beryl Lange was a lovely and loving Passionist, gently pruning away the shy blankness in her husband, and cheerfully encouraging the playful whimsy in her daughter. Whatever she did, she did fully; never did she accomplish by halves. Her tone of mind was all-encompassing, and I grew to embrace, or pursue, or criticize, or reject, whatever she did.

This wise woman saw that I was snatching at my own existence and failing, because I lived only in hers. Believing in free cultivation, she granted me little independent chores, during which she let me have my way about them so long as they achieved their true purpose. She attended to me with great diligence.

Quite soon afterward, my father's spirit - not half so self-sustaining as that of his wife - began to droop. She was compelled to leave me a great deal in order to aid and encourage him. She did right.

At eight years old, I saw a traveling fair for the first time. For the surrender of fifty cents, you were escorted to a boarded pavilion and a boxed pit. There were many things to entertain. I recall a violin and clarinet, gymnastics and feats and military maneuvers, horsemanship and human pyramids, and a strange goblin of bones and gills they called the FIJI MER-MAID. That thing frightened me even more than the painted men who had tumbled about and grinned painted grins. I was never done looking; I dragged my father hither and thither, examining all in wide-eyed silence.

There were many children. One of them ventured close to me. Stimulated into wildness by the wild scenes about him, he caught hold of my long hair, yanking it in the spirit of rude play.

Anger at this presumption welled from my hair-roots to my toes. I did not hold back. I gave such a yell as could quake *der Teufel*. My noise spurred a nearby stallion into action.

People have said that such moments pass in a blur. Not so for me. For me, it passed by in perfect clarity.

The stallion's painted hide trembled, his nostrils flared, his ruddy mane became a cloud of bristling thunder, and he ate up the ground in three lunges. In two more I would most certainly have died... but my father forced his way between us, throwing me to one side. He was trampled beneath the star-studded hooves.

By Fortune's good favor he did not die at once. He breathed long enough to bid his wife and I an affectionate farewell. He called me his good girl, his pearl of a daughter. This praise I did not deserve.

Yet, couldn't God have controlled that stallion even if no man tried? What had I ever done to the Deity, that He should treat me thus?

It was the first time since infancy that I shed tears. Previously, Temper was a mystery to me... it was oddly content to sit beside me, now and then knocking upon the door of my emotions, but never admitted entry. Now it took up sudden residence in my soul.

My spirited mother took up the management of the restaurant. In one point, and *only* one, did I detect in her a flaw. She was compassionate to our detriment. She gave the working positions to anyone and everyone, failing to prioritize ability or experience. In three years all was over.

Having closed the restaurant, we took up a soup cart and rolled it down the streets. It was not *all* bad. We kept each other company with ease and drank whatever was left over. Truly, we were not quite miserable. We had little food, but what we did receive was consistent. Peddling through town made us aware of all the places of shelter that we could use. And then, far sweeter to me than shelter was the constant companionship of the worshipped parent. She taught me to build fires and to mend clothing; she continued my English education with tireless passion; she helped me read every new sign we passed. In the early morning, she exhorted me to strengthen myself by running through the chilly streets. In the evenings, she encouraged me to sing German tales and to recite family history.

One evening she placed me upon a box and told me to sing to the passerby. Her pleasant, fireside German resonates in my ears to this day.

"Do not think, heart's dearest, that we do this in hope of money," she had said. "Let us make them happy. Reach out with your kind little voice, and their hearts will warm, making warm your heart!"

I did not approve of showmanship. I broke down halfway through, stumbled off my perch, and flatly refused to ever do it again. At first she scolded me, but my petulance won the day.

Beryl Lange always smiled upon petulance, for she had it herself.

Chapter Four

RINGMASTER ERBANHUE

In 1860, my mother fell prey to consumption. Although the battle was long and valiantly fought, the foe won at last. I see her now, carefully folded in both her own worn coat and mine, propped up against our soup cart. We spoke to each other in close, low tones. Exhausted and heart-sore, our minds could barely manage English. We meandered between languages.

"Heart's dearest," she sighed. "My little girl, thou must be very brave. In this, however, I am confident, for my Yassy is brave without Mutter... but..."

She was spent with groaning. I waited for her to catch her breath. "Yassy, dear, listen to me. Thou must culti... cultivate" (her tired tongue struggled with the word), "Cultivate happiness."

"But how?" My voice trembled, faltering with anxiety. "How can I do that?" I folded my hands together, picturing in my mind's eye a tiny Yasmin attempting to cultivate happiness, as one would cultivate a potato in the ground.

"*Mit Vertrauen,* Yasmin. *Warum misstrauen Sie den Menschen?*[1] "

"Mutter has taught me that people are sinners, and that no man is good. *Nur ein Narr vertraut den Menschen*[2]. I will not be a fool."

"Darling, you must learn to be a little foolish. Thou art too young," My mother's sorrow fell in gentle drips, "Too young to live alone. You will make friends, *Ja?*"

"*Ja, Wenn ich muss.*[3] "

"*Du wirst, du wirst!*[4] "

She gallantly wiped away her tears and gave me a hearty kiss. Her temporary glow caused me to glow, and it was only when I found her stiff the next morning that I lost my newly-formed determination.

No one is prepared to be orphaned, but I had been carefully taught. I wandered about, still peddling soup. I did not forget my mother's wish for me to grow in happiness and compassion. Indeed, I interpreted that as giving away soup for free when the opportunity arose. My dispassionate ministrations led where one might suppose them to lead, and supplies fell short. Falling inevitably from bad to worse, I joined a host of orphaned beggars within a month.

---

1. "With confidence, Yasmin. Why do you distrust people?"

2. Only a fool trusts in mankind.

3. "Yes, if I must."

4. "You will, you will!"

Still led by my mother's lessons of industry, I encouraged the other children to aid me in sweeping streets, washing windows, and running errands in exchange for pennies. The work roughened my hands and confirmed strength in my limbs. I tended to the other children when they fell ill, as I was rarely ill myself. As "necessity is the mother of invention," I often amused myself by scraping together abandoned hooks, rusted nails, old rope, and broken buckets to make climbing apparatus, or small weapons of defense that could easily be concealed.

Again, it was not a bad time, though its overall effect was bad. The days were peaceful (though hungry), and profitable (though dull). But the streets have never been kind to beggars and orphans. One by one, the other children vanished or passed away. One of them, little Charlotte, was snatched by a pale man with long features and black clothes. She was never seen again.

I was alone except for a stocky boy half my age. He had no name. I called him August.

August and I were of the tougher caste, quick on our feet and good for running errands in crowded streets. I was particularly nimble and slender. This was very useful when ducking behind objects or around corners to avoid crude personages; I could also out-maneuver any post carriage, even in the busiest of streets.

One businessman actually paid us three cents per errand. My, didn't we think ourselves rich! Didn't we barter and chuckle and put on airs! We delighted in trading watery soup for cold coffee, and the stale crusts of penny buns from the baker's.

Eventually, a pair of soft russet slippers posing regally in a shop window caught my eye. I coveted them. I cultivated a careful hoard to obtain them. August, however, continued to spend liberally until he was rendered bankrupt. Every so often, I caught him attempting to rob me of my coinage, leading to frequent quarrels. However, in due time I succeeded in purchasing the fashionable footwear.

Another traveling circus visited. This one, much to my delight, originated from pervasive New York. Its laughing, carousing performers passed me by, bright and painted and brightly smiling.

My fancy was recaptured by the delightful, wild control of the pleasure troupe. I made a decision at once, and it was impulsive enough! I commanded August to come with me and join them.

He objected in his own stubborn way. Selfish little Yasmin, weary of taking care of a willful child, announced that she would go with or without him. To the circus she went, with August trailing reluctantly behind.

Approaching a stuntman, little Yasmin requested direction to the circus master. She was ignored. After running front and back, Yasmin pinpointed that authoritarian man herself (so she assumed). She confronted him.

"I don't want any street urchins," growled the bearish, tattoo-inscribed fellow. "What use is your dirt to me? Go back to where you came from, or I'll hail a policeman!"

"No need to be harsh, Master Hue." Thus spoke a soldierly-looking man with a long mustache. "I was watching her. She ran from the end of Dancourt Street through the length of our procession without slowing once. She's strong, and looks capable." This speaker turned to me without awaiting an answer. "What is your name and age, and what do you wish to do?"

"What does that man do, the one I saw with the rope?" Yasmin asked, pointing with one dirty fingernail.

Her accent ever betrayed her origins. "Ah! She's a German urchin. Well, perhaps there's something lasting in her blood by breeding." (Thus spoke Master Hue.) "Stop the procession! And get Harry, he'll show her the tricks."

"She must be tired from running, sir. Her feet bleed-"

"And what of it?" Hue roared. "All the better to task her strength. Quickly, now!"

Mr. Harry, the current aerialist, came in a rush. His endeavor to conceal his bottle was not successful. "Get your drunken limbs over here, and show this German dirt the ropes," said young Master Hue. (A charitable man, this!)

Later, this prize among men was reintroduced as Ringmaster Erbanhue.

"Very good, sir." Harry's flushed faced glanced at Yasmin in bewilderment. "Well, then. What's your name?"

"Never mind my name," she answered, not in the mood for any more insults against her heritage. "Let me see what you do."

The ringmaster chortled. "Ha! Knees knocking together, and yet her pride is here and well. I may use that presently."

First, he set about examining my dexterity and muscular coordination. It was, to say the least, alternately painful and humiliating. But I had come this far; I would not turn back. It was not raw talent but pure fortitude that won me in the ringmaster's strict eyes. A few weeks of training sufficed to route Mr. Harry horse, foot, and artillery, and I was installed in his place.

One person resented it. That genial body was none other than August. He had been received also, but in the position of a lowly stable boy to clean up after the animals. In our younger days that might have troubled me... I may have made a stand for him. But I was hardened. Fierceness, self-interest, and pride had procured a future for me, and I placed my faith in them.

To survive – thus said I to myself – I had to be like the ringmaster. If he liked me, he would see to it that I was kept in the troupe. For the ringmaster was the true ruler of the circus. Kirkland Lovell was owner in name only.

Chapter Five

The Diary of Madame Tola

There was a certain fortune-teller in the traveling circus.

Contrary to expectation, she was neither mysterious nor particularly illustrious. Her skin, bronzed from travel, glinted in the scattered sunlight reflecting from her multiple bracelets. Massive earrings weighed down her lobes, swaying carelessly when she moved. She never walked per se, but rather swung about, swishing her fringed skirts and plucking at her ill-fitted bodice.

Madame Tola could be glib, and even witty, in the sultry commendations and declarations expected from her trade; but by nature she was the reverse. I believe Erbanhue tolerated her partially from laziness, and partially from a penchant for cheap members. She was known to smoke a pipe in her leisure hours, and to care very little about much else... even money. Therein existed her best feature (for Erbanhue, at least). It caused the ringmaster trouble and trepidation when she vanished.

All that is left of Madame Tola's illuminating legacy is her scrapbook and diary, fished out from among her objects of crystallomancy.

I have copied a few sections here. I only added what I felt the reader should know, as Tola speaks a little about me from her own point of view. It is not flattering, so do not accuse me of vanity *this* time.

From Madame Tola's Diary

March 16, 1862

It remains unusually busy for the early season. Perhaps our new location is lucky. I've also put our new stable lad, August, to work for me in setting up my divination tricks. He ought to be taught sleight of hand by Sallix; he's got natural flair for it.

That August is smart, more obedient then most, and fast on his heels. His lanky friend, Yasmin, certainly stands to contrast. She has the air of a female Jonah. See if something doesn't come of *that*. Erbanhue is harsh with her. I've seen him batty-fang[1] the girl from one side of the big top to the other. Someone should keep an eye on her, but I don't have time. Just hoping it'll blow over.

March 19

I suppose the husband divination games must be brought back, but I've gotten terribly bored of them. These mindless games are accepted by the menfolk a little better, as apparently crystal balls are "agents of Satanic

---

1. Victorian slang meaning to thoroughly thrash

influence." From what I've seen, marriage is quite the same thing, so they might as well have a go!

This morning I commissioned August to swipe some oil of gladness from Sallix. Before I could stop that ridiculous child, he tipped up the bottle and took several giant swigs. Not certain it won't kill him, but he seems hardy so far. A mite half-rats[2] at most. Told him the Old Scratch will get him if he does such a thing again. He is a good kid, and I don't want him ruined at his tender age.

Spied Yasmin at work today. She was right-side-down, about twenty feet in the air and as homely as a bat. She tied a cloth around one leg to the ankle and knotted it in the tree. Her gray gaze was focused on the ground as she made various passes with her hands, as if casting spells. I wouldn't much like it, being at the mercy of ropes and ribbons. She seems to like these high places. Perhaps because Nastyhue can't reach her there. He's good for heights, but he isn't the battish kind. Only batty in the head.

August was watching her, too. He seems to like to see her at work. Once I had overheard him ask her a question while they were eating (and Yasmin was in tolerable sorts). "Yes," she replied, sliding her finger along the bowl and applying finger to mouth. "I *am* afraid of falling. I'm afraid of nearly everything."

She tossed her gray-blond locks, put down her bowl, and walked away. August stared after her with the oddest look... a mix of malignance and admiration.

I asked him if the two of them were related, for sometimes they quarrel just as a brother and sister might. A funny gleam came into his eyes. "No. She isn't my sister... or my friend."

---

2. Partially intoxicated

March 28

Getting settled at A----- town. All concerned are relieved; it has been easy pickings for dinner lately. Population is better here. Sallix found some second-over ham and had it done to a turn. While eating, I was able to tempt August with some leftover rind and get him to tell me something about Charlotte… some little girl he used to know. Seems to me he mentions her a lot.

"What do you want to know about her?" he asked as he wiped greasy fingers against his shirt.

I knew how to manage him. Acting careless gets you more information. I shrugged, taking off my shawl. (It was a warm day… hot thunder raged a few miles distant.) "You mentioned her more than once. I suppose she was a special friend of yours?"

"Yes… but she's dead, I suppose. Went missing before Yasmin and I came to the traveling fairs." August greedily sucked at his fingers, savoring the last bit of flavor. We haven't had decent meat in ages.

I asked if Charlotte had been kidnapped or had run off. August frowned. "I don't know. She was walking away somewhere fast, but I think I saw a man some distance away. He was beckoning to her." The lad shrugged, yawning and patting his stomach. "Before she left, she used to say that a tall, pale man talked to her 'through the thunderstorms.' Not sure what she meant."

I suggested that she must have had a fever and wandered off. "Did Yasmin take care of you before?"

"No! – Y-e-e-s," he muttered, adopting a what-good-cometh-from-Nazareth tone. "For a little while, anyway. She did teach me how to sneak supplies from factories." I would have asked more, for Yasmin's oddities are the gossip of the troupe, but I was interrupted by Nastyhue's threatening voice.

"You, August! What are you doing? The horses need to be fed. And Madame Tola, lark the second! Where is my percentage? I swear, if things didn't run past my two eyes, all of you would be in the streets as you are - useless, mafficking[3], and starved - better start hoofing it this instant, you!" etc. etc. Charming.

April 3

It's not that I hate her exactly, but it *is* rather hard to smile upon Yasmin. But as we are all selfish here, including the expostulating victim himself, I shan't preach on about it. Her show routines, however, are really quite go od... though she is certainly no "lamb without blemish" being sacrificed on Erbanhue's grand altar. She does have a trick which comes in quite handy – a look of hard, cold, striking intensity – and with these weapons for eyes, she can fire enchanted bullets straight into the souls of the audience. It is the trick of fascination. August is good company, sometimes as chattery as a church-bell[4], but Yasmin is a born actress. I should like to read her fortune.

---

3. Fighting in the streets

4. Slang term for a talkative woman

Chapter Six

YASMIN'S FORTUNE

Diary of Madame Tola Continued

April 4

I knew she would be difficult to approach. But, nothing hindered, I used Yasmin's gift against her and "fascinated" her into submissiveness.

I took her palm into my hand. "Hmm. A short life line. Not surprising... You're lonely. That's obvious. Hmm, not as cryptic as I hoped for. Ah, *here's* the good stuff. You miss your mother... you had a strong bond with her, yes?"

"Yes."

She avoided my eyes, fastening her cold, clear optics onto my forehead. In that moment, the most eerie sensation permeated the air. The aura of my tent changed completely. It felt as if... it evoked a sensation... of standing within the bower of an empty garden... at midnight. I was lying in a rock garden... haunted by spirits.

Yasmin's eyelids flickered as she blinked. The mental imagery changed. Now I was shipwrecked... marooned on a weather-beaten shore, battered by thirteen years of miserable tempests.

With great effort, I gulped down a breath and continued to speak. My voice seemed to emanate from afar. "You miss your mother with such intensity... you are haunted with agony. But... you don't want to be like her."

"*Nein*."

At Yasmin's word – that one word – the power of her influence intensified sevenfold. My hands shake as I write of this experience... I began to wonder if I would escape from it alive!

Lightening flashed around me... the rock garden was on the stormy island. My ship... the only home I had on this darkened sea... was roiling further and further away... a ghost ship.

Lost... lost... lost! I would be here, living on this island of bare rock and morbid rain, for all eternity.

The voice that *seemed* to be mine spoke again. "You think your mother was somewhat foolish?"

"She believed in things that I cannot believe."

Yasmin's speech is like her features: short, severe, and to the point. Somewhat distorted, always too concentrated. I hesitated, then nodded. "I understand. And your father?"

I braced myself as the island wind rose. The frozen gusts blew salty, icy crystals against my feet, green and glistening. Through the storm, Yasmin's thin mouth betrayed irritation. "Of my father, we need not speak." (Foreign tots do such neat things to English.)

The cold air clapped around my skull like a vice. I breathed hard, forcing myself to release her hand in spite of my deepening awe and curiosity. Instantly, all was made clear and real once again. There was no spell.

"You could speak to your mother if you wanted to," I told her, trying to smile (I was shaking). "Surely you do not fear the dead, do you? You are thirteen."

Yasmin smiled. For a second the visions returned; derisive waves crashed against the shore pebbles, rattling them, then settling them again. This vision was different. Her temper and mind had reset; I lost the connection. "What are the dead to me?" Yasmin asked. "What can my mother tell me that she did not say before? How could she help me?"

She whisked away, her lengthy hair floating like a veil. I saw her cool, pale hands lift and let down the tent fabric. She departed.

I shook my head. "I am sorry if I offended you." The selfish thing, keeping all that natural competence to herself! What would she do with it, then?

April 7

It is very early in the morning, but I *must* write of the fun! Last night Erbanhue went to cot with a bad cough, and so we had a regular rouser. Sallix and Kirkland were downright jolly, and even Yasmin didn't abandon us for her private ventures, but watched them at their tough-and-tumble contest.

"Bravo! Bravo!" August, Mathilda, Chaske and Demarion shouted and applauded. I sat nearby with a bug net, inspecting my latest catch.

"What are you doing?"

I was surprised. Yasmin very rarely initiates a conversation. At least, not with me. "I catch them to keep in my tent," I said. "Their wings are very beautiful. I decorate with them."

"I saw them; I wish you would not kill them."

I glanced at this cold child with some surprise. "There are gobs of them, my dear. One or two will not be missed." Feeling irritated in turn, I abandoned her and joined Mathilda. Yasmin drifted over to Chaske and

August. She sat at the Indian's feet. (Odd happening the second. Normally she avoided Chaske like the Plague.)

Chaske was telling August the story of the Ten Children. It was August's favorite, but Yasmin turned up her nose at tales of sacrifice and strange gods. "And this very god I have seen!" Chaske always finishes thus. "Tall and white as the winter snow, pure and radiant with the strength of the Ten Children, who died that He might live forever."

I sensed, more than saw, Yasmin's customary sneer. She laughed... a high, short, dry sound. "If he really was a god, he would not need the lives of *children* to live forever. He would live forever whether people sacrificed to him or not."

August turned to her in disgust and told her to go away, lest she provoke this great forest spirit; he may come and claim her life in the dead of night.

"Oh, would he?" Yasmin leapt to her feet, sneer now widely visible. She may be the older of the two, but sometimes she is just as childish as August. "Even if he took me, at least I am worthy of a god's sacrifice! He wouldn't want *you*!"

August proceeded to yell. Chaske commenced a rebuke, but Yasmin ran to escape it, leaving Sallix and Kirkland rolling with mirth. Anything is funny when you're drunk. Even arguing young beggar-performers.

May 21

I have taken to knitting alongside Mathilda. I hear so much interesting troupe gossip from her. I finally know a little more about Erbanhue's past. Mathilda actually asserts that he loved a girl once, but his case was spurned by the woman's father. Apparently the falling-out was so bad, Erbanhue took to drinking and aimless traveling, eventually wasting his fortune. He pounced on Kirkland near Chicago, neatly adapted himself to the delicate art of blackmail, grasped the circus in his controlling claws, and thus it is to this day. Not very romantic, but typical.

"I've always wondered whatever made Kirkland agree to call it Erbanhue's Traveling Circus, when Erbanhue is only the ringmaster," I said.

"Well, it's said that Kirkland is a bit of a softie. And he isn't good with business. Erbanhue, however, can run anybody roughshod." Her clicking needles slowed and she quieted her voice. "But frankly, Tola, we're better off. Erbanhue is a terror... but if Kirkland was in charge we'd *never* have any food."

"So we prosper *because* of him rather than *in spite of* him," I chuckled. "Although *prosper* is not quite the word."

I coughed into my sleeve.

July 1

Our street performance was the best we've ever given. Erbanhue insists that it's better to have one quick grand opening, and then several side shows going at once. Kirkland amuses the men with challenges of strength, Mathilda entrances with her equestrian grace, and Yasmin and Chaske astound with physical feats. Yasmin, now fifteen and much taller, looks *almost* pretty during her new routine of ribboned flight. An aerialist's work is quite mesmerizing when done well. She also made a new costume. It's a bit funny, however, seeing her white and gray, sober personage clad in bright scarlet and blue and purple. Those colors look uneasy on her, and she looked no more comfortable in them.

Despite my fatigue and coughing, I am happy. Erbanhue let us have an afternoon on the town, so pleased was he with our success. I shouldn't have had that tumbler of apple lady... I keep thinking I see someone in the corner of my eye, but when I turn, no one is there.

August 5

I am confined to my tent. I have nothing to do but write. I am restless and cannot sleep... Trinna has insisted that I rest as much as I can. But woe unto us all if Erbanhue gets wind of it! If I were dying, he would insist I arise and work. Work, work, work... all we ever do... but we must act as if we enjoy it. Wouldn't the rich folks be surprised if they lived one day behind our gigglemugs[1] !

I am quite out of sorts. Ever since my séance, in fact. Of course it was all staged! – nevertheless... I believe I felt a *presence*. And it has not left me alone since. I have nightmares now. I wonder when Mathilda will bring me my knitting. I'll go plum crazy, sitting here alone.

August 19

I am better today. I feel stronger. If only this confounded thirst would leave me! August risked life and limb to steal some fresh milk from town, a rare treat for us, and even that does not satisfy me... my skin is as dry as old bones, and my eyes look hollow. I'm a dreadful sight.

September 9, Nighttime

I am awake due to unquenchable thirst. But this is my first night in months without any bad dreams. Feeling much better other than thirsty... sort of dry and stretched. Will go for a swim, perhaps. Goodnight.

END OF DIARY ENTRIES

---

1. Habitually smiling faces.

Chapter Seven

When Talent Awoke in Earnest

Yasmin Lange

September, 1862

It was an odd day to travel. First Demarion, and then Madame Tola, were suddenly gone from our midst. Yet Erbanhue persisted, so not a creature among us attempted confrontation. After all, even the tiger Darius seemed eager to depart. That place smelt of evils.

I folded my Kostüm into its homely sack, caught up my slippers, and grasped spare poster paper between my teeth. I pattered out of the tent. From the side of mine eye I could perceive August engaging in customary glares, but I paid him no heed; I had no time for him. The Dragon Emperor was likely nearby... Ah. Hail, the looming shadow!

Emerging ahead of me strode His Masterfulness, Erbanhue. I knew from his gait that avoidance was requisite.

"Rope – girl!"

I answered him as seraphically as I could, still running.

"Are ye late? Where the devil is-?" He stuttered and quieted; the mere act of speaking seemed unable to cope with his gait. One arm splayed in my direction, bending like a felled tree. I dodged. Smothered laughter from August punctuated my partial success. I redoubled my speed to avoid the Dragon's angry curses. One never crossed Erbanhue the morning after a performance.

Do not suppose, however, that I was frightened by "Hue." He might be best described as a necessary evil. If I were to pick a fruit and find it small, unappetizing, and half-rotted - but find it my only supper that day, so I *must* eat it - this would be an apt comparison to my young thoughts of the ringmaster. He was intolerable, so very two-and-three faced! And yet our audiences ever adored him. It was quite enough to make one choke.

As a child, I convulsed August with laughter by calling Erbanhue nicknames to his own red, drunken face (for he would remember them not). Some prime examples included Silvertooth (his teeth gleam in certain lights), the Dragon, and Sir Lopwalker. With shamed surprise, then, did I one day learn of his hard past; I temporarily repented of these titles. But I could not neglect the former moniker now. Sallix endeavored in vain to resurrect the fallen one. I turned while running, extracting my bite full of papers. I hissed "Good day, Sir Lopwalker!"

I reflected, peeping comfortably from behind Demarion's abandoned wagon, that Erbanhue was not a bad-looking fellow. He was handsome in a dragonmold, irascible, inscrutable way. In dress he was acceptable. In cleanliness he was catlike, deliberately fastidious. He boasted of shoulders thick as thirty-cent beef, and eyes much like gemstones... one a rich brown tinged with red, and the other a shimmering oceanic blue... with both of their troublesome gazes as scalding and brilliant as molten lava. He wore a sneer all superb and monstrous, and brows like sable thunder glowing with briny pique and wax. His manners might toss sparks at any moment and catch fire directly.

I rather liked him when he was angry. It made him distinct; it chiseled him into a certain vital distinction from amongst phlegmatic humanity. I never saw him in a rage without musing on the avenging angel of God.

Brooding on the question that weighed troupe gossip, I addressed Sallix from afar. "Are we to leave without Madame Tola?"

Sallix shrugged. He approached me and, wholly without ceremony, dropped a penny paper into my hands. "I found this in the gutter. Yesterday's paper."

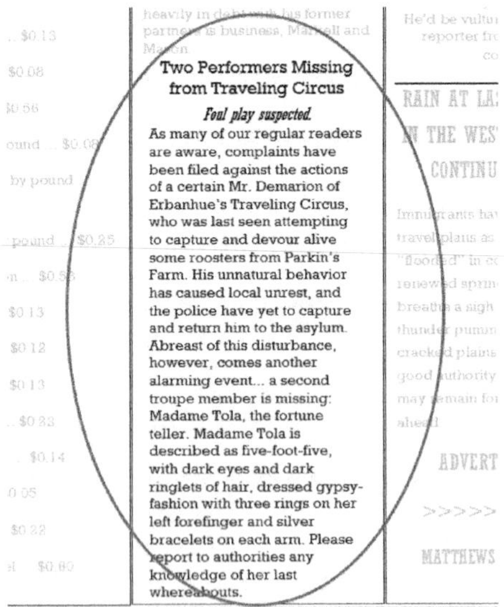

Two Performers Missing from Traveling Circus

Foul play suspected.

As many of our regular readers are aware, complaints have been filed against the actions of a certain Mr. Demarion of Erbanhue's Traveling Circus, who was last seen attempting to capture and devour alive some roosters from Parkin's Farm. His unnatural behavior has caused local unrest, and the police have yet to capture and return him to the asylum. Abreast of this disturbance, however, comes another alarming event... a second troupe member is missing: Madame Tola, the fortune teller. Madame Tola is described as five-foot-five, with dark eyes and dark ringlets of hair, dressed gypsy-fashion with three rings on her left forefinger and silver bracelets on each arm. Please report to authorities any knowledge of her last whereabouts.

Sallix saw the trouble in my eyes and nodded. "First Demarion, and now Madame Tola. I suppose I should say the *late* Madame Tola."

"This does not say she is dead, Sallix."

"No. But she is missing, and her illness was much worse, they say. Trinna is inconsolable. She feels she didn't watch Tola with enough care."

I returned the paper without further comment.

"That's life in a traveling circus," Sallix muttered. "Illness, thievery, poor luck... By the way, child, can you sew and mend? Tola did most of that, and now we will need someone to take over-"

Now, Reader, the mere *mention* of sitting still for long periods of time, doing any chore at all, was unwelcome news. I spent a great deal of time outdoors, stretching and posing to test my physical strength. It amused me to see how well, or how far, or for how long I could maintain a particular routine. I also enjoyed knotting my ropes in the tallest and most forbidding trees, and practicing my art from them. But to tangle with miniscule, exhausting rows of stitching, or to confine my country-loving eyes to a white page for hours... *Nein!* This, I could not like. I sank my stare into Sallix's eyes, signifying my response and escaping before any brute force could be exacted upon my person.

"How old is she now?" I heard someone ask.

"Fifteen."

"You had better send her to me; I knew how to sew extremely well by the time I was six. What a lazy upbringing she must have had!"

"Lazy enough, I should think. But hush – here is the Master – small talk is not in his repertoire." And Sallix began to order the men about. The Big Top must be brought down.

I could amuse myself in my own way. While hating most ardently to place a book or a piece of embroidery beneath my nose for perusal, I wrote stories in my own head and thoroughly enjoyed it. I suppose I did not like other people's stories, but with a type of satirical pride, I liked my own.

In them, I pretended I could be fearless. Chiefly after a row with the Master, I burned with every quart of my bitter blood to have recourse to strong words... Proclamations that would be every bit as insulting as the Master's own. I was inspired like so:

Erbanhue would be on the ground before me, having just fallen over in a drunken fit. I would be dressed in my prize uniform, standing straight as a matchstick, fingers neatly linked behind my back. My hair would be combed clean, extending down my back in full glory. I would peer down my nose at him, and oh! How I liked to imagine what I would say. I would take out his sins and polish them. I would set them gently, one at a time, in due order, on the shelves of his closed cabinet of oddities. Then, I would thrust open the doors. I would air them out for every passing ear and every curious eye. And everyone would know him for a fraud.

I would commence a soul-shattering speech. And I would end with, "You see, Master Hue? You are as rotten as Schweine. And I won't waste another thought on you. *Ich verabscheue dich*[1] *!*"

I would turn on my heel delicately, as light as a cloud. I would turn my back to him. He would be appalled by my sternness and shocked by my brevity. Furthermore, he'd be amazed. He would wonder why he never appreciated my strength of articulation before. Such keen and truthful insults *must* secure the Dragon's respect and admiration! Shaken in his soul, his very tattoos would frown; weakened by his excesses, he would tremble; he would implore my mercy and my forgiveness.

He would see me as I was. Not a child, but a young woman to be admired and praised.

---

1. "I despise you!"

For some reason, the play would halt just here. I could never devise Act II or properly envision what would happen afterward.

I see now that it was my logical self rising to its own defense. My subconscious acknowledged that this was a scenario utterly impossible and ridiculous. In spite of this complication, I wiggled with delight. It was a kind of mental sustenance, every bit as satisfying as fresh porridge and cream. There were moments when, as he was scolding me and clenching my arm tightly enough to produce imprints, I could hardly keep from smiling.

If you only knew what I could say! I longed to express it. *You would not treat me thus if you knew me. I only abstain because I know I can learn much from you, despite your moral failings.*

But my tolerance of his treatment was not the sole restraint. There were two flies in the ointment. Problem the second: To keep his station as ringmaster, Erbanhue *must* possess a particular talent for inspiring compulsive flight into the realms of fancy. It is the ringmaster's duty to capture each individual mind and meld them into a ceremonious whole. "To make a success of a circus troupe, one must paint the stage for every observer." I heard him say it time and time again.

Therefore, I am forced to admit his own portion of claim to an artistic spirit, an animalistic sensationalism, the power to seize and fuse and recreate. He does not lack the proper cerebral supplies. As I have intimated above, even in my imagination I have trouble defying a sober Erbanhue. The "dragonism" I have waxed eloquent on would arise and pitch tent in the souls of his eyes. I believe my well-crafted speech would fall flat.

In conclusion, I admit that between Erbanhue and Yasmin there exists a certain likeness. Yes... we are cut from the same cloth, though I shudder to consider the full implications. Yet we *could not* be friends.

I would have better luck seizing lightening and winding it into a necklace than in securing his happiness, trust, and (above all) respect. Besides, I am no favorite myself; and for reasons good, I aver. Our strained friendliness would cause celestial and planetary panic. One idle word, one false step, one ignored gesture, and we would be at each other's throats. Such hot-bloods cannot be companions and survive the attempt.

At any rate, Erbanhue's wicked criticism is hurtful, lashing, and poignant. But for my part, I can better endure harshness when it is sincere than I can endure flattery from lying lips. Do you doubt this? As an example, I shall transcribe my first sincere lesson in training, led by his good self; shall I ever forget it?

No more, I think, than it is possible to forget the final pleadings of my good mother.

No one was watching us. At least, I do not remember anyone laughing or speaking. Erbanhue was my sole audience... righteously angry, potent, and utterly unwise to batter down. A lion that one must not corner.

In those days, we were both fresh with the tender green of youth. My head hardly reached his shoulder. Master Hue was lank and suave, more inclined to laughter and taunts than furious curses. Although I cannot precisely recall the words we exchanged in that stormy interview, I do recall his insensate intolerance to any performance except the one where each gave his all.

Poor fortune deteriorated him for some years... but then! Ah, then! What a spectacle he was then. I hid myself for hours just to watch his stride, absorb his confidence, and even admire his shameless falsehoods when his firm, angular lips spoke them... lips that so finely inscribed a flawless contrast to my tremulous *Schmollmund*[2] .

To recommence: At regular intervals, Erbanhue tied the coarsest ropes in the highest of locations he could secure. He instructed me, ordered me about as a Rajah might. A dislocation, a scream, a whole array of scratches, never wrought from his mouth one twitch of sympathy.

In that first lesson - terrible to relate! - my temper was every bit as bad as his own. In the same manner dislocation, screams, and scratches - not to mention three-and-twenty bruises - never penetrated to the brain that the body was in distress. I learned in that one day what is yet the most valuable to my whole career... the trick of resurrecting a stronghold within the mind.

It is more than simply not looking down from a high place. It is looking down, but not blinding oneself with fear. You face Terror as it comes, acknowledge it, and diligently nurse the resulting blight and lesion far away from all prying eyes. Before the masses, you perform as a goddess.

The Master bid me to throw myself from rope to rope, to balance my body correctly, learning to time each leap and judge the distance in a fractional second. Each success dangled my frail self even higher.

Reader, I was afraid. Never had I feared heights more until that forced climb through air and space. Peevish stubbornness, however, did for me what bravery would not.

Although I fell at the end, the end was not bad. Master Erbanhue coolly pocketed his watch (his sole ornament of value in those early days), marked

---

2. Pout

the height to which I had last attained, and remarked as he strode away, "The petite *Fräulein* has the correct spirit. *Wir müssen auf der Hut sein!*"[3]

Shocked to hear my language on his ever-*Englisch* tongue, I compelled my aching limbs to hoist me up in order to stare after him. What sort of a creature is this?

How many faces had it?

How many spirits sought for purchase within that tattooed frame? What true mastery and might beams secretly beneath that sullen moustache?

Yes! Erbanhue, what art thou? What thoughts construct themselves in that high, spiked cranium?

Vain question! I did not know then, and I do not know now. But even at fifteen years of age I had a strict, defining subconscious; I knew that beneath this cruel serpent's fangs, I would grow. Nowhere else on earth would I find a more apt subduant for my wrongs and woes than in this multi-haunt, keen tyrant.

---

3. "We must be on our guard!"

Chapter Eight

A Revelation

Reader, I suppose you are puzzled by these meandering expostulations. Let me clarify: I do not write as I think of him *now*, but as my impressions were at the time. Fifteen is a malleable age. My parents taken from me, *something* must fill the void. Erbanhue possessed multiple shades to color the dimness that Life had become. Dreadnought that he was, I never tired of seeing him, of hearing his emblazoned tones, or of watching him tackle the tent stakes with energy and fervor.

I yet treasure in my heart (such as it is) the time when he spoke kindly to me. He was driving a stake into the ground to pitch the main tent.

"Can I help?" I signified. I rarely spoke in longer phrases; my native tongue rendered lingual succinctness necessary. Erbanhue, perspiring from the mallet's weight, tossed its boulderlike matter to me. He laughed as it slipped hopelessly from my fingers. "I cannot burden you with such tasks, tiny *Fräulein*. Your doll-bred physiognomy could not bear the weight, and I'd crush my promising little mustard seed."

I may have mentioned this before, but he has truly magnificent eyes. One cast in dwarf-work of fireborn bronze and ruby. The other finely wrought by the elves with cool, steady, and soulless blue.

The left *Erbanhue der Edelstein* winked with subtle calm. He grasped the mallet and continued anew. I actually glanced over my shoulder to see at whom he had winked so genially – Reader, it could *not* have been me – and perceiving that I was indeed the recipient, I hazarded an uncertain smile and promptly slipped away. Such kindness, from such a source, confused me dreadfully.

Never mind that in the same evening he was as irritable as ever, just as difficult to please as before. In spite of this, my mind linked together envisioning to understanding, clue to logic, guess to hypothesis:

"We are irritable with one another," said young Yasmin to herself, "because we are both mercurial. We sense the competition to outshine and outrank. Where *he* has the gift to control, *I* have the gift to compel. Where he can command, I can accomplish sans magnification. He enforces autonomy, but I am naturally autonomous. He senses my independence because he has it himself. He wishes to choke it out, to feed me the coarse meat of dependent living until I am a subservient follower and a tamed spark. Well, I shall pretend to blind myself. I can play the game in my own way."

I forged every intent to render this revelation invisible. But I was wrong to ruminate that I could thus deceive him. He found me out and doubled his efforts.

Still, I cannot paint the portrait *all* black. Our compelled alliance fed us beneficial results. The harder Erbanhue became, the harder I worked, and the better I was at surmounting every pitfall. The better I performed, the more audiences I attracted, and thus I filled the ringmaster's pockets.

"You've become uncommonly quick," voiced Sallix. I had completed an especially hazardous and taxing routine. I bowed.

"But you did not make your turns very graceful, which you know is Hue's demand. They looked a mite unnatural. I believe you work better when he is watching."

I allowed myself to smile. A prince among magicians, Sallix boasted legerdemain of insight just as he sported sleight of hand. "Is there anyone who does not work better at his request?" I answered with sarcasm.

"Right you are, right you are." Sallix chuckled. "I daresay each of you makes the other flinty, as they say 'iron sharpening iron.' But I couldn't be paid to work within twenty yards of ye."

"Good. At your desire; you can go."

"Scornful child," Sallix mumbled, yet delaying a moment as I remounted the training bench. "I predict an explosion. And Erbanhue cannot agree to keep her then."

I do not believe he knew I heard this, for I kept my own council.

Dawn blossomed upon the horizon, spreading a mask of golden cleanliness over a gray mountain of dew and fallen leafage. I adored practicing alone on such glorious mornings.

I slid one leg after the other over the curved ropes. Cautiously testing the cloth I had wound around it, I let go and hung upside down from the knees. My arms stretched luxuriously beneath my head. I drank deeply the morning's pure draught, discarding all prior tugs toward misery and foreboding. Sometimes it *is* beautiful to be alone. Disdainful as I seemed, denier that I was, I yet loved life. I celebrated it with movements rather than words.

Reaching up, I grasped the rope entwined with cloth. Slowly, gracefully, I lifted myself upward, extending one leg to shift my weight. Sitting on the rope like a swing, I twirled lightly, controlling my momentum by extending and then retracting my legs. Once balanced, I released my grasp, falling upside-down once more and spinning in a tight, practiced circle.

I closed my eyes and freed one leg from the swing, arching it gracefully and drawing my arms in and out... in and out... speeding and slowing the turns.

A cool rush filled my blood, soothing my brain with incomparable goodness, promising me a day of enjoyment and blessing. Reason begged me to stop the ebb and flow of good spirits, but I shut him out, and played with Imagination. How beautiful the day is, how sweet and exhilarating! How challenging it was to live amongst the talented and the eerie and the rare! How freeing it was to perform wonders before the masses! And how much I enjoyed my morning exercises, bending and waving and feeling the soft bounty of my hair, all growing wild and lovely and happy, as I myself was growing!

Verily, *that* was a pompous desecration. I looked (for the sake of truth be it said) very much like a youngling banshee. My hair is still long and thick, as it was then. The color was anyone's apostrophe: Gray, some have said it to be, or gray-platinum. My proportions have always seemed all wrong. My head is too long for my body, as are my dexterous hands.

The pale feet are spectral, long, and high-arched, webbed with a delicate pattern of pale blue veins. Then there are the lips and nose, the cheekbones and the glacial, quartz optics, all far too pronounced; the thick down-turn of the mouth; the temper-responsive nostrils... all too substantial for my liking.

The muscles are acutely developed from the strain and contest of exercise in the ropes. But my neck, forearms, wrists, and feet all wax suddenly frail, vapid, and tinged with indigo veins.

The effect is altogether reminiscent of sickly-looking dollage or fragile porcelain pottery. I am a mighty piece of work, attached and complete... but by a careless, uncertain Maker who selected mismatched instruments. It is not a pleasing spectacle that arrests mine eyes in the glass or on the water-front. However, as I am so used to its unlovely visage, I shall not mind it.

So, I could not count on beauty to bring me a fortune. What did that signify? There are countless unfortunates who are worse off than I. It is no disgrace.

Reveling in the morning silence, I let my lazy hands comb through my hair. I surveyed the fresh, dizzying world. My feet had taken root in the sky, and my head menaced the ground below.

These precious hours are often interrupted by the cries of animals and the stirrings of the troupe, ready to fall in line for inspection by Commander Erbanhue. I yet hoarded each minute and snuggled them jealously to my chest, for they were all I had.

Erbanhue, for all his faults, did not mind this idiosyncrasy. He would leave me around twenty minutes to myself. But it always ended at the sound of his peculiar, wide step, blissfully wrecking all surrounding foliage. I would be quick to release my hold and swing to the ground.

This time, the gesture was naught but oil to flame. With a flash of silvery grin, the Dragon spoke. "Your form was all wrong. Do it again."

Ordinarily, I stalled. When dealing with the draconian temperament, one must not let it have its way with too much haste. A little procrastination is called for. On the morning in question, however, his accost was not laced with cruderies or snarls. Therefore I complied.

I repeated the routine. The ringmaster crossed his arms. His daily habiliment consisted of tan trousers and a white shirt, an omnipresent checkered vest, and a vulgar top hat yet unapplied, held in one masterful hand. Not unlike the whiskers of a cat, Erbanhue's moustache smoothed, twitched, or quirked in accordance with his mood; a glance at it informed me of his humor. That day it was straight and flush, well-trimmed, his lips relaxing coolly beneath it. While he might jeer me post-performance, he would not bite. I completed my work in equal calm.

"That was better. Your addled brain, however, is not awake. You need coffee."

This comment made me stop. I grasped at branches to suspend myself. "Coffee, sir?"

"Yes, coffee... are you deaf, Yasmin?... Don't move. I'll get it."

I was fit to fall from mountainous heights in astonishment. That the Master should thus fetch anything to apply to me - besides a lit match, or a rope, or a whip - was beyond comprehension. The only conclusion I could come to, as he returned and solemnly placed the steaming mug between my hands, was that my routine had been sensational. And as I (his machine) was running to his liking, the mechanism deserved oiling and other methods of preservation.

I sipped. Sitting up there in the branches, a rising sun at my back, a calling bird at my side, and a warm drink in my throat, a rare aura of peace descended. I regarded Erbanhue with complacent wonder.

"You need not stare in that way," Erbanhue gruffed, returning my look with a raised brow. "You've been producing paltry work recently. I do not intend to stand by and watch your signature force abate. A regular employer would grant a holiday, I suppose, and a regular employee happily accept. But as neither of us merit the labels, we can dispense with commonplace prudery."

His remark was too succinct to arouse my anger. "Sir, you have doubtless been hardened," I replied.

"How would I be otherwise? Would you prefer me mousy, fawning, liberal?"

My conviction was instant. "No, sir."

Arms yet crossed, he shifted his weight from one foot t'other. "So you see. We are outside convention, and just as much above it as we are below it. We are likened to the wild-born but newly-tamed animals. If I were to spoil you, you would waste beneath my hand. To treat you with tenderness would deny you the right and means of sustaining your own self. *N'est-ce pas?*"

After several months of training with Erbanhue, I learned that he was sporadically multi-lingual. Though the entire troupe was mad to discover the entire length and breadth of his education and from whence he hailed, I suspected he only knew certain words and phrases. He aired them randomly and without proper discrimination. I pursued, "And if I should die of your unkindness, it would be my own fault?"

"Assuredly. I must treat you within your means and station, more than all of the rest. Even at risk and peril. If you die it is not by my doing, for you are the type to die only when you lay down your life. It cannot be taken from you."

Reader, a strange thrill or shudder rent my frame as I listened. Most true this was, but more than true. It was not only bland, simple, Rockness Truth. He had polished the rock and exposed the gem. He held it to the cold morning air, counting its facets; he quoted its value to the last Thaler.

At that moment, he was shafting his glance deeply into my eyes. His talent of fascination was whetting its fullest spell. Even I was susceptible to his spells in some ways. My heart eagerly absorbed his declaration. I think, more than anything else, my desire was to be *understood*. This man's decree seemed the most correct I had ever heard regarding myself.

"Now," the Denizen of Caverns spoke. "Do it again. This time I want you to flip from the last rope and land on your feet."

To flip once from the ropes sounds easy, but I insist that it is otherwise. My arms were strong enough, yet they were no comparison to a man's strength, and the novice male artist has accidents aplenty.

It must be confessed that my hands trembled. "Please go away while I try," I requested.

"No." A calm parenthesee, but seething with threatening embers.

"Very well, sir."

I arose. In my mind I repeated his words, fortifying myself as it were. He reached up to take my empty mug. I cringed inwardly as his bronze fingers brushed against my pale hand.

"Remember to vault your force from the legs into the upper body," I barely heard him say. "Do not think of falling. Success and failure are essentially psychological."

Normally, blind hatred was the result of this statement. He said it more often than I or my fellow troupe members cared to tally. But for once in my life, I dwelled on their import. I believed I saw what he meant. Taking brevity and ropes into both hands, I launched into the air.

"Now, picture to yourself a surging pendulum. Imitate it with your body." A pause. "Not bad. Take your time here."

I took him at his word (not wisely but too well). The ringmaster sensed my hesitation. A sneer - effortless from practice - distorted his snakish features. "No dawdling, if you please. I'm waiting. Your future audience is waiting." He made a show of tapping his foot.

I frowned. Calculated, faltered, then leapt. I landed in shaky triumph, scarcely avoiding a twisted ankle.

"Faulty. Try again."

Reader, you must forgive me for omitting this description. I failed, and dismally at that. I was sprawling flat on my back, wincing far, far up into the looming countenance of the Master as he grimaced. "Keep at it until you have landed perfectly ten times."

"Yes, sir."

Old scratches were ripped open. New ones adorned their fleshy neighborhood. I knew my arms would be black and blue. But somehow, I had to smile. The subconscious, that carefully-crafted little stove warming the mind's dwelling, had decoded a glint of approval in Erbanhue's eye. I liked it.

He extended one brown, haughty hand to help me up. "Practice until noon, and then help Trinna clean the cages."

"Yes, sir."

"And don't default; I intend to craft you into the finest of freaks, strong and steady. Perhaps I'll put you at the center of the show. 'Tis a crying shame you are not more handsome, eh?"

"Indeed, it is a shame *we* are not, sir."

Erbanhue blinked his surprise. He abruptly doubled over, fairly roaring with mirth. I was again astonished, though this time at my own singular audacity. To form such a remark was completely within my capabilities; but to *deploy* it? Not so! I only did such things in the confines of my brain. "That is, sir... I do not mean..." I felt pink tinge steal across my face.

"Oh, shut up, and never mind! I deserved that, maybe, and all other slights I receive (though woe be to the man or woman who voices them). You tremble; you acknowledge that you merit a punch. I am affable enough, and will give it. You shall practice until noon *without stopping*. Do you understand?"

"Very well, sir."

"Humph! Keep your deceptive politeness to yourself. Your steely eyes dash curses at me. Do your work, and I'll descend from on high to grant thee rest. Good morning-" He spoke and vanished, leaving me to bask in my bruised glory.

What *is* Erbanhue?

Master; tiger; a Dragon; a silver-toothed, gilded-tongued devil; a scourge and a help; foul and unclean and honest. He was of the earth and of flame, not heavenly or precious or pure. Hopeless and devoid of granting hope, critical, cynical, uncaring...

Yet so determined for success, *his* success, that he'd beat it into being. He would force Fortune to visit, if not abide; he was foreign to the means of gentle growth and cautious fruition. His determined complexity, in short, was the main ingredient of a personage not otherwise tolerable. Unhappy man! And yet, darkly happy in his work, for the work's own sake.

He dreamed of phantoms and of fame. He was likely to summon both.

AVENGING ANGEL OR CURSED DEVIL,

HE WAS THE BLOOD-RED STAR...

AND I THE MOST AVID STAR-GAZER.

Chapter Nine

Two Hands of Shadow

"Trinna," I spoke, finally verbalizing what I had pondered all day, "is what I have heard true? Was Erbanhue in love once?"

"Erbanhue! The ringmaster? Well, that's been whispered before. But I think whoever said such nonsense must have been madly drunk," Trinna laughed. Her cleaning brush wobbled beneath the strength of her mirth. "A pretty story, isn't it? No, I hardly think it likely. He despises the feminine variety. A good thing, too; for if he liked them, someday one of them would be obliged to like him back, and a nice thing he'd make for a husband!" She broke off in order to chuckle again. "Yet perhaps I *can* imagine it if he knew a woman as naïve as a child, who didn't know what a temper was, and had no respectable education... and who supposed that all men lose their wits on a regular basis for no detectable reason - *especially* not from drinking."

Having seized upon the theme, she milked it for all it was worth. "Can't you just imagine it, Yassy?" Here she lifted her voice in imitation of a foolish schoolgirl. "Oh, no, Trinna! My dear Erbanhue isn't a drunk! He is a genius... A veritable genius! And geniuses always have their particularities!"

I coldly turned from her and placed more straw in the enclosure. I secretly *did* think he was something of a genius. Or he would be, if he would only apply himself. But I was not a silly schoolgirl!

"Do you think he is a handsome man?" Trinna questioned, darting a teasing ray of light in my direction as she opened the wagon window. I winced and glanced away from the sun. "No."

"Not even a little bit? I do *adore* a pair of strong, manly arms."

"I see him as I see Darius, the tiger... a thing strong and trustless. A creature that may pounce, and after pouncing, is certain to rip apart its prey." Seizing the pitchfork, I dashed away at the straw with more energy than strictly necessary. "He makes a handsome *creature*. But he is no handsome *man*."

"Well, my goodness. That's right," said Trinna, after gazing at me a moment in struck silence – I suppose for my long and pithy sentence (rather out of character). "To be sure. Erbanhue devours everything for the sake of his deities, Fortune and Vanity." She grasped her broom and began to sweep. "As his fortune benefits us, however, it would be irrational for me to speak in entire condemnation of it." She smirked, patting her patchwork pocket. The mild clink of coinage answered her touch.

"And Kirkland? Why does the troupe's real owner hide behind Erbanhue?"

"Ah, *Fräulein*, that is a sad story. I'm afraid it is not appropriate for young ears." (I, at the threshold of sixteen, glared at this nonsense.)

She waved her hand dismissively. "But Kirkland ought to be grateful. Things could always be worse. We get on, and we pull through, and that is the best the likes of us can expect." She nodded firmly at the broom and gave it a little shake. "Anyway, we're about finished. Yasmin, dear, would you-"

"I am hungry," I interrupted. "I'll see you later, Trinna." I departed without another word. *Yasmin dear,* without exception, preceded things either disagreeable or brimming with sentiments that I had no inclination to endure. Feeling truly hungry, however - suddenly remembering that, due to Erbanhue's harsh decree, I had not gotten lunch - I halted at the mess tent.

"Good evening, madame," chirped Aimsley as he slapped some manner of tangy, thin meat between bread. His knobby, round face grinned at me with imbecile satisfaction. Aimsley, I might here admit, was ill-endured by my impatient self. He was especially moody of late, as well... apt to explode for reasons known solely to himself. I took my meal, dispensed my thanks, and left. Conversation was really out of the question.

Navigating the disorder of cages, wagons, stamping stallions and babbling humankind, I selected a retreat comprising of a stump, pond-side, and weeds. I devoured my dinner in relative tranquility.

The weather on this day had been extraordinary for its dryness and chill, considering it was late summertime. I had not taken much notice. However, sitting still for once drew my eyes toward the nodding brown dreariness of the scenery... it was so vastly differing from the magical view I had witnessed that morning. I sorrowed over the delusion.

Cramming in the last bite of my meal, I evaluated my situation; I pondered life and life's moroseness. I wondered whether I was meant for obscurity for all time.

The wind gained more warmth. A steady fatigue dressed me head to toe. Sudden dizziness washed me in unwelcome waves. I spread my hands before my eyes... my fingers appeared to fluctuate in and out of my vision.

What was it? My tingling senses demanded to know, itched to inform the confused, enskulled organ what was happening. *What was it?* I was no longer cold, but blazing warm, my indigo veins pulsing with pinkish sparks.

My fingertips turned red. Vision slipped in and out. My fingers were there, and then not... my legs were there, bent over the stump, and then not; my body appeared to slip in and out of visibility, while the scenery in which I was placed stayed perfectly still and rational. Coughing, I put my hand to my forehead. "Help me," I tried to say, but nothing could be heard in that strange vacuum. A throbbing, sucking sound filled my eardrums.

I thought I saw two thin hands reaching for my throat. I strove to push them away. I saw nothing more.

They informed me later that Aimsley discovered me in the oddest of moods, places, and circumstances: Yasmin Lange was found curled up inside of Darius' cage, petting and patting his giant, clawed feet, and talking to him in calm murmurs. Darius likewise laid all soft, content, and collected next to the aerialist's defenseless body.

The dangerous couple was quite happy and amiable at first glance; however, when Erbanhue entered the cage to collect Yasmin from beneath the tiger's maw, she was pale as death.

I refused to move or to open my tightly-clamped eyes at any price. The ringmaster, having wrenched his burden from her encampment, thrust her into Trinna's care and adjured Trinna to "Make calm the blasted idiot; she's gone mad at last."

My own memory was of waking from a natural, lapsing sleep, and glancing into Trinna's aghast set of small eyes.

"Oh, miss! Such strange doings! Whatever were you thinking, going into Darius' cage?"

I sat up slowly. "Darius? Whatever do you mean, Trinna? And why am I in your tent?"

"You must have had a fit. Aimsley found you in the tiger's cage at Darius's very feet. What were you thinking? He could have killed you!"

The dear lady took the sinner by the shoulders and administered a good shaking. I lifted her hands and pushed them away. "My dear Trinna, do not shake me so. I assure you I know nothing in the world except that I have just woken up, and I am thirsty and dizzy. I beg of you not make it worse." In the midst of speaking, I recalled a vague memory... of a pair of eyes glaring down upon me... one blue and one brown. Erbanhue's eyes.

Had *he* done something to me?

But with what drug? I had not heard of anything that exhibited the symptom of coloring the blood in your veins... At that thought, I hurriedly examined myself. My skin was a bit paler, and my fingertips shaking and red. Otherwise I seemed normal.

Trinna, meantime, relished her sermon. "Worse! Worse, indeed! My tiny rebuke, making you worse? Far from *worse* is worst of all; we can talk of death, for you should be dead." She leapt to her feet and brought me a drink of tepid milk.

I took it eagerly while she resumed. "I declare, I am half mad with the reaction of fear! I don't know what I am saying. Darius has been growling and pacing a good deal this week, too. And there was Yasmin, tiger-tamer extraordinaire! You had best harden yourself, miss, for the Master will soon be in to give you his own brand of catechism... and it will be far more vehement than mine."

I took my dose without comment. Trinna's words, though mild, were too humid for my taste. I wished to be alone. I longed to analyze the mystery, to solve the puzzle. I could not do so while she spoke. "Well, Trinna, be a dear and don't scold me anymore. As you say, Erbanhue will do twice the job, and reap twice the enjoyment; the living and the dead may know."

"You speak sensibly enough, at the least. I was afraid you'd gone mad. Thirsty enough, too! Drained the canteen dry. Then you can have another. Only wait a moment." Trinna pattered off to fetch me more milk.

Had I been a bit younger, I would have pleaded for her to remain. I would have preferred to face Erbanhue with a defender at my side, however small she was... Nonetheless, I heard Erbanhue's stern step not a minute later. I steeled myself for the attack.

The Dragon lifted the tent's mouth and sauntered in. He coolly inspected the tragic victim, who was eyeing him with a look akin to defiance. He nudged the shabby carpet aside with his boot and sat cross-legged before me.

Erbanhue inspected Yasmin serenely enough, and even felt her pulse. An examination proceeded.

"Is Yasmin calm enough to share whatever idiotic idea entered her head?" was query the first.

Yasmin shrugged, intimating a proclivity for silence.

The silver teeth clenched beneath a sneer. Query the second: "What did she think she gained by willingly risking death? Was she suicidal?"

She didn't know. Didn't think so, but had no clear remembrance of how she felt at the time.

"Has she unknown talents? Can she train tigers and test their canniness with her own?"

She parted and closed her lips, fatigued. She felt hot and restless, either by literal temperature or by the additive of embarrassment. Yasmin cast the blanket off her strained form.

The queries evolved into a pointless stream of rage. "Is she sentient? Breathing? Of flesh and blood? No! She is a doll of dirtied wax who cannot speak! Is she a broken vessel, unreliable, worthless, to now be cast off? Can she hear with those stonish, unyielding ears? Can she be trusted to give her word not to do such a fool thing? No one in this whole blazing troupe can be trusted! The slightest compliment, the smallest kindness, the one greeting - They take all and sundry and enlarge them to impossible, stupid proportions. Trust is an impossibility in Erbanhue's Circus. He does not tolerate such foolery; not he! Well! Is she yet mute?"

She was. She had no explanation... could not attempt one.

"Then she would be wise to control herself in the future," anathemized the Dragon, his mighty teeth snapping and grinding. He retracted in complete dissatisfaction.

But what could I have said? Indeed, nothing but lies, for I knew nothing. Everything within me screamed to rush after him, to take his arm and, if possible, to soothe him; I write with saddened repentance even now, recalling how much I yearned to promise him plethora of sanctity for that one harrowing fault. That he should rake me fore and aft for diminutive faults, I could bear... and even perchance thumb my nose at. But this wrath so justly earned urged me to repent in sackcloth and ashes.

Sir, it is all a dreadful mistake... I am a child yet, and I was curious, and Darius was so calm... I deserve to be whipped with the lash... you may do it if you like, and I'll not flee. I will not make one sound, if only you'll forgive me. Do forgive me!

Reason, however... the veritable hero of my life... held me mute. To say these things would discomfort us both, and lift the mask from my face forever; his scornful reaction could not be borne, and I could work for Erbanhue no more.

As harsh as he was, I would not leave him. Where, indeed, could I go?

Chapter Ten

THREE YEARS LATER

The tiger cage incident ought to have been buried in the oblivion of time. I, however, did not forget it… and Erbanhue would not let me, nor did he fail to keep all records concerning any defaulting action of mine. Whatever had happened - supernatural or otherwise - I at length became convinced that Erbanhue was not of the guilty party. He brought up the subject with his typical fearless audacity. If he was the culprit, he deserved a trophy as the best actor ever produced in America.

My talents at the rope bloomed, however; how could they not under his perseverance?

With Trinna's aid, I also became useful at the needle and improved my own costumes. I chose the stage name Anmut, meaning "grace." I planned my own routine, dispensing with the celebration of power in favor of the show of delicate aerial dancing. At first, this was much to Erbanhue's displeasure. My infatuation for his good opinion, however, was much abated as I aged; I no longer concerned myself with his fuss and fervency.

After all, I was eighteen.

I surpassed all the troupe in health, strength, and resilience. I could not comprehend my good luck, or from which spring it flowed: good, evil, or indifferent. The rich and the poor came and went; I was untouched by thieves. Indelicate food was served; I ate the tiny messes provided and was as satisfied as if it had been a banquet. Illness surfeited and spoiled our best in the troupe, but my body was never besieged.

I continued undaunted, at one point putting on a one-woman show with Erbanhue as announcer. At which point he designated that a devil must live beneath the walls of my skin, lurking among the sinew of my delicate form.

"How do you do it?" Hue asked abruptly (tipping up his bottle post-equivocation).

"How do I do what, sir?"

I knew quite well what he meant. But like the main of humanity, I wanted my pride gratified.

"Go on like that." He wrinkled his nose, sneezing into his sleeve. A smattering of blood baptized it. "Everyone else is sick in this god-forsaken circus, including me. How do you manage? You must be a witch. A stalwart, sulking she-devil in human form, untouched by mortal woes. Eh?" He imbibed the remainder of the liquid, wiping his flushed face.

"It must take a demon to recognize one, sir."

"Ha! Typical, imperious, impious statement... all pagan, but true enough. I often despise you the most, Yasmin, for speaking truth in so fine and deft a manner. I've never heard your equal."

"Not so. You have heard my equal in your own self."

I marked the fact that he had finally begun to call me by my name as a matter of course. *Fräulein* was the cold, impersonable title he formerly attributed to me... when he troubled himself to dispense with unpleasant adjectives.

Hue gave me a look which I suppose I deserved... a look of hesitating suspicion. "Really," he rejoined. "Then, if that's how you perceive me, I would expect you to pay more attention to my lessons. You used to be the most impressive rope artisan in the county. You could be still, but you stiffen your neck to my instruction." He nudged the empty bottle at his feet, yawning widely.

"And you, sir, have the aptitude to don your vest each day, thereby filling it with the most striking, charismatic, and successful ringmaster that any vest could bless itself to decorate... but here you stand." I pointed tranquilly at the bottle.

I think my lesson must have cut. The ringmaster said nothing; he handed bottle the fourth to me and stumbled away.

Drifting off among the trees, I caught at falling leaves for a time to examine their various veins and colorations. The fine-tuned ear, however, could pick up the throaty complaints, threats, and perverse *Flüche*[1] of the drunken sufferer. I soon gave in to my hidden inclination to yet soothe, yet please, and yet serve... an inclination greatly diminished but not gone. I glided into his tent unbidden.

"What do you want?" Thus his kindly accost.

"To help you."

"I am not so drunk as all that. I may not see the knife, or the poison bowl, or the contortionist's native darts, but you have one from among that agreeable arsenal. Away with you! It is not in my plans to be killed today."

"You believe I am a murderess?" I could not keep my smile at bay. Erbanhue is the best fun in the world when he's in humor.

---

1. Curses or oaths

"And here is the perfect opportunity, *capire?* Nobody's around... No one will care... I'm too weak to move, I s'pose... Do go away."

He tossed and turned in childish vexation. I ruminated on his changing tones. I sensed an ill wind coming. But amusement was scarce, or at least the type of amusement I liked. I would yet stay for it.

"Indeed, I won't go. I am your humble servant, nothing more; but if it pleases you, consider *that* in practical application. If you die, sir, at whose feet must I grovel then? My primary occupation would be lost."

"No doubt, no doubt, gorgeous one," (and he laughed, for I am not gorgeous), "Witch that you are, you will follow me directly into Hades, and you will jeer me there. My eternity is not safe from you."

"Nor your present. I am the worst sort of witch, the type that retains empathy for base humankind... I shall not leave a sick man to die of cold and stupidity. Sit up, sir. You are soaked, and your shirt must be changed."

"What care I for the cold? Damn it... damn everything, and you most of all!"

I had not endured his vocal menaces some years for nothing. Off came the drink-soaked shirt. On went a clean, dry shirt. Away went the dirt from his coughing, grimacing countenance. As I ministered to him, my eyes could not help dwelling on the tattoos imprinted across his chest and upper shoulders: depictions of great war-ships, traces of mighty lions, dates and signatures of significance unknown (to me at least), maps and constellations, serpents and soldiers and swords. He was beginning to look like a walking picture book. I told him so.

"---- ------!" said he. (I shall not affront my reader's intellect with so coarse a phrase.) I requested that he hold his tongue.

Erbanhue grimaced, staring at me for some minutes. The narrow eyes put me under examination, attempting to burrow into my thoughts. "How long have you worked for me?"

"About four years."

"And you have been afraid of me all that time?"

"Naturally, sir." Not *afraid*, exactly... I would have to invent a word for the sort of emotion he inspired... but I agreed with the false stigma. I was curious to see where the pretext would lead him.

"You hate me?"

"As one fell demon is jealous of another."

"Then why don't you leave me alone?"

"Because I cannot."

"Why not, you brainless thing?"

I paused, considering my answer. It must be blunted. With wily Erbanhue, one cannot let a sentiment penetrate too far. Then again, in his current state, perhaps I would gain the upper hand through vocal force. "Because," I saucily put forth, "your well-being is so very repugnant to my soul, and yet so necessary; also, I find you singularly ugly, and long have I endeavored to calculate the source of the ugliness, more spiritual than physical."

He crowed with laughter. "I thought so! I knew it. You are in love with me, then."

The remark on its own feet did not phase me. Erbanhue is nothing if not vain. No, it was the insolent, flushed, watered-down, joking look that dressed the phrase. *That* drew my wrath.

I knew that any other young woman would have merited a semi-respectful sort of deprecation. He would have laughed with Sallix and the other menfolk, mocking the lady's misplaced devotion. Yet, while scorning her hapless goal, he never would have mocked her to her face.

And yet for *me*, the talented and serviceable Yasmin, for *me* he had nothing but bad-flavored raillery. My loyalty was strained and stubborn, but still I was loyal. Did that count for nothing?

Erbanhue had never truly maimed me before, only skin-deep. *This* treatment lanced my seventh layer. "That is a falsehood beggaring description," I said, rising and casting the cloth to his feet. "It only shows the depth and width – to say nothing of height and volume - of your vanity. Unless you wish to waken one night with a knife to your throat, you will never say such a thing again."

"You say so! Forsooth! She has more of a passion for me than I thought. What a loving glance is hers! What a soft embrace she longs to bestow upon me! However, I shall resist. At the end of the soft hand grows dangerous claws. Will you just stay with me? Will you nurse me through the night?" And he laughed again, enjoying himself immensely.

"I will see you in Hades first." Not exactly ladylike, but effective. After all, circus performers are not ladies.

He was rocking with mirth, delighted that he had truly roused me at last. It may have been only the drinking, but I cared not. I left him.

I swore that it would be last time I nursed him, or lifted my hands to assuage any physical suffering of his.

I avoided him whenever I could. Erbanhue was confounded. He could not remember the awkward insanctity of his words. He only recalled that I had come to him in his tent and done something about seeing to his comfort. My iron animosity puzzled him.

In attempting to solve the mystery he tried various tactics: wrath, raving, sulking, teasing, insulting, turning cold shoulders, and the like. At last, he even tried flattery. I was insensible to every approach.

At the end of the week he brought me coffee during my morning exercise, as he had done before. I snubbed him so thoroughly that he drained the coffee himself in two gulps and "swore by his ancestors to never instruct me again, I must just stand on my own feet." A rather amusing declaration, by the way, as I was already standing firmly "on my own feet."

In due time, the troupe could not help taking note of the flaming catapults. Formerly, they were kept in neat reserve. Now they fired on sight.

"Miss Yasmin, has the Master done something to offend you seriously?" Sallix prodded me. "Everyone has their own rows with him, but yours seems fixed as fate. What have you done?"

"What have *I* done?" I seethed at the words. But nothing short of immediate descent into damnation could compel me to relate what he had said that night.

Luckily, no one had the vaguest inkling of what may or may not have been the case... or so I surmised, until August deprived me of this sweet misconception. "I heard your voices raised," August affirmed, stopping me in my chore to feed the horses. "Is what he said true? Do you care for him, Yassy?"

"What do you suppose, August?" I turned on him sharply, actually seizing his arm and giving it a squeeze less than amiable. "Do you suppose that I am in love with such a man as that?"

"You are like him, you know," the boy protested, struggling under my firm grasp. "You are just like him!" He escaped from my hands and ran away, leaving me to ponder his statement and pour out the feed in heated, violent sweeps.

My chilly, dispassionate self, like the blazing Dragon? Bah!

Chapter Eleven

Nightmares and Decline

There are certain events in the life of a performer from which I do derive pleasure. On one occasion when we were permitted to leave the circus grounds and go into town, I saw a musician mounted on a self-made stage, playing Irish melodies with dramatic enjoyment and pleasure.

Reader, I see him yet. Light curling hair, shining and rich and well-tended, a clear and full complexion attesting to a good appetite for his healthy meals: so delicate and so tender a touch upon his musical servant, and two blue wells for eyes, placid and "full of soul."

This, thought I, *is the enfleshment of happiness.* This is what contentment is. I stood by and watched him closely. Let Master Erbanhue draw nigh and gaze his fill; let him contrast himself against this beautiful lad, overbrimming with cordial intent, fulfilled and pleased and pleasing others, one of the most handsome sights my beauty-loving eyes have ever been or will be graced with. Without speaking to me, or hazarding more than one cursory glance, that boy did me good.

Feeling more at peace than I had felt for many a month, I wandered down-stream with the crowd and looked in shop windows. As a child I had practically lived in costume, but now I was developing a keen relish for the ordinary fashions, and silently envying the ladies of the flowing, grave, majestic gowns and concealing veils. It would amuse my reader to know how often I turned over various projects in my brain to affect an exchange, thereby acquiring the cash with which to purchase such coveted and costly array. Costly it was, nonetheless, and I could only deck myself out via imagination.

I passed a certain shop. Faintly hungry senses sharpened at the scent of breaded fish.

Now, it happened that I was acquainted with Erbanhue's preference of taste. Not easily would he overlook a fish breaded and baked to perfection, at any season, day, or hour. Brief was my consideration; boldly did I refuse it. "A treat for *him*! It would be like me, indeed, to treat my jailor, as a prisoner begging release. He must just look out for himself."

Look out for yourself!

Such a cutting, doleful, hateful phrase! It struck out in my mind red and painful as a venomous blow. "You are just like him!" August's assertion echoed.

No, I am not! I heaved an involuntary sigh. Guilted into action, I entered the shop and withdrew several coins from among my hoard of earnings. Having purchased and bagged the snack - not without a twinge in my stomach and a hungry sniff - I reentered the circus grounds with alacrity. "Here is a test not comfortable, nor likely to result in comfort, but a test of some interest," I regarded it in this light. Doffing my shawl from my shoulders, I sought the victim out.

If I have not mentioned the contortionist Chaske in recent writings, it is because I personally had very little to do with him. As I passed his tent, I could hear his low melodic speaking in the tongue of his ancestors; I shuddered and quickened my pace. As a child, I had reflected too well and too often upon his eerie tales of gods in the woods. I had no desire to reawaken such musings now.

Imagination can be a tyrannous thing, all too ready to capture and control and persist, until you are led by overwhelming ideas into the lands where no mortals ought to go, even in speculation.

My search becoming wholly unavailing of its object, I sought out Sallix. "Where is Master Hue?"

"God knows," he replied. "He went to town himself today, strange enough for him. I doubt he will return in his right mind. I have half an idea to bring him back by force, if need be... but we know how well he would receive it, and how exacting his vengeance would be on the morrow. I do not think it would be wise."

I didn't care to fetch a reply from among my wounded thoughts. Morbid, unjustifiable womanhood! I felt snubbed (as if Erbanhue ought to know I would bring him gifts). I ate the treat myself. No doubt my reader reproaches this behavior, as I do now, but it was too late.

I had meant to appease him. Fate denied me the chance. But my punishment would come in due course... that very night, in fact.

Nightmares are not uncommon to those poor in fortune. I had seen many times, since my adventure in the tiger's cage, a cloaked and hooded man reaching for my throat. Time and again I attempted to view the full form of my persecutor, but I saw nothing but his shadow, and felt a burning in my eyes like hot needles. Habit compelled me to cease and desist, staring only at my own dream-hands. Whatever they touched, they distorted. Little as I possessed in the way of beauty, I lamented the disfigurement. Every morning I would awaken and eagerly examine my hands for reassurance.

They remained ghastly and pale, extending into reddish-purple fingertips. Something was not right about them. I took to wearing gloves.

In my youth I often stole glances at Erbanhue's hands, for in my heart I believed it was he who had struck me down and put me into the cage, as revenge for some imagined slight against himself. I recalled seeing in a brief glimpse the flash of Hue's angry, mismatched eyes. The hands in my dream, however, were too thin to be his own. As I progressed in age and therefore in reason, I objected to these suspicions.

I suffered from recurring visions. That was all.

Until the age of twenty, the years passed on wings of wind. Twenty and above morphed into seasons of rock and weight. They dragged on with ceaseless work, endless scarcity, frequent illness (among others), rapid decline.

As before, my own body remained virtually changeless as the members around me suffered. Due to this, and my natural bitter tact, the gulf between me and my fellow workers widened all the more. The flavor of Erbanhue's perception of me became so muffled and changeful that I knew not what to think of him anymore. The Master, once best interpreted by Yasmin's written word - better than any other study on earth - ranged beyond her comprehension; she knew not what to say in his presence.

I could almost believe he was frightened of me. But this was unthinkable! He developed the habit of watching me with an odd, sidelong gaze, neither hateful nor exactly despairing, but still quite gloomy... sad, frustrated, weary, and... hopeless.

I had never seen Erbanhue hopeless before. I did not like it.

Trinna noted it also and predicted failure for our troupe. Sallix took on more and more of Erbanhue's duties, as that affable man acquired a taste for hiding and sulking in his tent. "What is this emotion?" I asked myself in my bewilderment, "Am I disgusted and confounded? Yes! I am both; though why I should trouble myself about him, I do not know. What is anyone to me?"

The tumble of the Master from his masterful estrade felt like a loss within my own persona; where he diminished was my loss, and his decline tempted me to decline also. Whether he read my reaction or not, I do not venture to guess. I do know that he avoided me more than ever. He even sabotaged my ropes once or twice, as if in hopes of causing an injury. I calmly reattached new ropes and said nothing.

"Unresting, unhasting" without, and confused and wondering within, I agreed with Trinna in secret that we were not meant to last another year.

"Why doesn't Yasmin simply run away?" you may ask.

Well, Reader, there are not many avenues for an aerialist, whose whole universe comprises of rough manners, physical tasks, minor education, and general poverty of mien and mind. I could mend for my living, or perhaps learn to cook; but thanks to a perverse hatred of normalcy, I would rather be chained and tormented than succumb to the natural world. My fancy was my daily bread, and independent of the cruelties under certain keepers, there was a freedom in the circus that I would not part with for a fortune. I was convinced that giving it up for the grimness of reality would kill me faster than starvation.

It was winter. Darkness sang around the tents and we gathered together closer than usual, willing to endure the snarls and spits, curses and snores and coughs, rather than the piercing chill. I sat down and wrapped my feet in rags, intending to go out and dig for roots to flavor the soup.

"I will be back, Trinna," I said. In spite of her prattling nonsense, I did come to like her, and consented to share my blanket with her and no other. Lillias had perished some time ago.

Taking my reclaimed gray shawl, with Lillias' initials laced upon it like a ragged frown, I darted outside and ran through the woods. I hoped to make my excursion short, for the cold could not be borne many minutes.

The change from fireside to whistling cold energized me. I darted around mounds and trees with enthusiasm. Sallix, I knew, had begged of the Indian to set about making traps; he and Chaske were hunting nearby, so I was not afraid of being alone. Indeed, if my fancy had allowed it, a few of the nearest trees looked like the Black Tree of eld, but I shut my thoughts to the impression and refused to let darkness reform my reality. Sallix and Chaske were close. I took comfort in that.

My enthusiasm, like most of my daydreams, was quickly snuffed as the cold increased. I drew my shawl tighter and wished for the thousandth time that my dress was woolen instead of cotton. Spying a protruding cluster of good shape and size, I dropped to my knees and began to harvest. Most roots hereabouts do practically nothing as a soup additive - but desperation provokes action, however slight, and soon I had a handful of the unappealing improver.

As I scrambled to my feet, I saw a man.

He had the height and build of a tall spindle-tree, a very white face, and hands as sheer as ice. He was dressed in the darkness of the night, shod in shoes of silence, and cloaked in some softly folding hood. He... or it... had – this was the trait which caused me to halt as if precipitously dumb – no eyes, nose, mouth, or ears. That facial region was perfectly blank and smooth. I was staring into a beautiful, terrible mask of winter marble.

"Demon!" Reason shrieked. Imagination quailed and Pride quite deserted me. Anguish, Dismay, Nausea: these main and immediate attendants put me out of my mind. I was too horrified to run. My feet were hammered to the ground, numb and obstinate.

Neither I nor the Thing moved. Strangely, gently, a childlike curiosity began to edge its way into my brain. It carefully pushed away my fears. I took a step or two. A flash of something, unconscious insight perhaps, caused me to examine the creature's hands. They were long and thin, not unlike my attacker's hands from years ago. But they were not black and shadowed. They were white – I could say blindingly white, pure white, white as alabaster. They appeared soft and agile. The man-creature allowed me to examine them with immovable patience.

If it *was* a creature, it was certainly not afraid of me.

Another cascade of emotion, strong and swift, rose upon me – that of apprehension, wonder, admiration. A calm, self-assured, ancient power leaked from this creature's still body. As of yet it had not moved nor, indeed, made a single indication of being alive at all. Yet I respected its lithe quality, its stern silence, and its vast influence. It seemed a wise, potent entity, pulsing contorting waves of energy. I could feel him monitoring the ground, sensing every living thing around him.

It occurred to me that perhaps this was one of the ancient wood-gods that Chaske spoke of. But if that were so, could not the Being speak? Should I dare to deliver the language of base men to a creature of Tophet?

During contemplation, I had not noticed the crunch of approaching feet nor the murmur of men's voices. "Yasmin!"

The shout appalled me. I jerked upright (I had been leaning my head to one side). I peered and beheld Sallix and Chaske approaching. "I am here," I answered.

"It is too late for you to be out in this devilish weather," Sallix preached. "And did you not know we were out hunting? I might have struck thee. Have you no brains, woman?"

"It is indeed the Devil's weather," I responded.

"And no sane mortal should be out in it. I see that you have roots for the soup. Let us go back, and we shall have something with it!" And Sallix nudged Chaske, who dangled by its poor legs a small rabbit.

I turned away my face. Neither the sight of the gentle animal's glassy eyes, nor of the Demon hovering just behind Sallix (who saw him not), was much calculated to produce hunger.

Sallix felt generous with his luck, and consented to escort me back. I left the mystery behind with a good will. Nevermore would I hope, or plan, or believe, for Fate had cursed us all, and a Devil had been set upon our very tracks. We would indeed be finished before the year. His appearance marked the finish.

Chapter Twelve

THE CURSE FROM A STABLE BOY

Although I thought of the Demon often, it was with a passive morbidity. I knew He meant for me to see Him, and only the deadliest or the most stupid of predators would allow his prey to become alerted to his presence. Is He merely arrogant, or is He a harbinger of death itself?

In either case, I need not worry. If a wandering spirit, it was unnecessary to fear Him; if he was Death itself, there was nothing I could do. Pushing against Fate with weary, pale, mortal hands would not shake the power of eons.

It never occurred to me to doubt the evidence of my eyes. I may have been accused of being prone to visions, but I now I knew my attacker and the creator of my dreams. I know who drove me between Darius' paws, and who hunted down our troupe, and who rained down pain and hatred and misfortune upon a willing and hard-working group that ought to be as closely bonded as a family.

Within my soul, it never made sense that Erbanhue's Circus ought to have as poor a fate as ours suffered. While every man is portioned his serving of ill, ours was beyond the common lot. And if anyone is to doubt, I implore them to look upon the troupe as it was, and as it soon became within weeks of seeing the Demon. Draw the fatal conclusion.

For the Dragon's teeth were ground into sand, his claws into nubs, and his flame into dross. Erbanhue shivered in the corner of his tent, half-dressed, both bare feet tucked into his worn top hat for meager warmth. He hardly spoke more than three sentences in a day, and could not even drown in drink to escape, as there was not a drop to be had. August was too ill to go a'thieving, and I refused to procure it.

Speaking of August, it was gall to my feelings to dwell on the living August and to remember the dead Lillias. That the pure, sweet, harmless darling should be taken away, and the sour, scornful boy should remain, was but another proof that evil strove against us.

Trinna, the silly, simple little soul that she was, had attempted to nurse this promising male root back into health and usefulness.

But August spurned her offering, as God had rejected Cain's mass of ground-wealth. And not unlike Cain, August turned against the one of good intent, applying to her a fair dose of the poisonous language learned from the Master. The angry upstart seemed well-placed to pick up where our broken Master Hue had left off.

"Yasmin?"

I heard the boy call for me.

I did not wish to go. But after all, perhaps he may die; as much as I disliked him, it is bad to die alone. I would wait with him.

It was soon over.

Before breathing his last, this conversation took place between us.

"Yasmin," he said as I entered the tent where he beds, "before you mock me, I have not called you in to play nurse."

"Oh? Haven't you?" I settled some distance from him, not eager to catch his illness, whatever it was and however contracted. "We all know your distaste for it," he continued, "and I shouldn't like it myself. I've wanted to ask you something."

"What is it? Be brave; I have been distant, perhaps, but it is only my nature. I will listen."

After a short pause and a hard cough, August sighed. "I know your doubts of the supernatural, and your sneers for Chaske's stories. You know I have always believed in them."

Having not long ago beheld a Demon, I could not affirm what was once my belief, nor did I feel led to deny it. I kept my own counsel. "I understand. Go on."

"Some days ago, before I became ill, Erbanhue said he saw you early in the morning." He sought my face for information; I would not hazard any.

"He says you walked three times around the horse-tent. You threw a handful of dust into the air, let it fall to the ground, and walked once more around where I slept. A few nights later, I became very sick, and nothing seems to help me..." He coughed, spattering blood.

"Yasmin... Yassy..." His voice, recently deepened according to his attainment of age, went high again like a child. "Erbanhue has said that you are a witch. Is it true? Did you curse me? Am I... am I going to die?" Then came trembling, failing, sobbing. "Why? Why do you hate me so? Why do you hate everyone?"

I yearned to deny this. To say that I did *not* hate everyone. But as the reverse was much truer than I had realized, my lips could not lie. I mutely shook my head. Lillias no longer drew breath. Most of the troupe frowned at the sight of me. Demarion was locked up in an asylum, left far behind; Madame Tola was dead; I had never liked August; Erbanhue was no longer himself. Therefore, I *did* dislike everyone.

"I know I haven't been kind to you," he sniffed. "But I only stole from you when I was a child, and starving, and we were both snapping at one another. I have just as much right to curse *you*, if I could, as you have cursed me."

This was another truth that I could not deter.

He resumed. "But you will go to punishment when you die. You only want to send me first. Do you think I deserve a longer punishment than you? But you won't win," regathering his blanket and his pride, "for I have prayed to God for mercy. He shall use your curse against you. He will curse you in return! And you will suffer as I have suffered." His pitch rose to a yell, and his face became quite black. "I die in the presence of a witch, but the witch will die in the presence of demons!"

Reader, I was frightened. This was not the speech of August, the stable boy, the untaught and unteachable. This was another voice. Instantly, I knew who was speaking through him.

"I see in your eyes that speaking on my own behalf is worse than useless," I said. "Therefore, I will not attempt to deny what it is impossible for me to prove. But if I told you, for instance, that I was lying quiet in my cot, and saw sneaking past the shadow of Erbanhue; if I claimed I saw him stumble into Lillias' tent, and there mourn over her unconscious form as if guilty, you would not believe me."

August's eyes, bright with anger, began to appear glassed and fogged; he was going.

"And if you would believe it, I have not the time. Farewell, August..." My voice had changed in turn. I felt my hands shaking, as they had after the incident with Darius.

I rose and left the body. It fell upon me to tell Trinna that we must dig another grave. After speaking with her, I went in pursuit of the Chaske, who knew by his art that August was dead. He irritated me by pretending to know his cause of death. "You have a power beyond my knowledge," said he, between prayerful mutterings. "A power of which the bearer is not even conscious is the most powerful of all. I ask you again, will you let me teach you? Ah, to be in touch with that power! What could hinder it? You could save us from certain destruction, Witch Yasmin!"

Anger at such blatant imbecility fueled my response. I drew myself up to full height. "You are a foolish man! I wish you would cease all allusions to me. I despise the title you so blindly attribute to me. I, and I alone, know the true cause of the death of Lillias, by a hand I could not stop... by a demonic hand that was controlling *his* hand... But I know nothing of August's death, and I would never kill willingly. Let me alone!"

Halfway through this rejection, the Indian turned. For the first time I got a clear, close look into his face. Tanned and tattooed, like Erbanhue's, it secured an air of strength and cunning. There the resemblance ceased. In Chaske's high bone structure and the lines beneath his eyes, one read ancient faith, submissive abilities, and tamed fires. "No longer fear that I mean to use you. I may have meant it at the time. However, I now know the fearful power that I have sensed among us for many suns. Great Witch Anmut, I plead your mercy, and humbly ask that you devote your art to healing our fortunes."

To punctuate this ridiculous plea, he actually knelt before my feet, holding both hands in the air as if in worshipful salute. Tired, annoyed, and disconcerted beyond anything I had ever felt, I tore away from him and hid for several hours, trembling behind a large tree. I cannot remember what else I said, so wild and searching were my thoughts, but I do remember "*Mein Gott, bewahre mich vor dem Bösen! Mein Gott, bewahre mich vor dem Bösen!*"[1]

1. "My God, save me from evil!"

Chapter Thirteen

A Blessing from a Ringmaster

I woke behind the tree. My searching hands blistered against the bark, and I remembered where I was. I had concealed myself until I fell asleep from pure exhaustion, seeking its release from terror.

For a harrowing moment I believed I looked upon the long, bending, slight physique of my demonic attacker. I sat up on the verge of shrieking, only to behold the branches of the tree... It was only a hallucination, a spawn of panic. I calmed.

My first order of business was breakfast. I hoisted myself to my feet, wincing at the soreness and stinging pain that raced down my spine. Holding my throbbing head between my hands, I stumbled toward the tents. I paused to splash my worn face in the freezing creek. The spectacle in the liquid was anything but earthly. I looked calm, meditative, and spectral. My hair was cloudy and unmanageable, frayed with broken ends.

My cotton dress barely concealed the tall and bony frame it adorned. I did, indeed, look rather like a witch.

Pleasant conjecture! I shook myself for my doubts and got up again, refusing to stop until I reached home.

The walk took much longer than I had anticipated. I seemed certain enough of my direction, but it was as if my feet had other ideas. They had compasses of their own that they utilized in Knowledge's stead. Reader, I was simply disoriented and weak from thirst. But the wall I built restricting proper analysis - resurrected under Erbanhue's years of instruction - did not come down at the asking. After moaning, lamentations, and turn-abouts, I fell at the base of my tent and thanked whatever power that exists that I had made it safely.

I'd felt the Demon at my heels all the while.

"By God! It is the witch. Have you finished robbing graves?"

No need to look and confirm. The Dragon's spits were devoid of flame and spark. I motioned with my hand, commanding silence.

"All foul and strong, of course. We are moving on from this place, for while you were brewing and 'incantating,' I have been working. We are traveling to E----- Town. Get up! And gather your things. Witch or not, you can best the ropes - Aye, and gracefully, too, you heathen she-devil! We cannot do without you."

I stared at him. Call me void of sense, or simply desperate; use whatever adherent you will. I was *glad* to hear him talk so. This was the Erbanhue of old. He must have secured a good position for us.

I gazed up at him through my curtain of grayish hair. He towered above me, yet dirty and disheveled, chin covered with soap and a razor in one hand. In spite of his half-dressed glories, he beamed at me. The jeweled eyes, luminous with an unharmonious blend of recent illness and new hope, brilliantly proclaimed "Some good luck at last!"

The awakened Dragon spoke again. "Perhaps that brat's death was the turn of the tide, for the acceptance letter came directly after."

He leaned over me, confidentially adding in my ear, "I blame you not for doing it. He was a thief and a bore, and he bothered me with his ceaseless complaining. And devils and wood-gods, indeed! Didn't he beg the Indian for stories! As if we weren't plagued enough with superstitious foolery. Upon my word, I'm glad you did it, and I won't tell a soul."

I was quick to set him straight. "Indeed, I don't know what you mean, except that your own superstitious fancy has run away with your fine head. I never had anything to do with him, to live or to die. And as far as 'not telling a soul,' if you are referring to my reputation as a witch, you needn't trouble yourself. You are the last to accuse me."

"Ah. Her verbal darts are quick and sharp, as prior. I'm rather glad to see them." He stooped to catch me by the arms and raise me to my feet, christening me with soap suds in the process. "Be quick. We will depart within an hour." He walked away whistling.

It took a minute for my mind to catch up with what my ears had received. I reviewed everything that had happened.

To tally: Demarion was rendered insane by causes unknown. Madame Tola was missing and assumed dead. Later reports reached us of her bracelets being found by the lake; it is assumed that she drowned herself. Lillias was dead. August was dead. Erbanhue had nearly escaped death, for he had been remarkably ill.

Chaske and Sallix had thought it proper to fix for themselves a miserable fight. Sallix had been poisoned... though he yet retained life, it was not without weakness. Mathilda was recovering from a recent fall from the back of her horse, which had reared at a pinnacle moment.

Only the juggler, the fire-eater, the contortionist, Kirkland, Erbanhue, and I were fit to be seen by an audience... and Erbanhue's health was shaky.

What a magnificent caper we would cut! What a troupe to arrive in a new town! For a second, I was tempted to rush up behind Master Hue and knock him down. To have the insolence to stride off *whistling*, when we are in such a state! But the other half of me admired his resilience, for I had feared he had lost it to be seen nevermore.

Trinna broke my reverie by seizing me unexpectedly. "Yasmin," she pleaded, her voice tremulous and her eyes full of pained tears, "Chaske has just discovered that his pouch of darts and his fungal powder are both missing. You... *you* didn't take them, did you?"

"Whatever would I want them for?"

"Well, for your-" I dispensed a hard stare. She ceased. "I thought you might be interested in such things."

"No."

"Oh... I believe you."

The fear in her eyes betrayed her. She practically ran from me.

In leaving camp, the heavy work and the rush gave us all the warmth that watching and waiting never could grant. In spite of our hard lot, we cheered, and Erbanhue's passionate tunes continued to penetrate the bustle. And in spite of myself (for I was determined to be rude to everyone), I felt my spirits rise.

While it was idiotic to hope that any malevolent force would cease due to changing locations, it was pleasant to leave.

I helped attach the horses to Demarion's wagon, for it was meant to carry poor Mathilda. She was not permitted to walk. Being alarmingly short of working hands, Hue instructed me to lead these horses along and take care of them… a station which had once belonged to August.

This circumstance propelled me to consider the lad's demise. His illness had been very brief, and the symptoms rather unlike the sickness that had swept the troupe (in everyone but myself). When putting one thing with another, I considered the Indian's missing trophies were behind the death of August. The lad had poisoned himself.

Therefore, I was hardly surprised when the juggler, in folding up August's things, discovered the pouch and the empty papers partially hidden in straw. The juggler showed Trinna the items, and they looked at me askance; they whispered, doubtless believing that I had forced the lad to take them, or somehow hypnotized him… for where they imagined, they believed, and where they believed, nothing could dissuade. What could I do?

Again, I could do nothing at all. I had no proof.

We arrived at E----- after a few stops and only minor difficulties. The prospect was pleasing. Our encampment was settled near a farmer's plot, and we were offered the service of his own well, an occurrence which cheered us mightily. Then, our post was on a hill, looking down into the city valley in which we were meant to perform. Marcus, in going through town to distribute our announcements, reported multiple pleasantries. Included among these were a bookshop, not one but *two* bread shops, sweetmeat sellers who offered delivery, and a few good clothing shops that boasted bargains magnificent in the way of woolen dress and smart winter caps.

I longed to purchase something in the way of winter apparel. I was heartily sick, I assure thee, of my flimsy summer cotton, which was the only dress I owned (much of my salary being withheld due to Erbanhue's steady retrenchment of moneymeed). I went to the Master and calmly but distinctly intimated that I wished for my proper due.

Why I had *not* demanded complete payment in my history, I need not explain, as the reader has seen in more than one instance the happy relations between us. The "Witch Anmut," however, was to be more cautiously revered than the ordinary Fräulein of meager proportions. My request was complied with.

I wrapped the money in a corner of my shawl with the utmost care. I kept casting approving looks upon the smiling, shining faces, so nicely bedded in the tired gray folds, with a glance of appreciation and reverence. It had been many a month since I beheld so vast a portion in my possession. I descended, my makeshift purse cautiously guarded, to have myself measured for a dress and cap. Wonder of wonders!

A path most amiable and easy opened before my feet. The country trees fringed our camp, giving way before a gentle slope bedewed with foliage, as tender and shivering as raindrops. It was such a pleasant walk. A cheering zephyr blew, strongly enough to stir and encourage slow bloods, but not enough to chill or irritate.

I was ignored by the citizens. But this was a common circumstance, and not rare enough to disturb me. Not experienced enough to judge from window to window which shop was least detrimental to my shawl-pocketbook, I dove into the first one I came across.

The dresswoman, of course, treated me with condescension. However, having turned a corner of the shawl to reveal a slim but respectable hoard, that lady's mien was changed. She fluctuated between respect and doubt with a vacillation amusing to witness. Despite this social catastrophe, we came to an agreement. I was measured, the price was quoted, the material cut, and one week later I returned again. I left in state with a brown paper parcel hugging a soft woolen blend, maroon in color, with a matching cloth cap adorned in black ribbon.

On purpose, I had purchased a little extra material in order to refit (or at least somewhat repair) my old red slippers. The tint would not match, but in my case I preferred to rebuild some savings in coin… one never knew what turn things could take.

In the deep cauldron of my thoughts, I contemplated another course in life… a different avenue, a plan for which frugality was necessary. It was a brew both audacious and somewhat faithless, but now and again I returned to my cauldron, and gave the prospectus a turn of the spoon. I was not willing to let it blacken from inactivity.

Armed with dress, shawl, and a humble lunch, I returned to my tent in triumph. There I repaired my slippers in peace and industry in my spare moments. In due time a serviceable dress emerged, all whole and complete, though near vision proved some of the hurried stitching to be rather irregular… for I was no fonder of close work than I had been in my youth.

The result was a trim-waisted bodice, closed with small ebony buttons. It descended into a full skirt of appropriate length and swirling breadth. And best of all, I rejoiced in the pair of highly satisfactory puffs adorning the shoulders and tapering down to pointed sleeves, culminating in a rather aristocratic point at the backs of the hands.

I felt in my heart that nothing more could be desired. In truth it was simple almost to puritanism – no frills, not a pocket, not a tuck, the sole ornaments being the sleeves – but it gave me the greatest delight. To me, Reader, the rich color seemed nothing short of regal to their satisfied recipient. Having finished my shoes, I hastily donned the completed outfit. I donned the smart cap "fearfully and wonderfully made," rendered jaunty with a touch of ribbon 'round its circumference.

It must be confessed that I brushed my locks with care. Tucking the voluminous burden well beneath the hat, I marched out, curious to see what the well-water would say when I applied to it for a diagnosis. The result was not disappointing. I saw in the reflection a woman, not pretty but decent, with a shining ebony bow above one temple. The cap successfully concealed the wild hair in a proud woolen encasement. The witch's gaunt figure was well disguised, looking deceptively neat and tidy in a maroon gown of proper length. I made, I believed, a good and graceful figure. I no longer feared going into town as a disgraceful subject for human eyes.

For my own particular reason, I chose to embark on a second walk through the encampment. Kirkland stared, Sallix grinned, and Hue cursed.

Satisfied, I returned to the city for another walk, for city life pleases me in small quantities. Did the smells, the sights, the bustle, the purchasing and bartering and talking, confuse and dismay my solitary vestments? Not so! I was happy, dearest Reader, truly happy. I wandered there for hours without wearying, and ate a modest dinner with the air and deportment of a queen. It had been years since I was able to dine in a restaurant – an occurrence which tickled Memory and awakened her. As I tasted and was satisfied, I thought of my mother.

Chapter Fourteen

THE TURNING OF FORTUNE

It came in timid but certain steps. A peace unlike anything I had known since the passing of Beryl Lange stole across Erbanhue's Traveling Circus. Our troupe gathered might and health, we improved monetarily and morally, and amiable evening campfires were in fashion. At first, Erbanhue shunned these parties on plea of business. Soon not even he could resist the tempting cadence of laughter and storytelling that often rose among the smokes of warm, crackling flames. We enjoyed one another's company as any circus troupe should. It was forgotten that I was called a witch.

"You need not kill yourself vaulting at every performance," Hue was saying in one of his fits of fireside kindliness. Despite his wary side glances time and again, he persisted in addressing me when he was "being good."

"I have taken a liking to the subtler, more dancing style, and the audience likes it," he announced. "I think you ought to do it."

"If you say so, then I've no objection. I can do either." To hide a smile, I casually rubbed the back of my hand against my mouth. I had been using this method for six months!

Blissfully unaware of his blindness, Erbanhue nodded. "Yes, you can do both. You have improved."

Other people must have thought so. Sometimes methought I was being followed post-performance by an unwanted worshipper or two. I concocted various means of returning to camp unseen, and was debating within myself whether to secure an escort, when the Fates reeled me about again. I yielded to the inevitable.

Our Saturday performance was, almost without omission, the longest and most spectacular that we could conjure. As Saturday is the last night before piety is vicariously followed, human nature acquires an insatiability for the freakish and fantastic. It was our duty to satisfy.

Erbanhue opened with the darkest and most shadowed stage possible, with Marcus the fire-eater darting in without warning and deploying a shocking breath of the reddest flames.

After a brief but impressive manifesto, Erbanhue emerged decked out in a silvery, star-spangled costume of black velvet, surmounted with a silky cloak. His moustache was shaped with pomade, and his brows shone aglow, eyes smoldering alive as they borrowed from the ranks of fallen angels. He gestures, he pivots, he almost flies in the faces of the enraptured audience (targeting the beautiful ladies). He is before me even now! His voice alternates, now a soft tenor, now a brave and dark shout as passionate excitement is commanded by his tyrannous movements, returned threefold to its audience. Depending on the quality of his movements and the rise of his voice, the remainder of the troupe is either fired by his example or repressed by his lack of enthusiasm. In short, he determined our success.

One summer night, he was in especially superb form. All of us caught the transformation and performed as souls possessed by every Muse in existence. After Erbanhue's introduction came Mathilda and her splendid work, for though she was small she was quite pretty, and the tininess of her limbs did little to diminish how perfectly turned they were, and how gracefully employed. She twirled from horseback without fear, leaped and posed without flaw. One would never guess she had ever been injured. I, among the thrilled audience (we'd never had such an audience before), cheered boisterously for the little performer.

Next came the "ring," or the general deployment of several side shows at once, wherein each of us had a place. I towered above them all on my ropes, delighting those below with daring leaps and feats of elegant balance.

We ran backstage for the third act among generous applause. Chaske was next, and went beyond himself, folding his form in ways that truly suggested the aid of the supernatural. Once more I could not resist joining the audience in the execution of murmurs, shudders, and delighted clapping.

Kirkland depicted Act the Fourth, completing the last wishes of the men's hearts by means of strength and lances and giant hammers. I was next.

Now, Reader, I had prepared my own act without aid or direction from anyone else. I had shaken off Erbanhue's controlling intentions the instant he indicated them. I let him fuss and rave and storm; fight as he would, I would plan my own show.

After all... I still rather liked to see him irritable. Sometimes I couldn't keep my smile tucked away. It *would* betray me.

In the city, I located and hired a street musician whom I had seen wielding a violin with passionate skill. Not liking the classic, prudish, opera style, the raw and gypsy-like flourish of his contented me to perfection.

I crafted for myself a blended dance and rope routine and a new suit of purple and black.

I eagerly awaited its culmination. Would it be well received? There had never been a show quite like it. Most traveling acts did not bother with background music. But I intended for my act to be more like a dance, performed in the air among the ropes and the ribbons.

I stood onstage, awaiting the cue.

There!

The first strains of his beloved instrument were played. I bent my arm slowly with calm grace, then raised it along with one leg, touching my toe to my fingertips. Gentle applause praised the effort. My dance was quite gentle, but interspersed with feats of turns and balance and dexterity, merging ballet and contortionist elements. At last I approached the rope.

I grasped it in my right palm, wrapping it around my arm. In time to the music, as practiced, Kirkland (behind the scenes) gradually raised the rope until I was suspended from the stage. Many hours had been devoted to this, as absolute stillness was required for a professional effect.

As the violinist's steady melody increased, not in speed but in feeling, I turned upon the rope, making delicate twirls perfectly matched to the music. Applause increased, and just as it seemed I could go no faster and do no more, I added and redirected, all-consumed with the performance. Tilting my head back suddenly, I threw my weight, thrusting myself upside down. With my foot, I twisted the rope higher up, securing it around one ankle. I let go. I twirled upside-down, and in the midst of center speed, let the rope unravel from my ankle.

Falling, I barely caught myself at the very end of the rope, to the breathless joy of the watchers below. It rather burned my fingers, but this also I was prepared to endure. I landed onstage in a difficult position. Straightening, I dropped a quiet curtsey.

There was a whisper, a murmur, and suddenly a simultaneous, erupting applause... all at once they were on their feet, smiling, cheering, waving, even throwing coins.

"Bravo! Magnifico!" cried a familiar voice, my violinist. I smiled and turned my hand in graceful acknowledgment. I looked for the Master with the corners of my eyes, but he was nowhere in the pits, where he ought to have been.

Then someone ran out from back stage and was fervently wringing my hand.

"Brilliant! So spirited! Quite spectacular!" cried Erbanhue's voice, the breath of his praise hot on my ears. "A true enchantress in our midst! A spell you have certainly wrought. Take another bow. Stand, every one of you! This is our hour of triumph!"

I was unable to hide the beaming pride that I felt on my face. The cheers redoubled. Erbanhue held one of my hands in his own and bowed with me. "Ladies and gentlemen, our charming aerialist! Our spellcaster divine, our enchanter spectacular, the Lady-Witch, Anmut!"

Standing right next to me, so proud. My heart swelled with joy. In that moment, I was his equal. These loud, delighted words, the new stage-name so happily pronounced, both pleased and pained; it was bitter and sweet. I dwelt on them over and over as I walked back to our encampment among a dancing and leaping troupe. They were babbling and chattering, trading goods and tossing coins, congratulating, singing, executing leaps and handsprings. They were verbally living and reliving the show that was our highest triumph to date. I could barely think, let alone be heard in the uproar. I wondered what dimension I was thus launched into, for this, *this* congregation was certainly not Erbanhue's Circus.

This was an anomaly, a daydream, a vision. Surely I was dreaming, for in the palm of my hand I felt a pile of cold shining money, collected from the stage with a baffled, shaking, glowing, happy hand, that surely was not *my* hand.

And yet, so it was. The bite of the hard coins as I squeezed them assured me that it was true.

Overwhelmed by my first true victory, I walked a little apart from the others. I regretted that I had not properly thanked my violinist. He had kindly pressed my hand against his lips, treating me like a lady of the court, and vanished, apparently made nervous by the shouting of the crowd.

Erbanhue appeared without warning. His long, firm stride crunched the thick summer grass. "A fine night, is it not? And our routine quite precisely managed. I have done well."

I was not surprised to hear him apply all merit to his own self. "*We* have done well, as you say," I supplied, a bit disconcerted, and letting him hear it in my tone of voice.

He chuckled. "You must admit, even *you*, that if I had not inspired you all to take the bull by the horns, you would not have triumphed to-night." He waved one hefty forefinger in my face, grinning.

"I admit, sir, that we often wilt when you do, as plants bemoan a covered sun. But do you assign any credit to anyone? What do you say of Mathilda?"

"Oh, she does well enough, for a midget. But *you*..." And he waved his hands, smiling widely, indicating that he had no words for such a triumph. But I had merely been inspired by Erbanhue the Great, of course.

At that moment I was jolted by an unseasonably warm premonition. It was an eerie sensation, and I was ill-equipped to interpret it. I allowed his praise to roll off my head and down my back, as effectively as water flows from the backs of water-fowls. Returning to customary coldness, I said "I beg you to refrain from praising me. It is a rarity I might compare to an earthquake, and its effects are hardly more pleasant."

"But indeed, you have improved! My work has finally reached its zenith. The little rope-girl is grown, and-"

He stopped and released my hand, his bronze complexion paling. For running up to us, with the speed indicative of tragedy, came Marcus.

"Matteo is dead, sir! He's been murdered."

"Murdered! Who the devil is Matteo? What does he mean to us?"

"Why, Miss Yasmin knows him. He was her violinist tonight."

Reader, believe me or not, I knew he would say so before he spoke. That warm jolt was felt both before Lillias' passing, and again before August's.

I had already perceived that my onetime companion was dead. "How was it done?" asked a shaking voice (I think it might have been mine).

"Stabbed through the heart, Fräulein."

"And the weapon?" (Erbanhue)

"Missing, sir, along with the money he earned tonight."

My hands shook involuntarily. The coins rattled within them. And Erbanhue, fraught with horror and violence, struck at me, causing the coins to tumble from my palms. Seeing the wealth, his expression became so ghastly that I lost no time in abandoning the hideous scene.

Chapter Fifteen

The Master of My Soul

I buried beneath several blankets, curling up on my cot. I plugged my ears against the whispers and exclamations floating 'round me. They circled me as Darius circled his dinner. Once I even considered joining the tiger in his den. Whether God would shut his mouth against me, or allow me to be devoured, was of little concern. I felt I *ought* to be consumed alive.

What sins have I committed?

This is what was said among them:

I did not kill Lillias. But I *had* poisoned August. This I could not prove in either direction. I probably attempted to take Erbanhue's life. The charming man claimed to spy me in the forsaken mornings, when no other creature stirred, on the witchling prowl. I circled his tent just as these rumors now circled mine.

Reader, would you believe that this spite against Yasmin Lange, which she had previously ignored with such patient carelessness, was now her greatest sorrow?

That brief, brief moment! When Erbanhue's praise was at last genuine and solid, speaking as friend to friend, and talent to talent. I yearned with all my might that I had never heard it. The taste of his praise meant more to me than all the shouts of the crowd combined. To touch it was to relive Eve's ancient curse. I had fallen to temptation in the splendid Garden of Gardens... I knew what it was to taste of golden richness, to inhale a smell better than the most delicate of perfumes, and to have the whole of the treat ravished from my lips.

Yet, even after that solitary bite, my eyes were opened to the divide. I was now eaten up by the battleground, busily distinguishing good from evil. At long last, I knew what good was, having lived a life peppered with tribulation.

Mine eyes thus enlightened, I was driven from the Paradise, never to enter it more. The despotic dislike that Erbanhue kept in ready case was instantly resumed.

Hatred! Had I known what hatred was before this? No, I had only supposed I knew it. I had not seen it on its throne, fraught with dripping rivulets of poison, circled with a cloud of venom, protected from the siege of future repentance with spikes of metal soldered by angry, righteous blows.

Residing on this throne was the Master, my Dragon, my Cerberus, my source of daily bread, my one protector from the hardships of the normal world (such as he was). For since that night of victory and despair, he would not plague me with cursing and confidential talks and abrupt changefulness of mood... not sweet but natural, obvious, customary. My precious study was closed to me. He swapped mere dislike for an anger so steady, a hatred so violent, and a distrust so rooted, that the Dragon not only hissed in my presence, but struck. Multiple bruises attested to the new state of things. I cannot speak more of this era, Reader; I cannot try!

Yasmin Lange, the immovable, the passionless, the heartless! That aerialist without care, or soul, or family! That hateful and hating object of statue-like expression which never varied, no matter the cries of the winter gale! That unwavering ship that sailed through the vilest of weather, without pitch, without wreck!

A cold, pale dawn that blessed not a single rosy face asleep in the cradle; nor warmed a single trusting couple in each other's arms; nor cheered the lonely widow watching for daylight with hopeful and sleepless eyes. Clouds rose over the dawn, spilling their contents over the land, by night drowning them all. She never spoke of her great trouble, nor asked for clearance, nor begged forgiveness, for Fate mastered her will above Yasmin Lange. She did not even allow her to seek purchase on that rocky and inclement shore. *Beryl's Daughter* - sailed alone.

When we left E----, I traveled by horseback. I had remained popular in the city and had amassed - not enough wealth to buy a steed - but enough to bribe Sallix to ride his. Barnabas proved a willing charger, and did not appear to mind bearing a witch. I fed him sugar whenever it could be filched.

Another year passed away in these modes and manners. You need not have details concerning their progression. It was as if I drank oceanic waters to quench thirst, and ate ash to appease hunger, and slept on a bed of nails to satisfy fatigue. I prospered financially, ate well, and slept better. Yet I was never more alone in my life.

In good weather, I took to wandering in whatever towns or cities were nearest in my reach. Once or twice I contemplated selling my body as a means of escaping the circus, for on some days the glances of Sallix, the fearful looks of Trinna, and the shafts of Erbanhue became too much to bear. Why I wasn't fired, I do not know. I suspect they really did believe me to be a powerful witch, and so they feared my wrath.

But utter shame, and the image of my trusting, dying mother, held me at bay. I retreated as often as I attempted; I could *not* do it. And then (strangely enough!) there was Erbanhue himself, who sporadically forgot his malicious views and would discuss the business of the circus with me. Mostly he did so to hear himself reason aloud, but sometimes he would even value my opinion. I never did wholly comprehend him, I find. His unexplainable sways of manner puzzled me exceedingly.

In one other personage did I find a measure of serenity. Chaske annoyed me with his misplaced reverence and devoted affirmations of my immutable powers. Nonetheless, he was kind to me in his own way. His way consisted of offering, with persistent arrogance, to teach me his peculiar art of contortionism, and thereby to "lead me down the sunlit path of peace, to the worship of the god in the wood."

Not a Christian, but not a confirmed pagan either, I rejected him. Nothing daunted, he kept his persuasion at the ready, tipped the plunging arrows with flattery, and shot with an accuracy that made me smile in spite of my irritation.

"He longs to be known, as you long to know Him more," Chaske insisted, looking as wise as mortally possible. "He has gifted you with the willing hands of the White Ten. They are serving you, working out your insensate will! Do you realize what you could do in conscious effort?"

The Ten Pale Children! I have heard this superstition before. These children of the woods had sacrificed themselves to an ancient wood-god. Under his command they summoned chosen mortals to work His will whether they wanted to or not.

I bore no scruple about telling Chaske what I thought of his pagan nonsense. But in my heart, and in the dark privacy of night, I often considered what he said. I compared and contrasted his submitted beliefs with the misfortunes I had suffered, and was suffering.

Reader, they were disturbingly similar.

One twilight during mushroom hunting, I stumbled upon Chaske in the midst of his prayers. He sat cross-legged before a bluish conflagration. In one hand he held a very thin, black tree branch, and in the other he held aloft one of his prized poisonous weeds. I turned to abandon this pleasing spectacle.

"Wait, Anmut! Your presence strengthens my ceremony."

I informed him that my presence had nothing to do with his ceremonies.

"No, Anmut! Behold!"

But for the note of excitement in his voice - quite sudden - I would have ignored him. By it I was mastered. I looked.

In a cove formed of towering, weaving vegetation, I perceived among the enigma of branches a tall and white form clad in ebon vestments.

This creature was no stranger to me. It was the very same that I had beheld over a year ago, and had since attempted to forget. Being closer than it was before, I could confirm that it did indeed have the appearance of a man, though extraordinary in svelte precision. The face, again, was white with the whiteness of ice, and it had no features.

I think the shock of its realness, its solid being, went thoroughly home; it had not been so the first time. *This was no vision.* I screamed.

Chaske immediately threw himself toward me to silence me, forcing a hand over my mouth. The Demongod vanished and I relaxed, sighing...

I had rejoiced too soon. Out of the thinness of air it reappeared. It stood directly before my face.

The conclusion was correct. It had no facial features. It had no true face at all. Its blankness terrified me, for it exuded a sort of malignant, unreadable power that I could neither interpret nor overwhelm. I wanted to scream again, for the sound of my own voice in that terrific silence would have been a relief. Chaske only held me more tightly, and in a cowardly moment he shoved me to the monster's feet.

A throb... a repulsive, quivering cadence, the very sound of malevolent power... trembled at my ears and forced its way into my head. I heard Him speak.

Anmut, du hast deinen Willen gegen meinen verhärtet.

(Anmut, you have hardened your will against mine.)

I drew breath. I resisted. "Ich könnte nicht! Beschuldigen Sie mich mit Verbrechen, von denen ich nicht einmal weiß?"

("I could not have! Do you accuse me of crimes I know nothing about?")

Hearing His voice, without seeing any mouth, made me sick. I doubled over, wretched. Generating from my insane fear came a vision of miniscule, sickening, contorting lights, writhing across a backdrop of sodden mud. Sometimes the bands of light struggled, caught in the gray thick, drowning in it. Throughout the conversation they throbbed in rhythm, pulsing with eerie heathen life.

A mantle of midnight billowed about Him as He spoke.

Deine Proteste sind logisch. Aber Anmut, du hast mir dein ganzes Leben gedient. Ich kannte dich in deiner Wiege. Ich habe dich besucht, während du geschlafen hast. Ich habe dich von Anfang an markiert.

(Your protests are logical. But, Anmut, you have served me all your life. I knew you from your childhood. I visited you while you slept. I marked you from the beginning.)

"How? I do not believe you! What fellowship hath light with darkness?" I spat, wincing with pain.

Ich dich gelehrt, deine ersten Schritte allein zu gehen. Ich habe dich gelehrt, Bitterkeit zu trinken und Kraft zu gewinnen. Ich habe dich unter dem Hass des Erbanue's festgehalten. Ich bin es, der dich unterstützt, dich lehrt, dich ermahnt, dich peitscht. Ich bin dein Anführer, nicht das Schicksal. Ich bin deine Zukunft, nicht Schicksal. Ich bin es.

(I taught you to take your first steps alone. I taught you to drink bitterness and gain strength. I have held you under the hatred of Erbanhue. It is I who support you, teach you, admonish you, and train you. I am your Leader, not Fate. I am your Future, not Destiny. It is I.)

Throughout this assertion, the throbbing music of His voice grew stronger. At the end it pulsed with a shockwave, convulsing my body, throwing me backward and blackening my sight. I felt a legion of thin appendages wrapping around my gasping form as He lifted me to Himself.

Beneath the humming of His voice, I heard the cries of several small children. Two of the voices were quite familiar. "Yasmin! We are here. Do not resist, Yasmin..."

My senses trembled, rushed, and then... suspended.

Chapter Sixteen

Minister Benjamin Lewis

Letter to Dr. Samuel Clark

G---- Hospital

Dear Sir,

I am gratified to receive your correspondence. My former pupil has indeed vacated his station, and his rooms are at your service. I understand that the typhoid has claimed many innocent lives in your neighborhood, and you must be anxious to remove them to safety. I beg you to consider my country chapel for anyone that is fit for travel. It is somewhat isolated, enclosed by a well-tended garden, and is well kept by my helper and brother in Christ, Thomas Gensing. Truly, God has made His Provision good.

Have the goodness to convey any information you know concerning my future responsibility, as I wish to serve him or her in whatever capacity that

I am able. If there should be any relatives living, I desire to notify them immediately that they may reunite.

May God bless your service!

Minister Lewis

Westford Chapel

Reply to the Minister of Westford Chapel

G-----, Arkansas

Dear Sir,

I thank you from the bottom of my heart. The situation in house is indeed alarming, and I write with grateful haste.

Your charge will be a young woman estimated at twenty-one to twenty-four years of age. After regaining consciousness, she gave her name as Yasmin, but beyond this we know nothing of her family or her former place of residence. She is believed to bear resemblance to the famed "Witch Anmut" of a traveling circus. There is no certainty, but should she be of their stock, she is certainly blessed to be receiving your care and Christian outreach.

She appears to be suffering from a nervous fever and dehydration. She is ill suited for the crowded situation she presently endures. With rest and regular meals, as well as the calming tonic I shall send to you, I am confident of a full recovery in time.

However, great care must be taken. Guard her from all disagreeable associations and memories, and divert her as well as you can with pleasant talk and easy reading. See if she prefers painting or garden work, for when she is stronger, she ought to be more out-of-doors. She is excessively pale.

I am sending her in the care of one of my most trusted nurses, Miss Nora Oliver. This good lady has been overseeing the patient and will carry out my instructions and prescription to the letter.

Do not hesitate to write to me if you observe anything that you feel should be brought to my attention.

Most respectfully yours,

Dr. Samuel Clark

Yasmin's Journal, Continued

June, 1875

Reader, I write what follows not as one who has witnessed, but one who has heard of these happenings below... with some imagination aiding me, perhaps. I got to know the Minister rather well in those days.

"Thomas, when is the carriage to arrive?"

"At 10:00 sharp, sir."

Thomas Gensing spoke with dry sarcasm. Both men knew quite well when the patient and nurse would arrive, but Benjamin still wished to revisit the fact. No oversight would be permitted, and no detail would be overlooked. He sped out of doors, yanked the well-aired quilt from the wash line, and ran back in, arranging it over the mattress with painstaking care.

"Ben, I do wish you'd settle yourself. You're making me nervous."

"Dr. Samuel is adamant that she receive the best of care," the minister replied. "I received word that she suffered a relapse last night. She needs rest."

"That goes without saying, Sir Perfectionist. You are like a tornado, a natural disaster of the sweeping and arranging brand, and woe be to the man who encumbers you!"

"Thank you, Thomas. I hope you attended to the garden yesterday evening, as I asked."

"I did, sir, and dusted it besides... placed a few doilies about, hung out some curtains. I thought perhaps a lace rug might suit. Unfortunately, there were none to be had." Thomas playfully wrung his hands in mock shame.

Minister Lewis ignored the barbs. "I am grateful. Please go into town and order a good luncheon from Darby's. I cannot cook, and Harris left not a scrap of leftovers when he departed."

"Yes, sir."

"Also, return this book to Mr. Johnson. I have finished it. Tell him it was immensely helpful."

"As you wish."

"Oh, and I must repaint the mantle. I forgot and let the fire smoke again, and no amount of scrubbing has cured it of its stain. Stop at Mr. Frank's and order some leaf green paint for me. Don't let him pawn off the latest color on you – leaf green, you understand? That shade, and no other."

"Very well, sir."

The harassed Thomas was ducking out the door when Benjamin poked out his head, saying "And Thomas, won't you-?"

But Thomas absconded with his current task list, departing in high dudgeon.

Patience, however, is firmly schooled in the life of ministers, and Benjamin resigned himself with a good-natured shrug. He drew back into his house and sat at the study table, attempting to calm his nerves with a few minutes of studious writing.

This bright little chapel, connected to a few private rooms, claimed a more homelike air than most churches. Its walls were not a strict, devoted white, but instead a mellow gold, like antique sunshine softly glancing on a mild spring day. The podium, desks, seat-backs, and pews all shone well-polished, and any seating arrangement was amply cushioned in solemn blue velvet. Matching curtains framed the windows. A frail blue vase, of odd and curious design, harbored crystallic water and curling vines. Neat piles of ecclesiastical volumes decorated many a corner. A stained glass window shot rays of blue, yellow, orange, and amethyst light down the tan-colored aisle.

The atmosphere was pleasant, clean, and bright. The air smelled of wood and lilacs, piety and health, sanctity and virtue.

Benjamin Lewis himself, seated placidly at his desk in a miniature side room, seemed the embodiment of the chapel: clean, healthy, virtuous, and good. In inches he stood rather below average height. His character was warm and discerning. His hair was blond, sleek and unassuming. His eyes were a clear, clean hazel that portrayed an open, determined spirit. The mouth was small and thin, but quick to smile, and beneath it reposed a clean-kept chin indicative of potential sensitivity. His lineaments were equally well-turned and well-matched, and his movements made distinctive to himself; he never dawdled or wandered about. He darted here and there, moving with energy and purpose.

His pastime was to plan – he took a prodigious delight in planning, counter-planning, and post-planning – sending clerical spies and receiving their notices – scheming in businesslike manner from Point Alpha to Omega, and every other sub-point that could possibly be conjectured. He also liked to read. To that end, he was frequently seen rummaging from steeple to cellar in search of favored volumes. His personal library extended from his shelves to tumble beneath beds and into flower pots, and from atop precarious perches to descend upon people's heads. Once, a distinguished visiting pastor was accosted by such a mishap on discovering a pamphlet (authored via William Booth) peeping at him from between the loaves of his sandwich! Thanks to this incident, Minister Benjamin Lewis was ever hailed as the most amiable yet most absentminded of all ministers in the county.

He liked people and was well-liked. He possessed *vor allem* the art of being spirited without being severe, and the talent of being led by a hardy temper without being overcome by it. His one fault, if he had any, was too much delicacy of feeling. He had the habit of getting "the sullens" and detracting into himself if any word was contrived against him (though *that* was rare indeed).

When the carriage pulled up, as it did at ten-o'-clock sharp, he came rushing out to greet and assist from the carriage his charge and her nurse. Reader, I wish someone had been there to paint that tableau. It would be a remarkable portrait: An honest, handsome little minister, handing out with suave respect the rope-artist, performer, and protégé of Erbanhue, the "Witch Anmut."

"You had a fine day for your journey," Minister Lewis began. "I am very pleased to welcome you. I fear your rooms will be small, but I can personally vouch for their cleanliness, and you will want for nothing."

"You are very kind."

Wan, feeble fingers were placed in his outstretched hand. His clear nimble gaze summed up the fair unknown as she dismounted. One slim, long foot followed the other. He noted her gentle, light step, akin to a dancer's gait. The shoes, or rather slippers, fit her ill; he could detect red painful impressions that the tight footwear inflicted on its pale wearer. "Pale," though, was not quite the word, for her complexion had a tinge of yellow in it. She looked sickly enough.

The figure was trim, strained, and somehow seemed put together wrong, though he could not understand why nor wherefore. The face was etched with the stamps of Hunger, Fatigue, and Want. The eyes were large, gray, and glassy. The hair he could not yet judge, as it was folded in hasty fashion into a mound of maroon wool she wore on her head. It was meant, he surmised, to fulfill the employment of being a hat... but surely it had seen better days.

He kindly offered her his arm. "I have sent for a lunch, I hope you are hungry."

"*Vielen Dank.* Not very."

"This is the front gate; through here is the garden. You may walk in it at your desire once we have repaired your strength. Here, this is the chapel. Be careful of the steps. Now we go toward the back through this door. It's usually locked. On the left are my rooms and the study room. Your room is on the right, and passed that is the kitchenette and a small living room. I apologize again for its meager size."

"It does not trouble me."

"Your nurse may take the couch. We placed it at the foot of your bed. Is that satisfactory? It's no trouble to relocate it."

"Thank you, there is no need to move it." Wearied by his solicitous prattle, Yasmin attempted to detach herself from his arm.

"Please, miss. Let me help you." He lowered her carefully onto the side of the bed, as if she were prone to dislocation. "Your nurse is bringing your things."

"I had little to bring."

"You forgot your luggage?"

"I had none."

Effectually quenched by the look of pure exhaustion that accompanied this assertion, the minister withdrew and shut the door behind him. "Not a patroness of social graces, that's certain," he remarked beneath his breath. "Quite a state of rigid propriety all round." Shrugging, he left in quest of Thomas, for their lunch was late.

Chapter Seventeen

RELIGIOUS SECLUSION

Lunch was served to me in bed. The minister insisted that "Miss Yasmin must take it in her room and not budge and inch more than necessary" - A proceeding which irritated me, as I had taken a violent fancy to his garden. I pined to walk in it. My termed insanity was routed horse, foot, and artillery by gentleman and nurse, and I was compelled to be submissive and sensible.

I had my vengeance by asserting quite volubly that Minister Benjamin had "*seine Zunge hing an seiner Mitte*"[1] , but as the stigmatized fellow had no knowledge of German, the dart rather missed its target.

While I sulked, Benjamin Lewis put the last touches to his lodgings and prepared for a long evening of scribal duties. His sermon was due on

---

1. "His tongue hung at the center", i.e. He talks too much.

the morrow, and nothing, not even a compelling curiosity concerning the identity and history of his patient, should force him to cease, or tease his brain back with the fancies of tragic circumstance and ghastly remembrances. He sat down to work.

Slowly but surely the afternoon wore away, as well as evening and most of the night. He extinguished his candle and retired late, forgetting entirely that anyone else was in the place but himself and Thomas.

The morning, however, restored him to reality. He whistled his way into the garden to delight himself in weeding before the sun's heat rendered the task miserable. He was stopped. His vision was arrested by the remarkable visitor, just then admiring his African daisies.

She wore a maroon dress that at once proclaimed the slender means of the wearer. Its thick material was most unsuitable for the season. Conscious of its objectionable warmth, the lady had rolled up the sleeves as far as they would go. Her hair, remarkably long and thick, brushed the stone garden path.

Heralding the minister's approach, Yasmin turned. Her eyes flashed across his face, mobile, stern, and piercing; the pupils seemed to dilate and retract at random intervals. He wondered at their intensity. What terrors had thus convulsed them into their present width and apathy? From what pagan land hailed this fire-witch, with eyes of dwindling flame and hair of spent ash?

I studied the intruder in turn. "Forgive me. I suppose you thought I was in bed."

The minister shook his head. "You struck me as an early riser. Or, at the very least, a light sleeper; your countenance told me as much. Did you sleep?"

"I did, thank you. I am much refreshed."

"So I see."

It was true. I had seen it in the morning-glass. My face, still pinched and hollow, had lost some of its yellow tint. The flesh looked like flesh instead of parchment.

Benjamin smiled. His hazel optics quite sparkled. "What do you fancy for breakfast? I can order it from town."

"Nora has taken care of me, thank you." I smiled in return, but quickly ceased, conscious of displaying a set of white but worn, short teeth. "Toast and tea is quite an extravagance. I have not had it since... in a very long while. What sort was it? Black?"

Incredulity lifted his brows. A young lady who did not drink tea! Unfathomable! "If you please, Miss Yasmin, have a seat on this garden bench. If you feel strong enough, I should like to hear about you and where you are from." I was sure he believed it was his duty to learn what wild species of womanhood he tended beneath his roof.

I seated myself, securing my eyes on the hills opposite. "I will oblige you as well as I can."

"Where were you born? To what family?"

"I am German, as you have surely noticed. My parents were Alarik and Beryl Lange."

"Forgive my presumption, but your clothing denotes your station. I perceive that you are in the midst of a hard financial situation. And you spoke in the past tense just now. You are an orphan?"

"Yes. I am without family."

"I suppose you were placed in a charity school?"

"No, I never went to school. I was taught by my parents before they passed on."

Again, the minister was obliged to suppress his astonishment. "You never attended school? Yet you are well-spoken. And your nurse requested my leave to bring you some books. Those that were selected did not lack information."

"My mother taught me well."

"Have you any siblings?"

"None. I was an only child."

"No other living relatives anywhere?"

"None that I know of, sir."

"Any friends that I can notify? Anyone who would be concerned by your condition or able to provide permanent shelter?"

"No one at all."

"You are sure?"

"*Sicherlich.*"

A pause intervened. I yawned and played with a stray lock between my fingers. Benjamin Lewis thought, struggled, and bravely ventured a more dangerous road. "And what have you been doing? What is your employment?"

This was quite audacious, for all manner of moral degradations were more than hinted by his tone. However, I restrained myself, turning to him with a pair of troubled but innocent eyes. "I do not remember."

He lifted one fine, blond eyebrow. "Your illness has robbed you of your memory?"

"I fear it is true. I clearly recall most incidents from my childhood. But from thence it is... it is a blank."

"That is most extraordinary."

"*You* say so!" A sarcastic smile curved my lips. "Imagine what I must feel in such a position. Reliant on a complete stranger, three of them in fact, and not understanding the nature of my malady, and still less knowing how I came about contracting it."

I arose and paced the garden. "Where will I live? What can I do to support myself? *Mein Gott*, what will become of me? *Was soll ich tun?*"[2] Tears threatened to drop from my eyes. I hastily blinked them away.

Compassion spoke in the tenderness of Benjamin's mien. He knelt by me and tried to encouraged me with pastoral goodness. "God has preserved you, Miss Yasmin. He never leads by mistake, or calculates in error." He put my hair from my face and handed me his handkerchief. "Until we find a place for you, Nora and I will protect you. You need not feel unguarded or abandoned."

"Thank you, sir, that will do." I managed, wiping my traitorous eyes. He attempted to put an arm around my shoulder. "No, only let me alone if you please, and I shall be myself in a minute. Indeed, you must not touch me, for I may be in disgrace."

"Alas, it may be the truth. But that is enough of the past. Rest now, and we will work toward cultivating a future for you."

"I am grateful, sir."

FROM THE DIARY OF BENJAMIN LEWIS

It is perfectly ridiculous that I should be so "jumpy," as Thomas says. I do not know what makes me this way. I refuse to consider that it is the advent of a young lady guest, arriving all in mystery and pert moodiness...

---

2. "What should I do?"

But as she *is* interesting, at least, I intend to write about her and inspect my theories later. Right or wrong, they will amuse me, and a clergyman's life is lonely at times. Writing keeps me out of the doldrums.

Yasmin Lange arrived two days ago. I did not know what to make of her at first, beyond the obvious facts that she was poor and hated small talk. She is fitful; I heard her upbraiding the nurse with a piqueness that did me good to hear. She is not pretty, thank heaven (Thomas has no intention of dying a "solitary bach"). If she *was* pretty, I would be obliged to send her back.

In other respects, however, she is very well equipped to fascinate mere masculinity. Of course, Nora guards Yasmin like a tigress, and Yasmin is often spared the trouble of being rude for Nora executes it in flaming style. I expect they'll become thick as thieves in time.

Miss Yasmin has spunk, I suppose, but it is a type I have never before encountered. I don't yet know how to make head or tail of it. It is grave, tempestuous - anything but conducive to hilarity and fun, which is a trait I have often attached to "spunk" before. Yet her methods still make one smile... if one does not feel offended.

Never mind! It turns out that spunk has a blue side to which I have been entirely blind ere now. It will take a good deal of pain and purgatory to comprehend when she is joking and when she is serious, for she seems serious all the time. I wonder if she knows how to dance, or cut capers, or fly about, or commit a prank. I wonder if she ever laughed in her life.

June 9

Today I made a discovery. Having attempted to make breakfast, I ended up reading instead, leaving the eggs to burn gaily on the stove. I assume the smolder awoke the sleeping beauty from her fairy's slumbers - Yasmin rushed in with alacrity amazing, hair billowing behind like a grand gray ghost. She put out the smoke with tact.

"What do you mean by burning the house down?" was her flattering remark. "I was led to believe you are a man of sense. I was mistaken." She dumped the blackened contents out of window.

"I was performing experiments," I meekly replied, catching up the pepperbox in one hand, as if intending to perform wonders with it. She flew to purloin it. "Unhand that at once, if you please, and don't terrorize me with the actions of a two-year-old. Give me a clean pan. I'll make breakfast myself."

Result being: She presented her culinary offering very much flustered, glaring down upon the contents (very much burnt). She is a worse cook than I am. I ate away manfully, excused myself, and assigned myself a far corner, restricting the elements of my mirth to secrecy. I laughed until I was ashamed. In some respects, the poor woman knows next to nothing. It is like having a child about the place. Lord, give me patience! Help me to guide her!

June 12

The patient does not enjoy being a captive in her bedroom. Delicacies, stitch-work, fresh novels, German lyrics: All and sundry were spurned by her thin, calloused hands. She therefore found it convenient to be as trying as possible, so Nora rapidly reported her patient much stronger. The new recommendation was more air and wholesome scenery.

I proposed a short walk in the adjacent fields. Nora wrapped Yasmin in her shawl and took her out for an hour. Unknown to them both, I watched them from my study window, hazarding snatches of view between editing a manuscript.

It appears to me that Yasmin might be the circus performer that the doctor described. It is rather early, I admit, to make such a declaration, but today has convinced me of the hypothesis. By now I have had time to study various hints.

For one, upon her descent from the carriage, I noted that it was not a fastidious carriage. It had a faulty wheel; it wobbled and leaned sideways. This confounder of balance did not phase her in the slightest. I privately remarked that her center of gravity was practiced and intimately controlled.

Point two: She knows practically nothing of the common knowledge of daily life, such as English teas, social gossip, current reading, setting tableware, advanced cooking, fancy sewing, embroidery, or the artistic accomplishments of music or drawing. She has, however, a keen taste for rustic tunes, and a fine dancer's form... muscular, gracious, and enduring, though coarse from malnutrition and overuse. Her existence has certainly been very hard. Two nights past, on setting table for supper, she stared as Thomas put down the butter. She asked what on earth the yellowish block in the dish was, and what it was for... a curious query, that!

Point three: Today she was propelled into manifestations of profound glee in discovering that I kept a kitten. From that identical second onward she has cuddled it, crooned to it, petted it, given it half of her meals - from eggs to sausage to the milk for my tea - and proclaimed that it would sleep with her every night, in her own bed, from now until eternity. Her attachment amuses me, and it is rather suggestive. As a circus worker, it is natural that she would be fond of animals and prone to immediate bonding. I am fond of the miniature feline myself, and am loath to give it up, even to her. But I must strive to "love thy neighbor as thyself," so I relented.

Tomorrow, in sending Thomas to town for groceries, I shall instruct him to inquire after the nearest traveling circus troupes. They always send on announcers and posters ahead of their arrival. Surely if I am correct, and I produce an advertisement for her inspection at the right moment, it will release her memory. But I must be very, very cautious of when I produce it. A sudden intelligence could prove disastrous.

June 18

A sad diary-keeper am I! There is a substantial blank in the books. But things have been increasingly interesting in my little chapel, and "Yassy," sorehead as she is, is much improved... Though by her temper, one would think she dislikes being better. If any human on earth suffered primarily from malcontent and not much else - at least at the moment - it is this piqued and plaintive Germaness.

I mused, in my previous recordings, that an intimacy was liable to strike up between the patient and the nurse. This has indeed come to pass. Yasmin is active, impulsive, and willful, and heartily demands modes of freedom, in the most impossible manners, and during the most extravagant hours. Miss Nora finds her amusing, often indulging Yasmin in ridiculous style. I do not approve of it, but it is evident that Yasmin is not used to being fussed over. I will allow it in consideration for her condition.

I do not pretend to like Yasmin any better personally, but of late... Ah, here is a contradiction!

In spite of her own avowals to the contrary, she *is* tender and affectionate. One needs only to peek into her shadowed room and see her crooning to "Kitty Liebling" to know it. She has, too, a certain undefinable grace and strength to her, that I cannot very well describe. She looks terrible still, all wan and desultory, but she is "brimful of vim and vigor." She *cannot* be kept down.

I caught her... listen, now... I caught her actually *dancing in the chapel* (she insists on keeping it clean as she likes to be busy, no matter how small the chore). Her movements were decidedly German – stout, athletic, decided, yet charming. I liked to watch her. As strange as it seems, she reminded me of the celebrating daughters of Israel. She ought to have had a veil and a tambourine... And, of course, beautiful dark hair and eyes, instead of her part-granite, half-transparent shields of white and gray.

I begin to comprehend where she got her show name. That is, if she *is* the "Witch Anmut." She has a certain aura, a tenacity, and a sober antiquity that well befits a witch. She is just the sort of lady to crone ancient spells at midnight, spurning meat, drink, and sleep as things to be vilified, burning the candles at both ends until her caster's net is fully woven and tossed neatly over the brink.

If only she were happy all the time! For sorrow is her main visitant, and no joke of Thomas', nor any gift from my hands, has raised up a smile for longer than one minute. She is quite grave, even while she dances. It was as if she was dancing *at* someone... someone visible to her eyes alone.

Chapter Eighteen

You Know Nothing of the World!

Benjamin Lewis

June 19

The trouble that I have most feared is commencing at last. My congregation, small as it is, is in the main a kindly set. They are eager to help the "poor dear" that they soon discovered Thomas and I were sheltering. As in any flock, however, there will be gossips. My wolves of sheep's clothing *en masse* tend to be the gossiping sort - short of fang, perhaps - but for Yasmin, all the more damage resides in their tenacious jaws. I must be vigilant.

More posters like the specimen Thomas brought back to me have been handed about within my set. I have not written about it until today, because it elicited not a single clue as to her identity. Thomas found a poster depicting "Erbanhue's Traveling Circus," the troupe associated with the name "Witch Anmut." But there was no picture of the witch.

There was only a great, shining image of a ringmaster taking up the whole of the canvas. And my, didn't he do himself justice? Didn't he sneer gorgeously, waving his glittering cape of ebony gold? What doffing of his gleaming top hat, measured carefully to mask his devil's horns! What regal placement of his polished boots, black as night, staid and masterful! What a beautiful mustache had he, and what crafty, volcanic eyes! I admired and despised him with all my might.

Although there was no sign of Yasmin anywhere about this fantastic demon, somewhere in the depths of my spirit, I knew this man was no good to anyone who ventured near him.

June 21

Today, I had to be a little stern with Thomas. Good pupils are hard to come by, and pupils devoid of curiosity are in even shorter supply. But after all, he led me to the discovery of important information. I shall not be cross.

Having got hold of one of the accursed ringmaster's posters, Thomas apparently elected to take it upon himself to show it to Yasmin. On the whole, anyone who looked upon the image of this Erbanhue attributed to that dashing serpent his due wages of admiration, expostulation, and fascinated loathing. They also, of course, whispered that Yasmin had been a woman of his, and he had cast her out on finding that she was with child. Gossip continued to assert that Yasmin had refused, and he had beaten her, and so mistreated her that she lost the baby. The ringmaster left her, weak and half insane, on the bottom of the hospital steps.

I believed that this story was perhaps half-true, but I doubted it as a whole. Yasmin bore no resemblance to a mistress robbed of child. Her recovery was too fast and entire, and her form, though sorry and thin, did not bear any lasting wounds except for the chafing that would match the use of circus ropes. As far as the whispered charge of insanity is concerned, I oppose *that* completely. She has one of the strongest minds I ever witnessed in a woman's head.

Her encumbered memory, however, is yet a mystery... for when Thomas showed Yasmin the poster of Ringmaster Erbanhue, she merely shrugged and said he was *"Ein bemerkenswerter Mann ... aber wahrscheinlich unheilbar."* A remarkable man, but likely beyond salvation. We agreed with her, but I wished I had caught Thomas and shorn the poster in two before her eyes perceived it.

June 22

"You have spoiled Madame Purrer terribly," I averred, watching Yasmin sort a brew of broth and fish for her " liebling." I grinned. "Do you not begin to fear that Kitty will become something of a vulgarity in weight and breadth?"

"Now, don't condescend. You spoil her yourself when you suppose we are not looking." She dropped her spoon and bent to stroke the cat, smiling as she never smiles for mankind.

Yasmin's constitution, I have since found, is perpetually icy. Her paleness is not a signal of weakness. It is simply her natural constitution.

She has been with us nearly a month. Her memory, I believe, cannot be as poor as she pretends. I have determined to make a test... but for reasons I need not explain, I have been putting it off. As curt as she can be, when she is friendly she is pleasant in her own way, and I liked talking with her on happy terms. Today I finally relinquished my selfishness. I took the tumble.

"I suppose you will train her to do tricks." I submitted in a nonchalant manner. "Did you learn many things from Erbanhue?"

"Oh, if you call meanness many things-"

The culprit stopped cold.

Her face looked as if I had tiptoed up behind her and thrown ice down the nape of her neck. “So you *do* know him,” I continued. “Very good. We shall have a long talk about it, for I am curious. I mean to know all about it. How is life in a circus?”

I came to lament my bluntness. I ought to have been more patient, more forgiving, more tender, as befits a messenger of the Almighty. However, I cannot erase what was done. I can only inscribe what occurred.

The witch was angry. Her eyes lit with a keen ember that I had never before seen in her face. It entirely cleared and magnified the dull orbs that her eyes had since been. Her act was finished and the curtain closed, the stage quieted. Her expression was cold, open, and living, her hidden passions all awake.

“You think you are very clever,” said she, “And you do not understand my reasons for lying to you. Very well. You shall listen! A bold-faced lie might be forgiven, but could my lifestyle be pardoned at any cost? No! You and yours can never understand what a woman... what a girl... what *I* must do to keep victuals at arm’s reach and a sip of water near my lips. You, sir, can do what you please, and be what you will. He,” (I supposed she meant Erbanhue), “*He* can be cunning and foul and malignant, and be praised for it. I... we... my troupe was hard-working and honest. We were abused and forsaken, and our names spoilt by lying conjectures. Did you think I would thus confide in you, minister, who knows nothing of the world I know?”

Thus she continued to apostrophize myself. Her hands clenched. “You, with your happiness and your security and your fond, loving God! You, with your constant prattling of contentment and patience under persecution and wrath, and you have not tasted an hour of such things!”

She had expelled all her breath. Her chest heaved with passion. Her eyes were silvery cups overflowing with disgust and rage. I cannot say how it was so, but she who had never before been lovely, now almost glowed... A pagan goddess who thrived on anger and injustice and remorse. The false, stiff, careless woman was gone, ravished away. And what was the woman in her place?

A mortal tragedy who had undergone evils and seen Pain and Privation – perhaps helped to cause them – in order to partake of daily bread and of life. Yet, if I hated the sin, I cherished the sinner. My next speech appeared to astonish her; before I was half done she was quite subdued, and her eyes wide with amazement.

"I see. You judge rightly to suppose that I have never seen an hour of pain, or been the recipient of vile actions. My heavenly Father has raised me among the roses. My earthly father has always been fond, sweet, and joyful. He never once rose in wrath to strike me, or to pile upon me word upon word of blame for a mother's abandonment."

"My darling mother I have always known, from my cradle onward; she never deserted me. My childhood has been gilded with many friends, and even now blooms with the tenderest of memories. I am never lonely, or friendless, or hungry. I never sacrifice meals for those hungrier than I, for all about me is gold and sunshine, and I have never been touched by evil anywhere. In attaining manhood I have known love, and in desiring a pure love from so beautiful a woman, she doubtless honored me, and she loved me in return... however... However!-"

I said more than I intended to. I slowed, conscious of my own growing bitterness. It would do her no good. "May you forgive me for my strong words, Yasmin, and may the Lord forgive me also. I repent for my hasty condemnation of you. But I ask in return that you consider me as I consider you."

She said nothing. I continued, "I have also tasted of the dregs. I have been given salt to drink instead of fresh water. I have been fed the shells and the crust, the mere rinds of the meal of a cunning and evil man. I do not say that we have experienced the same tribulations, for God crafts them to the individual to grow us as we can best be cultivated."

Her face softened. Taking heart, I resumed "You have been through harsher fires than I… therefore, a harder and more proud nature I have never been blessed to call to repentance. I pray you will consider my words! Instead of darkness and evil and cold, you can yield your life to hope and good and grace. God blessed you with protection and talent to keep you through your darkest hours. You have worth, you have strength, you have intelligence… You have a life and a future. I beg you not to waste them!"

Longing, confusion, bitterness, and annoyance wrestled for purchase in her face. Among these emotions was an odd flicker of recognition, as if someone else had told her these things before. No more was required for me to say. She had been captive in an adjoining room during all of my teaching and preaching. She knew to what faith I was referring. I waited.

"I will leave you," she finally spoke, "I will leave you soon. I respect you, and I am sorry for the pains that you have endured. But I cannot accept a God that I do not know. I am assured that He does not know me, nor does He wish to."

I opened my mouth to recommence, but she hastily rose a hand to deter me. Then she said something very odd. "I have been marked by a lesser god than thine; lesser, but crafted of a potency that man cannot resist. He has marked me from my youth, and I cannot escape him. As every word of false hope is more torment to my mind, I ask that you will never speak of your God to me again."

Thus profaning, she fled.

I looked down at my hand, which in my excitement had been clutching hers. My heart was yet beating with tremulous force. I had been so certain that this was the hour of salvation... that presently I was to hear the dearest confession that ever rang true in my humble chapel.

Instead, to hear such a repulse from a woman I have begun to care for! For this untamed flame of the East, so unlike me, has bound me captive far more than she was ever *my* captive. But the revelation startled me. "For what fellowship hath light with darkness?"

I suppose it is good she will leave me, but I have not prayed myself into submission yet.

The Diary of Yasmin Lange, Continued

July, 1875

A barrier has risen between us. Let no man speak it... I adjure thee, let no one know it or consider it, or seek it in its lair where it lies all serene and fat of flesh, well-kept, but well-hidden... But it is true.

I never experienced a friendship quite like his. It was calm and unspoken and solicitous. He read very early my longing for clear, charted waters, and we sailed along at peace, talking when we felt like talking, resting when we did not. We were able to sit together in the miniature kitchenette, and yet we could comfortably keep still.

It was my first sample of stable sincerity from an adult source (since my parents), and how glad I was to receive it! I could not have abided a noisy, demonstrative friend. In Lillias it could be born, for she was a child. But then Benjamin Lewis – with alert, passive, frank kindness shining in his looks as well as his words - *he* became my first real friend.

"Don't put that in this cup, it's Miss Yasmin's, and she doesn't prefer it."

"Won't you tell that story, Thomas? Yasmin would like it."

Or even "I ordered beef as it is Yasmin's favorite." I had indicated a preference for beef, in somewhat vague terms, no less than three weeks ago. The instance of his remembering such a thing astonished me.

These were a few instances of his lasting compassion. Just as Erbanhue had been the catalyst of wrath, frustration, condemnation, pain, despair, subjugation, hypnosis, discomfort; so was Benjamin a herald of peace, contentment, mercy, comfort, interest, wholesomeness, wisdom, and knowledge.

But every word from his God dropped like millstones upon my ears. They were mocking, vain, and cruel. How can such a kind man believe that half of the world's population was destined for eternal hell-fire... And how can such a man, thus believing, still be kind? Especially to me.

I attempted by my actions to show him that I was not of his flock, nor would I ever be. He saw it; I knew from his worrying, gentle glances. But he is stubborn, too. He would not be deterred.

Upon discovery, I promptly quenched him. Our friendship is practically at an end. It hangs by a thread. I do not believe it will ever grow back. But it is his fault! If he had left me and my history well alone, we could have continued friendly as before, and parted ways on the best of terms. But, no! He could not. Men must always be fixing, chaining, instructing, designing. I do not know what they would do if they did not have wayward women to fix. Their favorite employment would be gone.

In spite of this misfortune, he rendered my convalescence a time in my life that I do not recall with regret. The tiny chapel was neat, orderly, and colored with low, pleasant voices that spoke pleasant words in pleasant, reverential tones. The kindly fellow (thus I denominate Mr. Lewis) could not sing, so the song services were something laughable, but he never let that profound handicap disturb him. He warbled away like a stunted blackbird. I liked to hear him because it showed he had some fight, though he strenuously imitated an all-perfect serenity.

In walking past his rooms one day, during one of my "housewifely rampages," I put aside my broom to get my brushes and buckets. I saw, perched on his chair, a dejected minister.

Across his omnipresent Bible reposed the poster of Erbanhue. Hanging disconsolate over the image, Benjamin's face was delicately tinged with envy, and he appeared to be having mental calculations over the depicted handsomeness of my old master. (It had been grossly exaggerated in that poster, by the way.)

Not having the decency to keep quiet, I went ahead and laughed. Benjamin colored up to his ears. He crumpled the poster, shoved it into a drawer, and obstinately turned his back to me as he lifted his Bible in both hands. What an amusing chap it is! It looked daggers at me afterward whenever I so much as mentioned anything to do with Erbanhues. Eventually, even the minister laughed at his seeming vanity.

"I begrudge him not his lot in life! However, Yasmin (tell it not in Gath!), I do despise him for his mustache." Here the silly man stroked his bare face, still dimpled, fresh, and childlike. We really let go of propriety then, causing the empty chapellette to ring with merriment.

But what good, after all, comes of those memories? I was all packed, ready for departure on the morrow. I desired to journey into town and see what sort of work I might attend to. I must support myself.

Benjamin seemed sorry, and earnestly pressed me to take anything and everything, down to the shirt off his back and half the kitchen wares. It was kind of him, and I halfway apologized for my ill humors... But nothing would detain me. My heart ached for freedom. The Westford chapel, while pleasant, was confining.

Chapter Nineteen

TOWN LABOR

I left Westford Chapel before dawn. I left behind a short note thanking everyone for their kindness, particularly Nora. Originally, I had planned to slip it onto the minister's desk. Upon perceiving candlelight flickering beneath the door, I knew he was awake. I fled in fear of discovery.

You may not comprehend why, but I understood myself as I trod down the road to town. He had been exceedingly vacillating of late – tender and helpful one minute, speaking calmly and hopefully of my departure – distant and vague the next minute, a little emotional, a little grumpy and dissatisfied, as if I had failed him in something. In taking my leave, I felt like a spoilt child snatching a forbidden holiday.

The warm, sweet wind! The feeling of freedoms to the utmost! For uncertainty, dear Reader, is not always an evil. You wake up with it. It stirs the mind and provokes it to contemplation, and thus to action. My step was light and firm.

I felt well indeed, quite well and strong. My well-rested limbs yearned to leap for joy, or climb a thousand ropes. I was excited all through, and I knew I could work hard.

I would find respectable work. These calloused hands would be put to honest employment at last. I clutched the little monetary hoard I had managed to keep with me (though I wondered with wholesome perplexity why Erbanhue had withheld his hand from it).

The night before, I trimmed the broken ends of my hair. For many days previous I had liberally romped in the sunlight of the garden. Light ashen hair, silky and smooth, was now well-tended, properly braided, and coiled on the back of my head. I wore a new dress of brown lawn (courtesy of Nora), and dark brown shoes made to measurement. I was confident that nobody would know me as the Witch Anmut.

Having studied the new image reflected in the mirror's face, I knew I must not go by my own name. Who would hire me? I selected an alias of Emma Bauer. It was a common, modest German name, proper for a humble start.

As I walked, I murmured the name to myself several times. I wished to familiarize my tongue and ears with its lineaments. Before I had half done, I found myself tucked within a swirling mass of humanity, carts, and cart-horses, with shops leering above me on either side.

This threw me into a bewilderment. At once I was pushed, tossed hither and thither like a branch in a typhoon. Having enquired in a confused, wild way of the baker, milliner, the general store, and a restaurant – finding no purchase or welcome in any – I finally stumbled across a tidy dress shop's threshold. Here I took heart, for having made my own clothes all my life, my foot was not on strange soil (though it was hateful soil). Beggars cannot be choosers. I gathered courage and knocked.

The lady of this place looked upon me with more grace of favor. As woman to woman, I claimed one sympathy; by my pitiful, confused glance and low, shy applications, I claimed a second; and I promptly claimed a third when the matronly woman professed to discover that I was very thin. My victuals had been plentiful enough at the minister's, of course. Yet I had only recently salvaged a normal appetite, and half a month does not undo the damage of many years.

Mrs. Bentley (for such was this lady's name) invited me in at once.

By way of acquainting ourselves with one another, she invited me to partake of tea. The cakes had the make and lightness of a pastry, "vanity cakes" she called them. I'm afraid they did not accomplish much in the way of satisfaction in the stomach.

But her kindly, unobtrusive questions and her genteel lady's ways put me at my ease. I was soon able to answer with confidence, although I made fearful blunders in the recitation of clothing materials, committed sins in ignorance of the latest fashions, and made confessions terrible as to my lack of the knowledge of hattery or the tending of gloves. Mrs. Bentley was not altogether deterred, however, for she liked Germans and knew their fastidious natures. Also she required a help, for the town's population was expanding and her sewing was falling behind.

"Providence is certainly on both of our sides, my dear! You will find me a gentle employer, though perhaps an absent-minded one. If you will just be so kind as to tell me to stop talking, or to put up the teapot, just say so. I won't mind a bit!"

Providence! Here was another Christian to sermonize me. I kept my vexation of spirit to myself, for I needed a place. I must only manage to still my abominable tongue.

My new station was quiet... almost too quiet. But perhaps it was best for me at that time. I was kept placid in my work. I had little to amuse myself with, but I was safe and could earn my own keep.

Emma Bauer had friends, too. Mrs. Bentley never neglected Emma, making sure to set her up with gossip and dessert, regarding Emma as a thing of grace and a joy forever.

Our humble peach-and-white parlor was not empty, either, for that interfering Minister Lewis soon found me out. He and Thomas Gensing persisted in visiting once a week. During such unwelcome moments I restricted my comments to the weather, keeping my fingers busy with stitches while Mrs. Bentley debated politics, theology, and recipes. Thankfully, I was always at liberty to excuse myself, withdrawing to the seafoam blue sleeping-closet that had been assigned to me.

Life on a circus campsite granted me a keen ear. One was always listening for orders, accidents, or escaping animals. I may not have spoken often, but I could listen well. Whenever I eavesdropped on their conversations, I cultivated a higher respect for my employer. Voluble and chattery as a magpie with those of her own sex, with her gentlemen visitors she waxed docile and charming. Her statements were well informed. Her sentiments were bridled, slowing the stream of her talk to a gentle tide. It was gratifying to listen, for I learned many useful things without risking my own interjections or making naive remarks.

"Good evening, Mrs. Bentley. Is your husband at home?" progressed Benjamin Lewis. I sat concealed behind a window curtain, quietly mending a pair of rosy gloves.

Mrs. B: I fear he is not, sir. He has gone into Whitwell with my cousin for supplies. I declare, Nicholas cannot do anything without my husband's aid. Can I offer you gentleman some tea or coffee?

Thomas: No, thank you, madame, for we have taken both. We've been to Mrs. Taylor's.

Mrs. B: That blessed lady! How does she get on? Her cousin Lidia is quite well again, I believe?

My ears perked up at this, for the name Lidia reminded me of my lost Lillias. In an absurd moment of subconscious parallelism, I instantly hoped for good news.

Benjamin: She is completely well, ma'am, thank you. The Lord answered our prayers. He is always faithful! The three of them stole quick looks at the stony German heathen, sitting primly by the window sill, sewing as if deaf and dumb.

Mrs. B: Thank God, indeed. Lidia is the sweetest young woman I have ever beheld, and by far the prettiest. Is she not engaged to marry Mr. Dan Henderson, minister? (Whereupon she looked most proper and innocent, her inflection rising. Not being a boring perfectant, but a womanly little mortal, she liked the marital gossip vine as much as anybody and frequently refreshed herself with picks at its silvery grapes.)

Benjamin: I believe so.

I leaned forward somewhat. The short dryness of his phrase rather interested me. Its tone was not like Benjamin Lewis, minister. Ordinarily, his warm and gentlemanly style could not help airing itself in the presence of... well, anybody at all. This comment was neither warm nor genteel. I stirred imperceptibly, parting a peep-hole between the curtains to better ascertain his current physiognomy.

He had his reading spectacles in place (i.e., precarious upon his head), but his fingers tapped nervously within their cotton prison (i.e., the pockets). His hazel eyes squinted and his yellow hair fluttered. "Something," said I to self, "Something in his bearing denotes a pain. Is it conscionable that this lady alluded to is the 'love' whom he had failed to gain?"

Mrs. B: Do you know when the wedding is to be? I am so eager to see that dear girl happy, after all her illness and trouble!

The minister looked sober and replied in kind, with the same mode of shortness. I baited my bit of surmise, caging it in my mind for safekeeping. However, gossip is yet gossip; I did not wish them to know I had heard. I kept my fingers duly at bay. My eyes, however, I did not keep under the same oath… they lingered for too long, inadvertently resting against Mr. Benjamin's gaze. For a long minute we simply stared, and finally I nodded once. He nodded in return.

He turned back to Mrs. B. "Give my good wishes to your industrious Miss Emma, as she is too busy for company."

"Ah, yes! The blessed girl. What should I do without her? I am getting altogether plump and lazy, for she has all the work done and folded before I have my irons prepared."

And the woman beamed upon me from afar, or so I guessed, for I had dissolved back behind the curtains. I do not like to be praised by her, especially in front of a minister. Whenever Mrs. Bentley talked of her "Emma," the minister's countenance would inevitably seek me out, and impress upon me the wordless shame of once again donning a pseudonym.

I withered away from such looks. Furthermore, I did not comprehend his intent. Well he knew that if I was to stand and announce "This is Yasmin Lange, the Witch Anmut of Erbanhue's Circus!" that it would murder my days as a decorous, tame lady, sewing away my leisure hours in dutiful introspection, surrounded and hemmed in by all things proper.

Mrs. Bentley, to be sure, was too much of a lady to escort the disgraced one out of the house. But she would be alarmed nevertheless, and her trust in me would diminish. I would hunt out another place.

Benjamin Lewis might look pins and daggers all he liked; I would not budge. He may submerse those unspeakably adamantine spectacles, gazing search-bound into my layers of soul, all he liked. If "Witch Anmut" was a flexible specimen, to be put on and cast off at will, so like her was this woman "Emma Bauer." It was just another mask, but one that suited propriety much better.

"Well, as I see you are hard at work, we shall call again some other evening. Goodnight, Mrs. Bentley. Goodnight, Miss Emma." My latest appellation was stated caustically, with an amicable lift of the brow.

Mrs. B: "Goodnight, good sirs, goodnight!"

The childish precipitation of my tongue from between my lips was the only farewell the minister gained. I returned soberly to my work, leaving the consequences to fall where they would. I was not afraid of *him*. I only feared men that I could not read, and Benjamin Lewis was not such a man.

Chapter Twenty

The Devil Interrupts Theological Musing

I learned much under Mrs. Bentley's persuasive guidance. Fanciful stitching, practical cooking, and how to shop for bargains and wear hats (she insisted that ladies always wear hats and gloves). I did not mind hats, for their brims offered me multiple choices in varicolored and vari-styled safeguards. If I wished not to be seen by a personage, I simply pulled the brim low over the forehead, obstructing the face. If I wished not to talk to anyone, I could register the whim by keeping the brim down and demurely saying "Ja" or "Nein" until the passerby gave me up, taking me for an unschooled Fräulein who comprehended not a word of English.

It was rather like acting. I enjoyed it. Mrs. Bentley often chided me for such naughty megrims; I listened to her placations with something suspiciously like glee. Giving up on my sins, she gave me over.

On a particularly fine day, I amused myself out of doors. Not wishing to be social, I donned my widest straw hat, securing it with a lilac ribbon and trotting briskly through the streets, feeling quite fine indeed.

My feet were shod with fresh boots, so nicely seamed and stitched, encasing the proper laced stockings. Overlaying all this was a modest make of lilac-print cotton dress, multilayered and properly high-collared. I wondered if my troupe would know me at all if they spied me out.

Nine months had passed since I was surrendered to the hospital in G----. To me it must have been nine years, so changed were my circumstances, station, and look. My hair had become quite young and sunny, and it now stirred in the breeze like silk... an audacious thing that it had certainly never dared to do before. The proud owner of these tresses must plead guilty to many an enraptured surveyance of said hairs before a looking-glass. Perhaps, after all, some things *could* aid my appearance.

The minister himself seemed to approve of the change. He now called me "Emma" with a kindly intonation, passed me the biscuits with a kinsman glance, and met my eyes with confidence. It was a welcome change.

During this walk, I was carrying a volume the minister had lent to me. When handing it over, he fervently expressed a hope and belief in my faculties rather beyond the reach of my intellect.

"This is the current theological disparity of our season," Minister Lewis had said, cheerfully handing me the booklet, "and I know your eyes and mind to be as nimble as your fingers. You may spend some peaceful evenings in a little churchly education, if I might be so bold, madame."

I laughed, as I always did when he called me *madame*. "I have no choice in the matter, sir. I know you will pester me beyond my temper's threshold if I do not read it, and thereafter expound upon it."

"Your veracity has lost none of its sting, Miss Emma."

His hazel eyes glinted on speaking the false name, but this time without the old caustic smile (I smile I deeply despised). Over time, the nonchalant sobriquet had mellowed on his tongue. He admitted to me later that the name "suits you with a gracious softness that I enjoy better than voicing 'Yasmin.' You were Yasmin before, but now you are Emma."

My grip hugged the booklet as I thought of all this. What would Benjamin Lewis really think of my mind, if he could open its stubborn doors and dart glances about its rooms? They were not without trappings, but such trappings are best for show, not use. They are artistic rooms... crafty perhaps, but not deep... shining, but not practical. Whatever items practical they hoarded had been forced within them by trial and circumstance.

Turning my pupils onto the leaves of the book, I allowed myself a peek or two at its amusing preachments, so soft on the eye, so endearing to the trusting-minded. It must be admitted, however, that the sermons of Benjamin's choice carry a certain logical tone to them, only barely edged with sentiment, like a wreath of flowers lining a vegetable garden. Over the months, he had gradually introduced more profound themes in his gifts. Although I chuckled over them, I did think them over (at least when there was nothing else to think of).

I closed the booklet. I had reached the outskirts of town, and could freely deliberate with myself.

"In due consideration of these doctrines and creeds, sermons and beliefs, what is to be gained? What is the end of it all? It says here," I reopened the pages and sought the proclamation, " 'For the glory of the One True God, who devised and spread out all the universe as one rolls out a scroll, and who will indeed roll it up again at the end of time.' What have *we* to do with cosmic forces? I did not ask to be put out. And if man's nature is so evil, as these teachings say, what have I to do with an Almighty Wrath? Did He not cause my own make and design? Can a pot be blamed, when the potter himself ruined the clay with purpose? And, after all, I most certainly am not *evil*, though poor choices I may have made. One cannot be blamed for desiring to stay alive, even for a price."

Some of my bitterness of spirit returned. I strove to quench it. "No... no. Those are the deep roots of dark times, from whence a hopeless branch of thought still spreads. I must dig them out and expose the gritty soil to the sun. I must sift them with good work and gentle speech, until the soil is refreshed and can fructify. There is a healthy middle ground that many a man can choose. I need not be a devil any longer, as circumstances no longer necessitate it; I also need not be a religious fool."

So saying, I closed my conversation.

A well of manly laughter poured suddenly upon my ears. I turned in indignation, chin pointedly uplifted, lips parted to deliver righteous remonstrance. They were stilled.

Who was it that stood before me?

"It *cannot* be you who speaks such words. I would not have seen you at all, but for your particular step and crisp, cold levelness of voice... but stay! Yes, all doubt is removed by the flash of those flinty eyes. You are well, but your temper is equally nourished. You look very well indeed, Yasmin."

No, my brain could not accept this picture. Surely my imagination alone had grafted upon my senses... the *impression* of Master Erbanhue.

My logical half, nevertheless, was stifled by the truth. It confessed a cowering belief. I lowered a warm face, pink with embarrassment. My shaking hands clenched within my gloves.

Somehow, I managed to speak. "I am well and content, thank you. Forgive me if my manners were abrupt. I am... surprised to see you." (*Glad* would not have been appropriate, although to my own indignant shock, it was the truth.)

I advanced, offering my hand to the tall, black-haired man, whose ebony moustache glinted with mahogany sparks. "You seem hardier than before," he said, his wonderful mismatched eyes flushing over me in rapid patterns. "There seems to be more of you. You have found work?"

"Yes, good work, albeit humble." My bewildered brain struggled. I was impressed with the conviction that I ought to be quite a stately lady by now, and quite at my ease. I was obliged to suppress the multiple emotions now vying for release... long-suppressed anxiety being foremost. "I presume that the circus has folded up?"

Erbanhue shrugged. "Yes, we have disbanded. However, I am not without means, and I intend to weather the storm and gather an entirely novel set of performers when the time is right." He crossed his arms. "Take care that you do not get plump. If you fatten, you will not be chosen when I come a'hiring."

"I would not consider rejoining your circus, sir, no anyone else's... ever again." I stepped away.

Hue's thick black brow rose, along with his customary smirk. "You may be alive, my old friend, but you will not thrive with the common folk. I have seen it! I know you! Your true life throbs for the stage. The blood of a showman ripples in your veins. Your new friends my try to displace you... they can *attempt* to exchange your sticky native blood for the pure, thin blood of the masses. But you will wither away post-transfusion."

His heterochromatic optics flickered darkly. A shadow passed over them. My breath seized in my throat.

I AM YOUR LEADER, NOT FATE.

I AM YOUR FUTURE, NOT DESTINY.

IT IS I.

Oh, Erbanhue! You too?

But nearly a lifetime of command, of pressure, of hypnosis, cannot be thrown off all at once. Part of me still quelled in the stirring tones of his voice, unlike any other voice my ears had heard; I could sense myself shrinking beneath the brash omnipotence of his mien. But another part of me, light and strong as a spider's web, reached my lips.

Emma lifted her head. "That may be," she said softly, even kindly. "You can be true as the seasons, Erbanhue, and shrewd besides. That is your gift. But if you can pity me for joining the populace, I can also pity *you*, for you will never know the kindness and simple joys granted me by my friends. Do you know, Master Erbanhue, what it is to have a friend? To *be* a friend?"

I let out a little breath in conclusion. In speaking of a friend, I had been referring to the Minister Lewis, for who else had the sensitivity of mind and manners? Who else had such willing perception as he had shown me? I had not fully considered him a friend, until now. That patient, long-enduring, good man! I had not appreciated him as he deserved. Perhaps when I returned his book, the one I held even at that moment in my hands, I could explain... I could apologize...

I had actually forgotten Erbanhue. He stood wordlessly, staid and stubborn, but a quiet glint of amusement shone in his eye. "They have altered you already. Not, I must say, entirely for the better, but you are certainly more respectful than days of yore. Who is this great benefactor of yours, Yasmin Lange?"

"I am called Emma Bauer here."

"Emma, is it? Very good. That suits you somehow. Look out for yourself then, Miss Emma, for good friends are but for a moment, and I should be sorry to see you entirely lost, after all."

And Erbanhue shook my hand, as frankly as one gentleman bids good-bye to another. He left me, singing to himself about "Poor travelers on a summer's day, who trail'd a long and weary way."

I watched him go, wondering if I should ever see him more. The prospect left me feeling peaceful, with a sort of calm, placid, sad satisfaction. "Take care, Master Erbanhue. You were cruel, you were painful, and you were anything but good. Still, you represent a facet of my life that I would not scorn to bid a kindly farewell. I am strong because of you. I am *me,* because of you."

Chapter Twenty-One

LIDIA

The following spring, I was stitching away at the kitchen window. Ever and anon I refreshed myself with glances at the flower-box I was attempting to tend. My mellow project was presently interrupted by a Mrs. Bentley.

As I inscribe this occurrence, I cannot help but smile. It is so ironic that I would have been anathemizing my daily tasks at that precise minute. "You are a tired piece of work," I announced to the silk roses, reposing in rather boring fashion against a creamy glove. I had become quite adept at mending gloves, and was even accused of reinventing some and embellishing others. "You are a disgrace to the optic nerves. You are the height of fashion, and as a result, pathetically and hopelessly common. What a relief an electric-blue order would be! Or even a demand for the venomous arsenic green! I can brand it Hue Green gloves."

The weather that day was uncommonly good, and so was my mood. I laughed openly at myself.

To return to Mrs. Bentley: She flapped in, waving aloft some white square of curled paper. "Emma, darling! Do put that down and go change into something suitable. Your presence is requested at the Ladies' Society Tea in town!"

Baffled, I glanced first at the work of my hands, and from thence to my plain blue print with tiny ruffles at the wrists. "I present two objections, Mrs. Bentley."

"Why, whatever do you mean, Emma?"

"For one, madame, I am occupied in finishing Mrs. Lidia Henderson's rose-pleat gloves. And for another, I have just been thinking that I ought to have set my hair this morning. It will not be kept in order."

As a matter of fact, my hair had amassed such a startling abundance and satin-like quality that I was confounded. I did not know how to dress such a surfeit of hair. And being a sensible, mature bit of womanhood, I did not have any intention of asking for help or advice.

"Tish-tosh, my darling. I will set it myself in the latest fashion. But you must first change into your pastel-green dress with the puffs, and the pink camellia border. Oh, and you shall borrow my silver comb set and brooch, and my lace shawl."

Ensuing within me was an anxious soul-quake. I knew that particular tone. She would dress me no matter how I scorned or shivered or howled. It is not that I dislike being well-dressed. I disliked *borrowing* such finery, and being dressed with it like a doll. I lived in mortal dread of accidental and utter ruination.

"Mrs. Henderson's order must be completed by this evening!" I objected. "I promised her it would be ready tomorrow; indeed, by tomorrow morning."

In fact, I had promised no such thing. I was desperate to avoid such a lion's den as my dear employer was now proposing. A ladies' society tea, forsooth! The very place where my past identity was most likely to be unearthed. Likely these were all high-bred, highly-spoilt Misses who were accustomed to such pleasures as the parades, the operas, and the novelty circuses.

I held in my own trembling hands the gloves of one such angelic party-pleasurer, and to endure the delivery of said articles on the morrow was bad enough. But this tea was the very nightmare for a wretched witch.

As I shuffled and objected, Mrs. Bentley babbled on. "No more excuses, my Emma. You have been a veritable slave for over a year, and I will have no more of this seamstress hermitage. You have learned plenty of local graces and manners, and you have acquired quite a fund of wit and information. Surely it is time to air your trophies rather than be cooped up here! It isn't right, you know, for someone your age to live like an old maid." As she spoke, she swept me up into a whirlwind of powders, corsets, slippers and bows and bustles, until I was subdued by dress and hairbrush into societal decorum... albeit with a mournful countenance.

"Good heavens, do not look so much like a funeral! I am determined that you will enjoy yourself. You needn't fear that no one will speak to you. The ladies have been *so* eager to be formally introduced to you, and I have not attended a single party where you were not inquired after. Yours is a very popular name, indeed! And Mrs. Lidia Henderson has been asking about you particularly. In fact, you are to come at her own special request. Think of that!"

Mrs. Lidia was, of course, the lady who was recently wed to Dan Henderson, heir and recipient of the prestigious house on the outskirts of town. The Hendersons were said to be the bread and water of the place, for their social doings became the spine of local prosperity. This information was repeated with a delight evidently crafted to persuade me, but it shrank my brevity more than ever. Why should the eminently affluent, gracious, effusive bride Lidia Henderson have an interest in the lowly spinster, Emma Bauer?

Was it not likely to assume that Mrs. Henderson had heard, through some report through Westford, that I am obliged to be the estranged circus performer, Anmut? What food for speculation for a Ladies' Society! What a source of whispered entertainment!

No! No! Every feeling was repulsed. Every strain of my thoughts cried out against the expected cruelty of such a situation. I would become the gossip of the county for a month. "I cannot, Mrs. Bentley. I am feeling ill today." I anointed myself with a sour, puckered expression.

"You are being nonsensical, my dear. You're shy, no doubt, and I cannot blame you, but you shall not disgrace me in this way. If you refuse such a warm invitation to the largest house in the county, it will reflect on my management of you. You *shall* go!"

I ceased communication, snatched my buttercup gloves, and rushed out without further demurral. I left the gloves off as long as possible as a symbol of feeble protest. Whatever should I do?

I considered, as I hurriedly marched, that I might duck into the nearest store and amuse myself among the goods until I was too late for tea. But Mrs. Bentley was correct to plead for her name in this affair. My antics would reflect badly on her, and I could not be so childish as to treat that good lady with such poor taste.

Yes, I would go. But no force of the earth nor beneath it should extract from me a word beyond "Good afternoon," "Yes," or "No."

The road was damp and glistening from the morning rain. I stuffed my chilly, stiff fingers into the hateful yellow gloves, contemplating the female life. What absurd buttons fastened this bonnet! And how greatly I detest pink camellias! And how terribly stifling is this tan corset, caged in scholarly emerald-green girdle! And how rude are all the town populace today! They were glancing at the camellia border. I loathe pink, unless it is a deep rose pink. Sadly, Mrs. Bentley's honest soul delighted in decking me out with *pink.*

"Let us be sensible, and know our place," I said to the stubborn bonnet. (I never outgrew the old habit of talking to myself on walks... only now I normally addressed myself to my hat or gloves.) "It has been quite some time since you were the Witch Anmut of Erbanhue's Circus. *You* never knew or beheld such a personage, did you, you ridiculous bonnet? These delicate vestments clothe quite another sort of woman. Who are you to be so vain as to think Anmut is the talk of the country? Surely other gossip displaced you months ago. Just sit up straight, and simper over your tea, and silently munch the cakes, and nod pleasantly, and smile at all the nonsense. Nothing more can possibly be required of you in the space of one unpleasant hour."

So preaching, I had my bonnet ribbon tied and my gloves neatly buttoned. I was dusting off the leaf-green skirt under the emerald-green girdle when I heard a distinct *phud-phud-phud*... horseshoes on spring soil.

Curious, I turned my head. Behind me cantered a horse. On the horse's back was a lady, riding elegantly at side-saddle.

Naturally, I took notice of the animal first of all, for he was a beauty. The stallion pranced across the ground with eager cobalt hooves, panting, challenging the day in the satisfaction of his power. His golden neck quivered as he tasted the air, golden nostrils flaring, copper teeth flashing in the afternoon light. He was sure-footed and sleek, the true masterpiece of a horseman's collection. I stopped and withdrew from the road to admire him more safely.

In that moment, the graceful rider noticed me. She caught my eyes with a hurried but kindly nod. Her physical appointments displayed fashionable cunning, but in a healthy, keen, economical way. It enhanced her figure to perfection, for the horse was not the only beauty of the pair. One felt at once that she was both daring and delicate.

Her mane (never mind that of her horse, though it was lovely enough) shimmered in parallel sable gloss, not done up like one expected, but let down in thick waves to her navy-blue waist. Her light, dewy skin glowed from exercise. The pupils were wide, sparkling with excitement. Her irises glinted with the mild color of tea, amber, and cherries. I especially admired the full, sloping, peach lips; they were delicately parted to bestow a gentle smile. And it was not one of those "smiles for the populace" either. Those grimaces are polite, stiff, and entirely flat, never quite reaching the eyes. *Her* smile was complete, bright, and quite unconscious, the simple greeting of one active, cheerful spirit, to a calm and speculative one.

I smiled briefly in return. She raised a black-gloved hand, touching her fingers to her blue hat brim, and rode past, being careful to direct her steed's feet away from the hem of my dress. I thought of her as I continued my doleful march to Cotesbrook Hall.

The white columns of the wealthy house depicted elegance and strict servitude. However, I had moralized myself all the rest of the way, and felt prepared to be demure and polite.

I left my gloves with the butler (they pinched me dreadfully, and I could not endure them any longer). I rather imprudently wandered into the tea room... unbidden and unannounced.

I hid my bare hands behind my back. The fingertips were swollen and red. I told myself "It's only nerves," but that did not suffice. I felt the perspiration gathering in full force.

Before me frolicked the dreaded crowd of intimate honeybees. Slippers soared across the polished floor. Flowers waved, feathers drooped, silk floated, and delicate fingers grasped cups and saucers with intrinsic finesse. I felt myself tuning it out, quietly surrendering amid the pressure. The corner couch, I supposed, was the seating arrangement most conducive to my current frame of mind. I seated myself. I commenced with the typical play of strangers at teatime... the subtle observation and summation of everybody else... quite often to their detriment.

The tall, chestnut-haired one with greenish eyes, I predicted to be the beloved Mrs. Lidia Henderson. This lady was the most richly dressed of the party. Her long, lace gown sparkled at the neck with concealed gemstones, and her perfumed hair was gathered in modest puffs at the back of her neck. A rather matronly style, I mused, but becoming on her, at least. She was chatting in civil tones to a blonde neighbor, who brightened the room considerably in a violet gown of remarkable tint and magnitude. The lace woman is elegant, well-read, and has inherited or married a fortune, thought I. The blonde girl is frivolous, mundane, and vain, and has likely committed vast financial sins to obtain that ridiculous frock.

Having done with that pair, I coolly observed my other neighbors and their brown, blue, cream, and white raiment (all far more appropriate than that violet vulgarity). I was interrupted by the creak of the double doors. I turned my vision to the interloper, now the attractive cynosure of all eyes.

"Oh, I beg your pardon for being late! Bar-Nephthalti was overdue for a run, and I couldn't help losing myself in the splendor of the day. Do sit down, ladies! You shan't stand upon ceremony for the one who is tardy."

So she spoke, twitching her windblown collar into place, and smoothing the rumples from her silken riding habit. The other ladies warbled their compliments. I merely nodded from the relative safety of my corner. "I am glad to see that tea was served without me. Please, be seated! Miss Willhite, it is wonderful to see you." She glided (such a blasé term as *walked* proved an insufficient allusion to her gait) into the arms of the white lace lady, embracing her with sisterly affection.

As the multiple conversations resumed, I picked at a loose thread in my borrowed shawl. I considered the technicalities and ramifications of making good an early exodus. Perhaps I would not be noticed. I could slip past the butler with no trouble at all. And as to the lace-and-gemstone lady, Mrs. Lidia ... but halt.

That magnificent raven, the equestrienne, had addressed that lady as Miss Willhite. And so, which of these affable birds was the inevitable Lady Lidia Berenice Henderson of Cotesbrook Hall? I wished to identify her by sight. I meant to avoid her in the future, perhaps thereby preserving my standing as a well-mannered seamstress orphan by the name of Emma.

"And you must be Miss Bauer?"

I rose and made a slight curtsy. "She stands before you. But you have the advantage of me."

"I had forgotten that you would not know me from my wedding portrait." She laughed, her warm, amber eyes glittering with good-natured mirth. "It seems the whole town gazed their fill of it, probably memorizing every freckle I ever tried to camouflage! And then, my dear husband was possessed to go forth and hang it by the main staircase. I am appalled! But this is untoward; forgive my chatter. I am Lidia Henderson."

"The pleasure is mine, Mrs. Henderson." I spoke as formally as possible, but she surprised me by drawing me into a friendly embrace. "I've heard all about you from Mrs. Bentley, you poor dear. She told me that you worked your way in complete self-reliance, and even now you support yourself through your own efforts. I admire you with all my heart."

Miss Willhite overheard us. She rather wrinkled her visage upon hearing such (apparently unmerited) praise. "Ah, the mysterious Emma Bauer. I am pleased to meet you."

"And I, you."

Mrs. Henderson released me, still smiling. "Do sit down, Miss Emma, and I will bring you some tea. Would you prefer cream and sugar?" She took my hand and sat me down again... while subtly directing disapprobation toward Miss Willhite.

I smiled. "In truth, Mrs. Henderson, I was thinking of taking my leave. I confess that I feel uneasy in deserting my employer, with so much of the work unfinished... your own order amongst the rest." I worked with gentle caution to extract my hand from hers. My fingers burned like fire.

Suddenly she withdrew of her own will, frowning a little and briefly rubbing her hands together. She recovered instantly. "Well, if it is so pressing, I will not object to your spirit of economy. However, I will tempt you to attend dinner with my husband and I tomorrow. We dine at seven."

"I will come, if it be possible."

"Thank you! You are welcome, of course, to bring an escort, that is..." She hesitated and blushed. "If you find it convenient. I mean, if you know any gentlemen."

She beamed once more. Never did the word "beamed" seem so perfectly adequate when describing anyone's smile. She had the purest natural skin, diamond-like in clarity, and it mirrored the sunlight that her cordial expression enkindled. I found myself staring at her commendable cheekbones and fluffy, dewy eyelashes, and I wondered what sort of gypsy-fairie she had descended from.

Reader, I actually felt in awe of her. It is not a sensation that I have experienced often. In fact, not since Erban- never mind.

Normally, even the slightest of suggestions concerning "beaux" or escorts called up my prickles and thorns at once. But something in Mrs. Henderson's grace and frankness, and even bashfulness, was rather endearing. "I fear there are no single gentlemen of my particular acquaintance," said I, "but I have never objected to making trips by myself. In fact, I prefer it."

"I have observed you on your walks," Mrs. Henderson nodded. "I have often ridden past you. Indeed, you are a singular personage! I have seen you out walking beneath the moonlight, as I returned in my carriage from shows or late dinners... I was quite shocked, you see. I thought you were a ghost!" She giggled.

I laughed with her – for how could I do otherwise? I did not recall *ever* taking night walks. I was far too afraid of seeing *Him*.

"But it will be dark after dinner," she continued. "I do not doubt your bravery, but it is not safe for a young lady to walk alone at the dead of night. You really *must* give that up. At least, you must ask Mr. Bentley to come for you in his cart, so that you will not walk home alone. I would be all anxiety."

"Your suggestion is practical, madame. However, his cart is in use in the evenings. I loathe to ask him-"

"Well, never mind! You will have my carriage at your disposal. Indeed, I shall send it to you at six-thirty precisely."

Naturally I objected, citing the usual complaints of inconvenience (for her), the rashness of personal favors to unknown persons, and the possibility of inclement weather. All and sundry were overthrown. "And one more thing, please," the lady continued, taking me by the waist and walking to the door with me, "Call me Lidia. I was raised quite casually, you see, and I am not used to all of these curtsies and scrapings yet."

"Very well. Lidia."

"Thank you, Emma!"

Chapter Twenty-Two

THE CELTIC GODDESS

It was delightful to have a friend.

For the better part of a month, I was continually entertained in Lady Lidia's apartments ... her suave, liberal, unobtrusive apartments, not unlike her suave and cheery husband (who was often absent). To sit in the lady's company, all tea and cherries and sweets - are you not yet aware, Reader, that I am *quite* partial to sweets? - became both my chief delight, and my hesitant foreboding. Do you comprehend the opposing notions? Listen.

While taking tea in her morning room, I happened to fix my eyes upon the hills. Cotesbrook Hall had wonderfully crystal-clear windows and the view was favorable. As had become my habit, I took a little of my sewing work with me to justify my frequency at the Hall. That morning, I was working away on a delicate sky-blue handkerchief. I intended to sew some light pink roses (Lidia's favorite flower) into its corners. It was to be a gift.

My favorite sort of day is one of thunderstorms and dimness, all cold and dreary without, but all candlelit and snug within. However, I am guilty of enjoying a sunny, crisp day as well. This was such a day. I was considering the bend and sway of the trees, catching their flat, green baskets full of sunlight.

Suddenly, a foreign, stinging sensation penetrated my optics. I was forced to close them. I groaned inwardly, rubbing my burning fingers against the pained eyelids. Slowly, I opened my eyes again.

What was it?

The trees appeared to pulsate violently in an equally sudden and strange wind. When I gathered the courage to look again, there was a single Black Tree protruding from the green mist. I trembled, handkerchief falling half-finished from my hands. My fingers stung as if pricked with needles. I covered my mouth, sickened and afraid.

This was a summons.

Lady Lidia, kind hostess that she was, indicated concern for my startled actions. I responded in soothing fashion and turned my back to the window. We went on with our tea... not without some quivering fingers on my behalf, handing the sugar bowl and treats with unspoken trepidation.

I could no longer endure "sitting it out." My eyes were invariably drawn to the woods. I excused myself with the practiced calmness of Witch Anmut. "Get thee out of doors! Thou hast lingered too long. Thou art stout of flesh, ripe for the hand of the fruiterer. This summons shall not be disregarded."

Thus spoke the Witch in my veins.

I know not where my feet led me. I ambled half-blind as my eyes were sore, and my vision marred with tears. I was *not* crying, yet water poured from my eyes.

Before my blurred optics confirmed that thin, ghastly Tree, so poisonous to all surrounding life, I knew what it was that I confronted. The

Demongod had never left me. He had His hold on the Witch, and the Witch accompanied me at all times.

But before I saw Him, I beheld Lillias Vosquez.

She was standing as I had seen her last, folded carefully against the breeze in the faded gray shawl. Her little fawn legs were pale from the cold. She stood cloaked in an atmosphere that breathed chill and frost... her poor little eyes were swollen and black... her thread-like mouth was trying to speak, but no words came forth. There was only silence and a faded rattling sound. She stood straight enough, if stiffly... only she no longer had either arm.

As I stared at her empty shoulders, she began to fluctuate in and out of vision. I reached out to her, calling her name piteously and grasping at the wind, as if catching it could lead me to her. I collapsed. I forced myself up again, feeling my pulse jolting and the blood quickening in my veins. I was excited and terrified. My fingers turned red with all the heat of my body. The rest of me was left deathly pale and cold.

This time, I was not so much afraid. I was *angry*. Here was the truth behind my darling's expired life! He had taken her from me, *He* had ripped from my heart the one and only child I had ever loved, and could ever tend as my own little one. And I hated Him with a hatred I had not yet felt in all of my days... even for my hapless fate, even for Erbanhue, even for hunger and injustice and fear. *He* was my enemy.

Although I would certainly die, He must not command every endeavor. He would extract me for a price! I rushed at Him.

And what happened next? What, indeed!

THE TRUTH CANNOT, DOES NOT,

WILL NOT, EVER MATCH THE EXPECTATION.

I had not noted that as I stood, contemplating my deep and profound hatred, I vocally swore infuriated reprisal and abhorrence against the Demon. I say, as I compiled these bitter invectives against Him, I began to run. In the corner of my eye, I viewed another person. But I did not stop! *He* was before me.

He vanished.

I stumbled to a halt, panting, enraged. My burning fingers turned from red to blue-black. Smoke rose from their tips. I lifted them to my eyes, throwing back my long hair and howling with rage like a wounded dog. Yasmin Lange was finally struck mad.

The person I had barely acknowledged winced, drawing back into the brush. "What on earth? *Cé atá ann?*"[1]

I concealed myself behind a bolder. I would examine this new phantasm. Surely it was only a vision. Was it hunting me? Was this another trick of the monster's? Which being's appetite would consume me first? For whom had I been thus conditioned?

Had He led me here with irresistible mockery so I would meet this... thing? It could not be a *real* human. Who would be out here, in the middle of Nowhere, like myself?

The vision was female. She was majestic. As Lidia is not unlike a princess, this woman was like the ruling queen. Her height perfectly complimented her limbs' rounded, exquisite make, swathed in the folds of a black dress made of swirling, hardy material. The hair was thick, braided, and wound about the skull in a tight crown, reflecting the spring sunlight like spun gold. Her lips, tightly compressed, were vermillion with health and deter-

1. Irish for "Who is there?"

mined life. Her eyes were the blue of the Celtic shoreline, piercing and glinting... they were neither hiding nor cowering, but seeking... seeking with harsh expectation.

This was no prey, but another predator. Very good. But what was it seeking in the woods?

If I was the besought prey of this forest goddess, I quickly resolved that it would be an honor to die at her hands. Perhaps this was mercy. I covertly searched those same hands. They remained still, quietly clenched at her sides. They were empty. No weapons... this was pleasant news, but what prey could those healthy but delicate hands ensnare?

Surely she was no threat to *me!* The Witch's anger fueled her with consummate powers, contorting her features and sharpening her vision. I felt my teeth bare. "Let her try!" Hissed the Witch.

The vision lifted her skirts to take long, elegant strides toward the clearing. I shuddered. Emma Bauer parted her lips to call out and stop her; she was walking directly into the Black Tree - which I felt, if not the woodsome familiar of the Demon, was at least the harbinger of His presence - but Emma's aching throat emitted not a sound.

The Witch merely chuckled (as she would).

I was silenced. The forest queen passed through the Tree as if she, or it, were a ghost!

My mind reeled from the shock. The Black Tree, I knew, must be real enough. I had seen it before; I had touched it. From here, I could even perceive the white strip of wood... the area where I had peeled off some of its ebony bark in the desperation of hunger, all those years ago... and in an entirely different county!

Was *it* a ghost? Was the woman a ghost?

Was *everything* a vision?

Succumbing at last to the hideous ache in my bones, the terror that seized my vocals, and the paralysis that numbed my body, a soft cry escaped from my throat. I laid on the ground, as quiet and helpless as a child. Emma desired release, was *begging* to be let alone to cry away her fears. Yasmin sneered, denying her that wish. The Witch laughed at them both.

I heard footsteps approach. I clenched my eyes shut, unwilling to see either the ghost or the Demon. (Although, come to think of it, the Demon's footsteps were ever mute.)

"I would bid you rise, but it would not do to risk you fainting away altogether. Lift up your head. Lean against me."

My body was shifted. I know not if I actively obeyed, but the regal voice seemed to appreciate my feeble efforts: "Thank you. Now, your arm. You may feel dizzy; best to keep thine eyes closed." I gladly did as was suggested.

"Now I can carry thee. Fortunately you are slight. You will be asleep presently. You will awaken at my house. I have much to ask you... permitted that you..."

More was said by that soft, strong voice, but I heard it not. The wet cloth she held to my mouth smelled bitter, but its effect was calming, channeling my mind's stunted thoughts into empty waves. Yasmin, Emma, and the Witch all slept.

Chapter Twenty-Three

In the Little Gray House

I woke with a start.

I was tucked in a clean bed stuffed with sweetgrass, my head supported by a thin flannel pillow. The Celtic goddess sat beside me. Her eyes roved from the fireplace to my face and then back again. One of her slender hands clasped a small, black volume, emblazoned with a cross of brass. The other hand rested on my temple.

"Welcome back to the world, *mo chara.*"[1]

Her voice, though gentle, radiated such sovereignty that I was startled and shrank away. "You did not sleep soundly. You had many nightmares in quick succession. Dare I ask of what you dreamed?"

"I... I cannot say."

---

1. Irish for "my friend"

I struggled to sit up. She put down her book to aid me. “You may sit up, but please do not try to stand. You are trembling in every limb. What did you see?”

Her directness gave me pause. I stared. The blue of her eyes deepened as her eyelids narrowed. “You remember what you saw. What did you see in the woods?”

“Pardon me... we are strangers, and I do not know what you mean.”

“Do you equivocate with me? We are strangers, indeed, but I have sensed a spirit - nay, I suspect a fallen deity - for some weeks. He has refused to unveil Himself to me, but I know He is there. Now. *What... did... you... see?*”

Well, Reader, clearly she was human. And clearly she was just as mad as I am. I respected her request, for I had seen much. But could I speak of it? No, I could not. She required too much of me. It was beyond my power.

I opened my mouth once, twice, thrice, and was stopped each time by a clotting in the back of the throat. My tongue was coated with dried blood. I choked, leaning over the side of the bed to expel the vile flavor.

There was a bowl of cleansing water on the floor. I briefly caught my reflection. My eyes had gone quite large and deeply gray. They were nearly black. I lifted my hands. The fingers remained fragile, turning from pale to indigo at the tips.

I interpreted the signal. The Witch had taken hold.

I had forgotten my rescuer. “Will you begin with your name?” She asked, her tone somewhat irritable and impatient.

“Water, please,” I managed, coughing again at the effort.

Sighing, she snatched a clay cup from a stand and lifted its contents to my lips. I sipped eagerly, wishing that I could leap into an entire fountain... a lake... a rushing, crushing waterfall... a fathomless ocean. I could have devoured a sea of water... would have gladly drowned in it.

The aftertaste caused my face to wrinkle. "It is a cold brew with some herbs," she explained. "It will encourage your body to heal and soothe your swollen mouth. You are in a perilous stage of dehydration. How you have survived this long, I cannot say."

She took the cup from me and set it on the floorboards. I licked my lips, the crawling feeling of dryness already stealing its way back. The relief had lasted mere seconds. "What is your name?" she asked me again.

Emma Bauer, I could have said. I ought to have said so. But some maddening impulse caused my cracked, charred lips to drop the appellation, "Yasmin Lange."

There! That incorrigible Witch, long suppressed, had taken her revenge at last. She *would* be acknowledged and recognized, no matter the cost.

"Ah, German. I suspected as much. Let us see." Leaning over me, she took my hands and inspected them fore and aft. "A worker, but not of strong work. Strange bruising at the fingers... Hmm." She turned my fingernails closer to the firelight. "A baker of your own daily bread." With a deft movement, she used her nail to scrape the morning's bread dough from beneath my fingernails - a presumptuous act followed by her observance of a miniscule scar from an old pin-prick.

"A seamstress. Tisk, tisk, Miss Yasmin! You did not wash your hands so deftly this morning. These fingernails! We have also-" turning the hands back to the palm side, "Ashes from cleaning the grate. More scabs from sewing and mending... and..." rubbing at my thumb, "A spot of hardened wax from dipping candles. You are industrious. But you are ill. Severely ill." She sat back again, recommencing her previous glare. "You ought to be in bed for a month. What on earth are you doing in the middle of the woods? *Cailín dúr!*"[2]

In my mind, I laughed. I could not reconcile this commonplace berating with her glorious, tall, queenly vestige and voice. I smiled. "If you must know, my fair lady, I was out gathering mushrooms." In spite of my instant respect for her, I felt a sneer curling my lip. A tale must be conceived and promptly told. "I amuse myself, I ramble about, I go calling, I pick vegetables. I enjoy a pleasant life. And, if you can excuse my rudeness, my friends are expecting me. I must leave at once."

I proceeded to throw off the bedclothes. She grabbed my hands and pushed me back down. "Indeed, 'my fair lady,' you shall not stir a step until I give you leave. I shall summon your host of friends myself... although how *friendly* your friends may be is coming rather into question, considering your physical state. What are their names and addresses?... *Please*," thrusting on politeness like a forgotten garnish at dinner.

"I do not wish to impose on you any further. If you would be good enough to contact Mrs. Eliza Bentley, that will do. She is the lady in ------ town, to whom I am employed."

"Hmph. You do not *sound* like an invalid. Nor a simpleton, either." She crossed her arms in one light, fluid movement. "I have happened... merely *happened*, you see," Here her eyes glinted with mischief, "To have seen you out walking through town with that most royal of Highnesses, Lidia Berenice Henderson."

Something in her tone stiffened me. "Lady Lidia, if you please. Why do you speak of her so?"

---

2. "Stupid girl!"

"What do you mean? Whatever gave you the notion that I dislike her?" Tossing her golden head, she moved briskly from me to the hearth-fire, and began dashing away at the embers.

Despite our rocky beginning, I felt admiration deeply rooting in my heart as I watched her bold, fluid maneuvers. There is a strength in the grace of femininity that no other creature on earth could match.

"I only marked your tone of voice," I sniffed. "It seemed less than cordial." For a second time I glanced down in the water, contemplating the Yasmin in the bowl.

It was a frightening prospect. I looked just as ill as I had ever been during the days of my poverty. This unpleasant change – unnerving, to say the least – was nothing short of supernatural. Hardly half an hour ago I had been a healthy young woman, as far as looks went.

The Celt raised herself from the hearth and let out a cheerful, bubbling laugh. "As the good Lady Lidia is my cousin, it would be not less heartless than insulting to my own precious reputation if I were obliged to dislike her. I am jealous of her, perhaps."

I blinked at her frankness. "Or, to be more precise, I was *once* jealous of her. Her ease of social grace is something I can never strive for with any degree of success. I am too blunt, too natural, to get along well with others. I get along better with the trees and the rocks."

"*That* I can easily imagine," I supplied.

Glaring into my face for a span, she laughed once more. "Then there is no need for me to prove my words, I see. You spurn me already, and in an instant! What classic judgment, and what proof of superior mind and manners! I read you in your sour face, indeed I do, Miss Yasmin." She stepped closer, grabbing and inspecting my palm again. She shook her head slowly. "And yet, we are so alike. You cannot deny that while we are separate cups of bitter dregs, we were poured from the same divine flagon."

I snatched my hand away, launching into a speech that was less than civil. My well-met antagonist was kind enough to interrupt. "There, now, my passionate one! Forgive me at once, and I can begin the supper. My nonsense is merely my way. Just as that yellowish, sour face is *your* way, and it cannot be helped in either case." Fluffing her skirts, she rose from her throne and tended to a stew pot.

It will do, Miss Yasmin, thought I to self, watching her bustle about and gather her homely dishes. You have at last met your match. She is neither warm nor effusive, though I'd be far from grateful for the latter, and don't much regret the lack of the former. She is piquant and reckless, hardly hesitating to expose her flaws, not to mention her odd beliefs. What a fine friend she would make! And what a character *you* would become by association! (Sarcasm, my dear Reader – in the beginning at least.)

Soon, the day would come when I would think of my first impressions and smile. For this very same woman was destined to become closer than any sister.

We took a meal together. Despite my mixed antipathy, I had to admit that she was a clever woman. Although her tongue shaped a surplus of words in an unbroken and steady pace - which I despise in most persons - she was never without information, and her comments displayed sense, if also ridicule and gossip. "Can you believe the state of womanhood nowadays? How we are expected to adorn the ranks! How we must simper and sniff and sigh! With what wavings of handkerchiefs and woeful wringing of hands! Yasmin may look a sour cat, surely, but even *her* company was an improvement! Did she not agree?"

More bright laughter, like an elven, silvery fiddle and bow. She was a vexed, naughty, haughty being, but she spoke in placid bubbling all the while like a soothing brook. I discovered that her prattle carried a sweet, somewhat lethargic quality. I dozed while I listened.

I stole another look round her cottage. It was certainly rustic. However, its solemn wood and stacks of stone did my heart good; I felt at home in them. In truth, Reader, I was more at ease here than in the halls of my friend, Mrs. Lidia Henderson... notwithstanding that woman's statelier company.

"Do you often wander the wooded places alone?" I queried, setting down my mug of lukewarm milk. Her face took on a more serious air.

"Yes. It is what I love best in the world to do. If the elements were a little kinder... a little less against the common needs of frail mankind, how I would wander all the days of my life!"

As if yearning for the mighty winds of the hills from whence her soul hailed, she reached up and loosed the pins in her locks. Down came one glorious rush of refined, golden hair. I allowed myself the liberty of gazing upon it, wishing I could recite an enchantment upon my own sad scalp-threads. I sipped my milk.

Chapter Twenty-Four

Warren Hyram

Part Two

Standing eagerly on tiptoe, I listened at the open window for treading feet. Warren normally came at about this time, and his was the sort of gossip I liked for evening tea. The news of the day rustled pleasantly like the dying embers, Warren's familiar tones warming and gentle.

The dying embers! I leapt across the living-room in one bound, stabbing the fire mercilessly.

I had been dwelling in my very own house for two years, but I was yet decades away from becoming the model housekeeper. My mind, prone to wandering, continuously forgot the half-kneaded dough or the hissing teapot.

I wrenched said object from the fire's hold, earnestly hushing the screaming, boiling water. The teapot's copper surface showed a giggling and smiling Yasmin.

My "houselet," as I termed the place, was nothing but packed dirt flooring and wood-and-clay walls, hardly anything to boast of. Still, it was *mine*.

Nobody lived with me, nobody meddled in my affairs, and I had my own dear fireplace and my own sweet little couch to rest on. Even my tiny dinner table, dressed with my miniature dinner-ware set, had launched me into thrills of delight upon their presentation (my house gift from Mrs. Bentley, for whom I still worked). Her place was not far down-hill.

A few meager watercolor paintings, my early efforts at creativity, hung against the brown walls. They had not gone well, Reader... But I felt they were better than bare walls.

As for myself, I fairly glowed in the evening's light, warmed pink and orange in firelight and general contentment.

Yes, I was content at last. Living free among nature, nestled safe in a woodsy cottage-loving hill, yet near the town and the town's necessities. *And* near my very few, but hence very dear, friends. I was yet poor, in the earthly meaning of the word. But I was happy.

My quick ears, self-preserving to the last, caught the sound of Warren's friendly steps. I stood from kneeling by the fireside and carried the teapot to the table, where two yellow mugs waited in state. I poured, stole some teacakes from the cupboard, and seated myself just in time to murmur a sedated response to Warren's "Hullo, the house! Are you there, Emma?"

He stamped in with a smile, blatantly ignoring the mud on his boots as it happily became one with my floor. I frowned at him, or rather tried to... Frowns no longer lurked beneath the surface of my face. Nowadays, they burrowed many layers down. It took a good deal of effort to raise them to the forefront. "Bah! What is *that* face, Lady Emma? You are no good at welcoming your guests."

He sat across from me, playfully mimicking my attempt at a grimace. "I suppose *this* is a welcoming sort of mein, hmm?"

I laughed. Warren Hyram chuckled, tossing back his thick brown hair. "And what news have you for me today?" I asked.

"Oh, all the best! A traveling merchant hears all manner of social priorities and indignations."

"Well I know it. Indeed, sir, you are bursting with sensationalism. Which brand have you brought your changeling today? Animal, vegetable, or mineral?"

"Definitively animal, my dear Miss Bauer." Warren leaned toward me, grasping his mug between two suntanned hands. His soft brown eyes gleamed with mischief. "I daresay you would be interested to hear about the latest and greatest entertainer of our county?"

"Entertainer, you say? For shame, Warren! You have given yourself away like a simpleton. You haven't been working at all, have you? You've been lounging the days away, traveling at your ease, and buying tickets to all the latest amusements!"

Warren flushed a little, his brown spray of freckles hiding under a pink gauze. "Who can blame me if I use a pinch of my earnings for some pleasure? You needn't scold me, dear Emma. We are friends; let us be friendly!" – Then abruptly changing tones – "Do you want to hear my news or not, you naughty little spirit?"

I laughed again. Warren was the best of friends, truly the brotherly sort. He had all of The Nameless One's tarty changefulness, but none of his painful stings. Warren was a brown velvet serpent, fangless and tame, who would curl about my arm and mutter all manner of secrets to Emma, his tamer.

"You would sooner cut off thine arm than leave this place without spilling your news, and you well know it," I answered coolly. "Let's have it, then. Who is this proclaimed mastermind of entertainment that Warren so adores?"

"I shan't tell you," he grinned, leaning back and lighting his pipe. "I shall make… you… guess."

"Very well. It has been a dull day, and I am in the mood for guessing." I mirrored his pose. "You mentioned that this news falls into the animal category."

"That is correct."

"So this entertainer works with animals? Or perhaps he *is* one. Is he a monkey?"

Mr. Hyram collapsed with mirth. "Wrong, Miss Bauer! But he would make the most daring, handsome, lofty monkey ever seen to man." Warren composed himself, huffing chuckles around the lips of his smoking pipe. As my fireplace smoked a good deal, I didn't suppose another whisp of smoke would complicate matters much, though I did part the heavy curtains to let it out.

"He's been in the business before," continued my playful tormentor. "Perhaps you have heard the name."

"What name, Mr. Hyram? Have the goodness to stop me guessing. My tea is rather useless for flavor as it is, and even more so when it is cold."

Warren sighed dramatically, raising his eyes (and his smoke) to the ceiling. "Very well. You have heard the name Erbanhue, haven't you?"

I controlled a sudden spasm, reducing it down to a slight twitch of the mouth. Unbidden, my hands became very cold and laced their fingers stiffly together. "I've heard of him," I assented. "He has traveled through here with his troupe in the past, has he not?"

"Yes, although I'm surprised you would remember. It was some years ago." Warren extracted the pipe, trying for the thousandth time to make a flawless smoke ring (and failing). "The poor economy ruined him for a time, but it seems he's back. His show is better than ever before! It's called 'Erbanhue's Fair of Phantoms.' It's the show for ladies, they said... but I liked it myself, as it's so new, and quite flashy. A few fancy-pants couples have actually hired his show for private parties, if you can believe it."

He folded his gangly legs beneath the chair. "I rather balked at the ticket price, but everybody said it was worth seeing. And I can't say I regret the monetary loss."

His playful tone returned, lending sparkles to his witty demeanor. "I'd gladly pay again if you would come with me. There are such a lot of pretty girls in his act. I need someone to play the goody... to keep me in place. And you, you dear, strict dragoness, are just the person to keep me sane."

With that, he re-applied the smoking pipe, taking long amused puffs and glancing lazily at me.

As the reader may be pleased to recall, I had bidden Erbanhue goodbye years ago, for once and forever. I felt, in my soul of souls, that Fate had decreed I would never see that man again. I would never again exchange words or looks with him; I would never cross the path of his sight.

Why? My mind pondered while I worked to steady my hands. Why, after all these years, would I be forced to disturb myself again? Why be dragged along by none other than the kind but clueless Warren, to see my old nemesis in all his glory?

It was too cruel! Why would the gods punish me thus?

It was true that I had been bad enough, in days long gone. But I had been so unerringly *good* lately. While it was true that I still looked rather strange... my hair was never to be completely tamed, and my eyes remained wide and of the deepest gray... in action I was a confirmed lady about town. However, I suddenly recalled, there was the fact that I had woken up in the middle of the woods more than once, utterly and completely unable to explain how I had gotten there, or what my sleeping brain meditated on doing out in my night clothes.

I was always reaching out with my bare arms, as if longing for something far out of reach.

But I dismissed the memory. Those were just night-walks, like some other people had. I was normal otherwise. No one screamed at the sight of me. But I would never be a beauty. My figure remained bony and tallish, like a filly that never matured.

Aislinn didn't seemed to mind being seen with my homely self. We often held hands and strolled through the town or the woods together, murmuring secrets and laughing.

Sometimes we made up songs and sang them. Her voice was deep and throaty and full – the cello. Mine was high and icy and thin – the violin.

"Stay, ye laces, falling slow,
Gently kiss with cold.
Swift beneath the ice shall flow,
Waters cool and calm.
Mothers, let ye children know,
Wounded is the sun.
Fathers, tend thy fields of woe,
Spring shall ne'er come."

My eyes and smile both widened as I quietly hummed the tune. It was our favorite. Warren rose a brow and "a-hemmed."

"Emma, you're doing it again. You are daydreaming. Well? Will you come?"

As I sat mute, I considered that I *did* have the advantage. My hair, though silky and wild, was stylishly arranged. (It had never been so in Erbanhue's day.) My stature was the same, as stated, but there were ways of arranging coats, scarves, hats and such, to hide the familiarity of my shape. Add a parasol atop this plethora of ingredients, and I was certain to pass unrecognized beneath his very nose.

In fact, I could even borrow some outfit of Lidia's, and ask if she would accompany us. The more the better in my case. I could simply melt into the crowd, an unknown and perfectly respectable stranger attending to the Lady Lidia Henderson. Also, Warren was not altogether unimpeachable in some respects. He could use two pairs of eyes on him... especially since my eyes would be somewhat engaged.

I made up my mind.

"We shall go," I announced, "but I should like to invite Lidia. You need more than one pair of eyes on you, my risky young friend."

"Oh, to have a fashionable young lady on each arm! My lucky day!" Warren sank in his chair, pretending to swoon away with delight. I sighed, casting my eyes down into my stone-cold tea.

After all, even if the worst happened, what could my old Master do? I would slip out early, and he'd wonder evermore if I had been another of his phantoms, receding into the night. I was not afraid of *him.*

I was afraid of myself.

Chapter Twenty-Five

ERBANHUE'S FAIR OF PHANTOMS

"Those are our seats? At the front?"

Lidia smiled her sympathy but continued to hug my arm, as if worried that her little gray fish would dart free from its net. "I am sorry, Emma darling, but my husband always orders the best seats. It would be strange of me to refuse him."

As was often the case, Dan Henderson had business elsewhere and would not be attending. He and his wife were most pleased that she would have a companion, and as a showy display of gratitude (that I would gladly have done without), Lidia had taken me shopping for an entire new "set."

At least we had dispensed with the dreaded borrowed plumes. I had succeeded, however, in keeping to my own tastes in the matter of the palette. I was dressed in regal navy silk, the first silks I had ever owned in my life.

Reader, I wished I was enjoying it more.

Nervous aches trembled through every limb. I glanced down at my gloved hands and was relieved to see that any unladylike sweat was well disguised in the dark gloves. Elbow gloves, however, were a bit too princess-like for my station, and I felt positively ridiculous in them. I tugged at them again, feeling like a convicted robber of finery about to be brought before the gallows.

One object of wisdom did grace my addled person, and that was the hat. I had seized upon it in a paroxysm of joy. A marvelous, swooping brim ducked low across my forehead, and anointed my face with a blessing of navy star-studded veiling. Its crystal beads twinkled in the courtyard's firelight, causing all about me to float in diminutive stars. Lidia had declared that this hat was made for me. For once, we agreed on something fashion-wise... though perhaps for entirely different reasons. Yasmin loved it because it hid her face beautifully.

We were seated in the dreaded chairs. I focused on the beauty of the floral, embellished stage, and reminded myself to be calm. I did not wish to draw people's stares by acting the fool.

That was what I most wished to avoid. A declarative, powerful Erbanhue, wonderingly following the collective stares... that for some odd reason weren't focused on *him*, but up in the makeshift stands... to one blue velvet chair... to one stiff, pale lady in navy silk, who was hiding beneath a large navy hat set with suspiciously close veils.

As it was a nighttime show, the parasol scheme had to be abandoned. I sat in my seat calmly enough, but lifted my fingers to the hat brim, bending it ever-so-slightly downward. *Just keep breathing. Stay calm.* Caution births reward, but paranoia destroys all aims. I tucked my hands into my lap and waited.

It seemed like waiting for the Judgment Day.

"I've heard this Erbanhue is very handsome," said Lidia. Having conveniently forgotten she was there, I jumped.

"Yes," called Warren from the other side of her, "The devil most certainly is. I bet he has all those lovely show ladies all to himself. The wretch!"

As Warren continued to blast Erbanhue for his handsomeness and his devilish monopoly on the ladies fair, I turned and covertly pushed one fingertip into my ear. This was the last, the very *last* sort of thing that I desired to hear. Part of me wanted to get up and slip away now, before it was too late. The cowardly part of me - Emma - wanted to run, no longer caring about what the favored Lady Lidia and her friends would say.

I am unused to so many people. I needed air.

I feel ill.

I was about to faint.

Perhaps I could simply *faint* at this very moment. There were a thousand reasons at my disposal. But I sat quietly, straight as a poker in the velvet blue chair. Curiosity *does* kill cats, so they say. Well, it would be an entertaining death.

Yasmin wished to see him. The Witch longed to either curse him or jeer at him... I never knew which horrible, hideous thing she would strive to do. And Emma was insanely curious. She longed to know if her memories of him were of the truth, or of imagination, plucked from the realm of fantasy.

Was Yasmin Lange's secret and strong admiration of him - his charismatic spirit, his earth-shaking, terrifying gaze, his proud yet abusive mastery – Was her admiration of him real or born of illusion?

Was Erbanhue a great Falsity of my own making? A tall godling whom I had called into the sanctuary of my solitary brain, and harbored there for a time... unless deliberate Scrutiny and plain Logic released the figment from the confines of my passion?

Or was he truly a great man, a mortal of resplendent talents, admirable strength, and enviable daring, poised to be the great Entertainer of our day, and vowing (like myself) to leave past woes behind forever?

If the former, I was safe from him; he was a ghost.

If the latter, I must guard myself. He would be stripped of godlike influence and immortal powers, as I had once half-believed him to possess. But he would yet be grand, his comeback miraculous, his health and energy awe-inspiring, the conditions of his showmanship ghostly and hypnotic. My Dragon unconquered, unconquerable, once again ensnaring my wretched heart to reign over it.

Yes, Yasmin Lange! I know you! I know you! You are weak; you have not forgotten him. You could fall again... you are falling now! Just wait. Only watch, and be calm. Breathe, and forget. You do not know him, you have never seen him. Watch and see, your Dragon is only a man.

Only a man!

Such a simple concept... *only a man.* But what is Man? An entrapment of smooth, knit Flesh, enriched by the mysteries of Blood, rushing to invigorate the Organs, the Heart, and the unfathomed and unfathomable Mind, capable of great and terrible thoughts. But encased somewhere... *somewhere* among the grit and gristle, the bone and the marrow, was something glowing and preternatural. Something undying and eternal.

A Soul.

A Soul, bearing the image of the High God, capable of Knowledge beyond the grave, Intimacy unstained from the wreckage of sin, and Hat red... Enough hatred to bind the soul to Hades for all time... or Adoration to lift it to the highest Heaven.

"Only a man" had these destinies. "Only a man" had so glorious and so fearful a fate. The beast, the insect, the flower of the field: All fade and are burned away! But each and every body of Man holds a Soul. And the Soul, capable of all these things, would live eternally.

IT WAS NOT THE MAN THAT I HAD TASTED, HAD LEFT BEHIND, AND NOW ANTICIPATED.

IT WAS THE SOUL.

THAT, DEAR READER, WAS THE DANGER.

A rush of wind startled me. The torches circling the pavilion flickered wildly. The audience hushed, leaning forward to determine the tall object, standing alone and unlit in the center of the stage.

It was only a man.

He rushed upon our senses, wafting close on the wings of his cape. The smolder of ghouls anointed our nostrils. We smelt his clothing as raiment that had been beyond the grave. He bowed before us, dark as sable glass, sharp and final in the night. He motioned powerfully, summoning soft green Spirits to his aid who fled to his side, beautiful and terrifying to behold.

He spoke. Everything surrounding him blurred into a confusion of shapes and colors. Erbanhue himself (I could not doubt in my heart that it was my ringmaster) remained clear, every outline sharp against the swirling, menacing beauties in Spirit form. He knew each of them by name, summoning them with his voice, commanding them in an unknown Tongue of the Dead.

They obeyed his every whim. They moved chairs, blew cold winds from their formless hands, and lifted ticket stubs from the pockets of astonished gentlemen. He caused one of them, a tall lady the color of jade, to sing. The lyrics were eerie and monotonous, repetitious, causing a stupor to fall across the audience.

I, however, remained but slightly affected; I was busied with Logic. Logic and I were conferring among ourselves. These were excellent, fresh, and amusing tricks. How did he conjure them? We were determined to find out!

We would pick him clean of his secrets. I leaned closer, infinitely calmer in the blessed darkness. My hands burned within my gloves.

Next, he introduced a fire-eater to perform new tricks among the spooks, weaving (seemingly) around and through them as he performed. The flames were of strange tints: green and blue and purple. A steady drum hummed in the background, along with low, dark chanting. I frowned; the fire-eater was not Marcus. Had Erbanhue truly done away with every last member of the old troupe? It was like him, I supposed. Why would he neglect to abandon the people whose very presence reminded him of the days of hardship? After all, he certainly had no qualms at leaving me behind in some strange, overcrowded hospital...

His third act proved the most alarming. He closed his eyes, stepping closer to the audience, waving a hand to silence the trilling moans of the Spirits. One of them, the ghost of jade, slipped away and then reappeared with a small book in her hands. She passed it to Erbanhue.

Eyes still closed, his fingers roamed the pages with calm deliberation. He seemed to feel the strange words or symbols inscribed within. The torch flames, now a ghastly blue, cast a weird coloring across his tattoos. The snake tattoo on his neck seemed to move. I blinked and shifted my gaze aside. When I looked again, his arm was raised, mightily clothed in ebony and alabaster textures, soberly gloved in something black and smoking, and he was pointing-

At *me?*

Fear predominated all else. I shrank back in my seat, suppressing a cry of dismay. But how? How, in this enraptured crowd, had he singled me out in the darkness, and from underneath the stolid protection of my hat? Surely, he knew me! Perhaps those Spirits had betrayed me, sensing my fears, pointing me out, laughing in their smoking green sleeves at the poor orphan girl, who hated public humiliation like the Plague-

His voice thundered into the stands. "Lady Lidia Henderson! You are summoned."

I blinked again behind the veil, stunned. My heartbeat had seized hotly; it was released from seizure with cool relief. I breathed again. Of course, he would recognize the famous Lady of the County, even in semi-darkness. She was the paramount of loveliness, clad in folds of lavender and lace, a dark lavender cloak sweeping to the floor in regal swaths. She stood, quite calm and angelic, and descended to meet his outstretched arm.

An unexpected rush of... something, some emotion of bitter tang, coated my tongue with disgust. Stupid, vain, paranoid Yasmin Lange! As if he would notice *you* next to the county royal! I straightened myself in my seat, poking out my chin with defiance. How typical of a man. And how senseless of this woman to be so startled! The Witch was laughing at me.

I felt my gray eyes flashing storms, summoning the rains of pitiless disdain... just as they did years ago.

Chapter Twenty-Six

He Speaks

As I rested in Lidia's guest chamber that night, I could not remember the rest of the act. I vaguely recalled the torches changing from blue, to green, to purple, and to pale, and then back to blueish-green again. I remembered the crowd's building enthusiasm, the crash of applause. I remembered Lidia's admiration, too... sharp and plaintive, painful to my ears. The Witch had snarled... she had tried to lunge. I held firmly onto the arms of the chair, refusing to give her an inch.

And of course, I remembered Erbanhue's final bow and smile. It was the smile of the unconquered Dragon, leering and bursting with pride. Yet, I applauded him too. I couldn't help it.

Sleep evaded me. I rose to pace the room. Logic had been carefully shoving out Envy, piece by piece, and now she had a word to say. I splashed my face at the carafe, willing Yasmin to be put aside, willing for Logic to speak at last.

She spoke to purpose. "Yasmin Lange, a more selfish and colder woman never walked the earth. You hate him, and why? Because he is meant for success. From the very beginning, even in the Hungry Days, you knew this. His cool, trampling disdain for others, his wretched determination, his serpent-like methods of hibernation – suffering, yet exulting in the knowledge of the spring to come – His character readied him for the realities of the cruel world. Realities that *you* have fought to ignore, *he* has embraced in his heart. This is his reward. Do you desire such a reward for yourself? Ha! You have not paid the price! What do *you* deserve beyond your slice of daily bread, and your hourly wage of work?"

"But I have suffered more than he," I cried out. "I have loved and lost. When did *he* ever love anyone? When did he even *like* anyone (who did not suit his purpose)? Did he not, at first, show some measure of preference for me? And did he not abandon me, his pet project, his hope of future fame?"

"Yes, and it was well for you that he did so. What did instruction beneath his guidance ever teach you besides a bloated sense of your worth? Did you really imagine yourself destined for fame? Did you think a mere aerialist could go far? Did you think you'd ever be more than his trained servant? You needed to be humbled. You needed to be shown that longing for pagan fame would only corrupt you."

"But I am poor and faceless," I sobbed (crying for the first time in years). "Surely I have been humbled long enough. Is it not time to raise my sleeping practice? Should I not strive for higher things? Haven't I been too contented with my lot?"

"And who would help you to rise up?" Logic countered. "You have no family, no friends who could help you beyond what you have been given. You have no talent, no fortune, no vocation. What will you do?"

"I could apply for another troupe. I could use these new ideas and forge a new plan-"

"At your jeopardy, Yasmin Lange. That is all!"

I quieted my sobs, not wishing Lidia to hear them.

As the dawn warmed my tear-stained face, I was ashamed of my outburst. I had been so calm, so happy. Why should one unexpected incident throw away all my months of tranquility? I rose, washed and dressed, and took a long walk in the Henderson gardens.

Lidia had insisted that I stay overnight and for breakfast the next day. Although the garden walk restored my sanity, I was not in the mood for idle chatter. I took my breakfast in haste. I made my excuses, and took the long road to town on foot.

The road was friendly, familiar. I wore my usual cotton print, my shoulders wrapped neatly in a close-knit shawl. I carried a small suitcase and hatbox containing my navy finery. As I walked, I puzzled. I wanted to pinpoint the exact cause of my night disturbance.

It was normal to feel disturbed, restless, ambitious and envious, after what I had seen and described to my inner self. It was the life I had dreamed of. I had longed to be part of a successful, thriving, talented troupe that traveled anywhere, did anything it liked.

In my dreams we wore costly garb, ate well, and were hired out to fancy pavilions just like the one I had seen. Our audiences were not shabby, stingy, and coarse. They were groomed, glowing, and affluent... like Lady Lidia Henderson and Co.

Thus entered Envy, frowning mightily. She thrust her hand before her in disgust. She disliked Erbanhue because he was living what I had wanted. She wished to drown him out.

But why had I been disturbed to such a drastic extent? Why, in Heaven's name, had I *sobbed?* I was no child. Yet there had been moments when my heart seemed torn from my chest.

The answer continued to evade me all the day long. I walked to Mrs. Bentley's, puzzling. I knitted, sewed, and greeted customers, still puzzling. I went home and made porridge, stirring in an abstract, puzzled way. The riddle would not be solved.

Logic, as always, had been right. I was merely a cold and selfish woman, angry at a man who had hurt me, angrier still that this man was now successful. He gathered fame as easily and naturally as bees gather pollen. And where was I?

At the moment, I was sitting before my fireplace. Something moved in the corner of mine eye. I leapt from my chair with a start of fear.

What was that shadow at my door?

It was that of a long, thin man.

As I watched, he grew longer and thinner, stretching himself into impossible lengths. Screaming, I dropped my bowl. Porridge splattered across my shoes and dress. I cringed from the heat, still staring. It was a terrible, sickening sight! And yet I could not turn my eyes away.

Previous suffering has its claims. Starvation, exhaustion, and weakness can do something for you. In my previous hallucinations, I was too weakened and exhausted to register what I was seeing, what was conversing with me. I was too tired to believe it. I was too sick to comprehend it. But now, relatively healthy, neat, well-fed and sane, Yasmin Lange viewed it with perfect clarity. The Demongod of the Woods.

Instinctively, I fell to my knees. I knew that His eerie, marked pain would rack my body in the following seconds. I did not care to be standing when He struck me.

The Shadow became a whisp of black threads in the air. It solidified slowly, the Demon stretching itself into shape. A godless, black, blinding, alabaster-skinned shape that twitched and turned in a manner that sent bile to my throat.

The ebony cloak of yore materialized, casting shadows across His blank, featureless head.

I did not cry. I was too anxious to make a sound. For the first time, I looked up at Him quite steadily.

Two golden points of light (where the eyes ought to have been) slanted from the smooth, empty sockets. Two thin, icy hands, fluctuating in and out of reality, reached out for me. They grasped mine. A shock of thunder flooded my flesh and stained my blood.

It didn't hurt. I cocked my head slightly... Fear was steadily, steadily being drained away, sucked out of me in a thrumming cadence. *What was it?*

If I listened closely, I could hear the voices of children humming... humming the song Aislinn and I had written.

"MOTHERS, LET YE CHILDREN KNOW,
WOUNDED IS THE SUN.
FATHERS, TEND THY FIELDS OF WOE,
SPRING SHALL NE'ER COME."

The Witch came forward and spoke. It was as if my body was controlled, my tongue forced to speak by some invisible puppet-master.

"Warum hast du mich allein gelassen?"

("Why did you leave me alone?")

He answered. When He spoke, it was in a deafening chorus, originating in my brain instead of from hearing. The children's voices spoke with Him, operating as one. I sobbed now, but silently, sipping on the offending tears. Listening was one of the worst pains I had yet suffered in life, but the controlling thing in my body forced me to hear. Blood trickled from my eardrums.

Du warst noch nie allein, mein Kind. Du bist von meinem Design.

(You have never been alone, my child. You are of my Design.)

At these words, my temperament changed. The tear's flow stopped at once. I stood on my feet. His voice became more bearable. It was dread music to my ears.

Du hast in meinem Namen viele gute Dinge getan. Ich bin gekommen, um dich zu segnen.

(You have done many good things in My Name. I have come to bless you.)

Yasmin struggled against Him, but the Witch held her tight. There was a pause.

Es ist notwendig.

(It is necessary.)

Some miniscule shred of relief, a cooling sensation, slipped down my throat. I resisted the urge to force it out of my body. It felt cold and foreign in my stomach, but not painful.

Auch das ist notwendig.

(This, too, is necessary.)

His form began to quake, as if rent by lightning and thunder. A loud chorus of shrieks filled the room, rising and falling, crushed ghost ships in a storm. A long, black, tunnel-like appendage reached from among His many arms, plunging into my chest.

It felt as if my lungs were being torn apart. My vision darkened. Black shadows, tinged and tensed, replaced the objects in the room that I should have seen. The aching pulse expanded, and the odd drift of His Voice. In it, I traced a certain derision.

I sensed that Emma was being laughed at. The alien sound was sharply distorted but connected, patterned, and regular... yes, this was HIS LAUGHTER.

My tormentor was no immethodical being. He commanded His will with utmost confidence - calm, exacting, calculated - a surgeon performing a precise operation. I could hear nothing else but the ringing of my ears. I knew, trapped in this growing tunnel of exquisitely orchestrated torture, I couldn't hear myself, nor could anyone hear me.

Parting my jaws, I attempted to scream... whether for help or at the Demon, I was not sure. Intent, purpose, and even will, were being sapped away from me. My attempts at cries were animalistic and senseless.

Chapter Twenty-Seven

RETURNING STRENGTH

Emma.

I stirred.

"Emma?"

No... not yet.

"Emma! Emma Bauer, wake up!"

An earthquake supervened. Groaning, I opened my eyes. Pain laced through all my nerves.

Warren Hyram was bending over me. Worry played in all his features. He held a cloth in one hand, which I assumed had been recently applied to my forehead. "I'm all right," I said, sitting up and stifling a yawn. "Just sore. And sleepy."

Warren frowned, gesturing toward the front door. "I found you unconscious at the threshold. The door was open, too... I thought someone..."

"What do you mean, Warren?"

His soft eyes widened, betraying surprise. "Do you not remember how you ended up on the floor, as cold as a statue?"

I sighed, irritation still in excellent working order. "Obviously not, Mr. Hyram. Would you care to hand me some water?"

My lips were cracked with dryness. Warren hurried to comply, nearly spilling half the contents of the mug. I drank deeply.

"You were nearly dead, you know," said another voice, this one female. "You were hardly breathing."

I turned on my couch, examining the source of the voice. She brushed back her bright hair, perusing me with sharp blue eyes. "It seems this makes the second time I've saved you from peculiar circumstances, Miss *Emma*."

I smiled wryly. "Good day to you, Miss Aislinn."

The Celtic paragon nodded and winked, whisking the empty mug from my hand and replacing it with a mug of herbs steeped in hot water. "You seem much better now, at any rate." She stepped back, looking me over. A troubled expression settled over her countenance. "Warren sent for me when he found you."

"How did he know anything about you?" I asked, swinging my feet to the edge of the couch. Perhaps I'd mentioned her once or twice, but the two hadn't met. Aislinn pushed me back down, shaking her head at me. "Believe it or not, Miss Impertinence, I've been getting quite a reputation as a healer."

"And a beautiful woman," murmured Warren, glancing at Aislinn with smile golden. I summoned a glare. Warren shrank his head into his shoulders, mimicking a shame that he certainly didn't feel.

Aislinn pretended not to have heard him. "Miss Emma, I wish you to stay in bed until Doctor Lancaster comes over to see you."

"I'm all right, Aislinn. I'm sure I was only tired from... too much excitement lately." I suppose that would account for that bout of sobbing. Annoying, scathing, disgraceful Erbanhue!

"Do not argue with me, dear. Drink your tea."

I sipped and made a face. Warren laughed, a little too loudly for my strangely sensitive ears. Aislinn noted my reaction and shooed Warren away. "And don't show your face until you hear from me," she finished, shutting the door on his protesting form. I hid my smile behind the mug.

Aislinn sat on the floor beside me, gently stroking my forehead. "Are you hungry at all, dear Yassy?"

I considered the question. "Ravenous, as a matter of fact. I don't suppose I would be allowed a full meal?"

"I cannot say until the doctor has been here. He should arrive soon." Aislinn rose gracefully, taking the mug from my hands. "It loses its potency when it's lukewarm. I'll reheat it, but you should drink it faster."

Waiting until her back was turned, I permitted my feelings to indulge themselves with a roll of the eyes. Healer, indeed. Witch is more like it!

She sensed my sarcasm and turned on her heel. She smiled... a cool, delightful, penetrating smile.

I know you, Miss *Emma*.

I answered her eyes with mine. *Perhaps we know each other.* On a strange impulse, I got up from the couch and crossed the room to embrace her.

We were sisters, not in blood, but in spirit. Somehow, I knew it from the day we met. I fought the meaning of the similarity... of what it signified... but no longer. There was no use in resisting anymore. She knew.

If someone were to ask me for one lesson that I learned from orphanhood, I would comment that every disadvantage, no matter how severe, brings with it some slight reward... the merest catch of sunlight amid the depths of blackness. Even while drowning, one can submit a quarter of one's brain to the delight of the beautiful liquid world around them. Every deprivation has strengthened me in some small way (albeit a slight and meager token for such suffering). And here, rumored to have fallen victim to some species of fit, I had a small return for my pains. I was visited by old friends.

Minister Benjamin Lewis and I had drifted apart. But now he inquired after me, having heard from Mrs. Bentley that I was ill. A few days later he came to visit, Thomas Gensing at his side. I was pleased enough to see them. I didn't even object when Benjamin led one of his kindly but anxious prayers.

"And how have you been, Miss Ya- Miss Emma?" Mr. Lewis cleared his throat, earnestly examining the soles of his boots. I smiled, graciously thanking him for his inquiry and informing him that I was quite well. "Certain stubborn Celts refuse to release me from imprisonment for a season."

Aislinn smiled her compliments.

Benjamin chuckled, taking my hand in both of his. "It is good to see you. I am sorry that it's under much the same conditions as when we met."

"It does not pain me to recall those days."

"I daresay you rather enjoyed yourself. I think you liked teasing poor old Tom and I."

"Old! Old, indeed!" Benjamin had a smooth, classically youthful face, not much deterred by the advance of years. He almost looked younger than he had three years ago.

"Miss Emma seems healthy and blooming to me," Thomas piped up. "Why don't you let her loose? I want to see her spit fire from her eyes, as she was wont to do."

Aislinn frowned at him. "It is difficult enough to keep her down at all. Why must you stir up trouble? She was as cold as ice not two days hence!"

I laughed, settling down among the pillows. "You needn't fret, Aislinn. I will not stir. After all, I have not been able to bathe properly, and I see no profit in encasing my friends here with a cloud of noxious fumes."

Chapter Twenty-Eight

The Visitation

Visitor the third proved to be none other than the Lady herself, Lidia Berenice Henderson, armed with specially-ordered tea and scones.

Upon entry, there was a subtle contest between Lidia and Aislinn. However, my chatter and Warren's cheerful nonsense smoothed over the two beauties, and soon enough we were all gossiping away like a nest of noisy magpies. Aislinn and I listened, laughed, and mocked; Lidia dispersed her provisions with pleasantries and piquant jokes; Warren chuckled and jested, his admiring gaze lingering first on Aislinn, then on Lidia, blissfully wandering to and fro between them. He had found Paradise.

"The last wish of my heart has been granted," proclaimed that shameless man, once Aislinn had graciously escorted her cousin to the gate. "I have beheld both beauties of the county at once, and I was the only gentleman present. I can die happy."

"At your pleasure, sir."

"Emma, you're such a *cold* person!"

"Kindly refrain from praising regal women who are basically strangers to you. What do you think it makes you look like? And what good does hearing it do me, a gray-haired hag?" I amused myself with melodramatic sighs.

Warren cocked his head. "Was that a knock at the door, Emma?"

"A knock? Nonsense. Who would visit at this hour?"

No, he was right – there was a distinct knock. The sound denoted authority and purpose. "Ah, very well. Coming!" sang Warren, bounding up to open the door.

Erbanhue's massive presence loomed in the doorway.

It is strange how at stressful moments our brains only think of the silliest things. Of all the thoughts that could have tumbled into my head at that moment, I thought of how underdressed I was in my plain white house gown, and how my hair was not "done." It draped across my couch in its full ash-blond glory, only halfway up, and carelessly tangled by the slightest breeze from my humble clay windows.

I could not have possibly looked more witchlike. I longed in vain for my navy silks.

Erbanhue strode in sans invitation. He was more masterful than ever. His hair and superb jawline were neatly trimmed. Vest, pants, boots and collar, were in their turns spotlessly black, snow-white, and crisply clean. He wore his new ringmaster's cape made of some wafting material that, like my hair, danced in the slightest of breezes. Gleaming silver stars were stitched along its length, matching the silvery gleam of his teeth when he smiled. His keen irids flashed fire, sparkling 'round his pupils in multicolored majesty. The Dragon was... no, not smiling... *beaming* at me.

My heart fluttered to a stop – much to my vexation. It *would* betray me.

Master Hue fetched up Aislinn's abandoned stool. He perched beside me, one hand planted firmly on his knee, the other pointing sternly into my face. "Shirker! Slitherer! Trifling little traitor!"

I stared into his flashing, draconian eyes, beyond mystified.

"I have been lingering in town for months, on purpose, waiting for *you* to come and see my show. And yet here you are, claiming to be sick - faking illness! - just to avoid me. I know you, you witch! What the deuce have you been hiding in here for?"

I smiled.

"Don't smirk at me, Anmut. I know your tricks. You're pink and rosy like a little china flower, fairly alight with health. You are *not* ill." In fact, I was blushing deeply.

Erbanhue rose, throwing back the stool and pacing the room in angry huffs. Each stride was as long as three of Warren's steps. "Why did you cause that report to ring through town, making all of your friends – if they *are* your friends to you, you sorceress – making everyone believe you were dying?" He ceased his mad run of the room, panting, hammering down all the strength of his offended glares upon my baffled person.

Reader, the most unexpected sensation was welling beneath my lips. It bubbled and sang, attempting to dance out of control. I yearned to laugh. I looked to Warren for aid; he could not aid me. He kept staring up at Erbanhue's massive height, unable to utter a syllable.

Erbanhue resumed his tirade. "Well, your secret is out, little witchling. And your insolent snubs will not answer. You *shall* see my show before the month is out!"

At length, Yasmin Lange found her voice. "I have seen your show, Master Hue. I saw all of it."

"Blows and botheration! You did nothing of the kind."

"I can name all the Spirits whom you summoned."

"Humbug! One of your friends told you. You have spies."

"I can describe each color of the torchlights."

"There, again. You have informants. Do I look like an imbecile?"

I smiled softly, having purposefully saved this proof for last. I keenly delighted in his familiar, lusty anger. "I can sing the Ghoul's Litany."

There, he was silenced. His thick brows creased in astonishment. "The little baggage can sing, eh?"

"You never knew *all* my talents, sir."

"Then, go on. I want to hear this 'gray-haired hag' sing."

He sat himself again, choosing to dutifully ignore the return of Aislinn, who was glancing from Erbanhue to myself in proper confusion.

I sang.

Erbanhue listened with critical attention. Surprise at this entire proceeding was slowly but surely leaking into my conduct, however, causing my voice to falter. He merely rose an eyebrow, a slight, ever-so-slight smile, encouraging me to continue.

I finished. No one said a word. The wind alone spoke, breathing away whatever spell I had rendered. Erbanhue assessed me intently, regarding me as a potter examines his choice of clay. "Well done," he finally said. "Your pronouncements are correct. 'Tis based on Latin, as you noted, with the chorus RESURGAM, but it is essentially a nonsense language."

"Do you believe me now?"

"I do. You had to have seen it... and more than once." He stood again, straightening his vest and snorting, "But where the deuce were you sitting? I looked out for you every-"

My smile widened. Erbanhue stopped himself, grunting. "It's of no matter. Well, you wore a disguise. You thought you'd have a go at fooling me?"

"Yes, I 'had a go,' as you put it. And you see that I succeeded."

"Ah, yes, wound me how you can, if you must! But amuse me with this knowledge. To what lengths did you go to conceal yourself? Were you a *grande grosse dame* in masquerade attire?"

My slow-building merriment gave way at once. I burst into a full and animated laugh. "Aye, sir, that sounds like me, does it not?"

"For a skinny little witch, anything must be an improvement."

We both laughed then... Yes, my devilish Master and I both laughed. I hadn't really heard him laugh with kindly meaning before, just chuckle, or sneeringly chortle. His true laughter was bold, loud, and careless, utterly disregarding peoples and circumstances. It bounced off the walls of my humble mud shack, jovially quaking the ears of its listeners.

Erbanhue offered his arm, telling me I must "come to the fireside and warm your cold witch-bones." I accepted and followed his frank tread to the fire.

Warren rummaged about arranging the chairs. Presently we were all by the fireside, brutally overcome by Master Hue, but oddly content to be thus bullied. He amused us. His stories were fresh and bold, his movements lively and exciting. The entertainer in him captivated us all beneath the sorcery of his voice.

The hours of the night stretched on long and unheeded. Passing shadows lingered in his eyes. My heart beat quick and earnest, filling my thin veins with rushing blood, causing my pupils to dilate, my breath to be frozen in suspense.

Humanity has a happy tendency of only remembering the worst parts of a person. What I had forgotten over the years was that Erbanhue was truly the best entertainer of his generation, and perhaps the best storyteller the gods had ever made. Envy gave way to admiration. Hatred was melting away, sloughing off to reveal...

"Dost mine eyes deceive me? Lo, it is the dawn!"

Erbanhue smiled, his smirk of pride giving lie to the majestic words. "I have kept our poor, sick little witch up *so* late." He heaved a mock sigh, laying a hand on my head. "She may suffer a relapse."

I pushed the offending hand away. He merely laughed, exiting as abruptly as he had entered.

I was still blushing. Aislinn stared at me hard. Her eyelids crinkled as she slowly began to smile.

Chapter Twenty-Nine

A Summons Not to Be Disdained

His visit had done little damage. It could be borne. Benjamin Lewis, the Christian clergyman, already knew my true identity… I didn't suppose worse results could come from a few others learning of it. For I was obliged to explain Erbanhue's flattering terms of me, "Witch" and "Anmut," and also his eagerness that I view his new show… although I had trouble explaining *that*.

Warren was all wide-eyed admiration and profusions of astonishment. Aislinn, of course, was her steady self, grinning slyly; she had been given my real name and had known it all along. I liked her better than any other woman, but at times her uncanny grin was rather off-putting.

"How did he find me?" I asked the flowers growing beneath my windows, rummaging around half-heartedly in the dirt. I was born decidedly without a green thumb on either hand. "Only Benjamin Lewis knew my real name. And Aislinn, who wouldn't have told a soul. Everyone else calls me Emma Bauer."

Ah, yes. I had forgotten... I told him myself. He had stumbled upon me in this very town, years ago, when we bid one another farewell (presumably forever). I had given him my last words and went on, never considering that perhaps he paid attention to where I worked, and what last name I answered to. It would have been simple enough for a sly-boots like him. Oh, Yasmin! What a simpleton you are! I wonder if you ever had a brain.

And yet, it had been almost four years. He had traveled about, been in and out of town, but he had always returned at some point. Other things had occupied his mind (his own image to build, his finances to nurse back to health, his name to boast). Yet once he had acquired a suitable allowance of fame, he suddenly remembered that his former protégé was in *this* town. He expected her to come applaud him, as a dutiful old pupil should.

Confound his audacity!

But then, I had ended up going... and admiring... and applauding. In spite of my persistent odium, I found myself caught in his traps, obeying his whims. Like my hallucinations, I had no control over what I saw, heard, or did, concerning Erbanhue and the Fair of Phantoms.

A month ran its course. I had fallen back into the routine of mundane village life, with my only entertainment the scraps of news that Warren brought me twice a week, and the visits and walks with Aislinn. But then, a summons!

Warren arrived with a piece of paper neatly folded in his hands – an envelope.

"For you, Yassy," he said, beaming as he passed the parcel to me.

"For me?"

I gazed at the paper in some confusion. The waft of new-paper-smell tickled my nose, giving me an odd scholarly feeling. I'd never gotten a letter before. Invitations, yes, from Mrs. Bentley or from Lidia. But not thick, enveloped, personal letters. Who would write to *me?*

I lifted the wax seal. I read. My emotions coiled like a snake to strike; I immediately recognized the brash, commanding tone.

"Dearest Silver-Haired Hag," (So this tender letter commenced,)

"I am in something of a spot. Seeing as how I basically kept you alive while you were a helpless nothing, I demand recompense for my labors. I know you've somehow memorized the Ghoul's Litany from one viewing of my show. (Did you really just go once, you witch? I harbor doubt.) It so happens that my vocalist, Janet, has found it prudent to go and conceive a sore throat from somewhere. I had thought once or twice of training a backup, but it never seemed important enough to be worth the trouble. You know I am no public singer myself. I have no taste for it. I implore – and of course by implore I mean *command* – that you fill in temporarily for this addlepated personage.

Now, don't get it into your head that you can *sing* – in fact you're rather dreadful, all wobbly and unsure of yourself – but you can *chant* it. The Witch Anmut chanting a Ghoul's Litany would certainly curl the hair of my obliging audience, come what may. If you could conjure up a windstorm while you're at it, it would be all the better. I have all the necessary faith in your powers."

-Erbanhue

"And who is surprised by this?" I questioned aloud. "Not I, Master Hue. You believe that since I was your slave once before, I would willingly undergo servitude again. As if I had no life of my own!"

Yet even as I spoke, the ghost of that night... the night I wailed against Logic, pleading with her for a release from plain, normal living... rose again before the souls of mine eyes. Imagination put before me a vast multitude, easily impressed and amused by Erbanhue's machinations. Erbanhue called me before them. I stepped into the shadowed, eerie pavilion, my long hair wild and loose, my eyes wide and lined with dark, enchanting symbols. My dress, long, tattered, and witch-like, waved in the wind. I rose my hands dramatically, reciting the Litany in agonized yet controlling tones. As the recital reached its climax, I bent and swayed my body, floating, almost dancing to the rise and fall of my spell.

I knew my own powers. I could not *entrance* as Janet could. But I could *captivate.* After all, I was trained by Erbanhue himself, the master of captivity. I glanced up from the letter. "I'll go now," I said, hardly noticing Warren's response.

Dressing mechanically, I selected the plainest black dress. I braided my hair into one long rope. It is always good to look the part, even if the role has basically been promised. My milky skin pinked with anticipation. The mirror caught me smiling.

Heading through the Fair's camp, a host of ghouls peeked, peered, and tracked my movements at every corner. August ducked behind a pair of handsome white steeds. Lillias danced between colorful may-poles, a candle in each of her snowy hands. Madame Tola beckoned to me from between striped orange-and-gold curtains. I was anxious; I spared no glances for them. I slowed my pace, listening for the sound of the Master's irascible voice.

Having caught and cornered the sound, I moved in.

"Ah! The Witch." Erbanhue stood from a thin traveler's desk. He swept up his cane and pointed it at me. "I suppose you have come to barter?"

Yasmin Lange folded her hands behind her back. She spoke quite low and respectfully. It ever amused me to tease Erbanhue to sparks and flares, but now was not the time.

"I do not desire a wage, sir. My usual allotment of chance largess will do." By this term, I meant the coins that were perchance tossed on stage after a successful act. It was our old custom, "catch as catch can," but none the worse for that. I liked it.

"Good, good! That is sensible. But are you content? You are happy with your seamstress salary?" He lowered the cane, smacking it imposingly on the ground.

"Yes, sir. It keeps a roof above my head, and daily bread within the reach of my hands. I ask for nothing more."

"I see."

A look suspiciously like a frown creased the ringmaster's brow. *What could he want now?* I wondered, perplexed. He seemed dissatisfied. Erbanhue hesitated (something he rarely does). "He hoped Yasmin wouldn't find a few nights' work too much of a disappointment?"

"She believed she was no longer a baby, nor a child. She would be content with what was in her power to do."

"It comes to that! Yasmin brought it up herself - her powers."

Erbanhue strode up to me, looking sternly into my eyes. "Does Yasmin Lange bear a grudge against her former employer, though he has dared to give her a good turn? To offer her a place upon his stage once more?"

Yasmin hesitated. Dared she witness it? A certain softness, alien to his usual tones and commandments, underlined his question. "I bear no grudge," the Witch replied. "I will do my best to please. But you must have patience, sir. Your Witch has been out of the public eye for years."

Erbanhue waved his hand. "This I know, little witchling. You will do well nevertheless." He lowered his hand, his voice dropping another octave. "You must forgive it all, Yasmin. I have come from a rough place, among rough people. Combining with that, we knew each other in rough times. Thrice harried, kicked down... beaten... I was a monster, I will allow. But you must make allowances for me."

I inspected his searching countenance. His apology, as far as it went, was certainly sincere. But this softness, this entirely new tone of voice, struck me with suspicion. He had never once used it for *anyone* within my hearing. Why was it suddenly thus appropriated to me?

For I did not deserve it. In my heart of hearts, I knew that I had been fully as bad as he. The only difference was our station, our means of strength, and our manner of acting. He may have cursed me aloud, but his bark was worse than his bite. I had remained silent when accused of being a witch; silence became my advantage.

Ah. I saw it all now.

The Witch. *That* was the motivation behind this apology. Despite bluster and brevity, he remained superstitious. He believed I could tear apart his hard work in seconds, with one dark muttered word, or the wave of my strange hands.

I bowed, masking a hidden smile. "Your instructions, sir?"

Chapter Thirty

THE ROSE

Erbanhue led me through the throng, parting the Red Sea with a shout and the menacing wave of his cane. Workers scurried aside, staring after me in wary astonishment. I smiled upon them as I passed.

It was *good* to be home. Yasmin's anxious feet trod well-worn paths.

Clowns grimaced from the shadows. Tight-rope walkers practiced with care, shifting their weight. Stunning show horses stamped their impatient hooves. Their nostrils flared with my unfamiliar scent. Some of them reared, straining at their ropes in consternation. Reader, I smiled at it all. For I could no longer resist the call of the performance any more than I could deny breath to my lungs. I reveled in the engrossing atmosphere. I relished the pounded dirt, the pipe smoke, the sun-warmed hay, and the wildness of the animals. I heard the crack of the whip, the calls of the tamers, and the roars of exotic cats. Truly, I was never so happy in my life.

"No time to dawdle, missy!" shouted Master Hue. I quickened my pace. Erbanhue huffed his impatience, lengthening his massive stride. "Where are we going?" I inquired.

"To your quarters."

"Oh, surely I will not live here. I have a home, as you know."

"You lack transportation. I won't have you roaming o'er creation all day long, and you needn't disturb my horsemen, either. I expect you to stay on the grounds."

I did not care for this arrangement. "Must I, sir?"

Still walking, Erbanhue glanced at me and chuckled. "Is the princess balking at rooming among the commoners? My stars! How we have risen of late!"

"You need not wax sarcastic," I answered, lifting my skirts to save them from the mud. "I am accustomed to privacy, that's all."

"No doubt... no doubt! A witch must be alone to mutter incantations and try her hand at the cauldron's brew. However! You must sacrifice for a season. A little patience, a little longsuffering on your part, and we shall get along splendidly... On one condition!"

He ceased walking. I stumbled to a halt, darting surprise into his face. "Well, sir, what is it?"

Drawing up to full height, he pointed the nose of his cane at me. "I am obliged to extract a promise from you."

I sighed. "And what promise wouldst thou extract, *mein guter Herr?*"

The knob of his cane winked in the sun. A gilt serpent with ruby eyes cast speckles of scarlet light. "You must swear not to harm any of my workers. *Capiche?*"

Mild astonishment lifted my brows. "You needn't demand this of me, Erbanhue. I have no wish to harm your troupe."

"Tell me no falsehoods," he continued, narrowing his eyes. "If you have come to me with ill intent, I command you to confess it now. I will be lenient for honesty. I have come far, and would suffer much to defend my work. Should evil befall my Fair of Phantoms, I will not answer for the consequences... to *you.*" The ruby-flecked serpent stared me down.

My erstwhile awe of Erbanhue had alleviated over time. And yet, as he stood imperiously at attention, firing his multicolored gaze down the length of the princely cane, he seemed radiant to my eyes. Foreign delight stirred in my blood, lending an alien eloquence to my tongue. "I tell you earnestly, Master Hue, that I admire your work with all my heart. I could not destroy it for love or money. This-" Here I gestured over the whole of the circus grounds, "This is more magnificent than anything I had ever dared to hope for."

A subtle smile raised the corners of his lips. I resumed "You were born to illumine the imaginings of man. You are of the descendants of Helios, insupportably bright, unerringly passionate. You were meant for success. I've always known it."

Whatever Sphinx that had robbed my verbiage lost its hold. Catching my breath, I looked down in shame. Oh! What would he think of me after such a warm speech? I'd never dared to say anything like that before. Now would commence laughter and banter, blame and ridicule. What had possessed me to speak so? My heart, pulsing painfully with emotion, thickened with hot, embarrassed blood.

The Dragon watched me, his judgment stowed in neat reserve. Throughout my humble homily, he kept his cane pointed at my face. He did not sneer or chortle. He did not stir an inch. I slowly raised my eyes, querying his motionless stance.

"Your summation rings true," the Dragon said. (Reader, I swear I could see the flash of his ruby scales, and the smoke whispering from his ophidian jaws at every word.) "The Fair of Phantoms shall be the jewel of the county. And you, my dear little witch, shall be the jewel's fair setting."

He lowered the cane, planting it in the earth to lean his weight against it. He awaited my reaction with faintly amused eyes.

"To business, then," I coldly replied. "Where am I to live *temporarily?*"

Erbanhue swiveled on his cane, pointing to the right. "There be your quarters, gray witchling!"

The direction of his finger indicated a gypsy wagon.

It was handsomely carved, gleaming with polish and decked with fluffy paper lanterns. From hence I glimpsed the flutterings of soft curtains made of fairy-bred material. Their colors shone ebullient: mystical blue, glowing purple, forest green, and spiderweb silver.

I was dumbfounded, entirely struck with bewildered amaze. Even the Witch was quiet, silenced by her wonder. I pointed also, my hand shaking. "Is that... is *that* mine?"

"It is yours."

"Mine entirely?"

"That wagon is yours entirely."

I lowered my hand. "Whose wagon was this?"

Erbanhue shrugged. "It was Janet's, but she has taken extended leave. Whether she returns or not is of no concern. Her role is pliable."

I took a hesitant step toward the sacred wagon. I felt as if I were intruding. "You are certain I am to live there?"

He rolled his eyes. "Come now. Do cease your nonsense, woman! I have work to attend to. Go and settle yourself, and fiddle and rearrange to your heart's content, as all the women do. Unless witches do not care to homemake." He snorted, his draconian nostrils flaring. "The clothing and jewelry are yours to do with as you please. After all, *she* didn't purchase them." His hand tucked into his red vest pocket to withdraw a bronze key. He transferred its cool weight into my fingers.

With a final, befuddled exclamation, I approached the fairy queen's den. The lanterns greeted me with springtime cheer while the curtains whispered salutation. Delighted, I seized the handlebar and mounted the wagon's trim steps.

I turned the key in the slot and opened the door.

This was another realm. I removed my shoes to leave them on the stairs. I should die if I caused *one speck* of mud to besmudge this place!

I tiptoed inside on stocking feet. The first thing I noticed was the heavenly *smell.* Fresh wood and pristine lacquer, rich candles and sweet perfumes, leather and violets and tea and vanilla. I closed my eyes to absorb it.

Once I'd had my fill - sniffing eagerly like any dog - I opened my eyes to indulge them next. Two long windows, one on each side, warmed the gypsy nest with sunlight. Inbuilt shelves and cabinets dressed the windows, teasing the eye with hints of women's finery and costly array, interspersed with costume jewelry. Tucked into the far end was an amethyst-tinted couch, layered with silky pillows and featherdown quilts.

Featherdown quilts, Reader. Quite untouched in my line of life. After rinsing my hands at the porcelain carafe, I dared to lift them, caress them, and finally wrap them 'round my shoulders like a cape.

I returned to the charming vanity with the bright carafe and washbowl. My fingers tenderly brushed the bowl, the framed mirror, the rose teapot, and the silver hairbrush and comb, all tiny and perfect, proclaiming without effort their divine expense. I touched the ribbons, the perfume bottles, and the yellow beaded reticule. I touched the delicate, curved stems of the miniature teacups. I touched a wondrous ornament of glass, and seemingly *real gold*... A little elephant with a gilt blanket on its back, and small ruby tassels securing the corners. I touched the gleaming bronze knobs on the cupboards. I touched the half-melted candles. And last, I opened the slender chestnut wardrobe and touched the silk, the wool, the cotton, and the linen.

I touched them all because I could not believe the evidence of my senses. Mind refused the printed image upon the Eyes. Once I had firmly reported to the Mind that these, indeed, were real and solid objects, I fell into speculation.

Erbanhue did not set *this* aside for lowly Yasmin; he did not plan for her. Surely he did not know what splendors were reposing in state, beneath his very nose! One of his main performers – a lady whom he had spoken of with carelessness – was quite well off.

Oh, what he would do if he saw this richness! His malt eye would glimmer with desire, and his blue eye would glitter with ambition. Winning over this delicate dame would become his highest priority. Performances may descend to Hades.

I laughed at the thought. While laughing, my eyes strayed. They lit upon a single pink rose, withering away in blasting sunlight.

I crossed over to examine it. Folded against its crumbling leaves was a cream-colored note bound in red ribbon. I read it. I suppose it *was* rude of me.

"TO MY CHARMING JANET WILLOW. MAY YOUR LOVELY VOICE RENDER MILLIONS SPELLBOUND."

-ERBANHUE

Eureka!

My conclusion was not long in proving itself. I understood him well. I lifted the drying rose with care, perusing it fore and aft. It was neglected, locked in a coffin of finery to die in royal solace. One thing was certain,

Reader: Janet Willow did not suffer from illness of the body, but of the heart. I replaced the rose.

Perhaps, just now, the same thought crossed your mind that then assaulted mine. What did the dastardly fellow mean by feeding Yasmin Lange to the bowels of his ex-mistress' domain? What hints did this act imply? And how offended Yasmin must have been! What oaths she must have uttered against his impious soul!

I could not be offended. I was amused. The Witch was *very* amused. She reached once more for the rose, squeezing it tight between her fingers and laughing as the dry thorns punctured her skin. Indigo blood dripped forth. Tendrils of smoke rose from beneath the floorboards.

Yasmin lifted the mirror and looked at her reflection. The Witch, hollow-eyed and calm, gazed back.

"Two hearts, colder than the Arctic ices. Two minds, sterner than the mountains of Europe. Two souls, burning with fire and brimstone, doomed before the Second Death. Most merrily dost thou live, my children!"

I frolicked among the feathers and the sumptuous gowns. I was soberly arranging the folds of a funereal black silk (and holding a matching ball mask to my face) when a firm knock flailed against the door. Still in my stockings, I glided silently across to answer it.

Erbanhue jerked back in surprise. He recovered instantly. "Have you done with playtime, little imp?" the Dragon growled. "You're late for rehearsal. I expect you to toe the line in this circus!"

Being in hearty spirits, I laughed. "Do forgive me, your majesty. Your servant was considering which modest apparel best became her." I curtsied low, exaggerating the wide sweep of the ebony skirt. Erbanhue smirked. "It is well chosen. You have kept to your witchly tastes." He gestured. "Come with me!"

Dark had fallen. I pulled on my boots amid night-mist. As we walked together, once more side-by-side, my heart brimmed with tranquility and contentment. For one ludicrous moment, I reached out to take the Master's arm. The Witch, ever wise (if cruel), withdrew my hand at once.

What *had* possessed me that day? I know not. It seemed to me that my heart had been frozen in his absence. And now, the humid whisper of his mighty breath was slowly thawing it.

I remember hastening my step to keep up with him. I recall looking up into his face, observing his sharp eyes as they kept vigilant watch. One gloved hand flourished the serpent cane. The other tapped the brim of his hat in brief salute, in response to the call of his workers. His linen sleeves were rolled up. His bronze, muscular arms shone beneath them, lined with navy tattoos. He was more handsome each time my eager eyes beheld him.

He sensed me regarding him. "Do not think to menace me with your stares, witch. I am protected." And he raised his cane. The serpent's ruby scrutiny reflected moonlight.

I smiled. "Even if I *am* the almighty hex you thus denominate, do you think I am put off by such a trinket as that?"

Erbanhue nodded grimly. "I had it blessed by another she-devil very much like yourself. Its eyes harbor the Witches' Scourge."

My nose wrinkled as I abstained from laughter. "How can a witch cast a witch bane? 'A house divided cannot stand.'"

Erbanhue grunted, his stride quickening.

"In any event, it is very pretty," I continued, relishing my victory (small though it was). "Was this cane a gift from a generous lady?"

The ringmaster glared. I felt him accuse me of witchcraft and crystal-spying. Before he answered, enlightenment leveled his frown. "Oh, yes. I had forgotten the rose."

"Aye, thou handsome devil. The rose."

His eyelids crinkled as he smiled.

Chapter Thirty-One

Another She-Devil

Those were pleasant days.

In the growing town of ------, Erbanhue's Fair of Phantoms gained unprecedented popularity. He agreed to remain for two more months as I refused to travel with the troupe once it departed; I liked my home and my employer too much to give them up. For once, the ringmaster complied.

As I write, I wonder *why.* My service in his troupe was good enough, to be sure, but far from exceptional. I verily believe we *enjoyed* each other's company. Our campfire chats, our mutual love of storytelling, our practical discussions about the Fair, or books, or music... and our shared make of mien and mind, down to our deployment of speech. It cannot be denied, though I yet remain in awe of it.

I had caught lightening and wound it into a necklace.

It sparked against my skin, sometimes tickling and burning. But I had done it.

My part in the show proceeded very much as described. I chanted the Ghoul's Litany, as my singing voice was a successor of the Banshee. "It is too piercing, too plaintive! Like slicing an icicle in two," declared the Dragon.

The Banshee ceased and desisted, guarding her voice box under lock and key. The audience, undeterred by this change in the program, listened with enraptured attention to a chanting Witch.

I took to closing my eyes as the Litany reached its finale. I could see the Demongod's writhing tentacles extending into the audience, from *me*. He attended without fail... my most ardent supporter.

Anmut.

I was out late at night, amusing myself by walking on the ropes which enclosed our pavilion. I had been a vaultress; tight-rope walking came with ease. My arms extended, my eyes shut, I heard Him and considered His voice.

My bare feet slowed in their meandering.

"Sind Sie das?"[1] I called.

Mein Kind.

The voice hummed with a low, deep throbbing, like the purring of a leopard.

Pausing, I resumed my dance across the rope. *"Eins, zwei, drei... Eins, zwei, drei... und dreh dich um."* I pirouetted. My aching toes gripped the

---

1. "Is that you?"

ropes, chafing slightly under the strain. I grinned in satisfaction as my balance held.

Mein geschätzter Zauberin. Meine kleine Schauspielerin.

(My esteemed Sorceress. My little Actress.)

A slow, velvet smile grew on my lips. For once, I would rejoice in this alien affection. I would bask in it.

A winter-born breeze enclosed my body in its frigid embrace. Yes, that was Him. I summoned enough courage to ask Him a question. *"Was hat dir so gefallen?"*

("What has pleased you so?")

No reply – only the same low, echoing hum.

Then, looming from the silence, the words *Ich habe dir ein Geschenk gebracht.*

(I have brought you a gift.)

Familiar footsteps approached. I leapt off the rope and looked hard into the misty darkness. "Aislinn!"

"Hail, the beauteous Banshee!" Aislinn's golden laughter warmed me, followed quickly by her arms. Her lovely face was stained pale by the lingering starlight. "By the gods, you're cold! But you performed so steadily, as always. I am proud of thee, *mo chara!"*

"If only my other friends were as agreeable as you," I sighed.

Lidia Henderson had abandoned me at last, frightened away by the edicts of her high-born companions against a little circus witch. Aislinn slipped her arm around my waist. "Don't be troubled, *mo chara.* She was important to you for a time, to instruct you in the ways of formal society and behavior. You are not in need of such lessons now."

"'Tis true." I put my arm around her in return. We sauntered along the pavilion. "And how does my Aislinn find herself these days? Where does she wander?"

Aislinn chuckled. "She wanders away from the clearings of the woods, and ventures into their dimmest depths..." She quieted, stopping to face me. Her hands gripped my shoulders. "She strains to follow a great Voice, which whispers by day, and shouts by night like thunder."

Even in the darkness, I could see the flash of her exquisite eyes. "What voice do you speak of?" I asked.

Reader, I knew the answer ere her voice replied.

"I hear the words of a demon who appears in the woods. He directs me, preserves me, and teaches me many things... things beyond the scope of the natural mind."

I nodded. My collected countenance spoke volumes. Her blue eyes blinked serenely. "So, you serve Him as well. I knew it."

We smiled in tandem. She took my hands into hers and turned them palm-upward, studying my fingertips under the moonlight. Like hers, they gradually faded into a dark shade of putrid indigo. "You have practiced the craft longer than I?" I questioned.

She shook her head, releasing my hands. "You exhibited the symptoms far before I contracted them. And your fingers are more darkly stained by the Mark." She gazed into my eyes, her hands affectionately cupping my face. "Your powers must be great, indeed, little Yassy."

Her tone evinced worry. "No fear, Aislinn. I remain in excellent health."

A mischievous glint blossomed in her eyes. "Oh, really? In spite of the presence of the Witches' Scourge?"

"The *what?*"

Memory flooded my mind. I inhaled sharply, shaking Aislinn by the shoulders. "You blessed Erbanhue's cane? That was *you,* you perverse creature?"

Her frame quaked with mirth. "He heard of my medicinal and spiritual adroitness. He came to me with that ridiculous serpent, claiming there was a witch after his soul – he *must* protect himself – and would I oblige him?"

We clung to each other, devoured in shared laughter, its cadence mingling as threads of gold and silver. "I did not know for certain if he meant *you,* Yasmin," she continued, wiping tears of levity from her sapphire eyes. "But I suspected it was you. Either you, or some disdained and rejected lover."

I took a step back, shaking my head with wonder. "Janet Willow abandoned *him.* He knew he wanted to send for me in her place, so he paid precious coin in order to protect himself from my wrath." Contemplating, I leaned my head to one side. "It proves he has a conscious, I suppose... though he buries it several layers below the surface. Still-"

"Nay, he was determined to use you for your talent." Aislinn scowled and held me close in a protective manner. "What an odd creature he is! I wonder how you endure him."

"I am not so hopeless as I once was," I smiled. "Neither is this a permanent position. Two very good reasons to reap the benefits and sift the harms."

"And he *does* make for amusing sport," acknowledged the wicked Celt. "The very idea... No, do not laugh! Harken to me, Yasmin! This is quite serious. Picture to yourself the *wisdom!* A great and terrible man, lofty and powerful - *why* are you laughing, you silly woman? - A great man, I say, depending on the might of *the knob on his cane-*"

My stomach throbbed with merrymaking. I covered her mouth in an attempt to muffle the jollity leaping from her lips. It was apt timing, for a new set of familiar footsteps advanced.

"I perceive that my dear witchling has a friend," quoth the Dragon. "Greetings, sorceress the second." (Cue the sarcastic bow.) "However, may I present a question? Why is it that Yasmin is *choking* her friend, hmm?"

Aislinn and I shared a glance. Our laughter burst anew.

Erbanhue shrugged and moved on. If he recognized Aislinn, he gave no indication of it.

Chapter Thirty-Two

TO CURSE, AND TO HEAL

We waited with seraphic countenance until Erbanhue was out of sight. I took her hand. "Come, Aislinn. I cooked an acceptable stew yesterday, and some is left. Have dinner with me."

She nodded, her gilt locks gleaming in the mist. "I am *famished*. That reminds me, Yassy. Do you find that while you are hungrier than ever, the smallest of meals satisfies you completely?"

"Yes."

"Good. Further symptoms coincide. Then, whatever we are... whomever we serve... it is indeed the same master."

"The very same." I smiled, gently squeezing her fingers. "I have spent a lonesome life thus far. It means a great deal to me that we are friends."

"And our friendship shall always remain."

Aislinn and I traversed to my cottage, chatting in low tones or silently treading the paths of friendly introspection. Upon arrival, I noticed the glow of my table lantern, previously left unlit. I rose an eyebrow and darted Aislinn a cautious glance.

"Were you expecting visitors?" Aislinn whispered. We crouched below my window to observe the intruder.

"No, but it is not uncommon for Warren Hyram to pay me unexpected visits. He'll let himself in."

"How very like a man," Aislinn began. Warren's voice cut her off with a cheery call: "Ladies! *Do* come in. I loathe it when persons of the female variety whisper beneath open windows."

I arose with a grin. Aislinn grimaced. "I was intending to show you something of the utmost importance, *mo chara*. I suppose now we must wait."

"That mayn't be necessary. Perhaps he won't stay long."

"We shall see."

We entered, jointly rebuking Warren for his evening interference. He relished it enormously. "What cruelty I am subjected to! What would you have me do, then? Sit all alone by myself on such a lovely night as this?"

"Surely some lady companion would have leapt with joy at your summons," I replied, somewhat dryly.

"Ah, but of all those said companions, I prefer the company of Aislinn and Yasmin above them all. They are not just charmingly rude creatures, quite provocative of laughter and banter, but they are also mysterious. As mysterious as... as..."

He stopped, scratching his head. "My word, I cannot think of an apt comparison. You are rare creatures!"

Aislinn rolled her eyes.

I sat at the fireside and listened to Warren's country gossip with mounting impatience. His talk might amuse me on most nights, but tonight I knew I had something important to learn. Finally, I rose from my chair, signifying fatigue by a variety of subtle yawns and sighs.

Warren laughed at my demonstration. "The Lady Yasmin is the most formidable of foes when sleepy. I must bid thee goodnight, my fair ladies."

"Goodnight. Come and see us tomorrow," I added at the doorway. I felt a miniscule prick of conscious over dismissing him thus. He was, after all, the most cheerful male company I knew, and his company had made all the difference in the past year.

"Very well!" He trudged into the dark, waving his hat to us cheerily. I smiled at his boyish face. "Simple-souled he may be, at times. Yet his openness does my heart good."

"That it does, my dear." Aislinn crossed her arms, her elegant sleeves delicately rustling. "I have watched you and listened with care. Have you not noticed your growing peacefulness, your blooming complexion? Thou art vastly prettier than thou wert when I met thee."

I glanced in the mirror over the mantlepiece. "You mean to say that I look a proper human now, instead of a despicable entity comprised of sour milk, poured into a human-shaped mold?"

"And trimmed with unsufferable pride and stiffness." Aislinn giggled. She reached out and smoothed my hair. "Yes, your friendship with Warren has done you good. But I suspect there is more behind this gradual change in you."

"Yes, and I meant to tell you... But I had to be sure that you would understand."

"I can prove that to you now."

Aislinn's sky-blue skirt whirled about as she turned. She stepped into the kitchen and began to arrange a few pots, a mortar and pestle, herbs, and water left from the tea kettle. She hummed to herself, tapping her trim little foot to some inaudible tune. I thought what a charming wife she would be someday, her movements so adroit, her intentions ever melded into the most graceful of actions. Aislinn Bláthnaid, in *my* mind, ever outshone the more popular Lidia Henderson.

As she ground a select choice of herbs, she sang,

"AND SHE,
QUEEN OF THE FAE,
BESTOWED SWEET TWILIGHT
O'ER LIGHT OF DAY;
FOR SHE,
FLOWER OF THE FAE,
SAVED THEE, SWEET CHILD,
FROM HUMAN WAYS."

Aislinn drew out the lyrics with a certain lilting, playful sweetness, rather violin-like. Her words rippled around and over themselves, rushing like water. I blinked myself out of drowsiness.

She glanced at me over her shoulder. "Tired, Yassy?"

"A little. What are you making?"

Aislinn's glowing lips parted in a peculiar smile. "I'm afraid that is a secret. However, you shall see the results. Come here."

I arose and darted eagerly to her side. I inspected the bowl's contents. Within the mortar reposed a bubbling, tan-colored paste, looking rather like a mistake. "Dessert for the evening?"

Aislinn laughed, nudging me with her elbow. "You would find the flavor particularly unpleasant, my dear. Watch carefully."

Drawing up her sleeve, she took up a knife and, to my shock, made a swift cut along her forearm. It was a shallow cut, but I was frightened nonetheless. "Aislinn!" I stole the knife away, regarding her with horror.

"Don't be alarmed! Watch." Humming softly, she scooped up a fair amount of the paste onto two fingers and applied it liberally to the fresh cut. She winced slightly as the paste bubbled with new vigor, as if reacting with her blood. "And... three... two... one."

She fetched a towel and wiped away the paste. The cut was completely healed. Not a single trace of it was left. She held out her forearm for closer scrutiny. "Behold!"

I gently touched the perfect strip of flesh. "Wonderous. What talent do you call this?"

"*That* is your first question? You *are* strange! Have you named your inexplicable and wholly unnerving talent, my dear girl?"

I smiled impishly. "Do *you* know what it is?"

"I don't know what anyone would call it beyond the overly-dramatic title of 'black magic.'"

"Ah, black magic. I had not thought of that."

"Hadn't you? What else would you call the ability to curse your enemies?"

"Curse my enemies?"

My mind stuttered to a precipitous halt. I fled back into my past memories, visiting victim after victim of the troupe's misfortunes. I had truly thought it all a tragedy, a mistake... Fate.

Charlotte. Demarion. Madame Tola. Lillias. August. The street violinist, Matteo. Erbanhue's virulent illness, which he had barely recovered from.

My father. My mother.

"But, Aislinn..." My voice itself paled. "I did not wish them *all* ill."

"I know you did not, Yassy." Her voice gentled, and she touched my arm. "You were too young to be gifted with such power. You knew not how to control it."

"But... *Lillias*... an innocent child!"

My lips quivered. I fell to my knees, wrapping my trembling arms around them. Aislinn sighed. She bent over me and stroked my tears away. "Oh, my Yassy. If we could but know this great and dreadful Master who wields the power of miracles, I daresay we might understand His purpose, even for this."

For the first time, we differed. I believed I would never understand.

And I knew I could never forgive.

Chapter Thirty-Three

Erbanhue's Warning

Carnivals were often the only source of entertainment that any given family could look forward to, and the overall popularity of circuses continued to grow in leaps and bounds. Aislinn and I spent as many quiet moments alone as we could, tucked into silent forest corners. I observed with profound interest as she explored her talent with new herbs and flowers. She termed it divine herbology.

"I *can't* explain it," she'd say, despite my manifold requests for clarification. "I look at them and know precisely what to do with them."

I spent most of my free time with Aislinn. However, I was obliged to set aside time for my own private practice. Now that my friend had revealed the truth to me... painful as it was... I fully intended to gain control over this *black magic* that I supposedly possessed.

Yet the key to the lock ever eluded me. How can one conjure without spells? I had no books, no symbols, no mentors to guide me, and no priest to explain the origin of my sin. I could not even be certain that mere hatred was the facilitator, for people I loved had been led to death.

There was but one connection that linked every fatality.

I had spoken to each of them. They stood in my presence, heard my voice, and replied. I had conversed with them all.

Was the curse of death *my presence itself?*

"You were quiet this evening, Yasmin."

I shifted in my chair, smoothing the black folds of my costume skirt. "My apologies, sir."

I kept my eyes chained to the carpet. The orange-and-red stripes of the tent stirred in the wind.

Erbanhue leaned forward. The curling smoke from his evening pipe formed a wreath around my face. I coughed, waving it away. "Do you remember what I told you years ago?" he asked, his blue and brown eye each glittering, serpent-like. I flushed at his proximity.

"You told me many things. To which declaration, threat, or manipulative speech are you referring?"

Immune to my stings, he laughed. His bronze hand brushed a wayward strand of hair from my eyes. "I refer to the time when I told you I would never spoil you. I said that treating you with coolness - even harshness - would help you thrive. To pamper a woman like you would be the equivalent of drowning a plant with water, or cooking it dry in the sun, or overwhelming its roots with an excess of minerals. It is fatal extremism. Do you not agree?"

"I suppose there is *some* truth to that statement."

"Aye. But more than you think, little witchling." He leaned back again, puffing complaisantly.

His mood was cordial enough. He'd invited me into his own tent to "pick my brain," as he said. Perhaps his friendliness was due to smoking his favorite pipe. Or perhaps his new, dashing pair of shoes gave him joy. Or perhaps his workers didn't disappoint him too much that day. At any rate, it was one of the three or a combination of them; it was often a little thing that caused an eruption, and then a little thing that rendered the boiling lava inert.

I considered my rejoinder. One does not leap into the spoken word with a Dragon. One must pause, and interpret, and ponder the safest elocution.

I studied his pipe. It was new and quite handsome, constructed out of some manner of scented wood, carved with a fancy swirling "E" and a blossoming vine running up the stem. "What are you staring at now?" Hue demanded. "Those steely eyes are always deconstructing *something*. Are they never still?"

"Does it anger you?" I smiled. "Are you now contemplating a well-timed strike to the witch's lowly forehead?"

I bowed, bending my head toward him with exaggerated humility. Erbanhue's hearty laughter billowed through the tent. "Come now, Anmut. I'm not so rough as I used to be."

"A valid point, sir."

In fact, it *was* true. The Fair of Phantoms had filled his pockets and emptied his malevolent quirks. "But to return to your opening statement," I continued, coolly raising my eyes to meet his. "You think I did not call up the ghouls loudly enough tonight? Perhaps I should have rolled my eyes madly about, or screamed, or fainted dead away. That might have raised another cheer or two."

"Humph! *That* would have been the scene of the decade. And yet I verily... believe... you... are," tapping the stem of his pipe on my arm with each word, "At heart you are the queen of dramatic performance. You screen it as well as possible to avoid ridicule."

"Ridicule, sir? Is drama not expected from every woman whose lungs yet draw breath?"

"To you, Yasmin, the gossip of the masses is the same as outright ridicule."

"And yet I perform 'before the masses.'"

"For money! You need the money."

"I am a capable seamstress with a cottage of my own, even if it *is* humble. I do not suffer for the necessities of life."

"A seamstress, forsooth!" He huffed, absently tracing an invisible picture on my arm. "It does not satisfy your love of the dramatic. My carnival does that."

The trace of the pipe prickled my flesh. I strove to ignore it... to ignore that his warm lips had just enclosed it. "Ah, *now* we've come to it, sir! You think everything revolves back to you. The whole world ought to be clamoring to kiss your shiny shoes for the remarkable good you've done for it."

He chuckled again, drawing back and stretching out one well-shoed foot. "Yes, they're shiny enough for my demanding self. I can see my face in them. I never had so good a pair..."

His voice trailed away, and a shadow darkened his eyes. I saw him revisit his own stricken past. Like myself, he was seeing better days and could hardly credit them to the accounts of reality. Erbanhue noticed the soft, unobtrusive sympathy in my countenance. He waved it aside with a good-natured nod. "I shall not forget the subject I meant to pursue. You've been visiting that other lady witch, have you not?"

Thinking of his serpent-headed cane, I hid a covert smile. "You mean Aislinn. Yes. Should I not?"

He grunted. "What use has one witch's company for another? Do you meet to chant dark spells in the dead of night? Or perhaps to split a twin pair of giant black cauldrons between you?" He snapped his fingers. "No, I have it! You are sneaking off to place an order for two black cats. Witches must have their familiars."

I affected shock and dismay. "What is this, Master Erbanhue? Have you sent spies to report upon our proceedings? For shame!"

His playful smile broadened. When he smiled that way, irids shining alight with good nature, he was unbearably handsome. "There you go again! You've always been adept at distracting me from what I'm trying to say. *Do* pay attention, Yassy."

Yassy.

He realized his error. Erbanhue turned a delicate shade of red, starting at the ears and working into the face. "It... it isn't anything. I heard Lillias call you that countless times."

Lillias? By his own admission, Erbanhue was a consummate hater of children. Had he really paid attention to her plaintive little voice?

How interesting.

"Yasmin, I don't want you to spend so much time with Aislinn."

My reflection rudely interrupted, I merely stared. He lifted his cane (previously resting on the side of his chair) and pointed it at me – the cue for an especially heartless comment or command. "I've seen how she caters to your whims, and escorts you about, and fusses over you. I don't know what spell of worship you've cast over her, but I thoroughly disapprove of it. She's spoiling you. Your signature force is abating."

Antagonism stirred in my heart. It was immediately followed by anxiety and alarm: What if I should lose whatever tenuous control I had over the curse? I compelled myself to smile, folding my hands in my lap in a peaceful, womanly gesture. "In other words, you think our friendship is a distraction from my work."

"*My* work, Yasmin. Believe it or not - and I can hardly accept it myself - you cut a stunning figure in the Ghoul's Litany. You're not pretty, but you can be fascinating. If you're properly inspired."

A childish impulse caused me to retort, "Aislinn says I'm pretty."

"Well..." (grudgingly), "You do *look* better. Your hair isn't so flat, and your skin's got more life in it. Used to look as thin as parchment."

For Erbanhue, this was a compliment.

"But don't let that get to your head. You're still an eyesore."

I grinned.

"Your smile is positively morose... strict as the Mona Lisa. Not at all what a woman's smile ought to be: warm, confiding, and natural. And your hair is gray."

"Ash blonde."

"Gray." Erbanhue stood, knocking ashes out of his pipe. "Anyway, I know I can't possibly keep you two apart for good. Besides the fact that I believe it to be an impossible task, I would likely be cursed out of spite. I have no wish to die at the peak of my career."

"I don't imagine you would," smooth as cream.

"Instead, I *request* that you limit the time you spend with her. Use more of that time to practice your routine. You're getting lazy. I won't have my performers working like automatons."

"Very well."

"Goodnight then, mine Anmut."

He brushed my hair back once more, then stomped out for his evening walk, smacking the tent-flaps aside with his cane. I waited a few minutes, staring at his cluttered cot, then left also. As I strolled down the path to my wagon, I wondered if he'd ever be done ordering me about.

But if I disliked it, why did I stay?

Chapter Thirty-Four

The Awakening

It was about two in the morning. I tossed and turned on my couch, incapable of sleep. Erbanhue's conversation kept toying with my mind, as a cat paws a ball of yarn. At length I chose to take a walk.

The moon kept the paths bright enough to navigate. I sauntered at my ease. The sleeping animals stirred as I passed them. Darius, stalking in his cage, appeared to be battling insomnia as well.

The tiger growled. His yellow eyes were trained on something behind me.

I turned. All was still and empty.

The quiet whimper of a child met my ears.

I looked toward the woods from whence it came. Again, I could see nothing, despite the brightness of the moon. I approached the woodland's entry.

You must forgive me, Reader, for all the following vagueness. To this day, I am not sure if this truly happened or if I was suddenly compelled into a dream.

The woods melted, morphed, and re-formed. They collapsed around my ears, dragged down my neck and body, and pooled around my feet. They shot up again in a mass of thin, weaving, black trees speckled with thorns.

I was frightfully dizzy. I fought to maintain my balance, gasping.

In the midst of the rise of fear, awe, and dread, I *knew*. It was the trees, which were smaller replicas of the Black Tree I knew all too well.

MY BARE FEET STOOD UPON HALLOWED GROUND.

The corrupt forest floor was shielded by an irregular pane of black ice. Shreds of frozen leaves mingled with dead grass, crackling with frost beneath my feet. I winced, for the pain was that of miniscule thorns menacing my flesh. They drew blood, indigo blood that colored the ice below.

A harsh aroma of Scots pine cloaked the atmosphere. Elms, beeches, and ancient oaks bent noiselessly within ashen, grim gusts. Snowflakes of a pale blue shade were tossed slowly, slowly, to the ground. As they died, they became sheets of ebony ice, coating everything they touched.

Although my vision bore witness to a mild wind, the winds were silent with the silence of death. My ears could not distinguish even the slightest sound. My eyes, however, absorbed much.

I glimpsed the shapes of little children running to and fro beneath the endless trees. Their bare feet emitted flashes like flecks of lightening. I turned to stare after this anomaly in wonder. Yet no matter where I turned, I gazed at them amiss. The shadows bordered the very edge of my view.

The incessant silence of the corrupt wood gave me pause. I could scarcely breathe in such quiet. To draw every breath caused pricks of pain in my throat, hands, and feet. I gradually ceased to breathe at all.

Incredibly, the terrible silence leveled within my brain. The weight in my lungs was expelled. A cloud of black frost blossomed from between my lips. It vanished behind me as I walked onward, no longer breathing, but infinitely more comfortable.

My bare feet became numb; they no longer hurt me, either. I progressed through the wood. Now and then, I came upon another black frost-flower, precisely like the one my last breath had created. They swayed around me, as if imbued with mischievous life. I wondered if each frost-flower represented a prior visitor.

I was drawn in deeper. In the center of a shadowed clearing rose a throne of forest barbs. It was twisted and torn in countless places. This was a sickened, mad Tree, replete with sinful knowledge, basking in a multitude of sparkling thorns... iron thorns so dark and shining, the dim sun's effect on them could almost be heard in high, piercing shrieks.

My ears felt crushed by the impact of noise, and my eyes were confused by such awful malevolence. They rolled madly within my head. I quickly turned away.

To the left of the Tree sat a creature cast entirely from moonstones. Each stone was painted to look like a human eye. It seemed to be sitting in judgment. Finding the spectacle nauseating, I turned again, uncertain of where to look.

To the right of the Tree of Corruption stood its keeper.

Yes, the Demongod was there. He was starkly pale, appearing and disappearing in rapid succession, yet seeming quite at His ease. His form was severe, every corner of it solid and precise, shining like icicles. I regarded Him quite calmly.

He spoke, raising one thorn-like hand. He reached for me. Supposing He meant to feed, I closed my eyes to the dreadful sight that was certain to come...

Expecting a wail of rage, I instead received a whisper of comfort. His Form stretched above and beyond me. I felt embraced by the tension of restrained power. Throughout the embrace, His image began to change.

In the place of darkness shone the light of winter stars.

His milk-white skin melded into diamonds. He was glittering, sheer, and spotless, shimmering like the purest glass as pale blue snowflakes anointed him. He grew *eyes;* dazzling ice-blue irises encircled each white pupil. Thin features flowed over his empty face. There was a translucent quality to the lips and the high, angular cheekbones, and a calm serenity in the elevated, glacial forehead. His marble-smooth scalp was concealed by a head covering of Sabbatical design.

Two wings drooped from His sharp shoulder blades. The wings were splendidly dressed, encrusted with precious gems: blackrock diamonds, ebony tourmaline, zircon, and moonstone. The twin blades of treasure dragged along the ground in dense grandeur. While it was certain he could not fly with them, they were incredible nevertheless.

The Dread Angel wore neither jacket, nor shirt, nor shoes. A long, gray skirt was his garb, secured at the waist with gray rope. At the hem of the skirt, directly above His feet, were the dark stiches of outlandish words. I know not how I comprehended them, but the translation haunts me to this moment...

"LET THE LITTLE CHILDREN COME TO ME, AND DO NOT HINDER THEM."

A chorus of voices broke the realm of silence. The children chanted softly, and only twice, "Rothadamas! Rothadamas!" in dreadful voices of whimsy and trust.

I fainted… not from fear, but from an overpowering sense of relief. I was not here to be claimed, but to worship, as the children were worshipping. I was safe.

"You damned witch! You cursed halfling! What is it you are doing?"

I was startled by the agony of empty lungs. I panted and received but little air, for Erbanhue's cane was held tightly against my throat. My hands instinctively rose to grasp it, making a feeble attempt to thrust it aside.

Erbanhue's voice continued to shout curses in my ear. He stood behind me, my back pinioned against his chest as he held me prisoner.

I coughed, blinking in confusion as my eyes streamed water. Where was I? And why in Heaven's good name was I being murdered by asphyxiation? And by Erbanhue, of all people?

Well, Reader, I grant he was never wholly my friend; I didn't trust him enough. But neither did I deem him the homicidal type.

He increased the pressure, bruising my throat. I winced through a flood of tears. Through the dim, watery rush, I saw a small boy running away from us as quickly as his diminutive feet could carry him. He glanced behind once or twice, his wide and fearful eyes reflecting the moonlight. They were full of horror.

"What were you doing with him?" Hue shouted.

"Him?" I warbled, barely managing the single word. I desperately clawed my hands over his, trying in vain to pry his massive fingers loose.

"Him!" Erbanhue turned the cane, forcing me to look directly at the little boy. I could hear him crying as he ran. "Where were you taking him?

And for God's sake, Yasmin, where did he come from? When did you start stealing away children? And why? *Tell – me – now!*"

He cemented each word with a stern shake. I could not speak. A multitude of colors flashed in my eyes... I was going to faint in earnest now. Erbanhue leaned in, speaking low. "I tell thee now, you are the devil's child, and I never wish to see you in my presence again. You will leave the grounds at once."

My hands continued to pry weakly at his fingers. I was consumed with dread, sorrow, and helpless astonishment. Dark specks peppered my vision and closed in. I cast one suppliant glance into his eyes.

Something crossed his countenance... dare I say it... *pity*, and other emotives. Consternation. Remorse. Confusion.

It seemed that one glance had been enough to convey my plea. Erbanhue released me. I fell to the ground, gulping up air with shameless greed. I rubbed my throat, feeling it pulse with a rush of blood.

Erbanhue watched me silently. All at once he fell to his knees, passing his hand over his eyes in exasperation. "I know not what haunts you," he began, eyes somehow stern and kind at once. "But you must give up this mad chase. Whatever the prize may be – power, control, or money – it is not worth this awful work."

He meant kidnapping, I suppose. But I had never seen that child before in my life! What did it all mean? Who was to blame for this abduction? Certainly not Yasmin Lange!

Nevertheless, I was in no position to defend my honor. The scales weighed against me. With Erbanhue's worrisome face probing my deportment, I merely nodded.

He stood up with a sigh. "I have amassed a plethora of sins myself, God knows. But don't let yours take hold. I couldn't... I could *not* bear to see you fall so low, Yassy."

He looked noble and kind. My lungs continued to revel in their regained freedom, further baffling my senses. I said nothing. I was utterly consumed by staring with shock. This was not the same Erbanhue from but seconds ago. Not only that… This look, this demeanor, had *never* belonged to him.

He waited patiently while I breathed. "Will you help me?" I gathered the strength to ask.

He held out his cane for me to grasp, chuckling as he pulled me up. "In due time. I've done enough lifesaving in one day. Go to your wagon, thou witchling, and don't let me see you stir from it until showtime!"

The moment was indeed gone – it had vanished in smoke and ash. "What a strange, callous, changeful, hasty creature you are!" said Yasmin to Erbanhue, within the safety of her wagon.

For the first time, it finally dawned on me that *something* plagued, arrested, and controlled him, just as *something* harnessed me. But what was it?

Chapter Thirty-Five

The Scryer

Something had changed the ringmaster.

He did not seem to recall what took place. He remembered catching me out after hours. He joked about how he had scolded me and banished me to my wagon. He laughed, anathemizing me as a "truant" and a "childish little rule-breaker." His eyes twinkled when he spoke to me, rather as if I *was* a childish breaker of rules, and one that he was rather proud of than the reverse.

Confusion reigned supreme. Did he mean to confound me to insanity? Was that his new diversion?

Still, I was glad enough to play along. I gave cool, respectful answers to his jeers and jabs, or snubbed him in the same playful spirit. He answered to both with resounding mirth, and we got along better than we ever had before. Indeed, we became quite well known in the troupe as being the very best of friends.

I felt in my bones that it wouldn't last.

I tried not to remember my deep blush, that aloof but sudden prickle as he traced my arm, looking earnest and open as he called me *Yassy* and blushed himself. But, Reader, it was very hard.

Some mysteries are never solved. Mankind will perish sans solution. I resigned myself to the inevitable: I spent the next week under a strict curfew. I obeyed with alacrity every commandment; I stayed when told to stay, sat when told to sit, and performed my aerial arts with caution. Erbanhue was as pleased as Christmas pudding. Praise upon praise was heaped upon me... still, I was unhappy.

The incident in the Corrupt Woods prowled in the confines of my brain. Was I mad? Did I yet suffer agonizing visions? And if it was indeed real, what then? It wanted proof and understanding, or at least the smallest dawning of comprehension – I felt I was wasting time. If only Aislinn would come!

Despite the mounting strength of my wish, Aislinn's visit was delayed. Two weeks passed. There was no word of her. As I had promised the Dragon that I would stay on the grounds, I could not seek her out. I took to pacing between the shows, feeling as caged as Darius. At last I spurned my pride and resorted to begging, pleading, and the wringing of hands, etc. Erbanhue smiled but refused; he liked having me all to himself. (Not that he ever *said* so. But he *looked* it.)

After much anxiety and inward perspiration, she came.

I recognized her knock. I opened the wagon door. Aislinn swept in, looking like a veritable queen. At first glance it only inspired vague amusement. I longed to inquire "Why the primping and preening forthwith? Do you fancy the ringmaster?" But the teasing fell dead on my tongue ere its exit.

Every centimeter of her body glowed with health. Her hair, ever rich and lustrous, shone as powerfully as a miniature sun. Its regal length actually brushed her feet. Her optics, once a somber ocean-blue, were now light and frothy like seafoam. Her creamy eyelids were framed with perfect, doll-like lashes, and her lips were also as perfect as a china doll's mouth.

She was always beautiful. But now I was actually struck dumb. I felt I could fall in love with her myself, let alone every man in creation.

"Don't stand gawking like a goose," Aislinn said, seating herself on my couch and submitting a coy smile. "We have much to discuss, you see."

"Indeed." I sat next to her, still absorbing the vision before my eyes. "You look-"

"Magnificent? Angelic? True. It's only the herbs, my dear."

"Only?" I managed to exclaim.

"Yes, *only*. It's another use of divine herbology. I can enhance my looks. How do you like it? Am I the most stunning of visions?"

She smiled at me, a priceless gem glistening from the wrappings of its sky-blue dress. I struggled to find the words. "I'm inspired with awe, of course. Anyone would be. But... are you for certain... Does this harm you in any way? Or... or does it cause harm to others?"

"What a silly notion! Unless one bemoans the plants plucked from the ground, for *this* result," – here indicating her unmatched complexion – "There is no harm whatsoever."

"That relieves me. But-"

"But what?" she interrupted with some pique. "I came to show you Aislinn in the height of her glory, and all you can manage are cautionary statements and hesitations? What ails thee?"

Before I could construct a reply, her eyes brightened. "Ah! I see! You are envious, are you not, my dear Yassy? Never fear! I have brought the cure." And here she pulled from her reticule a small, thrice-wrapped parcel.

I held up a hand in mild protest. "No, thank you. I'd rather remain as I am."

She threw up her (perfect) hands in disbelief. "But you could have any man in the county! You would rule over every heart, captivate the coldest audience. You'd even have Erbanhue slaving away beneath your feet, begging you to be the star of his phantom parade! Don't tell me *that* wouldn't delight you to your very soul."

"Not through trickery, my dearest Aislinn." I put out my hand, quietly pushing the parcel away. "I'd rather earn those rewards by my own merits."

"Oh, very well. But I'll make you another the moment you change your mind. And you certainly will." Aislinn beamed, showing a line of charming little pearl-white teeth. "Now, what has been happening here? What have I missed?"

With a sigh, I revealed what had happened on the night of the Corrupt Woods. She listened with remarkable tranquility, only interposing with a question here or there. "And Erbanhue remembers nothing of this night?"

"He remembers catching me out late and sending me home. That is all."

"Is it possible he is only pretending?"

"I believed that, at first. But I don't think even *he* could keep up such a jovial deception, knowing he supports a kidnapper in his midst."

"And you don't remember at all who the child was, or where you were going with him?"

"Not at all."

"Well, Yassy, I confess I have no answers for you. But please continue your visits to me as soon as you're able. We may think of something later on, and I think more to purpose in my garden."

"Perhaps."

We fell into pensive silence. I went to the window. The dried rose, still chained to the note from Erbanhue to his former lover, looked more pitiable than ever. I took it up again. Its thorns pierced an old wound, and indigo blood seeped anew. "I'll wash at the creek," I said. Aislinn nodded, taking up a book and tucking herself into my couch.

At the creek, I bent to wash my hands. My blood mingled with the water.

It did not spread and vanish directly, as it ought to have done by all decency to science and physics. It *sank*. Once it hit the muddy creek-bottom, it spread very slowly into a perfect circle... then floated to the surface of the water.

I inspected it in silent amazement. It became like a dark mirror, with figures and faces and voices burbling out of it. The blood mirror bobbed at the surface, bending over the miniature ripples and waves. Curiosity overwhelmed my fear; I drew closer to study this new impossibility.

Two figures were outlined in the shimmering blood. Judging from their familiar positions, and the cane being held across the second figure's throat, it was Ringmaster Erbanhue and Yasmin Lange.

He was speaking in her ear, obviously very angry. Behind him, Erbanhue's shadow stretched and thinned, growing into a third black figure. It was tall, faceless, and still. The Demongod of the Corrupt Woods.

It appeared to be watching us. It waited until Erbanhue pressed harder, menacing the girl with his cane. Yasmin choked, her eyelids weakly fluttering. The Demon slowly raised His slender, dark hand, and touched the back of Erbanhue's head.

The ringmaster's countenance instantly changed. Rage and distrust were scrubbed away, replaced by pity and compassion. He released the breathless girl and stood frozen, empty-eyed and confused. He fell to his knees.

A guttural moan of pain startled me. I touched my fingers to my bruised throat, realizing the sound of distress came from *me*. For I desperately wanted to believe that the moment between us... the sudden compassion, the tender remorse and kindness... had come from Erbanhue himself. Now I knew that was not the case.

If *He* had not interfered...

No. I could not believe Erbanhue was capable of that!

As the blood mirror broke up and melted away, I returned to the wagon, reflecting in deep distress. I lifted my skirts, mounting the wagon steps. I opened the door. I saw the blinding beauty of my friend as she sat up in a hurry, asking me some question. I answered ambiguously.

"What did you say?" repeated Aislinn, looking as disturbed as I felt.

"The blood mingled with the water, and I witnessed the past. I truly am a witch, Aislinn."

Chapter Thirty-Six

BLOOD READINGS

PART THREE

The Witch Anmut rose from the stream, pinching the thorn-prick on her sore finger. She waited until the blood mirror melted into nothingness. Contemplating the scene it had played, she straightened her skirts, returning to the gypsy wagon with a quick, sure step.

A black silk scarf, interwoven with glittering circus scenery, danced from the young witch's soft blonde hair. Her ebony velvet gown was braced by a heavily-stitched bodice, dressed with golden threads in the shapes of various leaves and petals. A black lace shawl hung loose from her elbows, and her feet were opulently dressed in the latest silver-buttoned, high-heeled boots. Long dusky pendants shimmered and tinkled from her ears.

Aislinn Bláthnaid had her sort of glory; Yasmin Lange had hers.

Erbanhue's Fair of Phantoms had attained sufficient funds for Erbanhue to purchase a small tract of land. Although they could still travel during the late spring and early summer seasons, the fair now had a permanent location. Perhaps, in earlier days, Yasmin would have been surprised at the luck of Erbanhue choosing a site close to her cottage home.

Now, she credited all things to a subtle hidden power.

Besides her feats of elocution, gymnastics, tight-rope walking, and aerial art, Yasmin now added sangemancy to her list of performances. Women from all walks of life continued to demand scrying in the interest of determining the future. Although the continual supplication was wearying enough: "If you please, Madame Witch, show me my future husband!", the revelations of Witch Anmut never failed. A mere prick of the finger and a black bowl of creek water, accompanied with *"Sanguis subscriptorum animadvertebant,"* ever drew forth the result of the entreaty.

No matter the season, no matter the weather... and no matter whether the victim of the prophesy was pleased or otherwise.

The weather was promising. The troupe was gathered together for a party, organized by the previously stingy Ringmaster Erbanhue. A generous cheer arose as this self-same crabby gentleman passed around outlandish mugs of ale. "To Master Erbanhue!" roared Sallix the magician (recently reinstated and perilously endowed with drink). "May we continue to prosper beneath his critical guidance."

"To Erbanhue!" echoed the troupe, and drank deeply.

I watched from a nearby rock, preferring to observe at a prudent distance rather than partake. There are certain people, with certain secrets, who should refrain from drunkenness at all costs.

"You'll tell us a story, won't you, Hue?"

This sweet propitiation came forth from none other than Janet Willow, the once-displaced singer of the Ghoul's Litany. She had returned two months ago. Following a performance of wheedling never before seen, heard, or witnessed by mankind, she was able to regain her former place. However, her humbled self was relegated to a tent, while the more valuable Witch Anmut was permitted to retain the gypsy wagon.

Yes, Reader, it was true. After many years of training, hoping, and ultimately despairing, Yasmin Lange received the station and treatment she had once only dreamed of. And Erbanhue was not the sole vessel of commendation. The town knew her name; they turned when she walked past, and listened when she spoke. In aerial grace, her work was consecrated. In elocution she never once faltered. And in sangemancy, her word was concrete law.

And yet, whenever Janet Willow's musical voice was raised in placation before a certain ringmaster, the young witch would silently grind her short teeth. Janet's presence was a constant reminder that despite all her power, Yasmin could not have everything. She still wasn't beautiful.

Janet was asking the ringmaster for a story. Erbanhue bestowed a rather despotic smile upon his former lover. "What story do *you* suggest, Miss Willow?"

I relaxed, serenely tracing an invisible picture on my rock. Despite Janet's valiant attempts to reclaim Erbanhue's affection (such as it was), the ringmaster was proving as unbreakable as a wild stallion.

"Would you please tell us how you trained Darius to wave his paw at your request? You were *so* brave!"

Perhaps I had relaxed too soon; Erbanhue's pride could easily be appealed to. My jaw clenched imperceptibly.

The Dragon beamed his assent. The troupe gathered round, eager to hear of Erbanhue's colossal brevity despite having heard this story at least five times before. I tuned out the words themselves, though my ears still mechanically appreciated the warm charisma of his masterful tones. Mind and heart alike remained recklessly attuned to his voice.

I listened until I had my fill. Rising steadily to avoid attention, I slipped away to visit Darius.

The poor tiger was no longer the pawing, clawing fire-cat that he had once been. He had attained a "good old age," and was lazy enough as cats often are. Stealing a low glance at the enraptured troupe, I squeezed my right hand between the bars. I stroked the great cat's head, talking to him, calling him sweet names. Darius made the chuffing sound akin to a cat's loving purr.

"We've come a long way, haven't we, my love? It must have been hard for you. But now you can go to your final rest well-fed. You shan't suffer, my precious one."

Darius rubbed his cheek against the bars. I scrubbed his rough, straw-textured head, and his chuffing increased.

Aislinn's soft voice interrupted us. "You're always up to something naughty, aren't you?"

"Says the fellow witchling." I withdrew my hand. Darius continued to rub against the bars, this time in hardy protest. I smiled. "I am so glad you could make it this evening. You've been studying for so long."

"As you should be, my lazy sister." Aislinn embraced me, at the same time passing a tiny parcel into the palm of my hand. "I thought you'd want this tonight," she whispered in my ear.

I unwrapped the parcel. In its center was the "beauty powder" Aislinn had concocted and used on herself.

I shook my head, attempting to return it. She politely pushed it back to me. "You didn't know it, Yassy, but I was watching you just now. Every time that little priss, Janet, speaks to your Master Erbanhue, you flinch and get a cold, wistful look in your eyes. I know what *that* means, even if you don't."

My hands curled into fists, and I slightly crushed the precious parcel. "I will not stoop that low. If Janet could get her hands on this, don't you suppose she would use it in an instant? I shan't be vain like her!"

"Oh, hush, now! Someone will hear." Aislinn glanced nervously at the troupe circle. It remained trapped in Erbanhue's spell. "I know you don't approve of how far I have gone," she whispered, grasping my hand in hers, "but I've made it mild for you. It'll simply restore you to a blooming, fresh maiden, with your lovely soft-gray eyes as gentle as a dove's. It just *improves* you. It won't alter you by any means."

"How do you know? You know I have yet to determine the exact means and strength of my own powers. It may work triple wonders upon me, and then I'll be utterly indistinguishable, a living china doll who walks upon the earth and does magic tricks. I'll be ridiculous."

"Oh, you worry too much, Yasmin! Your plethora of anxiety is damaging to my trade."

I sighed. "Suppose it does exactly what you say. They all think me a real witch already (although I *am,* to an extent they know not). Won't this rapid change invoke calamity and alarm amongst them?"

"I tell you, it is most subtle. Only people who stand fairly close to you would notice anything different. And why would anyone have reason to do that? Except, perhaps," and her smile became quite witch-like, "if Erbanhue moved to kiss you. Then *he'd* notice."

I shoved her, my cheeks coloring with anger. "You know he'd never do that! He's told me to my very face how ugly he thinks I am. He called my hair gray... *Gray!*"

"And this would eliminate that assertion!" She caught my wrist, holding up the hand that yet clenched her little, evil parcel. Her eyes softened.

"My dear, I just want you to be happy. You've been given such incredible ability... far beyond anything a mere herbologist could conjure. I daresay you will reach greater heights yet. But despite this, you are unhappy. And I know this could bring you the happiness you seek."

I crossed my arms, scowling. "And what exactly do I seek, since you know everything?"

"What every woman wants, my dear. Companionship. Lasting companionship with the one you love."

"Love?" I chuckled. "I swear, I do not comprehend the meaning of the word. Obsession, maybe. Fascination, certainly. But not love."

Her angelic mouth smiled with compassion. "It may be hard to see the forest for its many trees. But what the wanderer misses, a wood-wise observer can detect. You're in love with him. You've loved him for many a year."

"Nonsense. I don't even know his real name. I'll admit to a certain degree of fascination, but I don't love him. He's vain and self-centered. In fact, I can list his foibles alphabetically, if you like. He's gifted and amusing in fragments, but detestable as a whole."

"So are you. But I love you anyway."

My eyes widened, but I couldn't help but laugh. "You're certainly in rare form today, you Celtic sprite."

Aislinn laughed with me, taking the parcel. "You're changing the subject. Nevertheless, if you truly and for good refuse this gift, I promise I shall never offer it again."

Despite my avowals, I hesitated.

My gaze traveled to the enchanted circus troupe, still spellbound at Erbanhue's feet. Janet's pretty face gleamed in the firelight. Her golden-brown tresses curled around her bare shoulders. Her eyes, the light color and shape of a golden fawn's irids, willingly followed the handsome ringmaster's every movement.

Yet I held in my hand the ability to outshine her. Or, if not that, to at least rise as her equal.

Was there no other way? I maintained there was not. In my particular manner of conversation, the Dragon had neither shown nor vocalized any disappointment in me. In my stature, my aerial work, and my scrying, he praised and admired me. He even hinted (though perhaps *per errore*) that he suspected I was highly intelligent. He lent me books and presented recitations he wanted me to memorize. Sometimes he made me practice them for his own pleasure, as we took an evening walk together, my gloved hand lightly touching the crease of his inner elbow. He'd smoke and criticize and dispense repartee, thoroughly enjoying himself.

Therefore, via process of elimination, the only barrier in the way was my lack of beauty. For a talented ringmaster who curated his shows to produce wildly beautiful and artistic scenes, it would be a tragedy - nay, a virtual impossibility - to love someone who was not beautiful.

Having perused that certainty... was it the *right* thing to do?

I was to combine this powder with water and drink it, becoming in essence a walking love potion. Aislinn insisted it would be inconceivably mild. But surely there were unforeseen risks. A price to pay. At the very least, it was sure to expire at some unlucky moment. Was that not the infamy of all such magic? No one ever said the Genie worked for good or for evil intent. Humanity doesn't consider it. We make our wishes and trust in the results.

Debating these points with my friend accomplished little. She surmounted each one of them as if she knew beforehand exactly what I would say. This disconcerted me. She laughed, insisting she knew me as well as "the back of her hand," and again assured me that there was no price, no expiration, and no risk.

"Just keep the powder with you," she said. "Take it when you're ready."

I tucked it into my bodice, still undecided. Aislinn took my arm and guided me back to the troupe, where we sat and listened to the end of Erbanhue's (grossly exaggerated) story. The applause was great, and Erbanhue's flourishing bow quite imposing indeed.

As we all rose to depart for the evening, Janet took Erbanhue's arm with a soft chirrup of delight, revisiting one of the most unbelievable parts of his tale. His chest swelled with satisfaction as he answered in his most booming, impressive voice.

After considering this subtle tableau of resuming romance, I drew out the parcel. "Go and get my scrying bowl, will you, Aislinn?"

Chapter Thirty-Seven

Vanity of Vanities!

While waiting at the creek, I applied only the smallest amount of Aislinn's powder to my forefinger. The putrid shade of skin gradually turned to the color of normal, healthy flesh. By then, the hurried step of Aislinn entered the woods as she arrived with the scrying bowl.

I withdrew a necklace tucked into my blouse, revealing the iron thorn I always carried. I pricked the healed finger. A small, bright red droplet fell into the water. As before, it rose to create a blood mirror, but this one was bright red rather than dark indigo as they had all been before.

"It does not harm sangemancy," I said. Aislinn smiled hopefully.

I knelt to study the images. Erbanhue and Janet, still arm-in-arm, were approaching her tent. I winced, forcing myself to keep spying. If they entered it together...

They lingered long, talking in confidential tones. After what seemed to be hours, Janet perched on tiptoe to give Erbanhue a playful peck on the cheek. She dove into her tent, affecting shyness. Erbanhue grinned, sauntering away like a satisfied cat.

"It hasn't happened yet," I murmured. "But it won't be long."

"What's that?" persisted Aislinn.

"Never you mind."

The images vanished. The blood mirror disintegrated. I motioned for Aislinn. "Give me the bowl."

She passed it to me. I mixed the rest of the powder with water from the creek. It bubbled and simmered into a light amber paste. "I've been working on making them more palatable," Aislinn mentioned. "It should taste much like tea."

"Thank you, Aislinn." After letting the mixture become homogenous, I drank it (or rather ate it, as it was quite thick) as quickly as possible. "How long until the change comes to pass?"

"A minute or two."

After waiting for a few minutes, I inhaled deeply. And I bent to look.

It was still Yasmin Lange who gazed back at me from the water's shallow edge. But she was healthier, fresher, and *attractive*. She remained unique to herself with blonde hair, only dark at its roots. Her eyes were yet gray but were softer, wider, and more innocent-looking, naturally achieving the doe-eyed look that many maidens used belladonna to obtain. Her lips remained curved into a natural pout, as of yore, but they were fuller and an appealing shade of peach-pink. The brows were smooth, slender, and regally arched.

Above all, the unnatural paleness of the skin was completely eradicated. In its place shone healthy, light skin, even and whole throughout to the formerly-discolored fingertips.

I held up my hands in awe, examining my fingers. They had been an embarrassment to me despite the mystic power they declared. I hid them in gloves most of the time. "You were right, Aislinn. I'm still myself."

"Why don't you learn to trust me, Yasmin?" Aislinn sang with delight, grabbing me by the waist and whirling me about. "Before long we shall have epic ballads written in our honor, the two most beautiful maidens in the country!"

"Don't spin me! You are making me dizzy." I pushed her away. "I'll admit I was in the wrong. But don't imagine I shall act any differently. I don't wish to cause a scene."

"Of course! Naturally, you wouldn't. You're a sensible girl." Aislinn pointed to the woodland exit. "I doubt Erbanhue has gone to bed yet. You might be able to catch him before then. Have a cozy little chat, hmm?"

"You're *terrible*, Aislinn!"

Said terrible one merely giggled.

A few days later, I hummed to myself as I undressed in the wagon. I popped my head out of the window. "Mary?"

The tapping of petite feet answered my call. "Yes, miss?"

"I'm ready for my bath now. Bring the hot water, please."

"Yes, miss."

Mary was a decent little thing, though not at all as interesting as my darling Lillias had been. She was hired to run errands for me and to aid me in dressing and setting my hair. I unpinned my locks, settling into the tub as Mary hurried in with the water, freshly warmed over the fire pit.

"I tested it just now, miss. It isn't too hot."

"Thank you. Pour it in."

She judiciously obeyed, watching the swift rise of the water with an anxious eye. I sighed in relief, letting its blessed warmth dissolve the ache of my muscles. "It was a difficult day, Mary. Erbanhue *would* propose to combine elocution and tightrope walking! Would you add some of Aislinn's special herbs?"

"Certainly, Miss Yasmin."

Of course, these were not just *any* herbs. They increased vitality, brought a warm glow to the cheeks, and erased dark circles around one's tired eyes. All of them traits that a good bath might deliver, but not to the profound extent that the herbs did.

"Take some for yourself, Mary. I daresay you'll want them on a cold night." Mary beamed with gratitude, civilly reserving the smallest portion for herself. She scattered the remainder of the fresh green herbs, dark curling leaves, and violet petals into the bath water. "You look happy this evening, Miss Yasmin."

"Yes. I am content."

So saying, I bestowed a furtive glance upon the abundance of flowers in my windows. Despite their restful, comforting scent, I wrinkled my nose in mild distaste. A fire-eater, a magician, and a midget: These were my admirers to date.

But, as Aislinn pointed out, at least now I *had* admirers. Before, my heart was as safe from robbery as the most destitute of persons. Well, no matter. Perhaps Aislinn could use my luckless bouquets in a powder or a brew.

I shifted my weight to lean my arms against the edge of the tub, dipping my hair into the scented water. "Mary?"

"Yes, Miss Yasmin?"

"Do you find me unapproachable?"

Mary, small blame, looked puzzled. "Unapproachable?"

"Intimidating, I suppose."

"Oh." She faltered, shuffling her feet.

"Don't be afraid to speak the truth." I softened my voice, raising my head to look her in the eyes. "I used to be in a position very like your own, when I was your age. I would never be unkind to you."

"Very well, miss. You are a *little*... intimidating." She held up an adorable finger and thumb, indicating the smallest possible gap. "Only this much."

Her petite, freckled face blushed behind her curls. I laughed. "Only that much? I suppose I needn't scry for a husband, then. One will come soon enough. I expect I'll be swept off my feet. I seem the type, do I not, Mary?"

"Um... well..."

"Nevermind." I laughed again, rising to my feet. Mary scrambled to find my towel and help me step from the tub. "Don't mind my prattling. Here." I opened a corner cupboard and extracted a slice of cake. "Have this with your dinner. Tell the cook to give you an extra serving, by my request."

She gave me a shy, toothy grin, and dashed off with her prize. The door slammed shut behind her. I shook my head, exchanging the towel for a white night-dress. It slipped over my head with its cool, silky texture, translucent flowered sleeves, and lace hemming. I admired its exquisite details in the mirror.

Unfortunately, the mysterious scar on the upper left of my chest marred the image...

The scar had appeared the morning after I used Aislinn's powder. I awoke from a deep sleep to find a small circular mark, a few inches wide, with two intersecting slashes in the middle. Concerned, I showed it to Aislinn, who parted her blouse to show me the exact same mark on her own chest. It refused to heal for either of us.

A knock at the door. "Yasmin? Gray witchling, are you there?"

Despite the amendment to my tresses' tint, Erbanhue insisted on using my old sobriquet. I cast my eyes to the ceiling, annoyed. "I'm here, Master. But I'm not proper. Don't you dare intrude!"

"I wouldn't dare in any case." Hue absently tapped a beat against the door with the head of his cane. "But pray emerge once you're fit to be seen. I need to talk to a woman with a brain."

"I am pleased to know you believe *some* women have brains, sir."

"Ah, yes. I believe all evil, conniving witches have brains. Comes with the territory."

"I see."

I snatched my navy coat from its hook and hastily donned it. "I'm coming out." Grasping the brass doorknob, I gave its stubborn self a deft twist and swung the door ajar.

"How can I be of service, Master Hue?"

Chapter Thirty-Eight

One Dead Rose Among the Flowers

The ringmaster's eyes traveled from my high collar down to my bare feet. "Go put some shoes on, you silly creature."

"Whatever for? We can talk right here."

"Just do it, woman! I have to walk while I deliberate."

"Very well." I darted back in, grabbed the first pair of shoes my hands met, and pulled them on. "I'm ready now."

"Thank'ee. Your alacrity suits me. Come."

He stomped away in Hueish fashion, striding as if he was in a rage although it was just his way. I hurried to keep up. "I was debating a very serious change for my Fair of Phantoms. I wanted your opinion."

Mildly surprised, I marched faster. "What change, sir?"

"We hold a pretty strong monopoly on the carnival here. We're medium-sized fish in a small pond, if you comprehend me." Erbanhue's sweeping gait was indeed trying to match. "But we'd reach far more people if we played in the big cities. Do you agree?"

"A logical conclusion. However, there would be more competition."

"Precisely. That is the debate. Competition." His thick brows creased as he meditated further. "But thanks to competition, would we not improve? I know my little troupe and I am proud enough of it! We would fight fire with fire. Ghostly, unnatural, paranormal fire." He cackled at the thought. "*We* would be 'the best show on earth,' not that upstart pug-face, Barnum."

"Are you certain of that, sir? I heard he boasts quite the menagerie. He even has his own *whales*."[1]

"Pshaw! What are natural creatures when I can call up the unnatural?"

"Can you, sir?"

"You yourself are an evidence to my claim. I consider you to qualify beyond the pale of *le naturel.*"

"*Assurément.* Yet *you* did not create me."

"No. Not your raw elements, at least. But I helped to form the clay."

I allowed him that triumph, as it was true enough.

"Then you agree, Yasmin? Isn't competition healthy for us? Should we not engage in it? Pursue it? Relish it, even?"

Lifting my head to answer, I noticed that subtle beam in his eyes that I knew all too well. He was practicing his favored duplicity, speaking one

---

1. Barnum housed Beluga whales in the American Museum in 1861. Unfortunately, they were killed when the museum caught fire in 1865.

thing that was true enough in and of itself, but also meaning it in a second (more devious) context.

My mind flew for answers. As we ambled in silence, I saw Janet peeping at us from the parted flaps of her tent. I caught her eye. She withdrew, shutting and tying the flaps firmly. I divined his alternate meaning.

"Competition is indeed healthy, sir," I declared. "It causes all parties concerned to do their very best. To *be* their best."

So, his game was to see if he could make me jealous. He would be disappointed. After all, I was presently disappointed in *him*.

The ringmaster's grin broadened. "I couldn't have put it better myself." He was clearly unaware that I had pieced together his vain little puzzle.

I shrugged with cool nonchalance. "You may take the fair wherever you please. Just understand that this is my home. I do not like large cities as homes, though they are pleasant enough to visit. You would have to find your Fair another witch."

"Not Aislinn Bláthnaid, I assume? She's still your precious golden sheep, following her witchling shepherd day after day. What does she do, anyway? Has she got a serious profession?"

"She has experience in medicines and herbs." (To say so was as close to the truth as I could manage.) "But you are mistaken. Having a blind follower such as you dictate is not friendship, sir."

"That's what all 'friendship' is, my naïve young friend. You pick the person you mean to copy and strive to imitate their best qualities, traits, and habits. She will tire of it one day."

I produced a rueful smile. "How skeptical you remain, sir! Aislinn has no need to mimic me. What could be her reason? She's far more beautiful, and gracious, and wise than I am."

"Beautiful, of course. Gracious, naturally! But not so wise."

"What do you mean?"

"As I said before (must I repeat myself?), you have a substantial amount of brains in your head. For a woman."

"Just so. For a woman."

I shook my head. He may be richer, more comfortable, and more devoted to the worship of Vanity, but at heart he was still the same old cynic. "I have a question, sir. If it would not displease you."

He flourished his cane. "Ask away. I am in a forthcoming mood to-night." He deployed his most dazzling smile.

"I have seen you out walking with Miss Janet Willow rather often. Are nuptial congratulations soon to be the order of the day?"

His cane dealt me a playful swat. He laughed. "Pfft! Janet Willow, indeed! She lacks quality. A pretty face is, after all, a penny a dozen; it alone would not satisfy. I require both a quantity of beauty *and* a quality of brains." He shot me a cattish grin. "To my great misfortune, all the women I've met have either one or the other, but never both. Present company included."

"But you cannot deny you're preserving a flirtation with Janet. You will break her heart again, Master Hue. Do you amuse yourself by breaking hearts?"

A mild spark of irritation lit his pupils. "Do not speak as if you know her. *I* know her. Most women like to have a gripe or two; Janet would break her own heart in two seconds if it could be affected. What else could she and her little friends gossip about, pray tell?"

"Oh! Many things. Feminine drama is infinite."

"Ah, point accepted. Their drama is indeed without limit."

"You intend to keep up this charade, then?"

He rose an eyebrow. "Why do you think I began it at all, Yassy?" And the dazzling glitter of his grin blossomed all the more.

I would not succumb to its glow. My exasperation overpowered it. "Such games should be buried in your distant past, Erbanhue. You shouldn't continue them as a man. It makes you so small, instead of grand and admirable and honest."

"Grand, forsooth! Admirable and honest, quite! Yasmin has a brain, and is infinitely more amusing." The Dragon stopped to roar with mirth. "By the gods, I shall burst! Ah, Yasmin, what would I do without your fine company to keep me clean and saintly, eh?"

"You'd do exactly what you are doing now: ignore everything useful that anyone 'with a brain' bothers to tell you."

Still cackling, he resumed our walk. I followed.

"Right again! You know me better than I know myself." Erbanhue abandoned his jeering, teasing tones, and said rather soberly "You're a valuable companion, Yasmin Lange. I know you don't believe a single compliment you've ever heard in your life, but I assure you, it's the truest word this scoundrel ever spoke."

"You've gone and consumed a pint too many. I'd vastly prefer another subject. Pray think of one."

"I'm as temperate as a priest, Yasmin. You'll have to think of another rebuff to weave your spiderly way out of my sincere compliment."

"Then you must have an ulterior motive."

"You've hit upon it! Yes, in a way, I do."

"Good! You're waxing honest at last. Well, out with it."

Erbanhue ceased walking again. "I noticed you've gained another sort of following, you wicked enchantress. You've cast spells on some of my workers, hmm?" He tapped one mighty forefinger against my cheek, smiling.

Well, if you dare to bring up the subject, I will dare to see if I *can make* you *envious.* This should be of great interest. Aislinn would relish it.

"Indeed I did, sir. I waited until your watchful eyes were veiled in slumber, and I whipped up a love potion that shook the very foundations of the earth with its potency. The entire world shall soon love me and worship at my feet."

"Including my humble, humiliated self?"

"Nein."

"Nyet?"

"I'd never want that. You'd make a terrible lover, as sincerity does not become you. And is not sincerity the bedrock of a lover's plea?"

"*Sicuramente!* Well, that's a relief of the profoundest order! Since you've admitted to your sin, I suppose you mean to amuse yourself for a little while with your floral offerings, and then give up the chase?"

"Just so."

"Then it is settled."

"What is settled?"

"We are the same. We have different ways of going about it, for sure and certain. But we are so alike it's positively distasteful!" He roared again, kicking at pebbles with his weighty boots. "We crave worship, and we will get it, by God!"

Chapter Thirty-Nine

THE SOCIETY QUEEN PAYS A VISIT

Evening drew to a close. I motioned Mary in to help me out of my bodice. She had just seized ahold of the strings when a tentative knock startled us both.

I heaved an inward sigh. "'Tis later than usual, but she isn't knocking after hours. Show her in."

Mary hastily aided me in re-dressing. "How do you know your customer is a lady?"

"By the knock."

Heaven knows I ought to be able to distinguish the various knocks, raps, and taps by now. Erbanhue had invented quite a flashy introduction for his "aerialist-gone-witch," and I was then his most valuable member… though his own performances ranked highly as well.

Mary showed my customer in. I closed the velvet drapes (customers, particularly female ones, liked to feel safe and secretive). Drawing out the scrying bowl, I arranged it perfectly center on my circular table. "Please sit."

My fair lady, swathed in the latest style of purple silk and an ostrich-feather hat, pulled fretfully at her snow-white gloves. The golden pleats of the glove tassels brushed the tablecloth. "I apologize for coming so late in the evening, Madame Witch."

I arched my brows wordlessly, sensing she had more to say.

"I beg your pardon also for feeling the need to veil my face. I do not wish anyone of my acquaintance to know I have come to you."

"I assure you that I have served many a customer with the most prudent discretion. All that is asked and revealed here never departs from these walls."

The veiled customer nodded her assent, dropping the required allotment of coins into the silver platter. I drew in a breath, covertly withdrawing the iron thorn. *"Sanguis subscriptorum animadvertebant,"* I whispered to the still water.

The blood took, swirling elegantly into a bright blood mirror. "Ask me what you most wish to know."

She wavered. I glanced up at her. "Please, madame. The mirror will only last so long. Make your request."

"I wish to know if I shall ever bear children."

In her emotional manner of asking, the deep falsetto she had adopted broke up, revealing her true tone of voice. Recognition pricked my memory; I knew this voice. I kept my eyes closely trained on the mirror, refusing to betray my knowledge. "It will only be a moment more. You shall have your answer."

The pool of watered blood muddled, then cleared.

An image of a woman, dressed in silk, leaned disconsolate over a baby's cradle. I looked closely, expecting the bed to be quite empty; lo! A baby, lovingly wrapped, *was* tucked into the crib. But the child's unnatural stillness soon betrayed the truth.

Reader, it never gave me pleasure to deliver such news. But I judged that it was always better to deliver the truth, and prepare the hearer for the harsh reality to come. Besides, I myself could not stomach being fed a lie.

I waited until the blood mirror was gone, choosing my words with care. "Let me prepare you first with the final word; your desire ends in tragedy."

The amethyst lady covered her trembling lips with her handkerchief, stifling a sob.

"You shall bear a child, but it will die soon after its birth."

She moaned, tears anointing the handkerchief's floral embroidery. "And is it... Is it the only child I shall have?"

I nodded. "If there had been other natural children in your future, the mirror would have shown them."

The dam burst asunder; tears flooded without pause. I stood and came behind her to pass my arm around her shoulders. "Take heart, my lady. It is well within your means to adopt."

"How did you know that? Do you know me?" She drew herself up sharply, tucking her handkerchief and her grief cautiously away. "I don't believe we have ever met, Madame Witch."

I smiled. "It requires but a moment to judge a woman's purse by her manner of dress, my lady. You want for nothing in this life. It can be the same with a child, if you have the heart to brighten an orphan's future by your goodness."

"But that isn't the same! My husband wants me to bear him a son." Wailing recommenced. I patted her back soothingly. Barring Lillias, I was never concerned about loving or being loved by a child. However, that is not to say I was opposed to the notion. I *did* pity her.

My case, however, was as cold as a northern glacier. (Unless I chose to wed either the fire-eater, the magician, or the midget.)

"You're wrong," the woman cried, clutching her coin purse and rushing out. "You must be wrong! You're a liar!"

Accustomed to such statements, I quietly watched her from my window. She stumbled as she ran, frequently applying the handkerchief, and not likely to return to the Witch who served Erbanhue's Fair of Phantoms. I judged this particular circumstance as for the best. That lady was none other than my previous friend and mentor, Lady Lidia Berenice Henderson – the society queen who had abandoned me as unfit for companionship.

Nevertheless, I did not wish her ill and would never harm her. Childbirth was a troubling thing, likely to result in tragedy many times over.

Anmut.

I stirred in my sleep, shifting beneath the blanket.

Anmut.

I sat up with a gasp, touching the burning scar. "Who is it?"

Wissen Sie.

Rothadamas. I leapt from the couch, lighting a lantern with a quaking hand. "What is it? What do you wish to say?"

Ich bin zufrieden mit dir.[1]

---

1. "I am pleased with you.

"Why do you call me Anmut?"

No reply.

I sat down again, searching every shadow within range for the Demon-god's dark form. He did not show himself.

Du bist von großem Wert. [2]

"Rothadamas? Is that what I call *you?*"

His strange, humming sound filled the air, then dissipated. I shivered, drawing the blanket close around me. It was no unpleasant sound, yet it was cold. I felt its vibrations through my body.

My scar burned and itched. I clawed at it in discomfort. "Rothadamas! Please. You *must* teach me the intricacies of my power. I have misused it. Please... speak to me again."

The shadow of an angelic being, arching his wings in a dazzling display, arose before me. I shrank back, marveling and fearful. It sank away again, leaving everything as it was before – still, peaceful, painfully normal.

As I was lying down again, trembling, a shimmering sparkle caught the corner of my eye. I slipped down from my perch, picking it up, turning it in my hand.

A cameo. Pure silver, inlaid with tiny sapphires, pearls, and aquamarine. On the back was etched a strange saying which meant nothing to me:

"ANMUT, THE LIONESS OF KHEIMA"

"Kheima," I muttered, turning the precious jewelry over and over. The Corrupted Woods, wherein I beheld so many strange and wonderful things. Was that place called Kheima?

---

2. "You represent great worth."

But "lioness" left me confounded. In what way did I mirror this beast, a known prowler and master huntress?

I could not imagine.

Chapter Forty

A More Perilous Game

"Is that from one of your admirers, Yassy?"

Aislinn nodded toward the cameo. It brightly caught the noonday sun, throwing sparkles of blue, navy, and white upon Aislinn's inquisitive face. I turned away, pretending to be intent upon my stitch-work. "True enough, I suppose."

I did not share my vision with her this time. Some things are best kept tucked away in the heart. "It's a thoughtful gift, is it not?"

"Very."

But there was no deceiving the crafty Aislinn. Her head tilted. "I did not think either your fire-eater, magician, or midget had the means to purchase such an expensive bauble. How did he manage, I wonder? Which one was it?"

I sighed. Here was an admirable chance to dispense a fib... but I was unlikely to remember my story later. "It was left for me on the floor of my wagon. I do not know who the giver is." At least, it was part of the truth.

"Left... on... the... floor. With no name. Hmm."

The Celt's wicked tone caused me to stiffen in self-defense. "It was *not* Erbanhue."

She prudishly curved her lips downward, mimicking one of my infamous pouts. "If you say so, my dear." She continued her sewing.

I waited in silent agony, knowing from past experience that Aislinn was far from finished with the subject. "I've just concocted a new blend of tea," she announced, catching me off my guard. "Will you try some with me later?"

"Of course."

I pulled my final stitch into place, holding the gloves up in the light and hoping they were the correct size. "It's been so long since I made a pair of child's gloves. I hope they fit Mary well."

"You measured her at least two-and-twenty times! They'll fit to perfection." Aislinn stood and helped me rise also. "It's time for tea. Let's enjoy it in your beautiful wagon."

We walked through sunlight arm-in-arm, a picture of health and textbook amiability. She nodded and smiled to the workers, tactfully acknowledging the murmurs of approbation being deployed right and left. Even Erbanhue, too occupied with staring, ceased instructing one of his workers.

I smothered a tiny stab of envy. I recalled when, years ago, he had tossed his mallet to me. He had winked as it slipped helplessly from my uncalloused hands. He laughed with delightful amiability; his blue eye sparkled, and his brown eye shone. He had never looked so handsome as he did then, though he was garbed in common workman's clothing, his robust arms sweating in the cruel sun.

Reader, he *could* be so full of goodness and charitable cheer! The sharpness of that memory was painted with great care onto the canvas of my mind. It might have been better if I had blotted it out... Painted it over with some more worthy remembrance. But what mortal heart only recalls what it ought to?

"Yasmin! Yassy?"

I started, realizing I had drifted off into mournful musing. "I beg your pardon, Aislinn. What did you say?"

She huffed. "I was merely introducing a subject of some importance. Do I have your attention now?" She pinched my arm in good humor. "You can make faces if you like, Yasmin, but listen." She pulled me eagerly into the wagon. "Look at this! I made it this morning."

Reaching into her reticule, she extracted a folded tissue paper with the utmost care. Unwrapping it, she proudly presented its contents.

A tiny, but perfectly-formed blue rose. I examined it with growing fascination, noticing the artistic curl of every petal, and the slight shimmer along its stem. "It's lovely! If you begin producing miraculous gardens instead of pandering to your own vanity, I might have more praise in store for you."

The Celtic goddess laughed, snatching the treasure away from me. "If those are the sort of comments you're planning to distribute, I shan't show you my creations."

I pleaded, reaching for the flower. "No, I beg your forgiveness! Let me study this work."

"Oh, you can do far more than *study* it, Yasmin. It was crafted for your convenience. That delicate flower you're holding is the receptacle of a powerful spell. It's truly the work of an accomplished enchantress."

"Oh?" I waved a finger at her. "This better not be another attempt at matchmaking. I tire of your insolence in that regard."

"I agree. Matchmaking is for amateur witches! I am far more proficient than that."

"Very well. For what shameful commission is this rose intended?"

"You won't pry it from me so easily. Can't you guess? Does that exact shade of blue stimulate any likeness?"

I held it up, turning it with care. It struck me immediately that it was the exact shade of a certain ringmaster's bright blue eye; but I would have preferred a sudden death rather than admit how quickly the comparison came. "I'm afraid it doesn't remind me of anything in particular."

"I don't believe you in the slightest. Nevertheless, I'll pretend I do." She plucked the flower from my hand. "It has been infused with a delicate but alluring scent, causing any person to inhale deeply in its presence. That scent harbors an airborne relaxant and a dream stimulant. In short, this rose is the gift of sleep and dreams."

"I thank you, Aislinn, but I don't feel I need this-"

"Not for you, Yasmin. For Erbanhue."

I frowned. "I confess I don't understand your intention. He does have restless nights now and then, when he goes for long walks or smokes his pipe. But I haven't heard of him suffering nightmares or overwhelming insomnia."

She shook her head. "I have more to explain. If you think of what sort of dream you want this rose to communicate, and exhale softly on the rose, that is precisely what the victim will dream about."

I paused, thinking. "Any dream at all?"

"Any dream at all. Even a nightmare, if you chose. But my idea was that you could use this rose to influence his decisions regarding the Fair of Phantoms. If he threatens to move us all to the god-forsaken city, for example, you could influence his decision this way."

"Oh, I see." I smiled. "You have your own agenda to defend."

"You know you don't want to live there, either!" Aislinn passed the rose back to me. "And… of course, you *could* use it to influence the desires of a gentleman. If you so choose." She ducked to avoid the threat of my hand.

"Aislinn, thy name is Temptation," I sighed. "But, once and for all, my dear friend. What use is romance if you have to charm a person into it?"

"The human mind is a singularly deceivable organ. He wouldn't know the difference, and given time, neither would you."

"We shall have to agree to disagree."

"It isn't a love potion, you know. It's just a dream. He'll wake up, and like any other dream, will likely dismiss it. But it'll linger. Certain things will call it back to mind, and it might turn things in your favor." Aislinn waved her finger at me in return. "Or would you rather sit back and watch him escort our bland Miss Willow down the aisle? At the very least, he's certain to play the love scene with her. Could you abide that?"

No, I was sure I could not. I turned, dumped the fire-eater's bouquet out of window, and placed the rose within the emptied vase. "No, that would be unendurable."

"That's my girl!"

"But I will not take your suggestion, either."

Aislinn frowned. "Why not? I think it's brilliant. Don't you see, he'll only change his actions after the dream because *he already wanted to?* The dream is a suggestion, a hint, a *teeny* push in the right direction."

After some meditation, I revealed my decision. "He *will* be caused to have a dream. But he'll simply dream of a shared moment in our past, which I recall with perfect clarity."

The conspirator beamed with anticipation. "You never told me you two had a past."

I shrugged. "We've been half-way friends, *very* good enemies, and then decent friends again. Nothing more."

"How insufferably dull of you."

"But..." I paused, not fully induced to share this information, "There was... a look."

Aislinn laid a hand over her heart. "Oh, my goodness me! A *look!* Sound the wedding bells! Call up the minister!"

I pelted her with a convenient napkin while she shrieked in protest.

Chapter Forty-One

Her Eyes Are of Steel

I waited until I saw Erbanhue depart his tent, smoking his fancy pipe and intent upon walking for the next hour. Blocking out the warning screams of my conscious, I tucked the blue rose into my blouse and departed in wary silence.

In passing Darius' cage, I noted he was pacing, growling under his breath at some unknown cause. Not exactly the most propitious of signs. But I had envisioned the alternative all too clearly: Sitting passively by while Erbanhue carried on an obnoxious flirtation, raw and ridiculous to everyone concerned. And partly, as I very strongly suspected, just to determine if he could rouse my jealousy! It was a hateful, discourteous game. This was just my means of ending it. My tender, kindly, floral means.

If he did not have a heart *entirely* made of stone.

The cool breath of nighttime cheered me as I crept along. I slipped between the flaps of the tent and located the target: Erbanhue's old top hat, which had been recently replaced by a star-studded felt alternative. Yet accustomed to the parsimonious life, he never threw anything out. The tent was a veritable hoard of odds and ends. I angled the blue rose into the brim of the hat, turning it out of sight, and slanting it ever-so-slightly toward the pillow at the end of his cot.

While rearranging the hat, I observed a miniature photograph of a young girl perched on horseback. Inquisitive, I picked it up. It was my Lillias Vosquez, smiling with deceptive patience as she balanced for many a minute to pose for the picture.

As you know, Reader, I have described the ringmaster as a verified "consummate hater of children." Here, then, was another anomaly. Why would a vain man so determined to hate children keep the photograph of a lowly child equestrienne?

My mind loves a mystery. I delved directly into theories, clues, and hypotheses – but I had not the time to sit and ponder! Speed was requisite. Having checked for observers, I crept my way out again.

A day passed.

Two. Four. An entire week trudged by. Nothing seemed to change in Erbanhue's manner toward me. He ordered me about the same as always, poked criticism at my routines, and called me "gray witchling" half-a-dozen times. I complained to Aislinn that the rose had not worked.

"I told you, it merely bestows a dream," she reminded me. "You have to give him time to mull it over, to see certain events resurface. You *are* planning on helping that along, aren't you?"

"Of course. I'm not a simpleton."

Although our fair's location was now permanent, the housing for our menagerie was routinely moved to provide the grazing animals with fresh grass. On those days, Erbanhue often joined the workmen to drive the stakes back into the ground.

I waited until such a day.

The sky was overcast. The hum of men's voices and the calls of animals rang in the air. *Puck-puck-puck, puck-puck-puck* sang the mallets. Three men worked on each stake, taking their turns to strike.

I approached Erbanhue's group, my rapid heartbeat reddening my face with agitated excitement.

Would he remember? Would he be cordial?

Would it strike a single chord in the instrument of his mind?

As I reviewed a multitude of disappointing scenes, Erbanhue's voice rose in song, powerfully swelling in time to the mallet-strokes.

"If I could but claim
A king's ransom or two,
I'd build her a galleon,
And hire a crew!"

"We'd sail to the mountains,
Of mythical fare.
We'd sail to the forests,
Where'ere we dare."

"For my lady hath no fear,
Her eyes are of steel!
Her will is a vessel

That ne’er shall keel.”

“I’d take her beyond
What her lost dreams have seen,
And sail her to gardens
Of heavenly green.”

A speechless surprise inundated my will, draining me of the power to proceed. I was ensnared, unable to walk, incapable of thought.

“If I were to battle
Along foreign shores,
She’d yet be kept safe in
Our land’s sheltered moor.”

“I’d give up my titles,
Resign from all fame!
To bask in her smile
Is one and the same.”

“For my lady hath no fear,
Her eyes are of steel!
Her will is a vessel
That ne’er shall keel.”

“I’d take her beyond
What her lost dreams have seen,
And sail her to gardens
Of heavenly green.”

A tingle rattled down my spine. My heartbeat, breathing, and consciousness seemed to slow...

Leaves showered leisurely around him. His eyes shone from the joy of his work. Resolute, vigilant, intent, his practiced skill was showcased by each crushing blow of the mallet.

The sun's stifled rays flickered through a break in the clouds. The deep tan of his skin was traced with gold, and his snake-head earring winked its ruby eyes in serene reply. His bronze, muscular arms stole my breath, as did the grandiose smile hovering on his steady lips. I stared at them. Wondered what it would feel like to press my own to his...

I had never applied the term "beautiful" to any man before, and have privately ridiculed others for doing so. But my confession remains; the thought crossed my mind. It was a savage, free, gypsy-like beauty.

Erbanhue hummed the tune as his task neared its end. Suddenly made aware of the closing opportunity, I compelled myself to move.

"Good afternoon, sterling witch. Have you a penchant for hammering stakes?" And he grinned a feline grin, tossing the mallet to me.

I barely caught it in time. But some years had passed between the original moment and this little reenactment; I was prepared for its weight. Deftly lifting it, I drew strength from my whole body as he had taught me to do over the years. Confronting the second stake, I swung the cumbersome tool and distributed a stern blow before anyone had time to object. Thankfully, it hit its mark.

"Excellent! A little stand-in, should one of us be taken ill!" exclaimed one of the workmen, chuckling in amusement. The others laughed as well. Erbanhue did not laugh, but leaned against the grounded stake, observing me with a pensive mien. "Don't harm yourself," he said.

“I haven’t.” Turning, I carried the mallet back to him, meeting his thoughtful gaze with confidence. “And I won’t.”

He took the offered instrument. An irresistible, subtle breed of smile melted his brooding look. “You are… a curious little woman, Yassy. Most… curious.” A flush of deep red began at his ears and progressed to his face.

“And I have brains, too!” I declared, dissolving him with hilarity.

Chapter Forty-Two

The Treasure of the Fair Arrives

The morning sun rose with speed, eager to be alive, happy to bless mankind with her golden gladness. I rose in kind. At the wardrobe, I donned a scarlet gown with crescent stitching and its matching set of moon earrings and seed pearls. Arranging a cream-tinted shawl across my shoulders, I leapt down the wagon steps and rushed across to the tiger's pen.

Darius stared at me, emitting a broad yawn before going to sleep again. He was alone in the pen. Where was she? Had she arrived?

I seized the magician's arm as he passed me by. "Sallix! Is she here? Has Erbanhue returned from fetching her?"

Sallix smiled, patting my hand in an unusual burst of morning good-nature. "We expect him back any minute. Her little entourage ought to arrive soon."

I arrayed a brief smile and turned aside. Sallix was a good man on the whole. Therefore it made me rather uncomfortable when the corners of his thoughtful eyes crinkled at me in that way. It was only Aislinn's enchantment that made him think such things. "I shall walk to the station to meet him."

"Be careful, Yasmin."

No need for a witch to worry, I chuckled in my mind. Waving, I trotted away with quick steps.

We would need a proper name for her. Would she really have spotless white fur, beautifully enhancing the streaks of her stripes? And would she truly have a glittering pair of bright blue eyes the shade of robin's eggs?

And what exactly had Erbanhue paid to get her? Surely the sum was nothing short of an outrage. My thoughts redirected to his cluttered yet homely tent... Yes, Reader. He had been hoarding funds – even the coins of his personal supply – for this mad venture.

She was to be delivered from the train today.

I nodded in wordless greeting to passerby on the road. One horseman's cheery salutation caught my ear with its known accents. I stopped to greet Warren Hyram. "What are you about, Lady Witch? And why art thou alone and on foot?" Smiling, Warren reached down to help me ascend the heights of his mount. "Are you certain Dexter won't mind the weight of two?" I asked, arranging my skirts to suit propriety.

"Not in the slightest; he often does it. Where to, madame?"

"The station, please." Warren urged Dexter onward.

The gentle weather of the day could not have been improved if it were custom-ordered. I did not suppress my smile as we cantered through an unending pool of sunshine, a chorus of songbird celebration at every turn. "Who are you meeting from the train?" called Warren, straining to speak to me over his shoulder.

"Ringmaster Erbanhue. He is bringing a new animal from the eight o'clock train."

"A new circus brute? That's news of high interest. Of what species?"

There was a decided thrill in my reply. "A white tiger cub."[1]

A slight pause. "A *what?*" Warren repeated. I laughed at his marked confusion. "A white tiger cub that was caught in India. She's an orphan, and she's going to live with us."

"I've never heard of a *white* tiger before," Warren muttered. "Are you certain your Erbanhue isn't the victim of a dastardly hoax?"

I stiffened, pinching his elbow. "First of all, young man, he is not *my* Erbanhue. Nobody ever said he was... or is... or is *going* to be."

"Of all sad words of tongue or pen, the saddest of all; What might have been!"[2] Warren quoted with glee. I distributed a second pinching.

Warren squirmed in discomfort. "There now, woman! I was merely having a go."

"Have the goodness to descend on some other companion with your nonsense. I haven't the notion to indulge you."

"Why ever not?"

"I am occupied." I revolved another two or three possible names. None seemed to suit. *Pavani. Qiyara. Parul.*

As I considered alternatives, I heard the furious clopping of galloping hooves behind us. Warren and I both turned to look. Lo! Behold Aislinn the Terrible, encouraging her mount to unholy speed, clearly bent upon overtaking us and seeing the tigerling first.

---

1. The first record of the capture of a white tiger was in 1915, when a cub was trapped by a maharaja.

2. *John Greenleaf Whittier, 1856.*

Skirts and scarf fluttered madly. Her heavenly eyes glinted with an appalling elation. "Way for the Witch-Queen of Éire!" Aislinn cried merrily. "Make way for her infamous Majesty!" The passerby shouted their disapprobation, throwing themselves aside to avoid calamity.

Her laughter trailed behind as she passed us. Warren's expression lit with desire, absorbing her flushed, greenleaf, madcap beauty. "An extraordinary woman," he murmured, quite forgetting my overshadowed presence.

"It's no matter. Surely Erbanhue wouldn't let an outsider hold her first!" I comforted myself, sighing. He may know Aislinn upon sight, and he may have commissioned a certain blessing from her some time hence. Yet she was no troupe member. "Sir Erbanhue of lands unknown, if you dare to hand the cub to Aislinn, I shall rain down molten curses upon thy wretched head."

"Calm down, Miss Yasmin! You are scalding my back with your menaces. If you arrive in a rage, it is certain he won't let you touch the cub."

Warren was sometimes capable of sense. I lifted my face to the wind, willing the breeze to cool my reddened cheeks. My hair whipped in tangled clouds around my face and neck. "Surely he *wouldn't!*" I whispered.

I slipped from Dexter in haste, nearly tripping on the hem of my dress. Erbanhue was there. The ringmaster was surrounded by the miniature entourage he had brought to receive our precious treasure. Aislinn stood close to him, talking in low, placating tones. A wooden crate was strapped to the buggy, empty – and something white and black was cradled in Erbanhue's stalwart arms.

"Schöne kleine!"[3] I gasped, stretching out my arms to receive her. Hue turned aside to keep the tiger out of my reach. He shook his head at me. "She's mighty nervous, Yassy. Just as hearty of a vixen as you are. I daren't allow it yet."

"Unsinn! I will calm her." I again made the attempt; Erbanhue held me off. "Stop, Yasmin! Look." Tucking the cub into one arm, he pushed up his shirt sleeve to reveal three long, bleeding gashes. "By the Hindu gods! She has claws of iron. I don't mean to anger you, Yassy," more gently this time, "but she is not to be passed around like a human baby. Understand?"

Quailing at the sight of his torn arm, I took a step back. "I understand, sir."

"Much obliged. Now," Erbanhue marched back to the crate, "I am going to keep her with me until Darius passes on (which, from the look of him, will not be long). I shan't risk putting them together. But that does *not* make her a personal pet, a toy, or a baby-plaything. Is that understood?" (Glaring at everyone present.)

The obedient chorus: "Yes, sir!"

"And no one is to touch her crate without my absolute permission."

"Yes, sir."

"If I fall ill and am unable to feed her, I will designate one person – a single person – who may fulfill that obligation. Am I heard?"

"Yes, sir!"

"Very good." Satisfied, he tucked the cub into its crate, maneuvering with wonderful tenderness. Her pathetic cries, muffled by a black muzzle, tugged at my heart. "I know, little Vainavi," Hue murmured, gingerly

---

3. "Lovely little one!"

petting her head. "But she has died long since. You are with us now. This is your family."

"Vainavi?"[4] I questioned, raising a brow.

"Yes. She is the treasure of my circus." Catching onto the challenge in my voice and demeanor, he rose a mightier brow in turn. "I am her caretaker. *I* have named her."

A pout creased my lips, but I could not protest. After all, she was bought with his own carefully-hoarded coin. "Yes, sir."

He approached me, grinning at my mournful face. "You are an amusing mortal, Yasmin. You could not care less for humankind, yet you fuss like a mother bear over soulless animals."

Wincing from the fresh wounds, he lifted a hand to force my chin upward. "Cheer up, gray witchling. Vainavi shall be enamored with your presence soon enough."

My countenance brightened. "You will let me come to see her?"

"Aye. That I will."

---

4. Hindu name meaning "gold."

Chapter Forty-Three

The Blue Rose Completes Its Work

Later that evening, I waited outside of Erbanhue's tent. "Sir? May I see Vainavi before I retire?"

"If you must," the Dragon decreed.

I pushed aside the tent's wings, moving silently, as one must move in Erbanhue's presence. Before me was painted a pretty, magical, but quite unlawful scene: The ringmaster sat cross-legged on his cot, cradling the mini tigress... and said animal wore neither a leash nor the aforesaid muzzle. "Ah, the almighty rule-maker has turned rule-breaker," I said, placing myself next to him. "How will you regain my respect now?"

He chuckled, careful to be soft and quiet. The velvet rumble of his laugh sent another queer shimmer down my spine. "I never said those rules applied to *me,* Miss Impertinence."

"This is true." I leaned toward the cub, longing mirrored in my eyes. "May I, please?"

"If you move slowly."

I extended my hand for Vainavi to analyze my scent. She wrinkled her tiny black nose. With more speed than my anticipation could master, she stretched out an oversized paw and batted my hand aside. I stifled an outcry, snatching back my hand and cradling it.

The Master smirked. "She tried to bite my ear earlier. High-spirited rascal, is she not?"

"Indeed." I removed my shawl to suppress the bleeding. Erbanhue crouched to place Vainavi in her blanketed crate, hushing her obstinate protests with soothing words. "Sleep now, you troublesome little thing." I watched the pair interact while applying pressure to my wound. Erbanhue stood and stomped past me, re-seating himself and lighting his evening pipe. "While you are here, Yasmin, might I trouble you for some words of womanly wisdom?"

"You may."

"You have heard of the carousel?"

"Yes. Imported via the courtesy of Germans, was it not?"

"Yes; you Germans are fiendishly clever." Erbanhue grinned, serenely expelling a black, scented cloud. "We ought to get one. What do you think?"

"I think the idea has merit." I wondered, not for the first time, precisely how and when I had become Erbanhue's advisor. "It's gaining popularity at carnivals."

"Then it is settled! We shall have one."

"Might I ask how you intend to pay for it?" I gestured toward Vainavi, who was cleaning between each of her toes, blissfully ignorant of the great cost she represented.

"Once I have planned her sensational introduction, we shall reap thrice what we have sown," Erbanhue replied. "People will travel for miles to see a snow-white tiger cub."

"I know." I smiled as she rolled onto her back, now fascinated by the twitching of her own tail. "But that will take time. You spoke with urgency."

"Did I? Perhaps that is how I speak when I am excited."

"You, sir? Excited?"

"You haven't beheld every mask of Erbanhue, Yasmin." And his countenance gleamed, his eyes twinkling with energetic mirth. "I can be just as excited and ambitious as a child."

I regarded him critically, and could not but agree. He launched to his feet, pacing 'round the tent. "My dreams enhance my daily visions with confident fire. I can see them, smell them, taste their overwhelming ash. It is all real *before* it is welcomed into reality." He stretched, his weary muscles straining against white linen.

I averted my eyes. I cast a subtle glimpse toward the withering blue rose, yet undiscovered in the brim of Erbanhue's old hat. Was it possible that it had affected *all* of his dreams somehow? Considering the consuming power of Aislinn's craft, it was not impossible.

"You'll think me mad, I know," he continued, his gaze simmering in a stern, resolute blaze. "But every dream I have had within the past fortnight *has come to pass.*"

I pursed my lips together, unsure of just how much to reveal. "I do not think you are mad, Erbanhue. Many people throughout written history have been granted the gift of prophecy."

"But it is sudden – and so unexplained! I have not had this gift before."

"Perhaps it required time to mature within you."

"Why do you speak so hesitantly? I know you; you understand these matters."

"Not as well as you think. As you so recently reminded me, I am only a mortal."

"You may pose as a mere mortal," Here he ceased his pacing and bent over me, frowning, "But you and I both know you are something more. I know not what. But you are something *else.*"

He was brazenly close. I smelled his sweat, his clothing, every lineament stewed in an otherworldly draconian musk. Even his breath somehow bore a smoking, saffron-tinted trace. He stared into my eyes. Commanding. Despotic.

Cruel. I lightly parted my lips, forcing myself to breathe through my mouth. I desperately wished I could suspend my lungs' operation, crucial as it was. My God, his wonderous *scent.* It was worse than his hypnotic stare. So, *so* much worse. The very blood in my witchling veins cried out for him; my cursed flesh crawled for his embrace. *I am going to hell when I die.*

I could only hope that my face did not betray my raging passion. By some unexplainable miracle, I could still speak. My voice trembled. "To borrow your own indication, Erbanhue, you have not beheld every mask of Yasmin. Despite my sullen, mysterious moods, I am just as human as you are."

"Let us put this declaration to the test."

The ringmaster bent even closer. He touched his lips to mine.

Our contact was fleeting. Mere seconds. I could hardly believe it happened at all. When he withdrew, the only testament to *the kiss* was my heated, embarrassed face.

He examined me with the studious look of a scientist in a lab. "What do you think?" he asked. His eyes snapped with suppressed glee.

Aye, Reader. This was also a game. Would I respond naturally? Would I be overtaken with long-repressed desire? Or would I be outraged and yell and scream, pushing him away and rushing out in a passion of fury?

I yearned to indulge myself in first one reaction, then the other. The tension radiated beneath my skin, fairly splitting me apart. It would be the *mortal* response, Reader, to take either of those routes. His driving curiosity wished to know: Which woman would I be?

I refused to give him the satisfaction. I would be neither. I cooled my face with great calm. I rose from the cot. I bent over him as he had bent over me. "Erbanhue, you shall never know the face behind *this* mask."

A beaming smile overtook the scholarly one. "I thought as much."

You see, Yassy? You are not a normal woman at all.

I left him, allowing the flaps of the tent to close gently behind me. I walked away with the utmost dignity. Once I was safe in my wagon with the door securely locked, I laid across the couch, and... bellowed passionate wrath into my pillow in plaintive English, steadfast German, and curse-breeding Latin.

Reader, I was frightened. I had never learned Latin. Now, entire paragraphs were falling effortlessly from my lips.

"You see, Yassy? You are not a normal woman at all."

Chapter Forty-Four

TEARS, TOYS, AND TREPIDATION

The day dawned insipid and cruel. I burrowed further into my quilt, resisting the morning call. I had not slept. Anger warmed my blood, stirring all manner of chaos in a ceaseless cycle through my brain.

Most unbearable of all was that I knew I *must* maintain control. I could not let this incident disturb my outward appearance. Once more I would act, both on and off the stage. Once more I was called upon to be measured, stoic, and emotionless. "It is the way of things; there is no use for melodrama," the Witch spoke. "Get up! And get to thine chores. Thou art called to higher things."

I obeyed. After scrubbing my face rather more vigorously than was necessary, I dried my hands and dressed. I turned the lock of the wagon door and stepped down. I almost smashed a parcel with the heal of my boot.

It was wrapped in brown paper and tied with a black velvet bow. Puzzled, I stooped and gathered it up, retiring into my wagon to unwrap it.

Another mysterious gift... although not mysterious to me, perhaps. Was it from *Him?*

I unfolded the paper with care. It revealed a wooden box, unlocked, with an ornately-carven lid. I lifted it.

A stern, glass-eyed doll gazed up at me from her bed of crushed tissue paper. It was just the sort of doll that young Yasmin of eld had mournfully (and hopelessly) observed from store windows. Its skin was flawless porcelain. The large eyes were a lifelike chocolate brown, framed by a veritable army of smooth eyelashes. The hair, curled and oiled into shining black ringlets, looked quite real. I cautiously pulled a lock and half-suspected it to be real, human hair. Its dressings were also indicative of quality: Proper stockings, layers of starched petticoats, and even a corset, all overlain in the swaths of a black velvet dress and a white collar.

In short, it was *not* a plaything. It was a highly expensive collector's item crafted of the finest materials. Around its neck was a thin black ribbon bearing the title *Thalia von Britannia.* [1]

She was a startling gift, impressive but odd. First of all, Reader, who on earth knew that I yet admired dolls despite my age? I had not told anyone; why would I? And secondly, who would have had the funds to spare on such a pricey bauble?

I lifted it into my hands. Yes, the beautiful stitchwork, the seed pearls glistening in her cold earlobes, the tiny frills of perfect lace on her sleeves... Thalia von Britannia was a priceless gift. A monstrosity, even.

---

1. A subtle reference to the history of Wicca, which began in England.

As I held her, an intense surge of emotion plowed through my fingers, up my arms, and into my heart and mind. All at once I felt strong, determined, and hopeful – powerful where I was, only minutes ago, powerless – entirely certain, where minutes ago I had been weeping hot tears of anger and pointless disillusionment.

Astonished, I dropped the doll. The impression yet remained, only dulling somewhat from absence of contact.

There was no use doubting it. *That doll* had caused the impression.

"Miss Yasmin?"

Surprised, I tore my gaze from the cold and lifeless Thalia, looking instead into the living, frightened eyes of Mary. "Yes, Mary?"

"Are you... are you feeling all right?" She looked from my (undoubtedly pale) face to the dead face of the doll, already believing wholeheartedly in the doll's possession. I could not fault her for that; it was likely she was not far off the mark. "I'm fine, Mary. I was just... puzzled. I'm not sure who gave this to me. Did you see anyone leave a parcel on my wagon steps?"

"No, indeed!"

"Hmm. Well, it cannot be helped, then."

Nodding, Mary backed ever-so-gently away, her eyes as round as dish plates. I sighed, picking up the doll and placing her on one of my shelves. Again, a thrill of fortitude and power crept along my arm.

"And what, may I ask, is *that?*"

I turned to greet Aislinn, who stood in my doorway with a suspicious expression.

"I do not know." I answered. Frowning, she swept past me and picked up the porcelain she-devil. "It has an aura," she said, turning it thoughtfully in her grasp. "She's a tool of divination. A tool for a witch... particularly," Here she rose a gilt brow at me, "For a witch with scrying abilities."

"Did you make her, Aislinn?"

"No. I work with herbs, not playthings." She replaced Thalia on her shelf. The doll stared with fixed complacence. I felt as if the room no longer belonged to me.

"It must be from *Him,"* Aislinn said.

"Yes. It's from Him."

We regarded the doll with more reverence. Aislinn turned from it to touch my cameo, fastened securely in my collar. "And this? This is also from Him?"

"Yes."

"I see." Distracted, Aislinn smoothed my hair. "Well, it's an unsolvable mystery, how this *thing,"* gesturing toward Thalia, "ended up on your doorstep. Yet there's no denying she has power. Will you use it?"

"I...I don't know."

"Let me be present when you do." She hooked her arm through mine. "It has a decidedly otherworldly presence. And I'm not so sure an inanimate object of her make and mien ought to have such *decision."*

"Agreed!"

Aislinn regarded my dress with a scowl. "Is *that* what you're going to wear to the festival today?"

I blinked in confusion. "Festival? Today?"

Aislinn laughed at me. "My, but your head has been in the clouds these days! Marcus ran all over the grounds yesterday, all but yelling the news. Erbanhue has declared an open festival today, and it shall run far into the night." She grasped my hands and twirled me 'round. "There will be musicians! Dancing! Wine and an abundance of food to eat! You must look your best, my dear."

"Then tell me what to wear, *teuflische kleine Fee!*"[2] I said, breaking free from her wild dances. "I have never attended a festival before."

"Well, dear, suffice it to say that color is a must," she began, surveying my gray garb with a chuckle. "This pitiful gown says 'I am a ghost; I do not wish to be seen, and woe to any man, woman, or child who dares to accost me!'"

I cast a wary glance toward my wardrobe, which boasted mainly of grays, blacks, a little navy or crimson, and some white. "Well, show me what will suffice, then."

"I can manage better. I've been working on these all night!" Darting back outside for a minute, she returned (amidst great huffing and puffing, for the girth of the garments was substantial). She carried two gowns: One of glorious morning-rose pink, sewn across with scenes of blue, gold, and green stitching, portraying pictures of dancing, gaiety, and merrymaking. It was a dress of springtime and gladness. Its sister dress was of bright, shimmering crimson, sewn with a daring design that gave a strong nod to Asian mystery. The incredible scenes depicted a dragon's carnival, with strange and joyful beasts parading through forests and along wooded hills, some of them playing odd instruments. She handed this dress to me.

I inspected it with a critical eye. "It's *very* beautiful, Aislinn. I'm truly impressed."

"Hold it close," she insisted, bringing the fabric to my nose. My senses were immersed in black currant and Indian tea, China asters, and a third musky, smoke-like scent, faintly reminiscent of exotic incense. "How did you accomplish this?" I asked.

---

2. Fiendish little fairy!

The Celtic witch smiled, her lips granting not a word. "Very well, keep your secrets. I suppose we'd better help each other dress."

"Why else would I have come at this hour? Here, turn around."

Aislinn set my hair first, braiding it into a long, free-swinging style, weaving tiny black flowers between the sections of hair. She then helped me into tight snow-white stockings, an under-dress, the corset, and the gown, tying a golden ribbon around my waist. Last, she dressed my feet with an odd pair of pointed, golden slippers trimmed with tiny bells.

I did not like them. "You'll get used to them after a couple of hours," she kept repeating. Reader, I had my doubts.

I helped her next, brushing her hair until it sparked and crackled. She forced me to leave it alone, saying she wished it to "flow as freely as my spirit shall roam today!" (I rolled my eyes at this proclamation.) I helped Aislinn into her own silk stockings, undergarb, and gown, tying a matching pink ribbon around her slender waist and glaring enviously at her pink satin slippers, dressed in tiny (silent!) rosebuds. "I thought you hated this color," she exclaimed, laughing. I shrugged.

"We're as fresh as flowers in May, and young, single, and beautiful," Aislinn remarked. "Mark my words, my dear. This will be a day to remember!"

Chapter Forty-Five

May Day at the Fair of Phantoms

We departed the wagon together. Aislinn had to hurry me along a bit due to my mincing steps; I attempted to dull the noise of the absurd little bells on my shoes. The identical second my friend turned her head, I planned to rip them off.

"A glorious Beltane!" the Celt cried as she greeted the workers. Mary waved to us in great excitement, employed in aiding the design of a brilliant May Pole. Musicians hurried to and fro, absorbed in a grand debate over which platform to play from. Even Darius, who had been winking disinterestedly for months, was wide awake, nostrils flaring from the quantity of meats, pies, and sausages being cooked with frantic haste.

"This is one of Erbanhue's more insane ideas," Sallix complained as we passed him. "A *free* festival! If only he'd agreed to sell tickets. Think of all the money that is lost!"

I rather agreed with him, but Aislinn stuck up her nose at this mercenary spirit. "May Day is *not* about money, Mr. Sallix." Taking me by the hand, she marched us away before he could debate the point.

My ears caught the tune of a violinist warming up. I turned eagerly to observe the band. Despite my natural stoicism, my feet were itching to dance. Here, though, was a question... whom would I dance *with?*

"Yasmin! Yassy, look!" Aislinn, as thrilled as any child, tugged at my hand, pointing toward a small group that was gathering around a solo performer. "That must be Arusi, our new dancer. She's wonderful!"

She was, indeed. Her exquisite cheekbones rivalled Aislinn's sculpted face. Her natural, thick lashes perfectly matched the shade of her eyes, dark with the star-studded depths of midnight. The dancer's braided, blue-black hair reached the soles of her feet, the long locks swaying against her golden skirt. Hoops of gold jewelry encircled her wrists and ankles, clinking as she danced.

The audience applauded as she completed her routine with a difficult backward arch, indicating some training as a contortionist as well. I clapped along with them.

"She's so accomplished! I wonder where Erbanhue ran into some real talent like that?" I overheard one of the workers say. I couldn't help but wonder, myself. First a white tiger. Now this lovely dancer, along with a free festival. Where was Erbanhue acquiring the funds for these enhancements?

Speak of the devil!

Master Erbanhue appeared at my side, smiling at the graceful curtsey of Arusi. "Truly inspiring, isn't she? Soon I'll have a whole retinue of dancers like her. She's the perfect advertisement to our growing success."

"Our success?" I couldn't resist echoing. Erbanhue chuckled, shrugging with casual good-will. "Yes. Our success!"

He looked quite fine in his scarlet ringmaster's coat. As usual, he wore the star-studded top hat, and one hand clenched the snakehead cane, gleaming in tandem with its twin snakehead earring. He flourished his cane and winked at me, belying a careless mood.

I smiled. *You should always wear red, Erbanhue.*

He read my thought. *Only if you enchant all my clothes yourself, sterling witch.*

I rose an eyebrow. We both laughed.

Despite his outward serenity, I knew he cared more about the festival's success than anyone else on the grounds. If it fell even one centimeter below his expectations, he would descend into morose dissatisfaction – This, the weakness of many a determined man.

"I must congratulate you on this decision, sir," I said. "What a crowd we're going to receive! They'll be certain to speak of us to all their family and friends."

"Naturally. And I have a surprise or two in store for our visitors," he claimed, striking a dramatic pose. I grinned. "Vainavi?"

"Vainavi. And another attraction that not even your witchling self knows anything about!"

I gasped. "Do *you* know how to dance, Master Erbanhue?"

Hue threw back his head, laughing heartily. "Excellent! You are in the spirit of the day. As that is the case-"

Tossing his cane to the ground, he imprisoned my cool, tranquil fingers within his torrid, passionate hand. Throwing me headlong into the circle, he did – he really did indeed! – proceed to dance, taking the protesting Yasmin by the hands and whirling her about.

As the ringing of the bells on my feet was a factual fear *and* annoyance, I begged for mercy... To no avail. Erbanhue was as tyrannical as ever. "Cease your protestations and *dance*, girl! Be a normal woman for once in your life!"

"He's right!" Aislinn called. "And I shall join you." Seizing the hands of the (considerably more talented and thus more willing) Arusi, the Celtic faerie joined in the mad fray.

I couldn't help but laugh at myself as I stumbled, again and again, and Erbanhue's bronze arms ever resurrected me. "You're really quite hopeless," Erbanhue crowed as I tripped over his foot. "However, I'm no Lord Fauntleroy myself."

"I should – say – not!" I panted.

He slowed our pace at last, and we watched Aislinn and Arusi weave a hypnotic spell over the audience with their elegant, wild, high-spirited movements. They made an astounding pair. "You know, Yassy. I bet you could dance just like that if you tried," Erbanhue stated.

I smiled, indicating a negative with the subtle drop of my head. His hand left my waist to tilt my chin upward. "Yes, Yasmin. *That* is you." He released his hold and pointed to the twirling, giggling, delighted girls. "That is exactly who you are on the inside."

I studied the double tableaux in perplexity. "If that is your interpretation of Yasmin, then she has recently been made a new creature."

"She has."

He motioned for the music to slow. He led me at a more graceful pace. If I stepped carefully enough, I could avoid the tingling of the tiny bells. I sighed in relief.

Erbanhue heard me sigh and followed my gaze to the pinching, noisy, idiotic shoes. "Just take them off."

"That's not exactly proper," I objected.

The ringmaster chuckled, nodding toward the motely circus crew surrounding us, many of them already unsteady from drinking. "I don't suppose anyone will notice, Miss Prissy. And if they did, it's even less likely they will care."

He had a point. Stealing a final glance at the distracted Aislinn, I sped to the outside of the circle, slipped out of the instruments of torment, and flew back to Erbanhue, who was waiting with a wide, naughty smile. "That's more like it, eh?"

"Ah, freedom!" I breathed, skipping with a dramatic flourish. The Dragon laughed. Eyes aglow, he took hold of waist and hand, leading me around the circle. His gaze betrayed an intriguing battle of emotions – Puzzlement, exhilaration, inspiration, inquiry, and friendliness.

Our gazes remained locked for some minutes. I flushed, wondering if he was thinking about the night before.

Just that morning, I'd every intention of snubbing him for the rest of our born days. And yet...

"You have the face of a man with a thousand questions," I said.

He nodded mysteriously. "I doubt it not. Still... I would rather divine the answers for myself than ask for them."

I tilted my head, smiling my comprehension. "I think I know what you mean, sir."

He touched one of the black flowers in my hair, smiling rather tenderly. Slowly, he brought his lips close to mine and stopped, an impenetrable barrier of restraint solidified between us. He would come no closer. Neither would I.

Draconian mirth glittered in his eyes.

HE KNEW PRECISELY HOW TO TORMENT ME.

AND HE *LOVED* IT.

Chapter Forty-Six

THE FESTIVE EVENING

"Ladies and gentleman!"

I sat hidden in the crowd, trying to put a little distance between myself and Mary. She was wiggling like an anxious cat in a basket.

"Boys and girls!"

The scarlet ringmaster tossed his silken cape, seeming to initiate an explosion of flames. The audience jumped, murmuring astonishment. "The Fair of Phantoms begs your attention for one magical moment." Erbanhue lifted the palm of his gloved hand, blowing glitters of "magic" across the heads of the children in the front. They giggled, reaching up to catch the falling stardust.

"I have summoned you here to witness the unveiling of a very special, very unique, very rare piece of artful wizardry." Drawing out a colored handkerchief, he tossed it in the air; a dove flew out from beneath it. "It is a mechanism crafted solely for the visitors of this fair – for those thirsty souls that crave the eerie, the exhilarating, and the odd."

He clapped his hands together. Ghostly attendants rose at his call, taking hold of the enormous sheet that covered this new attraction. "You shall wait with baited breath no more, my audience!" He called out, gesturing powerfully at the object. "I give you the Phantom Horses!"

His attendants pulled off the covering. A cry of astonished wonder arose.

A magnificent carousel, certainly the likes of which I had neither seen nor heard described, captured all eyes. Thirteen lifelike horses, each in a slightly different stance, hung from a silver revolving roof. Their hooves, also painted silver, burnt brightly in the setting sun. Each steed's bride and saddle was embellished with tassels and flashing jewels, ruby red, orange, emerald green, yellow, navy, and amethyst.

According to rising custom, the lead horse was the grandest, arrayed in gold and bronze paint and highlighted with glitter. By contrast, the last horse was given trappings of pure white and blue gems for eyes, instead of black painted eyes like all the others.

It was a unique piece, rivaling the carousels of the French gardens. I craved to abandon decorum again and rush up to the carousel to see such marvelous craftsmanship at once. However, that would be pushing the boundaries of decency twice in one evening. I kept my seat and contented myself with intense staring.

"Equipped by the latest steam technology, the Phantom Horses will guarantee you the smoothest ride every time without fail!" Erbanhue began to pitch his product. I barely paid attention, once again consumed with bewilderment. Where was all of this *coming from?* It did not make any sense at all.

Unless Erbanhue was involved in some kind of illegal activity, or blackmail. *Perhaps he's a kidnapper, too... of rich folks!*

Perhaps the desperate, conniving Erbanhue of eld was yet alive and well.

Awaiting the end of the pitch, I wondered how he would display our little Vainavi. Some maternal instinct in me despised the idea of her being introduced to strangers, but I knew this was ridiculous. Erbanhue was right. She was to be our reigning animal attraction, and would bring in unheard-of crowds. We were likely to become the most popular carnival in America.

I squelched my qualms, focusing again on the beautiful pale horses, and wondering how much Erbanhue would charge per ride.

I looked at the white horse, the thirteenth horse. Its jeweled eyes sparkled in the sunset. Behind the carousel, standing in line with this snow-white beast, stood a little girl.

She was soberly arrayed in a black dress with a white collar. Her long black curls fell across her petite, insipid face. Although at a significant distance from me, I could see her dark eyes trained onto the last horse as well. She saw me. Immediately turning her back, she slipped away without making the slightest of sounds.

"Did you see her? That little girl?" I asked, nudging Mary.

"See who, Miss Yasmin?" Mary asked, annoyed that I was turning her attention from the magnificent horses. "That little girl over there," I answered, pointing to where she had been standing.

"No, I was looking at the pretty horses."

The festival lasted well after midnight. At last, the audience departed in anticipation of the rising sun. Besides the occasional attempt at pick-pocketry and other minor annoyances, it had been an entire success.

A (mildly drunk and entirely shirtless) Erbanhue sat cross-legged in his tent, humming to Vainavi and congratulating her performance at an unwarranted level of volume. "That's-a my good little gal! What a princess! She behaved spec-tacular-lee! She didn't make any fuss! What a precious!" And other assorted nonsense poured from his lips as he cuddled and caressed her.

I stood silent at the threshold, waiting for my chance to finally hold the tigerling myself. Now was as good a time as any. Better, most likely.

"She's my little snow-white daughter!" Hue's absurd declarations continued. I closed in on my prey. "Give her to me, Erbanhue. You do not know which way is up at the moment."

"I most certainly do!" After a brief pause, he slowly pointed sideways, roaring with laughter. "Ah, Yassy, didn't you know - aren't you aware, sterling witch – that the world is *round?* There is no 'up' or 'down' when you're on a ball. It's either *inward,* or *outward.*" He distributed this mighty maxim with several prolific gestures.

"If you say so." Moving with great care, I got my arms around Vainavi and, little by little, extracted her from his grasp. "Be gentle with the precious," he insisted.

"'The precious' should be in much more careful hands than yours are at present, sir."

"Ha! You believe I am drunk. Confound it, girl! I'm as stober as the day is long."

"I'll believe it with all my heart if you will keep quiet." For the setting was all too familiar, Reader: A flushed, joking, cackling Erbanhue, who was quite likely to tease me about my poor little feelings for him. By God! If he started that again, or tried to kiss me, I'd run straight away with Vainavi in tow.

"Oh no, oh no! The Witch's claws are out. I'll be quiet." Erbanhue fumbled across the cot for his pipe, finally lighting it after multiple inefficacious attempts. "We mustn't disturb Her Majesty."

Although I had stroked Darius before, I yet marveled at the odd, straw-like texture of the tiger's fur. She tried to launch herself off my lap. I held onto her firmly, giggling as Vainavi squealed in protest. "Yes, you are very cute, my love. But you mustn't run wild throughout the camp."

"Try singing to her," The ringmaster mumbled, his own eyes already half-shut. "She likes it."

"Thought you didn't like my voice, sir," I answered, in some bitterness of spirit. Erbanhue shrugged. "Don't s'pose it matters right now."

I sang Erbanhue's song, *My Lady's Galleon*, in a low voice. The ringmaster stretched out on his cot, puffing his pipe with decreasing frequency until at last it fell from his lips. I pounced up to put it out before a fire resulted. "Men," I sighed, addressing myself to Vainavi. "They can be so remarkably careless."

She chuffed to me, her blue eyes placidly winking. Erbanhue snored. I gazed at him for a long time, then finally stood to crate the cub, afterwards covering Hue with his blanket.

I smoothed one hand over his handsome, flushed face. *Dream well, ringmaster.*

Chapter Forty-Seven

A Messenger

As predicted, both our miniature tigress and our carousel were pulling in crowds from many miles away. Even adults paid to ride the Phantom Horses, for the steam-powered mechanism was quite novel to many. I indulged in a ride or two myself when prying eyes were not watching. My favorite horse was the white one, shining like a star even at nighttime, when all was abandoned, dark, and silent.

Upon hearing my description of one such "night ride," Aislinn begged for one as well. I could not easily refuse her request when I was the primary transgressor.

We rode it together, stifling our laughter and delight, skipping about from horse to horse and making up silly songs to mimic the chorus of the circus organ. Of course, lights would come on, and people would stagger out of their tents to capture the night-riding culprits. Aislinn and I, deftly lifting the white skirts of our night-dresses, ran away as fleetly as woodland deer. We were never caught.

On one such night, I fled with her back to my wagon, swiftly closing and locking the door behind us. We caught our breath, giggling at each other, our hair wildly windblown, our bare feet splattered with dirt and crushed leaves. I poured the water left from my pitcher into the wooden tub. We sat on the edge to soak our feet.

"Have you tried scrying with her yet?" Aislinn was looking at Thalia, who glowered at us from her lonely shelf. I sighed. "No. As preposterous as it sounds, I think I am rather afraid of her."

"There is no shame in that! I fear that thing myself." Aislinn swirled her delicate feet in the shallow water. "Still, she was gifted to you for a reason. We ought to see what she can do."

I shuddered. "Please, don't talk about that doll as if it was a person! It lifts the hair on the back of my neck."

Aislinn chuckled. "My apologies." Our feet twirled in rhythmic dances in the water, brushing each other, then floating away. "We could try it tonight."

"Oh. Do you really think we ought?"

"We're alone. It's the dead of night. There's hardly any chance of interruption. I couldn't think of a better time to do it."

Sighing again, I lifted my feet from the water and dried them. "Let us put this nasty business behind us, then."

While Aislinn dried her feet, I took my ebony scrying bowl and filled it halfway with clean water. I withdrew my iron thorn from its hiding place and pricked my finger. The blood hit the surface, spilling into a perfect oval. "Hand Thalia to me," I directed Aislinn. She took the doll from the shelf and passed her into my hands.

I gripped the doll, staring into the motionless blood mirror.

The same sensation – a thrilling feeling of power and certainty – flooded my being. Aislinn drew in a sharp breath. I think she could sense it, too.

But her next words frightened me.

"Someone has just entered the room," Aislinn whispered.

My body stiffened in shock. I had never seen Aislinn so terrified before. Her lovely, soft countenance had gone completely white. "What?" I stammered.

"Someone else is in this room!"

I did not want to look. My neck strained tightly to keep me from looking. Suddenly, two tiny white hands covered mine. I shrieked.

"Do not be afraid."

The voice was childish, polite, but somehow anemic. It fell cold and hard against my ears. This was an empty, voided voice... a voice without a soul propelling its words. I leapt backward, my chair crashing to the floor. "Who is speaking?" I cried.

"My name is Thalia."

Horrified, I was staring fixedly at the floor. I forced my stiffened neck to bend upward. Yes, Reader, it was the girl at the unveiling of the Phantom Horses. It was the black-haired girl behind the carousel.

"There is no need to fear me. I am here to help you."

Gulping in a breath of air, I gathered my wits to speak. "Then... it's true. It is true that you are an instrument of divination."

"Yes. And more besides." She cocked her head slowly, as if faintly amused by our reactions. I say *faintly,* because I don't believe those pale, thin lips ever responded to amusement since the day they were born. "You require encouragement. I am here to encourage you."

"You were sent to me?"

"That is my purpose."

"... Oh." (What else was there to say?)

The raven-haired child would have looked ordinary if not for her awful paleness and the dark wells of her eyes. One could not determine where her pupils' boundaries ended, and where the irises began. Her countenance was one of the most unchildlike patience I had ever beheld in so petite a face: I could term it a *deathly* calm. Nothing ever swayed or perturbed her... probably because she did not care for anything.

"Shall we begin our work?" She asked, gravely pointing to my scrying bowl.

Aislinn, who had been driven purely by fear to the farthest corner of the room, resumed her seat. I righted my chair and sat down, looking once more into the blood mirror. "Yes, Thalia. We shall begin."

The child motioned for the doll, still firmly clenched in my grasp. I drew in a shagged breath and pried my fingers loose. I gave Thalia to Thalia (what a strange phrase to write!) and watched as the child cradled the toy, bowing her head and closing her eyes as if engaged in fledgling prayer. "Do not speak now. Only watch the mirror," Thalia said.

The blood mirror began to bubble in a hideous way. I had to turn aside for a moment to control the tightening of my stomach. Aislinn also wretched and turned her head away, disgusted. Fascination and curiosity mastered our wills, however, and we gathered the strength to look again.

"Kheima!" I gasped, clutching the tablecloth in amazement.

Outlined in the blood mirror was a portrait of the Demongod's realm. The silent, pale blue snowflakes yet fell. The strange throne-creature of painted moonstone eyes sat in exactly the same position, as if it had never moved. And the image of Rothadamas, winged and full of glory, caused the blood mirror to steam and bubble as lava might.

Aislinn and I lunged away as the hot blood splattered across the table, staining the cloth. Some of it landed on the child Thalia's dress and hands. She did not move... did not even raise her head from its humble attitude of prayer.

The bubbling subsided. There was nothing but a little water left in the bowl. "It is finished." Thalia opened her eyes and lifted her head.

"Was that... was that the realm you spoke of?" Aislinn asked me, her hands still shaking. Calmer now, I went to her and pulled her into a warm embrace. "It's all right, Aislinn. This is a sign of His favor. He is not displeased with us."

"Of course. I know that. It was merely... unpleasant." Aislinn gently broke the hug, addressing the child instead. "Did you come to us from that place?"

"Yes. I am surprised that you feel the need to ask."

"Well!" Aislinn broke into sarcastic laughter. "This is all just a little stranger than I expected."

"I have an odd question of my own," I said. "Are you a doll, or a person? Which is your true form?"

"A legitimate question, Yassy. That I cannot tell you, for I do not know myself."

I cringed when that soulless voice uttered my cherished nickname. "I would prefer that you call me Yasmin, if you don't mind. Or Anmut."

"Very well. It matters not to me."

As if sensing that we were too shocked for further interaction, Thalia turned on her heel to depart. On her way out, she stood on tip-toe to place the doll on the shelf. "I will come when requested," she said. And she tripped away. Her form went straight through the wall as if she were a ghost!

As Aislinn was far too frightened to return to her cabin until daylight, we made a sleepover of what remained of the night. There was very little sleeping involved. "Obedience is onerous once His blessings seem like discipline," Aislinn whispered. I could only agree.

Chapter Forty-Eight

Kadov and the Coven

"Mary?"

Again, no reply.

"Mary? Where have you gone?"

Thus my cry for the past half-hour. I frowned and threw my coat over my bare form, wondering where my dressing assistant had gone. I had sent her out to fetch more of Aislinn's herbs, and she had not returned.

I slipped into a pair of shoes and left the wagon, keen on beginning an official inquiry of the workers on the grounds. No one had seen her. I ventured to Aislinn's cabin.

The Celt's crown of hair glistened in the high morning sun. She was packing freshly-turned earth into a new plot for a garden, and singing.

"Has Mary come to see you this morning?" I asked, interrupting her chorus. She tweaked my ear in greeting. "I have not seen her, *mo chara.* Did you desire more herbs for your bath? I've been working on a new blend."

My frame of mind was reallocated by the design of the Celt's new plot. It was a perfect circle of red-brown earth, with an even five-pointed star in the center. Having completed the outline, she was now employed in the gentle disengagement of her precious herbs, planting them in a new and meticulous pattern comprehended only by herself. "That's beautiful, Aislinn. What does the symbol mean?"

"The five points of the star represent the perfect measure of nature, spirit, and energy," she replied, tenderly planting an array of blue leaves into the design. "The circle represents infinity." [1]

I crouched to examine the plot further. "But how did you learn about it, Aislinn? Who is your teacher?"

Aislinn sighed, raising from her crouched position and chafing the dirt from her hands. "Mind you, dear, the details of my craft are sworn secrets. But I daresay you will have secrets of your own soon enough. Come to me, Kadov."

I heard the flutter of wings. From among the tree-tops flew a white, slate, and dark gray raptor, with a fluffy white breast and striking eyes of dark orange. As it was small in size, it landed on my friend's shoulder with relative ease, its predatory claws finding purchase in the heavy shawl

---

1. The Pentacle became a symbol of infinite energy and a balanced earth with latter-day Wiccans. In some sects, it is used during magical evocations. Technically, this concept used in Wicca began in the early 1900s, not the late 1800s as described here.

Aislinn wore. "This is my familiar," She said to me, lovingly stroking his feathers. "Is he not beautiful?"

"Where did he come from?" I asked, longing to stroke those beautiful feathers also, but not certain he'd condescend to such treatment from a stranger.

"He was sent to me, along with a message from the Mistress."

My eyes widened with surprise. "Who is the Mistress? And why haven't you mentioned her before?"

"We are strictly forbidden from discussing her unless it is necessary," the Celt replied, bending once more to tend her plants. "As I believe it's become now... You never quite seemed to believe me, Yassy, but I spoke the truth when I said that my craft is actually most intuitive. However, certain recipes and instructions are conveyed by this means," she pointed to Kadov, "And once he brought me a tiny booklet of incantations. Sometimes he'll go away in the night and return with a small roll of paper in his claws. It contains instructions from someone who calls herself the Head Mistress."

Excitement outgrew bewilderment. "Then there *is* a learned witch in our region! Surely you've attempted to seek her out?"

Aislinn laughed, rising and patting me on the cheek, leaving upon it a baptismal smear of dirt. "You dear girl! I wouldn't dare to attempt such a thing, and neither should *you*. I'm certain it would offend the Mistress enormously."

"But why?" My voice was a little gruff, perhaps. I never did grow out of my dislike for being "spoken down to."

"If she wanted to be found, don't you suppose she would have left instructions for doing so? I believe she intends to remain anonymous. After all, both of us boast a strong and unique power, and witches are not marked for their loyalty to one another. We may develop an antipathy and turn our witchcraft against one another. Though that is impossible with *us,"* she finished, smiling warmly as she rubbed the dirt from my cheek.

I fought the cringe that begged to manifest through my countenance. Never before, Reader, had either of us openly given claim to performing witchcraft, still decreed by most as a dark and evil practice. There was a certain formality to labeling the powers we possessed. I did not like it.

"Why have I not been contacted?" I asked. "Have I displeased the Head Mistress in some way?" What exactly was expected from me?

Aislinn saw the disappointment and frustration I tried to mask. She dropped her trowel and passed an arm about my shoulders; Kadov glided away to a nearby tree.

"You know more than you realize, Yassy. That has made you what they call a 'late bloomer.' When once you begin your rise to knowledge and fame, you will doubtless eclipse us all... But the Mistress must have felt you were not yet ready for the coven initiation."

"But *you* were." I could not erase the envy in my tone. Aislinn Bláthnaid possessed surpassing intelligence, loveliness, and refinement. Must her gifts in the coven best mine, as well? I loved her to distraction, as Heaven and Earth may testify, but the facts could not be ignored; I was ever her inferior.

"As I have said, your powers are maleficent and strange. Mine are far humbler, but by that same virtue, also more easily learned and managed. There is a predetermined formula that I can follow." She stooped near a flowerpot and snatched up a booklet, waving it beneath my nose. Its pages were tattered and well-worn. "These are all related notes from other witches. Divine herbology is a more common talent than we supposed."

"How many others are in this coven?" I probed. "Or am I barred from that knowledge?"

My friend tapped her chin thoughtfully. "Well, I was never instructed not to tell you *that.* It was merely put forth that this is my path, and mine alone. To cast the secrets of my craft abroad would deaden its meaning and ultimately weaken the strength of my spells. So it is said."

I sat on a rock, my face stubbornly frowning. "Then tell me all you can."

The lost Mary was quite forgotten.

Chapter Forty-Nine

A Hierarchy of Witches

Aislinn sat beside me, armed with a sharp stick as a scribing tool. She made a lovely scribe indeed, her slender form bending o'er the sweet-smelling earth as it yielded its fruit to her with great gladness. My heart smote me for my envious thoughts. I repented of them at once (to no one in particular).

"We believe our calling descends from this being whom you have termed Rothadamas," the magnificent Celt began, forming His name in the earth with quick strokes. "He grants a chosen few certain powers, for reasons yet unknown to us. The first of these witches or warlocks - and the most learned, given time - establishes their craft and can sense the presence of other bearers of power, in the same way that you and I were drawn to each other."

She drew a vertical slash beneath His name, writing "Head Mistress" beneath it. "There is no lore for our particular hierarchy to follow. But it is a natural course to take; the elder witch aids the younger in whichever manner she prefers. Our current mistress seems to favor anonymity, as least for now. Not that I mind," she added, "as I cherish our independence."

"Are there any head masters of the covens?" I queried. "Do you know of warlocks in our midst?"

"I do not. But I only know for certain of myself, you, and the Mistress. It is possible we have yet to meet others."

"So this Mistress somehow sensed or observed you developing your craft. Then she sent you this familiar?"

"Yes. As protection, and also as a means of communication between us. It is... difficult... to explain," She paused, "But Kadov is no mere bird of prey. When one looks into his eyes, one can see a soul trapped within them. He represents a higher intelligence. I daresay it is human. Or perhaps *was* human."

"Can the Mistress tell us about Kheima? Has she mentioned any personal knowledge of the Demongod?"

"No. That subject has never arisen. If I were to venture a guess, I'd say that she knows no more about our origin of power than we know. In fact, you might know the most among the three of us. You've truly been *inside* His realm, yes?"

"For a short time. It may have been no more than a dream."

"But Thalia aided you in scrying the location. It *is* a real place... Wherever it may be."

"And Rothadamas is a tangible being."

Silence descended as we struggled to process that statement. A quiet skirmish – a brief echo of memory – and then, nothing. Kheima was a million miles away in that emerald-green clearing of garden sunshine, a veritable faerie princess at my elbow who dazzled the eyes in butter-yellow silk. I plucked a flaxen rose and tucked it into her hair.

Aislinn leaned her head against my shoulder. "As you now practice sangemancy well, and can invoke curses with more directness of intent, I expect your initiation will happen soon."

"How can I prepare?"

Her hand clasped mine. "There is no way to prepare for it. You just do the best you can."

"Oh," I said, not liking her sudden shift from confidence to nervousness. "Can you tell me what happened during yours?"

She closed her eyes, burying her face in my shoulder. "No. I imagine it will be different for you, anyway."

"What do you mean by *different?*"

Aislinn sighed and raised her head, her butterfly lashes cast downward to kiss her cheeks. "You have great strength, Yasmin. A strength I shall never comprehend nor achieve. You'll do far better than I was able to do. I am... I am jealous of your abilities."

Another moment of silence, and then laughter – *my* laughter. "My dearest Aislinn! *I* am envious of *you.*"

"Gracious! Whatever for?" She cried, blushing and laughing with me. "All I can do is grow things. You can see the past, the present, *and* the future. You can cast down your enemies without detection. And you alone have been led into the realm of Kheima. You have been given marked gifts of His blessing and preference. I envy you! You are favored by the Demongod. I shouldn't wonder if even the Mistress was intimidated by you!"

I moved my optics heavenward, deploying an unladylike snort. *"Gifts,* saith thee? I suppose the cameo was nice enough, but it's just jewelry. And Thalia von Britannia... Well, any human who terms her a nice *gift* ought to have their head examined."

We embraced one another in our mirth, each recalling our naked fear of a porcelain doll. "Furthermore," I followed up, "You are as breathtaking as a statue of a goddess, and could make anyone in the world follow you into the bowels of Hades, even to pluck you a clover you wanted. You sing, and plants come to life. You dance, and every eye is gladdened, every heart uplifted. Men worship the ground you tread on. You are daring, ruthless, and cunning, yet you are also gentle and sweet and lively. You embody the wild beauty and the delicate balance of nature." I paused, wincing at the contrast. "I represent its darkness, its chaos, and its death. The shadow behind the light."

As I spoke this, I realized with a shudder *why* I was thus favored by the Demongod of the Corrupt Wood. I was formed in His image. The doleful impress of the truth wrung a disconsolate sigh from my throat.

Throughout my little homily, Aislinn's flowering smile lessened. By its end, her grin had withered to an empty furrow. A single tear escaped the corner of one seafoam-blue eye.

She threw her arms 'round me and cried on my shoulder. "You are my dearest, *mo chara!* We are closer in spirit than sisters of flesh and blood. Do not ever make the mistake of thinking you are alone, Yassy. I will always stand by you."

As I comforted her and dried her tears, I gained another insight into the designs of Rothadamas. The deaths of those around me whom I loved had torn from me my support as well as my solace. He wanted me to become strong. He *forced* me to stand alone, whether I wanted to or not.

Erbanhue's prophetic murmur tormented me from afar. *"You see, Yassy? You are not a normal woman at all. No mere mortal, nor a kindly spirit, nor an angelic saint. You are a sterling she-devil."*

Well, then. Perhaps there were *two* people who appreciated me for what I was.

Chapter Fifty

Vainavi Leads the Way

One week later, I completed my business at the scrying table. Tucking the booklet of basic incantations into the folds of my purple dress, I considered returning it to Aislinn that night.

However, I knew that part of the discipline of her craft required her absolute confinement on nights with a full moon. It was such a night... She would be devoted to the practice. It would be unseemly of me to disturb her work.

I forced my weary eyes in the general direction of the possessed doll. According to Aislinn, I should also be studying on full-moon nights.

I'd received naught from the Mistress. As perusing Latin texts had done nothing but turn my stupid head round in utter confusion, *that* was no help. Thalia was the only medium left. But I did not want to touch *that*. Resolved to play the truant, I abandoned the booklet beneath my pillow and slipped outside to taste the night air.

The big top, carousel, and menagerie tents glowed blueish-white beneath the icy chorus of moon and stars. A handful of Erbanhue's performers smoked and chatted in a circle, trading stories of various trials by fire. Sallix was teaching himself a new card trick. Janet Willow and Brinna Sable were taking a turn on the grounds, likely gossiping about the latest peacock feather hat. Every lady who was "in society" had some variation of this particular hat. I myself had neither the funds nor the inclination to buy every hat that stormed the market.

I skimmed the circumference of the group, my gaze on lookout for one noteworthy set of bronze draconian appendages, heavily tattooed. I scouted for the moody moustache, the snakehead cane, and the flash of buckled, gritty boots.

Tell it not in Gath, I wanted Erbanhue.

Notwithstanding my resolve to be quite cool though friendly with him, I had been avoiding his presence when I could. On May Day I was in my element. Such festivals were frolicsome, cordial, and crafted to celebrate the peculiarities of human nature; I was not disadvantaged there.

But on a working afternoon as he surveyed my craft, my articulation, or my routines, I could *not* bear to feel his stare fixed upon me. I rushed through everything now, darting into shadows and behind convenient corners to avoid his heterochromatic study.

Yet, loneliness compelled me to seek him forthwith. Aislinn was too busy for me, and Mary had vanished from the grounds and n'ere returned. The Dragon may be slipshod, perilous company, but he was better than no company at all.

Anyway (I thought this with a private laugh), if Erbanhue was like a dragon, then was I not like a dragon-tamer? Could I, a mature woman of twenty-six, not deal with his smoke-ridden slights by this time?

It was then that I heard the chuffing squeal indicative of Vainavi's presence. I walked nearer to the outlying woods. There was darling Navi, and following her prances at the end of the black leash, was the Dragon himself.

He trudged after his charge with a face of tranquil forbearance. For once he was pipeless, caneless, *and* hatless, and the passing breeze ruffled his black-mahogany locks. His merry voice alternated between whistling and talking to Navi, instructing her to inspect this tree or that plant.

I smiled at the charming picture. I called out to him, "The lowly Witch Anmut seeks an audience with the Dragon King!"

Erbanhue turned his head. His eyes flashed. "She shall be heard. Send her forward!"

I glided obediently to his side. Hue liked this demeanor; he beamed upon me with amiable fondness. "To what does the Dragon King owe this unexpected pleasure?"

Ah, Reader. What a paradox! I cannot for the world describe to satisfaction the sheer span and profundity of the kindness that burned in his bearing, his eyes, and his rich curving smile. He was the best company under Heaven when he was in humor. If only he were always so, I'd have proposed to him on the instant.

Instead, I settled for briefly stroking the Dragon's scaled muzzle, taming him with persuasive though stark politeness. "I wished to inquire into the state of our mercenary affairs," I replied with suave cheer. "How is Erbanhue's Fair of Phantoms fairing in this fair season?"

"The Fair's fortunes multiply fairly in such fair weather," the Dragon King replied, not hesitating an instant. "Our majesty expects to provide increasingly sumptuous fare to the members of his phantom lands, as fair recompense for their labors."

"We are delighted to hear this fair and wondrous report," I answered, endeavoring with some trouble to maintain a sober countenance.

Erbanhue failed first. He laughed, and I laughed also. "What, Yassy! You are in high spirits tonight. I guess you have killed off another of you mortal enemies, hmm? Cooked him in a cauldron with an eye of newt, eh?"

"Certainly not, sir. That demise is explicitly reserved for you."

"Ah! Cannibal! Sinner of sinners! Lady of trouble and doom! I doubt it not, Anmut. Only make my expiration quick. On the double, an it please ye, thou sterling witch."

"Cannibal? You provoke and disgust me. I plan to serve you *à la carte* to Vainavi."

"In that case, I shall die to greater purpose. Very well! I house an abundance of well-seasoned meat; she needn't feast again until next winter, I am sure."

"Oh, dear King! I imagine you would require a great deal of chewing."

"Oh, dear Witch! Your imaginings are correct."

My heart swelled with pleasure and delight. I dared to do a thing which I had not previously believed to be wise. In the meek fashion of a Janet Willow, I tucked my arm intimately around his, letting my bare hand rest on his wrist. It was yet in proper taste, Reader - a common pose for a gentleman escorting a lady - but Hue was not a gentleman, and Yasmin Lange was not a lady.

The ringmaster darted a look from the corner of his eye... a light, subtle searching. I exhaled with inaudible relief. He was not offended, merely intrigued.

"How Vainavi has grown!" I exclaimed, wishing to put him further at ease. "That is how both animal and human children find a strong commonality. We have just a little time with them - just a brief season - and they no longer require us."

"'Tis true," he answered, regarding the cub thoughtfully. "It seems only yesterday she was - Woah, there, little one! Where are you taking us?"

For naughty Navi had lunged in pursuit of some undetectable scent. Before Erbanhue could rally her, she cornered a patch of furry creatureness, half-buried among the brush. The ringmaster scooped up the tigerling to distribute spirited reprimands.

I bent low to examine the animal. A young cross fox shivered in the bushes. It lifted its pitiful orange eyes, pouring its frightened soul into mine.

We locked gazes. I reached out for the vixen. She allowed me to gather her limp form into my arms, submissive as a kitten.

Erbanhue watched in stunned silence. I gave her a name. "I'll call her Adalhaidis." [1]

I nodded goodnight to Erbanhue and left without another word, intent upon warming the kit in the safety of the gypsy wagon.

---

1. German name meaning "noble appearance."

Chapter Fifty-One

Another Disappearance

From the first, my Adel was shy and elusive of every breathing thing except for myself. I kept her tucked in the lowered hood of my cape. She liked to see and inspect everything. Much like Kadov, my familiar had bizarre eyes, human in their intelligence and as brilliant as citrine.

Her marvelous cross-coloring, tinting fur as soft as gossamer webs, was a source of keen pride. At least, Adel seemed to think so! She groomed it on a most fastidious schedule. Every morning I wakened to the sight of her curled against the windowsill, grooming in the sunlight, yawning in my general direction as if to ask "Why dost thou lie abed at this hour, thou sluggard?"

And I would gather her into my arms - not without the puerile phraseology and unmeted praise reserved for pets - and stroke her as I gazed out the window, contemplating the day ahead.

As our open festival on May Day was an overwhelming success, carnival holidays were in fashion. Erbanhue (if troupe gossip could be credited) was already planning a summer jubilee. Such news thrilled me with anticipation. Truth be told, it was only on such occasions that I was able to shake off fear and painful memories, and dance in the shoes of quite another person.

Still musing, I fastened my cape and secured Adel into her place of honor. I would go and inquire about this rumored fete.

As I advanced toward the ringmaster's tent, I saw him gathered before it with Sallix, Marcus, and a few other members including Janet Willow. Her large brunette eyes were full of fear and worry as she wrung her hands in feminine distress. I quickened my gait.

"Has there been some trouble?" I asked, stopping at Erbanhue's elbow and directing my question to him. He glanced down at me and folded his arms. "I'm afraid so. Have you seen Mary at all in the past fortnight?"

"No. No one has, sir."

"Are you privy to the rumors of *where* she was last seen?"

I shook my head.

Hue pursed his lips together, probing my countenance. "Brinna saw her stealing a ride on the carousel late in the evening. Since Mary was your attendant, Brinna assumed that she'd obtained your permission."

"No... no! I had no idea. I asked her to fetch some herbs for me. She never returned."

"Herbs from your witchling friend, Aislinn?"

"Yes."

"Hmm." Erbanhue stared at me a minute longer, then addressed Sallix. "And this distressing plea from the parents of a-" He paused to snatch a paper from his vest pocket, glaring over its words, "A little boy named Harry Brunswick. You're telling me that this is *not* the first complaint of its kind?" He threw the letter on the ground, firing his malicious glare at the magician. Sallix (a brave man deserving admiration) glared right back. "No, sir. This makes the second case. And Mary is the third, though she was one of us and not a visitor."

"Children are going missing?" I asked.

All eyes turned to me... every pair of them displaying, at varying degrees, some level of distrust. As Janet spoke her voice quaked with superstitious fear. "The children who ride the carousel alone are never seen again."

I sensed their rising suspicion. Even Erbanhue continued to peruse me with a wary grimace. I reacted badly. "That is not so incredible," I replied. "Children are lost in such gatherings when they slip away from their parents."

"But someone *must* have heard them!" Janet objected, continuing to wring her hands in the most provoking attitude. "Someone must have seen them."

"Or just taken them," answered Sallix.

"Perhaps," Janet agreed in a hushed tone. I looked her in the eyes. She quickly fastened them to the ground.

"And what superstitions have *you* to add?" I asked. Janet's eyes struggled to raise themselves. They flickered to my face, then back to the grass again. "The white horse is cursed, Yasmin."

By *the white horse,* I knew she meant the thirteenth horse on the carousel, the glorious pale one with eyes like gemstones. "That horse is the same as all the others besides its paint," I replied. "Sheer mobile decoration. What nonsense has gotten into your head? Do you accuse it of coming to life and galloping children away?"

"That is a fairy tale fit for the Brothers Grimm," Erbanhue concurred. "But it is not to be denied that such missives," kicking at the letter on the ground, "Such tidings as these will blacken my Fair of Phantoms. Then shall progress investigation – Police – Lawyers – Charges! I will *not* permit it. That carousel is to be guarded at all hours. Organize yourselves and take turns. Is that clear?"

All present indicated their assent. The company departed; that is, all but Janet Willow, who turned aside to Erbanhue and whispered at his ear, touching his arm to stand on tip-toe.

Not in the best of moods, the Witch uttered a groan. Adel dispensed a snarl in response. I scratched her head to soothe her.

"There is no proof in the matter," I heard his lowered voice rumble. "Nevertheless, it is well thought of. I will consider it."

Janet beamed and hugged his arm with thankful warmth. I turned away, quite incapable of digesting the scene with dignity.

"'Tis a pity there is not much variety amongst womenkind," I remarked to Adel as I commenced our daily walk. "A lovelorn woman will take any distressing circumstance and intensify her panic. She then proceeds to lavish her velvet weight upon the arm of the man she hopes to ensnare. Ha! Shield me from such paltry missions and degrading weakness!"

I sat on a log, frowning, plucking at strands of grass and decapitating daisies. Adel was digging among the leaves with enthusiasm. At my sour remarks she ceased, tilted her head, trotted into my lap and nuzzled my cheek.

I laughed, wiping away the cold wetness from her nose. "I see you are not above the same method, little trickster!" She crawled about on my dress, snuffling in its folds. I placed a cheery kiss on her head. "Only a few days with you, and I hardly know how I survived this life otherwise."

Chapter Fifty-Two

REMORSE AND REVELATION

It was no accident that Adel was sent to me at that time. Over the next few weeks, I felt less certain of myself than I ever did in my life. I would pass Erbanhue's tent and either hear or see him speaking *tête-à-tête* with Janet. Her low giggles tarnished my brain with malevolent red stains.

And yet I could not blame Erbanhue *entirely*. When I at last forced myself to consider the matter with sense, I realized that Janet Willow was just the sort of girl to appeal to a man of his wild caliber. Opposites attract, so they say. She was pretty – no one could deny that. She was cheerful, trusting, and sensitive – other commendable points for a man who led a boisterous life. Her company presaged charm and tranquility, and the proud comments and statements of a Dragon impressed her.

She was also well versed in the feminine art of deploying those sort of gentle, compassionate glances that lift a man's soul. It was a special look that I was never able to imitate in my life, even if someone were to hold a gun to my head.

In other words, common flirtation was beyond my scope.

"Well, I suppose I am rid of his impudence at last." I addressed Adel. She squinted at me mournfully through the ring of soap bubbles; she did not like bath day. "It is something of a shock. Here he's demanded 'quality' and 'intelligence' time and time again, just to end up preferring *her!* But it does not surprise anyone else, I daresay; it all comes down to opportunity and demographics. Still... If I were to guess who he'd finally lose his black heart to, I would have imagined Aislinn to be the unknowing thief."

Adel shook herself. Water and soap flew through the air, and I laughed and pushed up my wet sleeves. "However," I continued, speaking at last the thrice-denied truth in my heart, "Is this not the way of the world? What man would unite his fortune with that of an acclaimed witch? He would have to be a warlock himself to disregard both his reputation and his soul. And after all... after all..."

I hesitated a long instant before admitting my fault. "This yearning is unhealthy. I have long wondered," scrubbing away at Adel's fur, "I have long wondered why I cannot seem to maintain control over my powers. They are as slippery as eels! Is it not possible – in fact, is it not *certain* – that my thoughts of him detract from my true pursuit in life? Fool that I am!"

Having rinsed her thoroughly, I lifted the fox from the tub and cuddled her despite her drenched state. "Of *course* my dreaming discontent would keep me from pinpointing the secrets of my craft. Do you not think so, darling?" I kissed her.

Adel sneezed, again pleading with her eyes that I abandon my scheme of torment. Reaching for a towel, I wrapped it round her and rubbed her dry. "It is high time I brought my fascination to a close," I declared, cradling Adel and rocking her as if she were a baby. "Aislinn is an exemplary witch's pupil; should I not follow her lead? *She* is not pining away for some imaginary future beau. In fact, quite the reverse! I never witnessed a woman so happy in single blessedness. She is always singing and dancing and working away in her garden, radiant as can be."

I giggled at the memory of her wild festival dance, when Aislinn caught hands with the exotic performer Arusi and twirled with her around the May Pole. "I believe Erbanhue was right," I assented, releasing Adel from her blanketed prison. "He pointed to those lovely, wild women of nature, and he said to me 'That *is* you, Yasmin,' knowing somehow that I have been given that strange, rapturous freedom. I only hesitate to act. Well, if I cannot make him happy, I can at least make him proud."

A cold, childlike voice stalled my speech mid-breath. "You fluctuate madly from one idea to the other," it said. "You are contradicting yourself even now by immediately returning your thoughts to *him.*"

I flinched in astonishment. There was the spirit-child Thalia, crouching in the corner, soberly straightening the black curls of the doll with a doll's hairbrush. "I thought you only came when I called for you," I said, not at all appreciating this intrusion.

She rose, clutching her porcelain doppelgänger. "That has not happened for many weeks. You render my service most dull." Bestowing a quiet, affectionless kiss on the doll's cheek, she replaced it on the shelf. "So I decided to tell you something."

"What have you to say?" I sighed, resigning myself to her marble gaze.

"I was created precisely for you, Yasmin Lange. If you do not use me, I will become the lifeless doll you supposed me to be. I would appear no more."

I spoke before I thought. "Would that not be a relief to us both? It is plain that you find no joy in your work."

"Heed your words," she warned, lifting a tiny forefinger. "I was bought with a great and terrible price. Rothadamas would be most displeased if I was neglected."

"What *was* the price?" I instantly regretted my question.

"Rothadamas is proficient in executing His will," Thalia said, "but He cannot create life from nothing. Existing souls must be manipulated – reformed – to beget new ones. Understand? A sacrifice was made, one that even He was hesitant to extract."

My flesh crawled with misgivings. "Was it a human soul?"

Reader, what terrible creature stood before me? A child perfect in form and in dress, every curl in place, lashes long and lustrous, boots free from even a particle of dust. Her starched collar avowed a puritanical life of its own. She was the most faultless – I daresay *sinless* – of all children on the earth. And yet... that made me terrified of her.

I vastly preferred the company of the playful, romping Lillias, whose frocks were endlessly torn and rumpled, and who snorted when she laughed aloud, her sharp eyes gleaming with mischief.

"It was a human soul," Thalia answered. "One child, beloved of Rothadamas. Do not treat His offering with scorn, Yasmin. All gifts descend from a prior source."

I nodded and extended my hands for hers. She gave them a blank stare. "I can't touch you."

"Oh... Well, I am ready. What have you to teach me?"

The tiniest of smiles grew on her face. I glanced away. It would take time to accustom myself to her dreadful expressions.

Chapter Fifty-Three

DARK MAGIC

Thalia's system of instruction was short, smart, and resolute. To my surprise, she also demonstrated a wealth of patience pleasant to behold. "Your spirit is caustic, cold, and wild," Thalia told me. "Therefore, your craft remains without a clear direction. You mask your own intentions from yourself. You must learn the art of meditation, of flushing out impure distractions and never bowing to the worldly view of yourself. You see, I am saying that the Yasmin Lange you *know*, is not the Yasmin Lange that you *are.*"

She liked showmanship. A glimmering interest in my circus career betrayed itself one night during our meditative exercise. I told her I would show her the grounds.

"Here," I wrapped her into a forgotten cloak of Mary's. "It would not do to have you be seen right off. People might ask questions."

Thalia peeped at me. Her dark eyes glinted from beneath the hood, a touch of childlike mischief sitting on the corners of her mouth. "You may tell them that I am your long-lost daughter."

"How amusing."

"Why not?"

"There is not one molecule of resemblance, my dear."

Thalia frowned. She despised terms of endearment. She shrugged off the cloak, letting it pile onto the floorboards. "There is no need. *You* can see me – any witch could – but to anyone else, I am invisible."

I studied Thalia's waxlike face. "Are you *excited?*"

"I like to go out," Thalia announced, marching her soundless boots out the wagon door. "You never take me out, Yassy."

"I asked you to *please* not call me that."

"You used to like it."

I hesitated at the threshold, staring at her. "That nickname did not originate from you, so how did you-" I caught myself in time. "Nevermind. An increase in wisdom is an increase in sorrow."

"You allow it from Erbanhue. And Aislinn."

"She is my friend. And he is my employer. So long as he pays me my portion, he may call me anything he likes."

"Old hag! Chilly gray witchling!" Thalia sang, mocking Erbanhue's flattering manner of speaking. I tried to push her out the door, but my hand passed through her.

We marched into the humid evening. I navigated past the carnival folk with great care. Erbanhue was smoking and chatting with Sallix. Janet stood at his side, though a little distant from him, with a secret and steady frown shimmering in her wide doe's eyes. I wondered if they'd argued again.

I felt Thalia's persistent tug on my sleeve. *"Waerloga! Waerloga!"* she whispered, and a crackling giggle escaped her pale lips.

I bent to hear her clearly. "What is it? What is that word?"

"A warlock!" Thalia laughed again – a radically unpleasant sound – and pointed...

At Erbanhue.

My bewildered eyes studied the accused. Master Erbanhue was staring... no, not at Yasmin... but at the pale, giggling spirit-child at her side.

He could see Thalia.

I whirled back toward the wagon, hastening as quickly as I could without running. I slammed the door behind us. "What does this mean?" I fiercely whispered, reaching for Thalia's shoulders (and again passing through her). I clenched my fists in annoyance.

"He's been marked by Rothadamas, same as you and me," Thalia sweetly explained. She tossed her dark curls. "Why did we come back? I wanted to talk to him and see what *his* powers are."

Motioning for her to lower her voice, I locked the door. "He can hear you, too?" She tilted her head, smiled, and nodded.

I trembled with shock and anger. "Did you already know? Tell me everything, child. What is he capable of? Does he know what *I* am?"

Thalia scowled and stamped her tiny foot. "You never let me out! I know nothing in the world about him except for what you've told me. So there!"

"Thalia, it is *crucial* that I understand this situation before you depart. Now. Attend to me!" I pointed to my vanity stool, indicating for her to sit. "He can see you *and* hear you?"

Thalia nodded again.

"He is marked by the Demongod?"

Nod the third.

"And he has powers?"

"It is reasonable to assume he does."

"If I let you talk to him, could you tell me what those powers are?"

"I can."

"Excellent. Now, do you think he is aware of these powers and from whence they come?"

"Judging from the rate of incidents in his *brilliant* Fair of Phantoms," she said (with unmasked irreverence for his vanity), "He must know he lives and breathes beneath an ill-fated star. Perhaps he is a clairvoyant."

"And... the children?"

"What children?" Thalia echoed, all innocence.

I dearly wanted to shake her. "The children! The children that have gone missing! Mary. Harry Brunswick. Did *Erbanhue* take them? Is he responsible?"

Thalia shrank from the force of my voice. "It's too early. I'm not supposed to share that information yet!"

"I am your mistress. Without my service to Him, you would not exist. *Tell me!*"

Thalia stared into the vanity mirror and heaved a long sigh. She toyed with a lock of her hair, stalling, but she finally submitted to my glares. "Yes. Erbanhue took them, but not *all* of them. You've had your share of the lion's hunt, though I daresay you were both unconscious. There! May Rothadamas forgive me, but I have spoken the truth. You are his beloved hunter and huntress, pursuing fresh souls."

I couldn't believe her. I couldn't move.

My very eardrums pulsed with rushing, crushing blood, propelled by the beating of my black heart.

I rushed to the vanity, seizing the cameo and rereading the inscription. *Anmut, the Lioness of Kheima.*

Though Thalia's sable eyes followed every motion, her icy lips yielded not another word.

Chapter Fifty-Four

We See Through a Glass, Darkly

An infernal tapping menaced my wagon door. I hurriedly wiped my eyes, attempting to raise my mournful countenance with a smile. "I'm here. One moment, if you please."

Thalia shrank into the stool, thrusting glares in my general direction with no small munitions. Ignoring her, I unlocked the door and swung it ajar.

"Good evening," Erbanhue stated, poking his nose into the chamber in search of surplus humans. "I wanted to meet your diminutive visitor. Is she in?"

Upon hearing his booming voice, Thalia immediately flew from her seat and observed him from behind my skirts. The childish impulse amused me despite my vexation. "How do you do, sir?" She curtsied.

"I am well, thank you, young lady. And how do *you* do?" Erbanhue administered one of his deep, flourishing bows, summoning Thalia's eerie giggle. One could almost see the uncanny sound bristling like sparks of lightening from her mouth. I suppressed a shudder. "Hue, this is Thalia. She is... an orphan that keeps me company sometimes, in Mary's stead. We met when she came to have her fortune told."

I'd never told Erbanhue such a bold-faced lie before. I did *not* like it.

Smirking, Erbanhue mounted the wagon steps and strode inside. His muscular bulk instantly shrank the room like a bottle of Drink Me. He offered his massive hand to Thalia. "No, thank you," she declined, smiling as politely as she could. "I don't like to shake hands."

The ringmaster chuckled, tucking his hands into his pockets. "Rather precocious, this one. Wherever did you find this miniature witch, Yassy? Custom order? Hellish brew? *Essence de Satan?*"

Yet his easy words were belied by his glinting Italian eyes, roaming over her in a halting, confused manner. No wonder! From her solemn doll-like face to her ghostly air of knowledge; from her mature deployment of speech to her sudden childish motions: All and sundry collided in her tiny, pristine personhood.

Erbanhue's draconian eloquence resumed. "Beware of fledgling witches, Yasmin, for their damnable glory is but trebled in their compact packaging. From what land dost thou hail, witchling?"

"From Kheima," Thalia replied. (I would have pinched her if I could.) Worse yet: "But you've been there before, sir."

Fear and rage surged within me at her bluntness. Hue's careless response quelled the storm. "Sharp as a tack! And quick to hail from imaginary lands! I shan't preach against it, as it suits her. Anmut, from what field did you glean this superb impedimenta?"

I had no answer to give that would satisfy. Thalia, not a whit disturbed, broke into a little faerie romp 'round the ringmaster to distract him. "You are a great storyteller, Master Hue! So Yasmin says. Oh, won't you please tell *me* a story, sir?"

Hue smiled. He would fain have swept her into the air on one colossal arm, but she dodged him. My face quite reddened from anxiety. "It must be past your bedtime, tiny imp. But since we are newly acquainted, I suppose a short one…?" He glanced at me. I bit my lip and assented.

The ringmaster sat on the couch. He beckoned for Thalia to enthrone herself upon his knee, but this of course she could not do. She sat at his feet. Strangely enough, contentment and affection radiated from her spiritless black eyes… Two sentiments, by the way, that were never for one second bestowed upon *me*. Erbanhue was, however, the foremost of storytellers, as I've doubtless wearied my reader by asserting; I was not to be robbed of listening also.

As he monologued to his heart's content, I watched the subtle play of emotions between them. Erbanhue was in first-rate form, modulating his voice to suit the rising and descending plotline. Thalia increased his confidence with her wide eyes and delighted smile. In my mind, a low yet insistent voice described the similarities between the two. Thalia instantly adapted to his demeanor and drama of expression. Something about their eyes, as well…

He clapped his hands together once, solidifying a shocking event; Thalia mimicked the movement and momentum a few minutes later, smiling just as he had smiled. *How curious,* I pondered.

The story concluded. "Sleep well, mini witch," Erbanhue murmured, yielding a fatherlike smile. After telling her that she must be good and get plenty of rest, he swept past me, menacing my ear with a tweak. "Yasmin, I must speak with you a minute." I followed in mute submission. Once we were outside he shut the door, crossed his arms, and stared at me.

A *warlock*. I no longer knew him. I couldn't guess what he might say or do. I was afraid of him, Reader, really and truly afraid of him for the first time in my life.

"I saw it when she mimicked me by clapping her hands," Erbanhue began. "It's small, but dark." He raised his mammothine paw and turned it palm-down, tracing a circle just above his wrist. "Did you notice it?"

"No, sir. Do you mean a birthmark? Or a scar?"

"A scar, I believe. In this *exact* shape..." He grasped his shirt buttons and unfastened them. (I mechanically averted my eyes). "Look, Yasmin. Is it not like my own scar?"

I restored my gaze. On his chest, merging with the dragon tattoo above the region of his heart, was a scar identical to my own. A circle with an *X* through it. "Do you know what this mark means?" he asked.

Reader, I had noticed it before, last time I'd seen him shirtless – but I hadn't allowed myself to dwell on *that.* I was... distracted. My lips parted to drop the declaration *"I don't know."* Erbanhue's stern, fiery gaze penetrated my defenses. The wall came rumbling down – crashing – wholly demolished, it dissolved into dust.

"It is the mark of the Demongod, Rothadamas by name. He grants skills of witchcraft to a chosen few in exchange for their loyalty. They are his hunters and huntresses, seeking prey in the night, bringing Him young souls to provide energy and to be reborn as His demented creations."

A long silence.

Wind stirred the loose hair framing my downcast face. This was the moment I'd been dreading since Thalia's abrupt revelation: He would laugh and label me a madwoman, and lock me up directly in a lunatic asylum.

"Rothadamas," Hue repeated, rolling the strange demonic name across his tongue with disconcerting ease. "I dreamt of a demon called the Wrath of Adam. Alas, I paid it no heed." He sighed, passing a hand through his hair. "And these young souls that He takes... or more truthfully, that *we* take... He changes some of them into... into...?" He waited for me to finish.

"He is attracted by the ironic and the extreme. He enjoys creating living, breathing oxymorons. Take Thalia, for example. His smallest and slightest of children is also one of the most gifted of all His servants."

"But why her?" Erbanhue whispered, passing his hand over his eyes. "Why? Why did he take *her?* Oh, God of ages, her *eyes!* The way she lit up the moment I entered the room. She was like... I can't say." He turned from me, blinking away the rising liquid in his eyes.

"Erbanhue, I *must* ask it, as cold as it makes me seem. You just met Thalia. Why are you reacting with so much emotion? It's not like you, sir... all due respect." Ordinarily, flagrant curiosity would eradicate concern. He'd scratch down all the facts and theories on his fine mental clipboard, elicit prophetic proclamations, then promptly close the frontal flap; *the final word* was his.

The ringmaster nudged my hand off his arm. Rage tightened the muscles throughout his body, culminating in his balled fists. "That strange little beast is... She's *my Lillias.*"

"*Your* Lillias?" Mingled disbelief and anguish descended. "Your Lillias, Erbanhue? She was yours?"

"Yes, she was... she *is* mine! By God, I will claim her now, though I was too much of a coward to do so while she lived. Lillias Vosquez is my daughter."

"Then you had a wife?" I gaped, at last able to credit the gossip that enclosed him in our younger days.

"No. She was not my wife." Subdued, Erbanhue crouched to sit on the wagon steps. He linked his fingers together. "Maria Vosquez was my mistress. I visited her whenever I could, but the traveling... *You* understand. Our relationship was sporadic at best."

"Couldn't have been otherwise, sir." I sat next to him. "And she bore you a child?"

"Yes. But several years passed before I claimed her, even solely to myself. Lillias endeared me to her with such mischievous sweetness. Although she favored her mother in looks, her eyes echoed mine, and something in her character was similar too. She was playful, roguish, and fond of showmanship. Thrilled by the performance. I had my doubts at times, but Maria's claim rings true. Lillias *is* my daughter."

"How did she come to work in your circus?"

"Her mother threw me off for another fellow. (No surprise to me, really.) Prior to then, she'd refused to let me see Lillias, even in the character of a 'family friend.' I complied. I could not add to the trials of my flesh and blood by declaring myself her father... A wretched, poor, immigrant scum failing miserably in his poverty-ridden circus."

My brows rose. The profound irony of life never ceased to amaze me. I expected a flaming, damning, self-righteous warlock; instead, Erbanhue rested his mighty head in his mighty hands, doleful repentance and abject humility sitting on each mighty shoulder. "You never failed, sir," I reassured him. "'Twas your circumstances that failed *you.*"

"Well, I thank you... And I don't believe you, you silver-tongued witch. Anyway," his supple mouth rose in a halfhearted smile, "For a time I resigned myself to Maria's wishes. I believed it benefited Lillias (at least in the eyes of society). But Maria abandoned her for her man, leaving her in the care of a doddering old nurse who could barely hear or walk, let alone provide for her victuals and clothing. I had to come and fetch her, harsh as I knew her life would be."

"She loved her work, Erbanhue. She was never happier than when performing as your star equestrienne. And she liked you. Indeed, I don't see how she could help it! For someone who claims to despise children, you're quite natural with them."

"Yes, she seldom complained. I was so delighted with her at times, paternal pride fairly leaked from my chest. I feared they would see it. To hell with *my* reputation – I don't care for it one whit – but I'd see myself hanged before hers was ruined." His fingers traced his scar. "So, I led everyone to assume she was just another parentless urchin I'd taken in to make money with. Like yourself," he added with a half-smile.

"Much obliged to you, sir."

He laughed, as I knew he would. "Why your taciturn, sarcastic dryness does me good to hear, I've never comprehended." He grazed his hand against mine.

"Listen, Erbanhue. I, too, have learned and done many things too late... and here is another mistake of mine, perhaps. But it is not – not quite too late – Only, you must discern that for yourself."

"What is it?"

"I *do* respect you, sir. I admire you with all my heart. Your rise to fame delighted me, even past my envy. I've not said so because I feared such praise would make me weak in your eyes. Yet, above everyone else... Far more than anyone else I know, Erbanhue... I desire *your* commendation. The whole universe could sing in my honor for a decade, but without your voice leading the chorus..."

My ringmaster's tan face burned hotter every second. "What nonsense!" He hesitated, then cradled my head against his shoulder and stroked my hair. "Just sit still like this a moment, Yassy. I'll recover in haste."

"And repent at leisure," I saucily added. He chuckled and briefly kissed the top of my head.

Chapter Fifty-Five

The Coven of Healing

Manifold revelations consumed my mind that night, encasing my thoughts in swirling, multicolored fires. *Now* I interpreted every gesture of his, as clearly as midday... Every charismatic, enunciated word... The beckoning motion of his subtle forefinger... The dark magic creasing his wicked gypsy's grin. *Of course, you simpleton!* thought I, twisting myself in the couch coverings, wincing with every recollection. He is a warlock. He is the master of charm and enchantment. Did you not see it with your naked eyes, day after day, year after year? Fool that you are!

One question yet remained. Did Aislinn know?

Did her elusive coven know? That coven remained closed to me, for I had received neither an invitation nor even a whisper of acknowledgement from any source. I'd gotten my familiar – for that I could be thankful – but it seemed to me that the Head Mistress executed the bare minimum of her station where I was concerned, content to lavish her attention upon Aislinn. (I couldn't really blame her, Reader. I'd have done the same.)

Disquietude racked my feelings. I reached beyond the couch and called for Adel. Rising from her pillowed slumber, she trotted to my side. I gathered her in my arms, happily burying my nose into her sweet, rich fur, which retained the scent of maple candy and autumn wind. I stroked her as she settled. "Aislinn *must* know," I murmured to Adel. "She is, by each and every account, a truly gifted witch."

Adel, unimpressed by this declaration, stretched her legs luxuriously.

"Perhaps my instability is the reason I'm excluded."

My familiar glanced into my eyes, blinking her citrine irids softly. "You're right, Adel. Patience is among the most priceless of virtues... but in my case, it lost its charm long ago. I'd better go see Aislinn."

Adel inclined her sleek head in regal assent. She jumped from the couch and pattered to the door, scratching at it. I smiled. "I need to change first, darling."

Aislinn's cottage shimmered with verdant creeping vines. The quarter moon provided plenteous light for my Adel. I tracked her closely, whispering encouraging words as we traveled. Her eyes glowed in nocturnal delight.

Low, musical chanting reached my ears. Adel ceased her trek, listening, listening, her long ears flickering toward the haunting sound. I picked her up. Creeping among the brush, I watched and waited to see what I might learn from this midnight incantation.

Aislinn sparkled in the partial moonlight. Her pearlescent skin and golden hair mimicked the stars above. I admired her graceful motions as she raised and lowered her arms.

My attention was detained by the second figure. It was tall and slender, wrapped in a heavy silk robe of deep maroon. A dark waterfall of hair tumbled from the crown of her head and down her shoulders, past her waist, reaching her bare ankles dressed with anklets of gold. This silken cascade arrested me for a good minute, for never was the verse more appropriately brought to mind: "If a woman hath abundant hair, it is a glory to her." It was raven, thick, and waved, tinged in the moonlight with oceanic blue. Quite rich and so regal! I was convinced from the heart that neither jewels, nor delicate crowns, nor beaded headdresses could add to her beauty.

I looked at her face. Exotic eyes flashed darkly in the night, turning regularly from Aislinn's face to the floral pentagram growing between them. Her lips were full, her nose delicately rounded, and the mysterious eyes were full of a gleaming light that rivaled the glimmer of her golden earrings. The stranger's long, slender fingers wielded fans of golden lace, and she moved them in silent, swift motions.

"Hush, Adel!" I whispered, for my eager familiar was stirred by this mythical performance and yearning to run to them both.

"You are welcome to join us, Yasmin."

The low speaking voice was quiet but most effective. I started, losing my hold on Adel. She slipped from my fingers and darted to the red-robed stranger. I came after Adel, but she evaded me, trotting from one witch to the other in rapturous displays of affection. I sighed, accepting the situation for the moment. "Aislinn I know, of course," I began, nodding briefly to my friend, "but of you, miss, I know nothing. Are you the Head Mistress of the coven?"

"I am." Stepping closer, the witch deftly removed her red hood. "That is to say, I am a Mistress of one certain coven, one that is most unique. And you *do* know me, you see."

Despite the dim lighting, her features were now exposed in the light of familiarity. It was the exotic dancer, Arusi, whom I clearly recalled from the May Day festival.

"I'm pleased to be formally introduced," I said, curtseying to her. "I apologize for my intrusion, but since I'm here, I have many questions."

"We shall hear them; we cannot promise to answer."

Arusi motioned for Aislinn and I to sit near her. Adel returned to my lap, amusing herself by snuffling among my skirt's folds as I spoke. "There are two matters in particular," I commenced. "My first question regards my training under the spirit child, Thalia. She believes I have progressed well in the control and management of hexing, as well as my talent of sangemancy. With the greatest respect..." I paused, rather uncomfortable beneath Arusi's predatory gaze, "With the greatest respect, Head Mistress, I wonder why you have not undertaken to train me yourself? As you instruct Aislinn."

"You are not ready." Arusi's eyes never wavered. I caught myself wondering if she ever blinked at all.

I shifted, pretending to be distracted by Adel's movements. "Yet it has been several months. Would it be prudent to know... Must I inquire directly what I am lacking?"

A dry wind rattled the waving vegetation. Arusi did not answer. "You contacted Aislinn almost directly," I dared to add.

"I will not speak to you (nor anyone else) of my pupil's progress. That is not for others to know."

"But why am I treated with indifference? I do not mean to sound rude or ungrateful. I'm grateful to you for sending Adel. But I don't understand why I am barred from further assistance. As I destroy (Aislinn's powers create and improve), I believe I am in dire need of guidance, far more so than her."

Aislinn's gilt brows lifted, but she kept her own counsel. Arusi nodded. "You have great powers indeed, Yasmin Lange. But they are not appropriate to initiate into my coven. They are beyond me, if I might make a full confession."

"Not *appropriate?*" I pursed my lips, incensed. "They were gifted to me by Rothadamas Himself. Is He not the source of this coven? You are merely the steward!"

"There you are mistaken, Yasmin. This coven is mine and mine alone. I am its only master." Her wolflike eyes menaced mine. "My initiates study the preservation and celebration of life, of nature, and of healing. Your *gifts,*" said with some asperity, "do not fall beneath these categories. You are a witch of death."

A witch of death. I pondered her statement. I accepted it, then savored it. "Yes. Though you speak with acrimony, you speak the truth. I am a witch of death, darkness, and chaos." Empowered yet humiliated, I rose. "Thank you for your time, Head Mistress. I shall no longer disturb you. Goodnight to you both." I departed, calling Adel to my side.

Chapter Fifty-Six

A Witch and a Warlock

"Yasmin?"

"I'm up here, Hue. What is it?"

I sprang from my perch on the high rope, untying my head scarf and shaking my locks free. "It astonishes me that you are *interrupting* my practice, instead of barking at me to 'Cease thine procrastination, woman, and slave away!'" I chuckled, more to myself than at him; Erbanhue seemed downcast.

"I've had another dream. The sort I can't quite shake."

"Have you?" I crimsoned in spite of my efforts to control it. I'd confessed about the blue rose some nights ago. It was an unpleasant altercation, Reader. But I had tired of any secrecy between us. "Any roses in your immediate vicinity?" I asked halfheartedly.

"Ah-*haa-haa-ha,* Yassy. I've yet to be convinced your little sapphire toy did anything to me at all."

Postscript the second: He absolutely, unequivocally refused to allow that the enchanted rose had influenced him in any way, not even to kiss me. (*"So there, you gray witchling, you unendurable hag, etc. etc.!"*)

Implication being, of course, that he really, truly, in sober earnest, *wanted* to kiss me. I wasn't sure which testament was worse.

Hue took my hand and drew me into a shadowed alcove. "I fear this is far more unpleasant than enchanted roses."

"They are not *always* unpleasant, sir. Have you not read 'La Belle et la Bête?'" [1]

"Pshaw! Woman, I have no time to read romantic fairy tales. I should be surprised at *you* doing such a thing, you hard-hearted, unromantic personage!"

"Gracious! I see you're in no mood for humor, sir. You'd best tell me what transpired in this dream of yours." I tucked my arm into his with a confiding air. Such sisterly actions, I had since discovered, served to calm him. It seemed Janet wasn't *entirely* clueless. "Tell me."

I felt his stern arm relax a little. "I was walking through a strange winter wood," Hue murmured, brows furrowed and eyes chained to the ground. "The snow was a pale blue color. And the ice... all the ice around my feet was a translucent black."

Kheima. "Did you see any children there?" I asked.

"Don't interrupt me, Yassy. It was a silent, eerie place. There were trees everywhere. Vines of thorns wrapped around their trunks, tangling in their branches... and children...Yes." He coughed, turning a sickly pale shade,

---

1. *Beauty and the Beast, originally published in 1740.*

"Children were trapped beneath the vines, secured to the trees. But they didn't seem frightened, or hurt, or even upset about it. They were quiet... *so quiet!* I thought they were dead."

I shuddered. To witness the bravest man you ever knew become deathly pale was horrible in and of itself. "One of the tree's vines began to move," Hue said, crossing his arms. "The child was slowly released. It didn't run away. It just walked over to this giant silver basin, guarded by four enormous, hooved beasts."

"Hooved beasts?"

"They were strange creatures to me; that's the best I can do."

"Go on, please."

"The child tried to climb into the basin, but it was so exhausted, it fell to the ground instead. One of the beasts moved to help it. The child was dropped in... and then..." The Dragon grew a shade paler. "That beast – that monster! – held the child under boiling water until it was drowned!"

I was not prepared for such a repulsive end. I stumbled away from him, clutching at my stomach, for now *I* felt ill. "Oh, Hue... how terrible!"

"That is not the end," Hue continued, grimacing. "The child was resurrected. It rose again from the basin, white as salt and with large, brooding eyes. It looked like a completely different child altogether. It looked much like Thalia."

"You've seen how the spirit children are born," I answered softly, looking up from where I crouched on the grass. "You have seen Kheima."

"Kheima? Didn't Thalia say... *Oh.*"

I reached into my pocket, playing with the sapphire cameo I kept with me at all times. "I've been there before. But, Erbanhue, are you *certain* beyond any shadow of doubt that Thalia is Lillias?"

The ringmaster scowled. "You don't think I'd instantly recognize my own flesh and blood? My *only* flesh and blood? And I've long believed in the supernatural. I thought perhaps she was only a ghost. *Only a ghost!*" Despite our mutual horror, he laughed at himself. "I'd gladly exchange demons for ghosts."

I nodded. A soundless, hopeless tear dripped down my cheek. Further piqued by my sorrow, Erbanhue ushered me to my feet and dried my face. "Something must be done, Yasmin."

I blinked. "What are you saying?"

"Something must be done! Rothadamas must be stopped."

I grasped Hue's sleeve. "We *can't,* Erbanhue! We've been marked by Him. He oversees our every move – when we are awake – when we are unconscious. We can do nothing."

"You've never tried it," Hue growled, his mustache curling like the whiskers of a furious lion. "*I* will help them!" So declaring, he cast off his coat and vest, rolling up the sleeves of his linen shirt. "That demon will rue the day he made Sergio Erbanhue Vincenzo a warlock."

"Wait, Hue! Please. We need to have a plan."

"We?" he snorted.

"Yes, *we.* I'm going with you."

"You'd better not, Yasmin. This is a man's job. After all," he chuckled darkly, "I am something of a devil in my own line."

"But what about Thalia?"

"What about her? I'm saving her first."

"Or you'll be killed in the attempt – or worse, turned into something else. What will she do without anyone to care for her? You're her father! You must keep safe for her sake. I will go."

"And what will you do?" Erbanhue sneered, his prior savagery resurfacing. "You can't even control your own powers!"

"Neither can you, sir!" I blurted.

Blank surprise crossed his face. He'd been walking away; he walked back to me. "Of course I can!"

"Was it your intention to enchant *me,* sir?"

"Enchant *you?* I… You think I enchanted…" Hue looked me up and down, taking in my silver silk dress and the five-pointed star nestled against my throat. "No. Why would I want to do that?"

"Because I was willful - sometimes quite unmanageable - and that is a trait you particularly dislike. You cast an enchantment onto me so I would be enamored with you and follow you wherever you went, no matter how cruel you were to me."

Reader, I had suspected it for some time. Erbanhue, like me, could but rarely control the direction of his craft. Subconscious whim alone was enough to nudge a mythical concoction toward its unsuspecting target. And I, believing my fondness for Erbanhue to be natural, stupidly recycled the inclination again and again!

Well, that would no longer be a pitfall for Yasmin Lange. She would not bear that cross anymore.

Erbanhue uttered a short, dry laugh. "You're a witch. Witches only succumb *when they want to."* Having dealt his blow, he turned his back to me.

"Are you leaving?"

"I am." He stopped, turned halfway, then walked away faster. "Goodbye, Yasmin."

I did not see Erbanhue for several days. I yearned to seek him out, but he'd wounded my pride. It wouldn't let me.

It gradually dawned on me that I knew his real name at last.

SERGIO VINCENZO.

Chapter Fifty-Seven

Aislinn Comes

As my pride was also wholesomely crushed by Arusi's refusal to accept me as her initiate, it was difficult for me to seek Aislinn out, either. She was the "gem of the craft," a beautiful and accomplished witch who knew her talents and followed the Head Mistress as religiously as any Christian followed her Bible. I, however, disliked the thought of narrowing witchcraft down to a religious order with a hierarchy, rules, and regulations.

"You don't know for sure if there *are* rules," Thalia decreed in reply to my complaints. "You don't know anything about the Coven of Healing."

"You would not say so if you had been there," I asserted. "If you were with me you'd know it, too."

The spirit child sighed. "Just when I think you're developing some measure of sense, you start jumping to conclusions again." Thalia removed herself from the stool, dragging her dollish facsimile with her. "Well, I do know Arusi a little; she ventured into Kheima before I was sent to you.

And you would do yourself a favor by keeping your distance. She doesn't really like you."

"What a surprise," I dryly answered. "I received only the warmest of feelings from her burning eyes."

"Don't misunderstand me. She respects you, or rather respects your craft. She thinks you're the most powerful of the four of you. But as she said, your talents do not fit her mold nor appeal to her taste. You are anathema to a coven of healing naturalists."

"Yes, I'm well aware of – Wait. You said four just now."

"To our understanding, there are four High Proxies to the Demongod. Arusi, Aislinn, you, and now Erbanhue, as it turns out. How funny!" She dissolved into a fit of humorless giggles.

"What is so amusing, Thalia?"

"I've spent the last forty-eight hours trying to imagine Erbanhue as a mighty warlock. It certainly gives me trouble." She laughed again, soundlessly this time, and curled up on my couch to snuggle her doll. "I thought you liked him," I said, nonplussed. *For all his faults, he* is *your father!*

"Oh, I do, I do! I like him better every time I see him. Still, he's so very full of himself. It's hard to imagine him doing anything real."

"What do you mean by *real?*"

"I refer to what the other three of you can do. Healing, potions, hexes, sangemancy. He experiences prophetic dreams, 'tis true. And he can cast charms on people and bend them to his will. But that is child's play. A baby witch can accomplish such things!"

"He will learn more and become stronger," I challenged her, frowning in her general direction. "And who told you that you could sleep on my couch, little imp?"

"That's what Hue calls me. Little imp! Little imp!" she sang, dancing away from me and stopping at my scrying table. "Let's see what he's up to. Why hasn't he stopped to visit you, by-the-by? Did you quarrel with him?"

"I'm sure he's fine. He's indulging himself with sulking, and probably flirting with the hapless Janet Willow."

"She's under his spell too, Yassy. You might consider securing your compassion for the poor woman."

Somehow, Reader, this had never occurred to me. Instant guilt supervened. "Well, then, let's see how the mighty warlock is doing." I had just seated myself with the scrying bowl when Aislinn floated into the room.

"Oh, Aislinn! What a fright you gave me. You didn't knock."

Aislinn folded her hands in a supplicating gesture. "I feared you would not let me in, Yasmin. You're angry with me."

"Angry? No! Why would you suppose it?"

"I *know* you are, dear. But I won't let it linger, for I've come to give apologies." She offered a filigree-handled bouquet of daisies so snowy and bright, they shimmered in the sun.

"Oh... thank you, Aislinn." I clipped the handle to the waist of my gown. "What have you to say?"

"Must *she* be present?" Aislinn (who never learned to like Thalia) pointed to the spirit child, who was slinking about from corner to corner and hissing in imitation of a feral cat. "Go and amuse yourself out of doors," I told her, lifting my forefinger in mild reprimand. Thalia hissed again and vanished, taking her doll with her.

"I simply cannot think with that child around." Aislinn sat across from me, motioning toward my scrying bowl. "First, I'm sorry that I interrupted your work."

"I was only doing it to amuse Thalia." I flushed, pushing the bowl aside. "She's been very... outspoken lately."

"She's always been that way, Yassy," Aislinn sighed, casting her eyes heavenward. "I do wonder why you indulge that *thing.*"

I stiffened. "I have my reasons."

Aislinn tossed her hands into the air. "You are quite impossible! But for the sake of our friendship, I will press on." She leaned forward and took hold of my hand. "Yasmin Lange, I am truly sorry I didn't explain more about the Head Mistress. I knew she had no plans to incorporate you... At least no immediate plans, but... I was at a loss how to tell you. I'd never wish to hurt you or cause you to feel inferior."

Her lovely eyes filled with tears. My heart softened. Aislinn continued, "Arusi and I mean you no offense. But a Coven of Healing has no place for a witch of hexes and sangemancy. They are talents that diametrically oppose our intentions and practices. Does that make sense, my dear?"

I nodded. Aislinn sighed in relief, releasing my hand. "Thank you. I ought to have spared us this dramatic moment and been honest from the start. You are a reasonable, logical woman... when caught in the right mood!" She darted a wicked smile.

"Well, catch as catch can, my Aislinn. I do my best."

"Then I am forgiven?"

I hesitated. Aislinn's smile beamed sunshine into my doubtful face, her tears turning into drops of hopeful light. I grinned. "Your flattering charms do not work on me! Nevertheless, you are forgiven."

Aislinn rushed 'round the table to embrace me. "I am so glad and grateful!" she cried. "Arusi is wise and kind, but she is quite formal and I cannot speak with her on equal terms. Oh, I have missed you!"

"I've missed you too, Aislinn." Immersed in her vast gown of crisp blue taffeta, I felt I was being drowned at sea. I gently detached her. "What can you tell me about Arusi? Without betraying any coven secrets, of course. I don't mean to cause trouble."

"Let me see." Aislinn drew her chair closer and reseated herself, lovingly petting and rearranging my hair as she often used to do. "She hails from Africa, as you must have deduced. She was trained as a dancer to support herself, and that's how she ended up in the Fair of Phantoms."

"I guessed all that. Anything else?"

"She can have a bit of a temper," Aislinn confessed, parting my hair in preparation for two long braids. "But one must make allowances for it."

"Why?"

"Because of what she is. She isn't a human, Yassy. She is-" Aislinn softly drew my head closer to hers, whispering against my ear, "Arusi is a lycanthrope."

Instantly, the vision of Arusi's flashing eyes penetrated my memory. "Ah. It did strike me that her eyes were quite wolf-like."

"Yes." Aislinn returned her attention to my hairstyle. "She can turn into a wolf at will, so she isn't one of those uncontrollable, wild beasts that go on murderous rampages. She says *some* werewolves end up like that, but most integrate successfully into society."

I amused myself by imagining her animal form. "She must make an attractive wolf."

"Oh, that she is. Such thick, blue-black hair, and such eyes! The darkest shade of silver you could ever envision, but so full of light." Aislinn withdrew two tassels from her reticule, using them to secure my braids. "She can travel anywhere, and has seen such a lot. Rothadamas prepares souls for reform as familiars, but Arusi chooses their species. She's extremely particular about matching each one to their master."

"In that, I certainly commend her." I rebuked myself for believing Arusi had done nothing but humiliate me. "So she *is* helping me, just from afar."

"She is, Yasmin. She truly is!" Aislinn seized and hugged my shoulders. "I know it does not seem credible, considering her cold greeting of you. But she does care for your wellbeing, just as she does mine."

"I am glad to hear it." I rested my cheek against Aislinn's. "Thank you for coming. And, Aislinn..."

"Yes, my Yassy?"

I quietly kissed her cheek. "I have something to tell you, too."

Sergio Vincenzo. I'd *never* get used to that.

Chapter Fifty-Eight

TO SAVE A SPIRIT CHILD

I reviewed the rumors I'd heard many years ago surrounding Erbanhue's life. From there I led up to Maria and Lillias Vosquez, and from there to Thalia's spirit birth, and thence onward to the fact that our ringmaster was, in fact, a warlock.

Aislinn inserted various short interjections and exclamations, but otherwise was a patient listener. When I had completed my incredible tale, Aislinn shook her head. "Is there anything you could do for Thalia?" I pleaded. "Is there any healing potion you could create to cure her resurrection unto death, and bring her back as Lillias? It would mean the world to Erbanhue."

There was a long pause while Aislinn prayerfully deliberated. She withdrew a small brown tome and muttered over various passages. She meditated, absently tugging my braids. Then she stood, emptied her reticule of its contents, and fingered through all the powders and tiny vials of liquid and paste.

"We could try an herbal bath," she announced, pausing at a clutch of herbs and flowers tied with pink ribbon. "You say she was submerged in water and drowned?"

"Thus indicated the ringmaster's dream," I replied. "But how can water heal the damage that water itself has done?"

"A good question, *mo chara*. But unless you propose burning her with fire, I know not what else may be tried. I'm experienced with healing infusions in herbal baths. I think it is our best guess at this stage, and it is perfectly safe. It cannot possibly cause harm."

I stated my agreement. Aislinn seized pen and paper to write me a list of herbs I must gather from her pentagram garden. She firmly requested that I obtain the plants with the greatest care, gently digging around the roots to extract them. "I need not explain that terrible consequences can result from mistreated beldam verdure," she said. "I would gather them myself, but I must cast incantations over the bathwater as well, and I should begin now."

Changing into a plain cotton dress, I took up my shawl and a basket. Aislinn had already heated the water and was making various passes over the steaming pot, reading and enunciating from her little tome. "I'll return soon," I called. She nodded without turning her head.

Rain dripped from a stone-gray sky. I shielded my hair with my shawl, tying it around my head and grasping the basket tightly. "Adel!" I cried. My familiar wiggled out from beneath the gypsy wagon (a favorite retreat of hers), skipping after me with glee, for rain bothered her not an inch.

"Stay close to me," I instructed. "I'll be more confident with you near. Nobody ever accused Yasmin Lange of possessing a green thumb."

I approached the garden with reverence. The herbs, flowers, and vegetables grew in a ruddy star-shaped formation, tangling together as if in a dance. All their colors were unnaturally bright and flourishing. The rose bushes gleamed like jewels.

I bent to admire some bright indigo berries that grew in bunches, surrounded by the petals of a sapphire-tinted flower. "By now, it may be reasonably concluded that Aislinn's favorite color is blue," I told Adel. Adel approached the berries and snuffed at them.

My work began. I checked Aislinn's instructions two and three times before touching any plant. "This is rather nice," I admitted to the fox as I churned the earth. "I never knew gardening was so pleasant." A whispering wind coaxed the greenery into shivering dances, shedding their glassy water droplets. Rain continued to fall. I tossed my soaked shawl aside. "Nevermind," I said to Adel, who sniffed it with concern. "Rainwater never killed a witch."

Having filled my basket with the required foliage, I rose to my feet and glanced about. Aislinn's stone cottage formed a charming backdrop for the rainbow of plants before it. Water *drip-dropped* from the multitude of towering trees, their branches rich with the dark green of late spring.

"I could linger here forever, Adel. See that clump of trees?" I pointed out a singularly close set. "Just inside the forest. They are formed almost exactly alike, those three. It reminds me of Arusi, Aislinn, and myself – the three witches of Kheima. And that tree, there. It could be..."

A torn linen shirt draped across the tree's roots. Dropping the forgotten basket, I ran to it and seized it up. It smelt of tobacco and draconian enterprise.

"Erbanhue!"

Chapter Fifty-Nine

The Wrath Against Adam

"It's him. I know it!"

Hot tears mingled with the sky's chilly remorse. I ran my hands along the bark of the strange tree, more confident than I'd ever been in my life that I could feel the ringmaster's firm outline in its structure. I dropped his shirt. "Adel, what can we do? He must have entered Kheima alone. Or perhaps Rothadamas forced him in. What can I do?"

Adel's sad eyes blinked up at me. I fell against the tree, despondent. "I'll have to go in, Adel. I must go in and bring him back."

My familiar whimpered. I caught her in my arms and snuggled her. "Stay here. I couldn't bear to lose you. Stay and look after Thalia, please. Make sure Aislinn finds her." Adel's gaze bore into mine and she cocked her head, as if to say *But how are you going to get in?*

"Thalia enters Kheima by prayer and meditation. I can try that; I am also a favorite of the Demongod's." I placed Adel back on the ground. "Bring this basket to Aislinn," I instructed her. "And go straight there! Do not stop for anything in the world." The fox took up the basket handle in her mouth and vanished into the brush.

I was alone.

As Thalia had taught me, I bowed into an attitude of prayer and began reciting incantations in the name of ROTHADAMAS. A shuddering, paralyzing fear washed over me every time I spoke His name, but I couldn't stop.

Dizziness clouded my senses. My vision distorted. Surrounding objects morphed into a black, wrinkled version of themselves. At last, everything fluctuated in and out of reality. I knew I had succeeded.

An adult female voice spoke to me. *He must not know why you are here.*

I whimpered something in return, baffled. The voice, though calm and measured, became more insistent. *HE MUST NOT KNOW!*

"He won't know. I promise."

Kheima melted into existence. The eternal snowflakes fell, silent and light blue, adorning my hands and feet with their icy kisses. Black ice crunched beneath each footfall. It was as if I'd never left.

My foremost desire was to call out for Erbanhue. Some instinct took hold of my throat and stopped me. As before, my lungs began to constrict, and I abandoned all attempts to breathe. Again, the black cloud of my breath followed me about.

A few shadows shaped like children ran beneath the trees, their noiseless feet shedding sparks. But most of the children of Kheima were secured to tree trunks, held closely by vines of black thorns. As Hue had described they neither cried, nor screamed, nor showed any emotion whatsoever. Their bleared eyes stared at nothing, empty and cold.

I could not stand the sight for long. I turned from them and began to run, wondering if Erbanhue could be reduced to that state by now.

Reader, you would not thank me for describing at length the dodging between trees, the hideous, terrifying faces of the Kheiman prisoners, or the frightening Creature of Many Eyes that guarded the demonic throne. Weak from terror and exhaustion, I at length came upon the demon's Twisted Tree. An enormous boiling cauldron was placed before it.

He was there. He acknowledged my presence with the slight inclination of His pale head. He motioned me closer. Trembling from head to toe, I approached the seat of Rothadamas.

Was wünschst du dir, Anmut? [1]

"To be shown about... please."

Fear laced my voice. The Demongod leaned over me, his form distorting and stretching. I cowered, covering my head.

Schäme dich niemals, mich zu fürchten, kleine Hexe. [2]

Rothadamas transitioned into his hunting form, black like the darkness of a night robbed of moon or stars, entirely featureless in the face, long and tall and awful. He pointed to the left, to a thick knobby tree.

Erbanhue was tied to its trunk. A myriad of thorns pierced his perspiring flesh. His bronze face was utterly stoic.

I swallowed hard, refusing to alter my expression. "What has he done?" I asked the demon. "Why do you treat him thus?"

The demon reached out, clutching my head with his long, painful fingers. I muffled a scream. My mind was flooded with memories and visions:

---

1. "What do you desire?"

2. "Never be ashamed of fearing me, little witch."

Erbanhue snuck into the gypsy wagon. He seized the porcelain doll and proceeded to search for Thalia. No small wonder, Thalia appeared to him, quite put out that someone else had touched her precious plaything. The two argued for a time.

Once Hue had used his charm to placate the spirit child, he drew her into deep conversation. I witnessed their lips sounding the name *Rothadamas*. Thalia consented to something Erbanhue was pleading for. It was by Thalia's means that Erbanhue had penetrated the Demongod's realm.

He stole the porcelain doll and tucked it under his arm. As he approached the cauldron where his daughter had been resurrected unto death, he smashed the doll against the side of the basin and threw the pieces in the churning water. The Creature of Many Eyes, along with the four giant hooved beasts, pinned Erbanhue to the ground until the Demongod arrived. Erbanhue was secured to the Tree of the Knowledge of Evil.

The Demon withdrew His hand. I backed away from Him, gasping, clutching my head which throbbed from pain. "And Thalia... is she all right?"

Rothadamas gave no reply. I knew He was regarding me with suspicion. He wanted to know why I was here.

"Erbanhue has broken your trust," I said, desperately wishing for Aislinn or Arusi. "But do not regard him too harshly. He acted out of love for his daughter, Lillias. Has he not been punished enough?"

A soothing sound, most odd and unexpected, throbbed from the Demon's throat. *Sie interessieren sich für ihn, nicht wahr?* [3]

---

3. "You care for him, do you not?"

"He is my brother, both in the Fair of Phantoms and in the dark arts," I replied, gathering courage. "He will be among your most prized bondservants once he matures. Please, do not destroy Him!"

I fell to my knees. I planted my face to the ground. "Please, Rothadamas. Spare him."

Du bist heute gewachsen, meine Hexe. Ich freue mich. Nimm dein Erbanhue, wenn du kannst! [4]

The Demongod's words climaxed into a roar of challenge. The Kheiman prisoners raised their heads, howling as one in a voice of great fear. I covered my ears. Rothadamas towered over me, thrusting me to the ground.

Again, the mysterious female voice whispered into my thoughts. *Yasmin! This is your initiation! You will be tempted with power, rewards, and gifts beyond reckoning. But it is all a trap! Do not listen to Him! You must rescue Erbanhue and escape. Do you hear me?*

"Yes. I hear you."

---

4. "You have grown this day, my witch. I am pleased. Take your Erbanhue, if you can!"

Chapter Sixty

The Tree of the Knowledge of Evil

Kheima plunged into darkness.

The snow stopped. Not a single breeze stirred. Not a single sound reached my ears. A sensation of horror unlike any I had yet experienced froze the blood in my veins. It was the sheer absence of all sound.

A shred of reddish, flickering light beckoned me. I stumbled in pursuit of it. My movements were awkward, sluggish, and stinging with pain, as if shards of ice impeded my muscular coordination. Irritation took the place of brevity, and I increased my pace despite the pain.

"Erbanhue!" I tried to call out. But just as it often happens in nightmares, I could not hear a word, no matter how much power I thrust into my voice.

My numbed feet caught on a tree root. I fell. Slowly pushing myself back up, I noticed a small childish figure on my left. It was one of the Kheiman prisoners I had noticed before, previously lashed to a trunk.

He watched me wordlessly, tiny red pricks dotting his body where he had struggled against the thorny vines. As I looked him over, his face broke into a thin and humorless smile.

I choked on the rising influx of terror. I turned, attempting to run, but the tree roots were numerous and the lighting extremely dim. I fell again.

The first sound echoed – A laugh. Another Kheiman prisoner appeared on my right, apparently goaded into gloomy laughter by the occasion of my fall. The adrenaline of terror finally resumed. I ran and was pursued by the tortured children.

As I ran, more prisoners appeared. Soon a large group of them urged me onward, drawing me toward the flickering red light. At length I recognized Erbanhue's tree of punishment, the Tree of the Knowledge of Evil.

I ran faster, crying out (I think, for I could not hear myself) as the pain in my feet increased. I reached the tree. The ringmaster was latched onto its trunk, staring stupidly, sweat thick upon his brow, and multiple angry scratches adorning his arms and chest, signifying his initial struggle against the thorns.

Oh, Erbanhue! Bravest and most foolish of men. I will do what I must.

Extending both hands as Thalia had instructed me, I spoke a deforming incantation against the tree. The tree shuddered and convulsed, but would not release its prisoner. Erbanhue groaned, his head lolling to one side.

"Greetings, Yasmin. It's time you knew what you are capable of."

This voice was familiar. I was not surprised to see Mary standing there, her skin deathly pale, her eyes perfect twins to Thalia's spirit child orbs. Her red hair shone in the feeble light.

"Did you know that you can extract and absorb a lesser witch's powers?" Mary questioned, tilting her head and yielding a mischievous smile. "If you would like to see the future in your dreams, and charm others into liking you and following your lead, it's here for the taking."

"You are no longer Mary," I stated (trusting that my voice, soundless to my own ears, indeed reached her own). "I will not listen to you." Hunting for a strong stick, I slipped it behind the vines and endeavored to break them loose. Spirit Mary chuckled. "You won't get them off that way, silly. But there's something nice you should know about craft extraction. Listen to me! You'll like this."

"I am sure I *won't.*" I darted a wary glance at the Kheiman prisoners who surrounded us, watching, looking as grim as death itself.

"He wouldn't remember one thing about being a warlock. He'll just be normal man again. Wouldn't he like that? He wouldn't remember this place at all. And he will think *you* are normal, too!"

"I don't believe you."

"But Rothadamas wants you to do it," dead-Mary coaxed. "It's why He's secured him to this tree for you. This is where it can be done." She bowed her head and joined her hands. The silent Kheiman prisoners mirrored her actions.

"Well, even if you *are* telling the truth, there's one thing he will never forget. His daughter!"

Dead-Mary cracked one eye open. "Ah, well. That is true, but he'll keep thinking she died of illness, like we tricked him into believing before."

Enraged, I turned on her. My lips parted and delivered some manner of Latin phrases that my lingual instruction knew not. Dead-Mary uttered a shriek of surprise and collapsed on the ground, expiring in a pile of ash.

Instantly, the unknown voice called out again. *Yasmin! You must escape this instant! Get Erbanhue out!*

He is coming.

Terrified, I caught up the vines and broke them apart with my own hands, doing my best to ignore the pain. As I worked, I chanted beneath my breath, multiple hexes piling upon the vines and twisting them apart. The mass broke away. Erbanhue, bloodied but free, continued to stare blankly at nothing.

"Come on!" I cried, securing his arm across my shoulders. His feet dragged on the ground. I was far too slow; it was certain we would be caught. As tears of defeat coursed down my cheeks, I felt Hue's heavy bulk grow lighter.

"Thalia?"

It was she. Her tiny frame, possessed by the strength of the dark arts, supported Erbanhue on his other side. "We must hurry!" she demanded. "He is angry with you because of Mary."

"I did not mean to destroy her." Sobbing, I dwelt miserably on the many lives I had destroyed without intending to. "I could have found a way to save her."

"No one can save a spirit child," Thalia firmly pronounced. "Hurry up!"

My slow, awkward movements infuriated us both. Thalia huffed and let go of Erbanhue. "There's one more thing I can try, but He will surely finish me for it. Close your eyes, Yasmin."

I reached out to her, still crying. "No, I can't. Thalia, you are... This man is actually your..."

"Be silent and close your eyes, or we shall all be dead!"

I covered my eyes with my free hand.

Chapter Sixty-One

THE SACRIFICE

Warbled voices assaulted my aching head.

"He could have found out!"

"But He didn't!"

"You are the most careless, disobedient, reckless-"

"No, stop. Yasmin is moving!"

I shifted on the couch, recognizing the texture of my featherdown quilt. Somehow I'd returned to my own wagon. A sweet-smelling rag dabbled across my forehead. I pried my unwilling eyelids open. "Thalia. You're all right."

"It was close, but yes. I am here. So is your Erbanhue."

"He's NOT my Erbanhue."

"Woah! Down, girl! Easy does it." Aislinn crouched at my side, smiling warmly. "You're lucky to be here, my dearest. Rothadamas must have changed his mind."

Erbanhue "guffawed" and entertained me with light friendly chatter during the short walk to the meal tents. I could hardly respond; I was so busy pondering the source of this amazing change.

He was... *human.*

And, strange as the admission was, part of me was undeniably disappointed.

It was but a little change to other spectators, mind you; he had his bursts of friendliness. But they were linked to some gain or purpose for himself. This had, as far as I could see, no purpose whatever, except... To be kind to someone he *liked.*

Sergio pulled out a chair for me and plunked himself right beside me. He seldom spoke to me through dinner – this was true enough – but he was lively with everyone. Everything he said resulted in tent-wide amusement.

I reacted mechanically. Reader, I was terribly confused. I actually entertained the notion that Kheima had been a nightmare, nothing more.

But then I glanced beneath his gaping collar as he leaned forward, slapping his knee and laughing. His scar had faded, but it was still there. The traces of painful thorn-pricks yet riddled his chest.

As he bantered and made jokes, he slyly peeped at me from the corner of his eye to be sure I was laughing, too. And I did laugh, Reader, for I could not help it. A realization began to dawn:

Erbanhue was under the Demongod's control for many years. He was marked as a young man and slowly influenced by the profound darkness of Kheima. His abrupt changefulness was heightened as his spirit warred for dominance against the dark arts waging battle for his person. His random outbreaks from brief kindness to physical cruelty were, perhaps, not part of his natural character. Weren't *Sergio.*

In short, Reader, demonic possession accounted for many things.

Since *that* was true, then the man I loved was...

The ringmaster traded cards with Sallix, taunting him in a friendly manner. He pretended to cast the magician's fortune, claiming that Sallix would soon be rendered moderately drunk. No cursing, no cold sarcasm, no insults. His fire-bred tongue had much softened. He heard me laughing and darted me a quick, low glance, eyes bright with good nature.

Thalia's sing-song tone dashed the warmth from my cheeks. "You're blushing, Yassy. Whatever for?"

"I'm happy, that's all," I murmured, trying to speak quietly under the roar of mirth from the circus men. "Hue can't hear you anymore? Or see you?"

"No, he can't." She pouted. "That's not much fun for me. I liked him. At least *you're* still here."

"For how much longer?" I whispered. *"He* will discover that I do not wield Erbanhue's powers. You have them. Won't Roth- won't *He* find out?"

"Yes. But I've prepared for that. I intend to play the part of a selfish little girl. I'll confess, but I'll say I wanted desperately to charm the other witches and warlocks into liking me. (It can be done if the target is already susceptible, as Erbanhue found with you.) I'm His favorite spirit child, when all is said and done. I doubt He'd do anything very awful to me."

She crossed her miniature arms. She looked and sounded very much like the ringmaster. I shook my head. "How can you be so flippant? You saved both of our lives, Lillias- I mean, Thalia."

I was too late. Thalia's arms dropped to her sides. "Why did you just call me that? Who is Lillias?"

I stood and left the table, speaking low as I passed her. "No one in particular."

Chapter Sixty-Two

SAVING LILLIAS

As I regained my strength, it weighed on my mind that Thalia was in grave danger. In typical childish fashion, she tossed her new powers to and fro, heedless of discovery and consequence. I rebuked her, pleaded with her, and even threatened her with punishments, but to no avail. I was merely termed a killjoy for my trouble.

I met with Aislinn to discuss what we could do.

"I did try the herbal bath," Aislinn admitted. "When Adel returned with your basket, I thought you decided to go into town. As you can see, Thalia was not healed from the resurrection unto death. But it improved her energy a good deal. She's more like a child, less like a waxen puppet."

"That's just what she needed," I muttered. "Now she's bouncing about trying her new talents in every corner of the earth."

"Well, she's a fledgling charmer now. She might manage to worm her way out of trouble."

"It will lead to her final death, Aislinn. Rothadamas will discover that she lied."

"How can we prevent it?"

"Take her to Arusi."

Aislinn shook her head. "Arusi boasts phenomenal powers of healing. I have witnessed her work in rebuilding the surrounding nature; the effects are profound. But Thalia – or rather Lillias – is no longer living. We cannot heal that which is dead."

"Have you never tried it?"

My friend hesitated an instant, tapping her chin as she thought. "Just with the herbal bath. However..."

"Then it is our responsibility to try it." Now *I* was sounding more like Erbanhue.

"I admit that her case is sorrowful, but her curse is not of your doing. I daresay she has only ever complicated matters."

"I have harmed many people without intending to do so, Aislinn. I desire to bring salvation for once, if I can. It may resolve the pangs of conscious... however slightly."

For Erbanhue.

The hot tears fell. Aislinn sighed, reaching into her sleeve for her handkerchief. "You have been crying a great deal lately. That is not like you at all." She gently wiped away the deluge. "I will take her to Arusi for you. But I must beg you to keep your distance. Your presence is highly conducive to the channels of death. It may interfere with our work."

"I shall not stir an inch."

"Good girl." Aislinn kissed my forehead. "I shall return with her directly."

I suffered in solitude for the next two or three hours. I paced. Adel watched me anxiously from her pillowed basket, her eyes moving from her worried Yasmin to the empty shelf where the porcelain doll had so recently stood in state.

The reader will not thank me, however, for a prolonged account of that excruciating wait. I shall resume with Aislinn bursting into the wagon, eyes wide with concern:

"Come with me!"

At once I planted my hand into her open palm. We fled the wagon as one. She did not yield another word as we ran, but further explanation was superfluous. Thalia was in danger.

Aislinn brought me to the Witch Trees near her cottage. I spared a quick glance for Erbanhue's tree. It was ripped apart as if a lightning strike had attacked it in a burning, sentient rage. Leading me past them all, she twisted deftly through the woods until far above our heads stretched the tall, thorned Black Tree of the Kheiman Realm.

It had grown since I saw it last. Its putrid aura sent a shudder through my limbs. The branches were hideously long and thin, thrusting skyward, then drooping until their crooked fingers nearly scraped the ground.

Beneath the wild growth, I saw the white naked patch where I had ripped away a portion of its bark for food. All those years ago, when I was another creature... A cold, wild, unsympathetic creature, not unlike the Demongod I became so willing to serve.

Staring at that Tree as it now appeared, I knew all.

Every truth I had ever denied flooded my mind. I knew I had powers – I strongly suspected the source – I cared not whom I destroyed in the exercise of them. *Apathy* was the poison that wrecked the lives of those around me. Apathy and denial.

No more, Yasmin Lange. Emma Bauer. Witch Anmut. You will no longer deny that which stands before you, breathes within you, shines bright in the darkness before your feet.

I loved Erbanhue. I loved him with a strength of adoration that frightened me. My fear and my pride scorned it. I would have *died* rather than admit it! While his charismatic mysticism had further tethered my heart - double-knotted and hopelessly secure in eternal subjugation - *I wanted the conquest.*

"Aislinn," I whispered, my eyes fastened to the Black Tree, "what have I done?"

"It was not you, but *Him!*" my friend cried. "I have been blinded by Him as well. You must enter Kheima."

"How did He take her?"

"There is no time. You must go in, carry her out, and destroy this Tree."

"To enter requires faithful prayer and a declaration of loyalty," I reminded Aislinn. "I can't rely on such sentiments now. I cannot enter!"

"Nay, Yasmin Lange," said Arusi's calm voice behind me. "You are the only one who can enter now."

Aislinn and I both turned. Arusi's tranquil mien gave us courage. "She cannot go alone," Aislinn insisted. "I must help her. Arusi, send us both!"

"You cannot go in, my blessed one," Arusi said, coming forward and placing her hand on Aislinn's pale, shivering shoulder. "Yasmin alone bears the keys to Kheima. We would lose you in the realm of death."

"Then *you* must go with her," Aislinn said. "You are far stronger than I. You will be all right."

"I shall not. It is death to disobey Rothadamas."

Aislinn would have sustained her protest, but Arusi narrowed her huntress gaze. A growl, ever so soft, rumbled from her throat. I remembered that Arusi - like Rothadamas himself - *was not human.*

"I am a witch bonded to nature, sworn to protect and preserve natural life. Rothadamas is a part of the sacred whole. I cannot go against Him."

Aislinn gaped in shock. "Then you are not..."

"No." Arusi parted her scarlet collar, showing us a pure upper chest unmarked by the Demongod. "I do not serve Him. We coexist; that is all."

Aislinn and I gradually absorbed the truth. "How can I enter?" I asked.

Arusi tossed her head, her glorious hair folding and shimmering down her frame. "As you did before, by prayer and faithful supplication. It is still within your power. You are frightened, but you know how to appeal to Him. You are still His favorite." Advancing, she held my hands and kissed my forehead. "Go and save Lillias, Yasmin Lange. Blessings to thee."

The last Diary entry of Yasmin Lange

Chapter Sixty-Three

Hades

Yasmin

I finished my meditations and closed my well-worn diary. I prayed. When the natural world fell away, I felt a suffocating dread that nearly vanquished me on the spot.

I was *not* in Kheima.

Although I stood on solid ground, the sensation of falling persisted. The earth upon which I trembled was black as night, devoid of any life. It was hot. I unfastened the collar of my dress, breathing great gulps of fetid air. This place was not kind to the living. Aislinn would have died within minutes.

"Thalia?" I cried.

"I'm here."

Her voice answered mine without hesitation. Eager and thankful, I quickened my pace in her direction. "Thalia! Where are you?"

"Here, of course... here. I've always been here."

"Where are we, child? I can't see anything."

I continued to speak to her, encouraging her to help me find her in the wicked dark. The spirit child's replies were short and remarkably cool. I wondered if she recognized me.

"Where are we?" I asked again, for this question had been asked and avoided several times. "Here," she kept repeating. "We've always been here."

I gave up in despair. "What are you doing?"

"I don't know. There's water."

"Keep speaking, Thalia. I must find you! Tell me what the water is like. Is it hot? What can you see?"

"I am in a cauldron, wide and silver. The water is very hot. I see a black star beneath my feet, perfect and sharp. I must not move."

Thalia spoke in a strange, chanting sort of cadence. It made me frightened of coming to her, but I would not relinquish my task. "Tell me more," I baited her. "How did you end up here?"

"Pale hands seized me by the Tree. Angry thorns took hold of me. I could hear other children, and they laughed. They said I was dirty."

"And me, Thalia? Do I sound familiar? What is my name?"

"You sound familiar. I don't know your name."

I believed this must be some manner of dark cleansing ritual, a way to restore Thalia to her designated station and with the powers and knowledge originally intended for her. It was clear that the Demongod had discovered her indiscreet lie. "I will find you, Thalia. Wait for me."

"It is... nice... in the water. I do not wish to leave it." She sounded sleepy. I called out loudly, "Don't fall asleep, Thalia!"

No reply.

"Keep talking to me!"

At long last, my hands brushed a large object that coincided with her description of a large cauldron or basin. My fingers burned against it. My sigh of relief was quickly replaced by a cry of pain. "Thalia," I whispered, "are you in *there?*"

"I'm here. I've always been here."

"I'll get you out."

"I don't want to come out."

Ignoring her proclamation, I inched closer to the basin and... plunged my hands in.

Boiling water engulfed me. I screamed. I could barely feel Thalia's tiny corporeal form against my fingers.

I seized hold of her dress and pulled. She mumbled feeble protests, but was limp and could not fight me. I dragged her to the edge of the basin. "Join me! It's nice," she said.

"Join her! Join her!"

Small, childish hands gripped my arms. I screamed again, both from the boiling water and fear of the children. I tried to dodge them, but I could not control my body; the children's touch numbed me and drained me of strength. My head was knocked against the searing basin. I fell in, the seething water closing above me.

"Thalia..."

With an enormous rush of will, I took Thalia in my arms and pushed her up and out. She tumbled from the basin. She rose to her feet, turned, and stumbled away as quickly as she could.

As I sank into the water (which no longer seemed so hot), a blue-white light shone from above. I muttered one final spell.

Thalia vanished.

The shadow of Rothadamas loomed over the surface of the water.

Erbanhue... Sergio. You deserve the truth. Hear me now-

Chapter Sixty-Four

DENOUEMENT

Sergio

Yasmin's thin, battered body was found near a blackened tree.

I carried her home. I left her to fetch Minister Benjamin. He came at once, full of tender compassion for the proud, fiery, once-defiant Yasmin Lange. He took the final rites in hand. I was deeply grateful... for I myself was not up to the task.

Much later, I dropped Minister Lewis off at his door. He was full of regret and sorrow.

"I suppose she died full of bitterness against myself, and against the God who granted her such a difficult life," the little minister said, thumbing through his Bible. "I pray her soul finally found rest in our Lord." And he rubbed his coat sleeve across his watering eyes.

I fumbled awkwardly with the reigns. Religion puts me on edge. "If there be a God, sir – and I believe there's probably more than one – but if there is one great creator God, He certainly dealt her a hard hand. If He is God indeed, why would he treat some folks fairly, and others so poorly? Yasmin did not deserve to die so young. My poor daughter's heart is quite broken, and she's but recently recovered from a long illness herself."

"Alas, I am not God, so I cannot tell you. His ways are infinitely higher than our ways."

I slowly shook my head. "She was a strange woman, indeed... thoroughly unique. I shall never forget her."

The Witch Anmut. The pride of my circus... and somehow, despite our skirmishes... my dearest, most faithful friend.

As I urged Belmont onward, an odd pang twinged through my heart, as if something vital had just been ripped from it. I looked up. A single raindrop fell from the gray sky. Gray as steel... gray like her eyes. It kissed my forehead with a brief, ice-cold prickle.

I swear upon my life, I heard *her* voice.

You deserve the truth. Hear me now...

I love you.

Wherever I am, whatever I become, I will always love you, Sergio.

I will find you.

Across the ocean, many miles away...

A thin black tree grew

in the Black Forest of Deutschland.

About the Author

Gothic thriller fan Richelle Manteufel grew up relishing the psychological deep-dives of Poe, Stoker, and the Brontë sisters. She discovered her passion for writing fiction at nine years old. Now a married mother thriving in Colorado, she can often be found reading or writing near a mountain view or walking around the park, earbuds blasting melodic death metal tracks.

Find all her latest publications on manteufelbooks.com.

Follow the Author

FB: Richelle Manteufel Books

IG: @richellemanteufelauthor

Printed in Great Britain
by Amazon

47421480R00233